THE MUSIC
OF YOUR LIFE

Stories

JOHN ROWELL

SIMON & SCHUSTER

New York   London   Toronto   Sydney   Singapore

SIMON & SCHUSTER
Rockefeller Center
1230 Avenue of the Americas, New York, NY 10020

For information about special discounts for bulk purchases,
please contact Simon & Schuster Special Sales at
1-800-456-6798 or business@simonandschuster.com

Manufactured in the United States of America

1   3   5   7   9   10   8   6   4   2

Library of Congress Cataloging-in-Publication Data
Rowell, John.
The music of your life : stories / John Rowell.
p. cm.
Contents: The music of your life—The mother-of-the-groom and I—Who loves you?—
Saviors—Spectators in love—Delegates—Wildlife of coastal Carolina.
1. Psychological fiction, American. I. Title.
PS3618.O875M875 2003
813'.6—dc21   2002045272
ISBN 0-7432-3695-5

For my mother and father

CONTENTS

Come away, O human child!
To the waters and the wild
With a faery, hand in hand,
For the world's more full of weeping than you
can understand.

—W. B. YEATS, "THE STOLEN CHILD"

"One should be the spectator of oneself always,
dear, a little."

—RONALD FIRBANK, *INCLINATIONS*

THE MUSIC
OF YOUR LIFE

THE MUSIC OF YOUR LIFE

You're ten years old. It's summertime. And you have Lawrence Welk damage.

You are, in fact, America's biggest little fan of *The Lawrence Welk Show.* You can't get enough of him, of him and his weekly television variety hour. Lawrence Welk: "Mister Music Maker," the leader of the band, a fussy, exacting man who sports a red or pastel blue polyester blazer that gives him the look of, say, the president of your father's Rotary Club, but that could never be, because this man is *famous;* Lawrence Welk belongs to America, to American living rooms, like some eccentric, musically inclined uncle from another state who suddenly appears in front of you— *"Hello, son . . . "*—bearing an undertaker's freeze-dried smile, lifting his baton and welcoming you to his show in a speaking voice that sounds eerily Transylvanian: *"Good-a evaning, everybody, I'm-a Lawrence Welk . . . "*

But you are eager for it, eager for him, because Lawrence Welk brings music into your home. From the television screen, Mr. Welk lifts his pencil-thin baton to conduct his big band— *"here we go, a one-a and a two-a . . . "*—and he might as well be conducting your heartbeat, because your little-boy heart accelerates with the thrumming of the tympani and the brassy blast of the horn section; it keeps tempo, marks time, this junior-sized metronome in your chest, and your entire body pulsates with the rhythm of the music; you can't help but be carried away by it as you listen and take it all in. You are mesmerized, you are utterly

I

JOHN ROWELL

fascinated, you are Lawrence Welk's Number One Fan. Is it love?
Are you in love with Lawrence Welk? Maybe; or maybe it's the
show you're in love with. Yes, you're in love with *The Lawrence
Welk Show*, if such a thing is possible. And it's not the dancing or
the stars or the costumes or the sets that have stolen your heart
away . . .

It's the music.

And because you love it too much, it has damaged you.

"Wunnerful, wunnerful," you say to no one in particular,
appropriating Mr. Welk's curious accent and employing it like an
actor. You whisper it under your breath to your mother as you
watch her prepare dinner. As she places the Sunday-night special
of Salisbury steak, green bean casserole, and mashed potatoes in
front of you at the table, you say: "Ladies and gentlemen,
tonight's dinner has been brought to you by Geritol—good for
what ails you."

"Just eat, please," says your mother, Connie.

Behind his sports pages, and without looking at you, your
father, Ray, says: "That'll be enough of that, son."

Yes, you're damaged, but no one seems to notice. Or: they
notice, they just pretend not to.

It's the Summer of Love in America, but for you it's the Summer of Discovering the American Popular Songbook, courtesy of
the musical selections on the Lawrence Welk program. You've
taken to joining Connie and Ray in the family room, plopping in
front of the new Zenith console television set, for an hour of what
Mr. Welk refers to as "champagne music." You've come to know
all the regulars on the program: the dancers Bobby and Cissy, the
accordion player Myron Floren (his upright, high-swinging rendition of "Flight of the Bumblebee" was a big highlight on last
week's "Songs of the Great Outdoors" theme show), Joe Feeney,
the Irish tenor whose signature number is "Danny Boy," and the
silvery-voiced, heavily hair-sprayed soprano Norma Zimmer.
(Connie: "I wonder if she uses Adorn or White Rain . . ." You:

" 'Adorn. To give you that natural look—all day, and all night.' "
Ray: "That'll be enough of that, son.")

Lawrence Welk calls Norma Zimmer the "Champagne Lady."
Before the summer started, you knew nothing about champagne—
now you pretend to drink it on a daily basis. Your grandmother
gave you one of her champagne glasses after she quit drinking last
year—a "flute," she called it, and then she said, "No, a *magic
flute*," and this caused her to laugh uproariously, a smoker's hacky
laugh, a laugh that seemed both happy and furious at the same
time . . . you'd never heard anyone laugh that way before.

So you have taken to tossing back ginger ale in a magic champagne flute and then asking, or maybe even commanding, your
mother to refill it, and repeating a phrase you recently picked up
from a *Dialing for Dollars* afternoon movie: "Hit me again, baby,
and don't be stingy."

And then you laugh throatily, uproariously, in your best
smoker's hacky laugh.

"Hahahahaha . . ."

In your Underdog shortie pajamas and striped white crew
socks, you sip ginger ale on hot August Sunday nights with Connie
and Ray as Mr. Welk and company serenade you, and when the
program breaks for advertisements of Martini & Rossi *("on the
rocks . . . say ye-e-es!")* and Pall Mall cigarettes, you inquire of
your mother, whom you have dubbed "Iced-Tea Lady," "Madam,
is there any *caviar* in the house?"

"Can you talk like a normal person?" Ray asks, as Iced-Tea
Lady serves the two of you her best version of caviar on a
moment's notice: Ritz crackers topped with discreet orange dol-
lops of pimento cheese. "How come you like all this old-people's
music, anyway?"

"I don't know," you say. "It has style." You must have read
that somewhere.

"Style," Ray grunts, flipping back pages.

"I think he has good taste," says Connie, hostess perfect in a pink and mauve sleeper set with matching short silk robe and mules topped with feathery puffs. Connie: tall and occasionally thin, blond enough, but blonder with a little help from Miss Clairol, not a former southern beauty-pageant beauty, like her sisters were, just always the "cute" one.

"And we know good taste comes from *my* side of the family," she adds, winking at you and gingerly tasting her own spur-of-the-moment Ritz cracker creation.

Ray makes a playful swipe at Connie, then grabs her and pulls her into his lap. You sit cross-legged on the floor and study them. It thrills you to see Connie and Ray like this, playful and affectionate; you imagine you're living with Rock Hudson and Doris Day from one of their romantic comedies, the ones you've seen on *Dialing for Dollars*. It's the final reel: obstacles surmounted, no more resistance, in love, *together forever*. From the TV, Mr. Welk's special guest, Miss Jo Stafford, sings: "Look at me, I'm as helpless as a kitten up a tree . . ."

"That's one of our songs, hon," says Ray, half-whispering in Connie's ear, pushing a few strands of her hair away with his nose.

Connie giggles and rests her head on Ray's big, round shoulder, running her fingers through his military-looking brush-cut and cupping his strong, shadowy jawline. In her moderately well-trained church choir voice, she sings along, something about left hand and right, something about hats and gloves; you don't quite follow it all . . .

And Ray joins in, and then so you won't feel left out, so do you, singing as high and as loud as your boy soprano will allow. What a trio: you're misty, they're misty, everyone's too much in love.

And what a fabulous night. Great American standards perfume the air, Connie and Ray are in love like movie stars, and you have a front-row seat, an insider's view, an aficionado's appreciation, for all of it. Even all the recent unpleasantness about your grandparents' divorce seems to have vanished for now. This summer, you and your grandmother have spent hours together, reading her movie magazines, *Photoplay, Movie Mirror, Modern Screen.* You feel as though you could be photographed, right here, right now in this very setting, for *Photoplay's* "Movie Stars at Home" section. You imagine that you are a child star, perhaps the youngest vocalist ever to perform a standard on *The Lawrence Welk Show,* and you become instantly famous, you become what *Photoplay* calls "an overnight sensation." You are photographed in your pajamas, brandishing your champagne flute aloft, and you consent to a few photographs with Ray and Connie, though you make sure the photographer doesn't snap Connie doing the ironing or Ray reading the sports page. You grant an accompanying interview in which you say you like it here in this house, but, really, it's too small, and the three of you will soon be moving from North Carolina to Beverly Hills, California, where you will be neighbors with Lucille Ball and Bing Crosby and Bob Hope. Once ensconced in sunny southern California, you are sure to attend your neighbors' smart cocktail parties, where you will stand in the crooks of their grand and baby grand pianos and sing, and everyone will recognize you from your appearances on *Lawrence Welk* and even Miss Jo Stafford will ask if she can sing with you, shyly revealing that it had always been her dream to perform a duet with an Overnight Sensation.

"Hey, sport, change to the channel for *Batman,*" Ray says, rattling the ice cubes in his tumbler, the finish of his second gin and tonic. He knows he'll get no resistance from you on this: you love *Batman,* too. In your hierarchy of entertainment, it is second only to *Lawrence Welk.*

And so: *Batman* . . .

Watching *Batman* is a different experience altogether: no one sings from the American Popular Songbook, no one dances in chiffon dresses and high heels. But *Batman* has something *Lawrence Welk* could never even begin to supply: men—handsome, grown-up men who live together in the same house, men who are each other's best friends, men who look out for each other in all sorts of strange circumstances. Also: men who wear tights. *Men in tights!* So why do the other boys in your class love the *Batman* show, too? They certainly don't like *Lawrence Welk*. But you're aware they watch *Batman*—you've overheard them talking about it in groups on the playground—and they watch it with their dads, too. You don't usually have much in common with the other boys in your class, and, for that matter, not much in common with Ray, either. So why *Batman*? Why is *Batman* common male ground?

It doesn't matter why, because you, being you, see it differently. Ray looks bored until the action breaks out into violent fights and scuffles *(POW!!!!! THWACKK!!!!!!!! BAM!!!!!!!!)*, but you're hooked way before that. You're hooked in the setup, at the woozy-music entrance of the villainess, Miss Eartha Kitt as Catwoman. You have memorized her lines, even practiced them in bed late at night, when no one could hear you. With the covers pulled up over your head, gazing down at your rolled-up pillow, you whisper: "You are *purrrrfect*, my little Boy *Wonderrrr!*" But no one hears you, of course; some things you must keep secret.

Watching *Batman* with Ray, you maintain a blank face so he won't see how you really feel about it. It's an acting exercise, this art of making your face Go Blank at key moments, and you've mastered it. And going blank doesn't work just for *Batman*: it's equally useful when you're caught in the middle of an angry argument between your parents, or the time you watched your grandmother tumble suddenly to the floor after too much wine, nearly hitting her head on the coffee table. Go Blank, and no one will know whose side you're on. Go Blank, and you can be as neutral as Switzerland. Go Blank, and you won't make enemies within your own family.

But this summer, for some reason, it's not as easy as it used to be to go blank in front of *Batman*, especially when a villain ties the Caped Crusaders to a plank, where they struggle against each other, bound, helpless . . . in their tights. You keep watching, but you keep reminding yourself: Ray is here. *Go Blank, Go Blank, Go Blank* ...

"No more music?" asks Connie, in the other room now, where she is spraying Niagara onto a shirt collar and steam-pressing *whoosh!* She pokes her head around the door: "Oh, I can't stand that *Batman* show."

"We watched all your girl shows, hon," says Ray, draining his third drink. "Gotta have something manly for us men now. Right, sport?" He doesn't wait for your response, he just shakes his tumbler in Connie's direction, which means: "Get me another one, babe?"

In tonight's opening segment, the Dynamic Duo are being lowered by a thick rope from a large ceiling pulley, which will slowly submerge them into a pool of hungry, snapping alligators. Batman and Robin are tied together, back to back; their legs, their calves, their feet kick together, their heads slide and knock against each other; if they were tied face to face, it seems to you, they could quite possibly ... kiss. Batman and Robin kissing each other ... the way Connie and Ray kiss? The way Rock Hudson and Doris Day, in the movies, kiss? Why would you think about such a thing? Why does your head suddenly feel light and balloony? Why does Ray have to be here? Why is Going Blank not working?

"*Lawrence Welk* is on the other channel," you offer quickly, turning to Ray but keeping the TV screen in the corner of your eye. Much as you want to, you're too afraid to watch it straight on. Oh, wouldn't it be great to have your own television set in your own room? Memo to Santa Claus ...

Connie returns with Ray's freshened drink.

"Wouldn't you rather see *Lawrence Welk*, Mama?" you say. It's a rally cry; you have to change this channel.

"Well, yes, I would," she says, sitting down.

"Oh, for God's sake," Ray says. "Just change it then, and stop talking about it."

And that's your cue at last. You twist the channel dial on the

7

Zenith back to the music. It's better this way; you'll just have to imagine the conclusion of *Batman* later for yourself, after you're in bed. You can do that; already, you're an expert at coming up with alternate endings.

What a relief to be back with Lawrence Welk and his orchestra! Mr. Welk is leading his musicians in the love theme from *A Summer Place*. You glance over at Ray—he's starting to nod, as he usually does after a few gin and tonics; perhaps it didn't even matter that you switched channels. You're listening, Connie is listening, Ray is half listening. The three of you sitting there, doing nothing but breathing and staring at the set, listening to an old romantic movie theme. And even though there's music filling the room, no one is commenting; there's just silence between the three of you.

And you're not a fan of silence. You prefer to keep conversation going, as if at a cocktail party; if you can keep your parents talking, and talking about themselves, they won't have as much time to notice you and ask you questions. *You* ask the questions, you get them to reminisce about themselves and the old days. These are the skills of segue, and you possess them in abundance; you have studied at the feet of Merv Griffin and Mike Douglas. Merv and Mike have taught you how to move guests along, how to fish for information, how to prompt a certain response. Also: How to cut to a word from the sponsor. How to thank everybody for watching. How to say good night.

"Does this song remind y'all of Chapel Hill?" you ask. You're aware that Connie and Ray would never recognize that query for what it is: a prompt. They don't watch Merv and Mike as often as you do.

"It does," says Connie automatically. Connie has no idea that ten years ago she gave birth to a small variety-show host, that she has a variety-show host living in her home. "Doesn't it, Ray?"

"Sure. I guess," he says.

The music on *The Lawrence Welk Show* often has the effect of making Ray and Connie nostalgic for the days when they first started dating as students at the University of North Carolina, and you've learned how to encourage that. It thrills you to hear the story of how they first met at the Autumn Ball where Kay Kyser and his orchestra provided the evening's entertainment. You have listened over and over to the tale of how Ray stood nervously behind Connie in the punch line, she in a blue-green taffeta party dress with sweetheart neckline, he in a white dinner jacket and waxed crew cut. Their first dance: "When the Red Red Robin Comes Bob-Bob-Bobbin' Along," and this number was also recently featured on Lawrence Welk's "Great Outdoors" show. You know it by heart now; quite possibly, you think of it as one of your signature songs.

On rainy afternoons this summer you have opened up Ray and Connie's wedding photo album, which contains in its broad binding a tiny music box that plays "Here Comes the Bride" if you stick a penny in the slot and twist it all the way around. You've studied the photos of your aunts and grandmothers in taffeta party dresses and sparkly jewels; you're especially fond of the ones of Connie in her big white wedding gown and Ray in his tuxedo. There they are, frozen in glossy, black-and-white Olan Mills perfection: Ray and Connie kissing at the altar, hurtling down the aisle, dodging rice, feeding each other cake, the cake where the tiny bride and groom dolls stood. (They now reside on your comic-book shelf; you're convinced this lends your room a touch of glamour.) Connie and Ray are the handsomest couple ever, everyone says so, and the fact of that makes you so proud.

Other photos in the album seize your attention, too: the snapshots—or are they portraits?—of Ray's groomsmen and ushers, his former fraternity brothers. You've memorized the photos of the "boys" grinning drunkenly at the camera, their ties gradually becoming more and more loosened with each subsequent flipped album page, the expressions in their eyes growing glassier and glassier, as they loop their arms around each other, shag each other's hair, corral one another in jokey chokeholds. There's even a shot of one brother pouring champagne down the throat of another brother. Their raucous, prankish spirits jump off the page at you from the slick Fotomat surfaces; if only some fairy-tale genie could grant you your wish to jump into the pictures as if by magic and enter those black and white scenes, to become instantly twenty-two, instantly one of *them*, an accepted, popular member of a good-looking boys' club, a prized VIP guest at Ray and Connie's wedding. You would be their instant new/old buddy, and you would suddenly share their entire history of friendship and fraternal brotherhood. You know all their names already anyway, and even their nicknames, the way they're described alongside the class photos in Ray's yearbook: Kip Carruthers "Esquire," Johnny "Meet Y'all Round the Corner, Girls" Armstrong, Hutch "What's Your Handicap, Fella?" Hutchinson. You've memorized these, too. You recall them more quickly now than Ray does.

But Connie and Ray always say: "That seems like such a long time ago." Perhaps it was. Yet in the photo album, it seems like it could have been yesterday. What you love about photographs and movies is that in them nothing changes; no one gets older, the images stay frozen and preserved between the album covers. You know you can always look at a photograph and plug yourself into that moment. You understand the lure of nostalgia. One day, you may even be nostalgic for Right Now: for these intimate evenings at home with Connie and Ray, for these hot August nights of *Batman* and *Lawrence Welk* which the three of you share; you look forward to someday reminiscing with Connie and Ray about these days and nights, in the manner of old friends gathered at a reunion. By then, you'll be old enough to knock back gin and tonics with them; the three of you will toast to your good old days.

For August will soon be a memory, and September will come along to carry you back to school. Oh, how easy it is in the depths of July and August to forget about school! These nights spent with Connie and Ray have nothing to do with fourth grade, fifth grade;

these nights are the anti-school. How natural it is for memories of the last school year to fade out over the summer, even for a highly academic child like you. On these humid late-summer evenings you don't dwell on the rejections and slights and hurts of the playground, the frustration of math (language arts are so much more important to you), or the rides home on the school bus when you sit alone, or maybe with one of the unpopular little girls.

Yes, you are damaged, but in the safety of your Early American family room, you are also one swinging little romantic guy, you with your upstanding, church-going, Good Neighbor parents, you in your beloved Underdog pajamas and crew socks, with your champagne flute and makeshift canapés, you with your ability to turn the family living room into the studio of your very own variety show, in which your guests for the evening are the glamorous Connie and Ray, the closest thing you have to Rock and Doris, perhaps even to Burt Bacharach and Angie Dickinson; Connie and Ray are the icons who happen to live in your home.

You can even dance. On the Zenith, Mr. Welk and his orchestra have begun to swing into a sassy, up-tempo jitterbug, and you recognize that it is time to offer your hand to Connie, to Iced-Tea Lady, which she girlishly, blushingly accepts, and the two of you jitterbug with great enthusiasm to that old favorite, "Cow Cow Boogie." Your steps aren't accurate, and there's the height discrepancy, of course, but the performance is, as always, genuine in its eagerness to please and entertain, and you are exhilarated by it. Any chance to perform. In the background, on the TV screen, you and Connie are shadowed by Bobby and Cissy, the professionals, the Fred and Ginger of the *Lawrence Welk* program; they're the dream dancers now, you and Connie are the real live ones.

And Ray is the audience.

Ray, your father, but also a dashing and good-looking former fraternity boy, is your audience of one, and he looks on, as audience members do. What perhaps you don't see, however, in the frenzied rush of your hard-working dance act, is that he doesn't so much look *on* at you and Connie—dance partners—but rather studies *you*, as if you were up there by yourself, as if you were a solo act and she was a prop. He doesn't need to study Connie, he knows Connie. But he studies you, and as he does, he sports a difficult smile, an aging fraternity-boy smile that endeavors— really, it does—to beam out delight and encouragement in your direction. But at the corners, the smile turns down, and that encouragement evaporates, and soon that smile, indeed his whole expression, morphs into something that is distinctly not a smile. It is a horror movie face of open-mouthed, frozen panic.

You and Connie bow, out of breath, of course, but flushed and beaming, and you look to Ray, confident that he will gratefully applaud, as audiences do, certain that he will bequeath that mysterious approval that audiences give to performers. The two of you wait, panting and watching: Is Ray a satisfied ticket buyer? Did he get his money's worth for this evening's show?

But after more beats of silence than an audience usually holds for, Ray only gives a couple of halfhearted claps and stands up, shakily, to get another drink, brushing past the two of you and turning off the television set as he makes his way to the kitchen.

"Go to bed, sport," he says, under his breath, looking away.

Oh.

And that's what you get for all your hard work. Ray is not only a disgruntled audience member, he is a surly talk-show guest. He didn't even give you the chance for the sign-off, the exit line that is always reserved for the host, which is:

That's our show for this evening, folks. Good night!

You *are* the host, right?

But it's OK with you, really, to be packed off to your room by yourself; in some ways it's a relief. You close the door behind you and stand looking around at your dimly lit room: alone at last. You remember reading in *Photoplay* something Judy Garland said: "An Oscar doesn't keep you warm in bed at night." You wondered what she meant by that; you weren't aware that Oscar winners took their Oscars to bed, though you're sure if you had one, that's what you would do. Of course, you don't need an Oscar to keep you warm; you have parents for that, parents who make sure you're covered up with blankets, safe in your single bed, in your darkened, hushed, boy's room.

No need for protective blankets now, though; no need for extra heat on an August night. Under a thin summer bedspread of generic cowboy-and-Indian scenes (Connie's choice, not yours), you lie awake, and you hear the faint sound of your mother's and father's voices in the living room, the occasional clinking of ice in their glasses, and from outside your window you hear the rumblings, skids, and honks of cars passing on the road, punctuated by the occasional whoop of rowdy teenagers, possibly fraternity boys, in convertibles, no doubt, approaching in the distance, then close, then loud, then farther away, then distant, then gone.

You turn over on your side, basking in the small, flattering yellow glow of your Rocky and Bullwinkle nightlight, a pin spot. Their bug-eyed cartoon faces intertwine around each other with the same Saturday-morning grins that grace your favorite cereal's box top; you had to collect four of those box tops, in fact, to send off in the mail just to get this very nightlight. Rocky and Bullwinkle stare at you all through the wee hours. You close your eyes and try to go to sleep, but what you count instead of, say, sheep, are Ray's fraternity brothers, and your mind jumps back to the image of Batman and Robin tied up together, stretched out, straining, twisting against each other, and then the Joker—was the Joker tonight's villain? You didn't watch long enough to find out . . .

Fine. Create it for yourself.

It's the Joker, standing over them, laughing, hysterical, as if he were himself a crazed, mischief-minded fraternity brother in weird costuming at the Campus Halloween Ball. And Batman, struggling against the Boy Wonder, implores the Joker to be released, begging him with his eyes but begging none too convincingly, and Batman begins to sing in a raspy, desperate bari-

tone: "Look at me, I'm as helpless as a kitten up a tree." You toss
and turn underneath the sheets, unable to sleep under the big
burly cowboys and Indians. You kick the covers off. You are still
dressed like Underdog, and Rocky and Bullwinkle still stare at
you, unblinking and unanimated. And somewhere in the background, on a distant Hollywood soundstage, but also in your living
room, a vocalist has stepped up to a microphone to thunderous
applause and has begun to sing. You can't make out the words to
the song, but the music is lush and dreamy, and you thrash around
and listen . . . and think . . . and conjure up pictures in your
head . . . and thrash some more, until, well . . . until you can actually imagine what it would be like to be a real, live Overnight
Sensation.

It's September, you're a fifth grader now, and—good news—you
got into Miss Kenan's class. She is the youngest and prettiest of the
three fifth-grade teachers at Linden Hills Elementary, and, to top
that off, last year a rumor went around the school that Miss Kenan
had once worked as a trapeze artist with the Ringling Bros. and
Barnum & Bailey Circus before turning to elementary teaching.
You try to imagine Miss Kenan in white tights, busty and big-
haired, with huge swipes of stagey blue eye shadow painted across
her eyelids, swinging upside down over a net, dangling, then
upright again, right arm high above her head: sexy, confident,
and full of herself, while below her, a lusty, common crowd cheers
in unanimous Big Top delight, greedy and hungry for all that she
has to give them.

But now Miss Kenan is just pert and pretty in a simple white
blouse and navy skirt, instructing you and your classmates to open
up your tablets and, with your metallic red, tubey Number 2 pencils, write in big, blocky letters: "My name is _____; Today
is _____; Our president is _____; Our principal is _____."
This disappoints you; you resent the act of writing reduced to

a mere exercise in penmanship. After all, this summer you authored a full-length play about your family, written in a week with ballpoint pen on yellow legal pads. You have never been one for pencils, preferring the look, smell, and feel of ink. It occurs to you that writing instruments, specifically pen versus pencil, are not something the other children in your class concern themselves with. Neither are they concerned with forging a special, secret understanding with Miss Kenan. But you are, and why not? You're a playwriting, champagne-loving ten-year-old, and she is a Teacher With A Past: loose-living, canapé-eating, martini-swilling, *all woman*. Miss Kenan is the type of dame—yes, dame—that you've read about in quick, secret perusals of *True Detective* down at the drugstore. You know, as the writers of *True Detective* would know if they laid eyes on her, what Miss Kenan really is: a shadow-dwelling refugee from the circus, a game-playing, lusty, busty babe, a juicy tomato, a hard-hearted *mantrap*. How many fifth graders are fortunate enough to have *this* for a new teacher? Miss Kenan may be outfitted conservatively in a plain blouse and skirt set, but you, and only you among the collective fifth grades, can see that that's really a disguise. You know this is not the true costume of swinging high-wire trapeze artists whose lives have been kissed by scandal . . .

You are so lucky. You and Miss Kenan will be a clandestine team. And if she doesn't comply with your request to be allowed to write in ink, you might even blackmail her with the secret information that you—and you alone—possess about her.

You develop a friendship with another boy, a new kid in your class named Eric Tuthill, who has moved to North Carolina from upstate New York. You suspect Eric would rather have been taken in by the popular, jocky boys, but they are selective and don't readily exhibit the gracious and welcoming ambassadorial skills that you extend to new schoolchildren. You figure Eric is probably glad anybody picked him to hang out with; plus you will talk to him about the state of North Carolina and reveal secrets of your town and clue him in on various shadowy intrigues of Linden Hills Elementary. He will feel, in turn, that he has been let in on something, guided, eased into his new situation by an unusually generous and giving host, and in gracious response, he will offer his loyal, lifelong friendship. What piqued your interest most specifically about Eric was his origin, upstate New York, which makes him something of an exotic in your area. It occurs to you that Eric's being from New York State perhaps means that he has had occasion to go to Manhattan, which, along with Hollywood, California, is one of your two favorite places in the world, despite the fact that you've never been to either.

"New York City is OK, I guess," Eric tells you in the lunchroom one day, over fish sticks and chocolate milk. "It's big, that's for sure."

"Did you go see Broadway shows?" you ask between bites. "Or the Rainbow Room, have you been to the Rainbow Room?"

"Nah, I never heard of the Rainbow Room," he says, which immediately disappoints you. "But we did go see a show once, for my sister's birthday."

"What show?"

"Uh . . . I don't remember. It was . . . something with a lot of kids in it. It was OK, I guess.".

Your mind races. "*The Sound of Music?*" you offer. "Or *Oliver!?*"

"Maybe. I don't really remember. My dad used to take us to Yankee games, though. Those are really cool." This finally lights him up.

"Wow," you lie. "I wish I could have done that."

And Eric launches into a breathless description of a Yankee game he recalls in vivid detail, and you give him your undivided attention, ever the accommodating host and gracious ambassador.

. . .

The feelings you have for Miss Kenan probably amount to a crush of some sort; most days, she reminds you of movie magazine starlets, like Sandra Dee or Annette Funicello. Plus, it's obvious she likes you as much as you like her. You stay after school and help her with classroom maintenance, you dust the erasers against the sidewalk or on the sides of the Dempster Dumpster. You water the plant, you feed the turtle. And Miss Kenan seems to have intuited that you prefer indoor activities to outside ones; she probably realizes how much you dislike the playground. Late one morning, as the other boys are gearing up to play football, she asks you if you would mind staying in from recess to help her put up a new bulletin board.

"I think we'll do an orange background, with a black crepe paper border, for Halloween," she muses aloud. It's just the two of you—alone together in the classroom—which has suddenly become hushed and quiet now that all the other children have gone outside. It is warm too, with the heat from the radiators, turned on now because of the newly brisk fall days.

"Yes, ma'am," you say, and then you add something you heard a Hollywood guest say on *The Mike Douglas Show:* "I think that will look divine."

She smiles at you uncertainly; she holds her gaze for longer than a moment, then looks away again. You offer to cut out jack-o'-lanterns and back-arching, torpedo-tailed cats from orange and black construction paper. While scissoring ever so precisely, your heart begins to beat, and you start to breathe in quick breaths. Is now the time to bombard Miss Kenan with questions about her past? To finally find out all the things you've longed to know about? Her rumored days with Ringling Bros. and Barnum & Bailey? You want to ask aloud if she wore tight white leotards and smoked and drank with the other circus people in the off-hours, if she dated handsome, but possibly slippery, carny types. You want to know if she ever had her heart broken. But you're too afraid to ask anything, especially if it might mean finding out that none of it was true at all. You don't really want to hear the possible cold hard facts about Miss Kenan, about Miss Rosemary Kenan. What if she is nothing more than a nice North Carolina girl from a good middle-income home, raised Methodist, an A student in home economics, an elementary education major at Saint Mary's College in Raleigh?

You keep scissoring, pasting, taping, and watching Miss Kenan out of the corner of your eye, wondering . . .

But you don't speak. You decide it's better to keep pondering the rumors.

After Halloween, Miss Kenan and the music teacher, Mrs. Curtis, choose you to do a solo song in the December assembly program. You are thrilled and hope that they will ask you to perform "Misty" or "Winchester Cathedral" or "Melancholy Baby," one of the standards you've heard on the *Lawrence Welk* program. This is it, you decide, your big break, and on the Linden Hills Elementary cafetorium stage you will perform and the children and parents and teachers will whoop and cheer and you will become an Overnight Sensation. You are certain Miss Kenan, with her show business past, probably knows an agent or two, and will arrange for them to be there for your performance.

The song Miss Kenan and Mrs. Curtis eventually give you to sing is called "Long John," and it's a children's folk tune about a legendary, Paul Bunyan-ish explorer and hunter in the Pacific Northwest. This is a little disappointing; you can't quite imagine that "Long John" would be a selection on the *Welk* show, or that this would be the type of number you would be asked to do at celebrity-drenched parties in Beverly Hills or at the Rainbow Room. Still, you accept the task with gratitude, and it does genuinely excite you to think about performing a solo in front of an audience.

But already you hear some of the boys in the class start to snicker and jeer about your being selected to sing a solo—even Eric—and you realize, or should have realized, that it was only a matter of time before he would move on, what with his first-hand accounts of big-league baseball games and his burgeoning athletic ability. But it doesn't matter, you tell yourself; he couldn't remember the names of Broadway shows anyway.

Your grandmother, whose name is Agnes but whom everyone calls Perky, spends more time visiting your house now that she and Grandpa Joe have split up for good, but she doesn't seem sad or moody, as you expected her to be. Instead, she seems her typically happy, upbeat, good-time-gal self, living up to her nickname, bedecked, as always, in diamond rings and rhinestone bracelets, with upswept, beehivey blond-gray hair and jewel-encrusted cat-eye glasses, as though she is always on her way from the beauty parlor or the country club. Often, she is.

"Hello, dah'lin," she rasps, kissing you on the lips (something Connie will never do), and blowing big smoky puffs of her Virginia Slim, bracelets jangling and sliding up and down her arms. This fall, Perky has indulged wholeheartedly in the current fashion trend of paper dresses. She features many different styles: a big white one with a red geranium pattern, a purple short one with yellow polka dots, a hot orange above-the-knee number. Connie has said be careful when you hug Perky that you don't tear her dress or go near her with a Popsicle because paper won't hold up in the washing machine. (Ray: "Connie, if you ever start wearing paper dresses, I'm leaving out the back door. I swear. Stupidest damn thing I ever heard of.")

One evening, as you and Perky sit side by side on the love seat in the family room, she tells you: "Dah'lin, the Capitol Department Store wants me to model my paper dresses for a photo spread in the newspapah. Isn't that wuunduhfulll? At my age?"

You agree with her that it is wonderful, *wunnerful, wunnerful,* and you're thrilled that your classmates, and especially Miss Kenan, will see what a mod, trendsetting grandmother you have. You and Perky sit together and thumb through new issues of her movie magazines, which she has brought over just for you to see, since Ray won't allow Connie to buy them for you directly.

"Which movie star hairdo do you think I should get for myself, dah'lin?" she asks, as you flip the pages.

"Like Elizabeth Taylor," you say, fixating on a page with the headline: *Liz and Dick: The Jig Is Finally Up.* "Or like this," you say, pointing to a raven-haired Natalie Wood, posing coquettishly in a "Toni Girl" flip, a publicity still from one of her old movies, *Sex and the Single Girl.*

"*Sex and the Single Girl,* oh my goodness," says Perky. "Well, dah'lin, that's what I am now, a single gal."

"Hey, Mother, why don't you take him out to the yard and throw baseballs with him?" Ray bellows from his tilt-back relaxation chair. "That's what he needs."

You look down quickly, pretending not to hear him. You know he's right; you probably should be trying to get the hang of throwing and catching instead of feeding eagerly on tales of Hollywood. You pretend to be engrossed in an article about how Doris Day's last husband has squandered all her money and left her penniless. The caption reads: *America's Sweetheart Turns Beggar Woman Overnight!*

Perky pulls a Virginia Slim from her ruby lips with carefully manicured, orange-lacquered nails, and narrows her false-eyelashed eyes at Ray.

"Now Ray-Boy . . ." she says. "He's just being a good little Grandma's helpah to give me his opinions. Don't say nothin' bad about my grandbaby." Ray eyes you both and goes back to reading his own magazine, the alumni journal *Tar Heel Pride,* smoking his newly acquired pipe, formed in the shape of a ram's head, the mascot of the North Carolina Tar Heels. This was a recent gift from the alumni organization as a thank-you to Ray for success-fully chairing a local fund-raiser. Connie has confided to you proudly that Ray is moving up, "way, way up," with the alumni group.

"Honey, tell Perky what Miss Kenan has asked you to do in the assembly program," says Connie from the kitchen, cleaning off the dinner table and noticeably troubleshooting through Ray's mood.

"I'm gonna sing a solo," you tell her proudly. " 'Long John.' "

"Oh, dah'lin, that's wuunduhfulll," Perky says, blowing smoke. "When is that?"

"In two weeks. On a Friday."

"Well, you can give me a special private performance, in case I can't make it," she says. You know that Perky goes to the Alco-holics Anonymous meetings every day, trying to be very involved, though you've overheard Ray say that he suspects she still has a nip or two late at night before going to bed, and that she's just going to AA for the social aspect.

"Why don't we go in the living room and do that now?" Con-nie suggests. "Perky, you can play for him."

"Dah'lin, I can't read a note of music, and you know it," she says, and it's true: she can't, she plays completely "by ear," and by ear her fingers fly over the keyboard in a way that reminds you of your other favorite pianist, Miss Jo Ann Castle from the *Lawrence Welk* program, who always plays on abundantly decorated "theme" pianos. (Connie has nixed your ideas for doing this in her home.) Whenever you place a piece of sheet music in front of Perky at the piano, she stares at it blankly for a long time, then finally manages to plunk out a few notes. Soon enough, she stops to light up a cigarette.

"But maybe I can read enough to pound out some chords for you, dah'lin."

"Ray," says Connie, standing in the doorway and drying her hands on a dish towel. What she means is *Will you please join your family in the living room and try to show some enthusiasm while you're at it?*

As usual, you set the sheet music on the music holder at the piano for Perky. She adjusts the bench for height before sitting down to play, and pushes her jangly bracelets up her arm. She does, in fact, manage to pound out some prompting big chords, and you stand next to her, singing: "With his shiny blade, got it in his hand; gonna chop out the live oaks, that are in this land . . ."

You haven't perfected it yet, of course, but there's plenty of time for rehearsal; the assembly program is still two weeks away.

"Real good, sport," Ray says, looking bored.

"Yes, honey, you're absolutely wonderful," says Connie, visibly excited. "You're a natural. As good as anybody on TV."

You love her for that. You love her for everything. You'd run and throw your arms around her right now, but you know that would look like you were playing favorites.

"Now how about playing something else, Mother?" Ray asks. "Let's have some real music."

"Well, lemme see," Perky says, flicking the flame of her gold lighter against the tip of a Virginia Slim. "I just know my theme songs, you know." She launches into a medium-tempo drag of "Red Sails in the Sunset."

"I'll never understand how anybody can play the piano simply by ear," Connie says admiringly, bringing you over to the couch, and positioning you between herself and Ray. They are both drinking gin and tonics, which always seems glamorous and movie starish to you, but you wonder if it makes Perky feel bad to see them drinking, since she can't join in.

"I swannee it's true, it's the only way I know how," says Perky, into another chorus, her tough, shiny nails clacking on the keys, as if to add percussion. Perky, a one-woman band. Ray has told you she once held a steady gig playing cocktail piano in the Capri Lounge of the Rembrandt Motor Inn on Highway 301, "before it went to seed and she was ashamed to be seen there, as who wouldn't be?"

"'Up a Lazy River,' Perky," you say, wiggling away from Connie and Ray, and pouring ginger ale for yourself into the magic champagne flute.

"Don't you know any other songs?" Ray asks, looking agitated.

"Ray," says Connie.

"Sing with me when I play it through the second time, dah'lin," Perky barks to you from the piano bench, and of course you will. You'd obey any command that came from her noirish cigarettes-and-scotch voice. Perky pounds the keyboard hard, her head thrown back and her eyes closed, hands flying and bracelets jangling, high heels pumping the pedals below. You imagine her in her musical heyday on Highway 301: *The Capri Lounge takes great pride in presenting for your listening enjoyment, the one and only, Miss Perky!*" How you wish you could have been one of her regular ringside customers, shouting song requests above the roar, and emptying change out of your piggy bank to tip her in the double old-fashioned glass on top of the piano.

"Here we go," she says, and you are ready; you know just when to come in. She has taught you, and all your instincts are musical anyway. The two of you do a bang-up rendition of "Up a Lazy River," complete with hand gestures you've created to indicate paddling, slow-moving river water, and an old mill run.

Even Ray applauds at the end, with more gusto than usual, which gives you a surprising little electric charge in your chest. The two of you meet each other's gaze, and he gives you a little nod and smiles, but then he cuts it short, as if catching himself, and you look away too, embarrassed.

"Y'all ought to go on the road, honey, you're so good," Connie says, beaming.

"Yeah, you might could reopen the Capri Lounge," Ray says, and snorts at his own joke.

"Oh, Ray," says Connie, with a sigh. "Now will you please go and see your son off to bed? I've still got a mess to clean up in the kitchen." She winks at him, and then she kisses you good night, and Perky kisses you good night, and you wonder why Ray has to see you off to bed.

It makes you feel nervous, almost embarrassed, to have Ray traipsing up the stairs behind you, neither of you saying anything. You open the door, and he follows you into your room . He rarely comes in here . . . what does he want?

He walks over to your closet and opens it. From a high shelf he pulls down a brown paper bag; in big letters on one side, it says *Nash's Sporting Goods.* Ray looks at you and makes a silly little "surprise" face. A surprise face? You don't really know how to react to that, you've never seen him make a surprise face before, so you just stare at him, with no reaction. After a second or two, he drops the surprise face and then glances away from you.

"Um . . . I have something for you, sport," he says.

He reaches into the bag and pulls out a brand-new baseball glove, stiff and shiny, tan-brown, the color of Sugar Babies. He holds the glove himself for a minute, looking it over and punching his fist a couple of times into the center of it; then, with a big smile, he hands it to you. You stare at it, in his hands, for a second or two, then, realizing that it's a gift and you should accept it, you do so. In your hands, it feels large and cold; the mild, aromatic scent of new cowhide leather fills your nostrils.

Ray clears his throat. "I know they've started to play softball in your grade at school this year, at recess . . ." he says. "Your mother told me . . . and . . . I thought . . . well, I thought you should have your own glove, sport. So . . . there it is."

"Oh . . ." you say, looking down at the glove, and not at him. "OK. Thank you."

"We can practice sometime, if you want to, out in the backyard."

"OK."

He clears his throat again. "OK," he says.

He picks up the Nash's Sporting Goods bag from the floor, and holds it. The two of you stand there; from the light socket, Rocky and Bullwinkle stare out, watching, unblinking. You hold the glove, it's still *in* your hand. Should you put it *on* your hand?

"Oh, and there's this. I got you this, too." He reaches into the bag again and produces a small 45-rpm record in a slick-surfaced envelope with a photograph of a baseball player in mid-swing. The song title is written above the picture: "Take Me Out to the Ball Game."

"They had this there, too, so I . . . I know how much you like music and all."

He hands you the record, which you take in your other hand and you say again: "Thank you."

"OK, sport," he says. "Well . . . good night."

"Good night."

And you remember to give him a hug. And he lets you.

On his way out of your room, he flicks off the light and shuts the door behind him, leaving you standing alone and still in the middle of the floor. The low, muted beams of the corner street-lamp filter in through your window, forming a silvery pool of light on the floor. You stand completely still in the circle of light, in the full-moon shape of it; you stand in it as though it were a spotlight, clutching the baseball glove in one hand and "Take Me Out to the Ball Game" in the other. Your room glows with the bluish, watery light, and suddenly you feel like you're living inside an old black-and-white movie, you're like a kid character in an ancient two-reeler. But you're another kid—a kid who carries a prized baseball glove, a kid who plays baseball with his dad, a kid who makes his dad proud of him . . .

And you stand here in the spotlight, holding your props, staring out the window at the streetlamp, not moving, as if waiting for your cue to begin the scene.

. . .

In November, a visiting music professor from the local college explains symphonic orchestration to the collective fourth and fifth grades in a special assembly in the Linden Hills Elementary cafetorium. You note that the man refers to himself as "Maestro" several times during his speech. He explains how instruments "come in" at a certain time during a given orchestral work; you think of Perky cueing you to sing after she's played her song one time through. The music man explains "vamping," how a certain musical phrase will repeat over and over until it is time for a more significant passage of the music to begin.

And this is how you feel: that you have been vamping for almost ten years, repeating the same phrases ("I hate math." "Can I stay up half an hour later?" "But I don't want to go to bed now . . ."), writing the same shopworn sentences ("My name is _____ ; Today is _____ ; Our president is _____"), living in your dull, non-Hollywoodish town, with its one tall structure, a fifteen-floor combination bank and insurance building commonly referred to by citizens as "our skyscraper." Eagerly, you have looked up New York City in the World Book Encyclopedia, you have looked up Hollywood, you have memorized the photos and imagined yourself into them. You see yourself thriving in the middle of a bustling crowd on Fifth Avenue, well-dressed and strolling with adult chaperones; you see yourself taking bus tours of the movie stars' homes, saying to the tourists on the bus, "That was where Doris Day lived before she became penniless," things like that, juicy tidbits the official tour guides would be too ashamed to reveal. You actually begin to pepper your conversations at home and school with references to Bonwit Teller and the Chrysler Building. You pretend your school cafetorium is the Automat, or the Brown Derby. You instruct your mother and Perky to pick you up "at the corner of Sunset and Vine." The other schoolchildren treat you, when they treat you at all, like a weird, exotic animal in the zoo. Sometimes, they seem to decide that the animal you are should be made extinct.

"You're a faggot, you faggot!" hisses Bully Number One on the playground.

"I'm gonna kick your ass someday, you little pussy," growls Bully Number Two.

If other bullies are around, bullies numbered three through thirty-two, they laugh and jeer derisively, conspiratorially; they are one.

You rationalize: Perhaps they hate you because you're not only talented, but because you're a good student too. Also: good in music, expert at spelling, accomplished and meticulous with arts and crafts. The teachers constantly praise you . . . And these are things that make the other children bristle in your presence. You feel their mistrust, their jealousy; you can practically see the venom rising out of their little fifth-grade bodies, rising like vapor, like unleashed, unsettled spirits belonging neither to this world nor the next: swirling in the air, hissing, monstrous, looking to attack. But they can't attack you in the classroom, because you *rule* the classroom, you deliver the academic goods, you have every teacher—language arts, visual arts, music, all librarians— in the palm of your hand. You sing, you draw, you spell, you write, you are a good ambassador for new children from other places.

But then there's the playground.

And this is where they get you. Other children thrive on the playground, they know how to navigate its terrain and use it to their advantage, but to you, the playground is a cruel, barren wilderness for which you have never had a map or guide. It's a desert where no one has thought to build a Holiday Inn. This is where your precious knowledge of Doris Day, arts and crafts, and all things Californian *(Californian!)* carry no weight. And just by running out so far into right field that you've practically exited the schoolyard won't protect you from their vociferous evil.

But it helps.

JOHN ROWELL

You can even sing out there, though not too loudly, you with your stiff, new, still un-broken-in baseball glove, a glove that covers your hand so unnaturally it's as if some monstrous, extremity-enlarging cancerous growth had formed there. You wait for a bell to ring, and you daydream and sing, all your favorite songs about lazy rivers, about red red robins, about getting misty . . .

"You're a big music fan, aren't you?" asks Miss Kenan one afternoon, after school, as you assist her with the daily eraser dusting against the side of the Dempster Dumpster. She is dressed in beige pedal pushers and a white peasant blouse, the kind of outfit you imagine a Hollywood starlet might wear on her day off from the set. You think Miss Kenan is like Barbara Gordon on *Batman:* dressed by day in casual, unassuming clothes, then one spin-around of that closet and: Instant Kinky Wardrobe. You feel you know exactly what Miss Kenan's closet must be filled with at home: go-go boots, discarded trapeze artist costumes (tattered but still spangly), real human-hair wigs, lacy bras from Frederick's of Hollywood like you've seen advertised in the back of *Photoplay.* You imagine she has a boyfriend named Dale or Travis who lies around on the bed late at night in nothing but cutoffs, sweaty and horny, smoking a marijuana cigarette, and saying things to Miss Kenan like, "Swing upside down for me, baby. Let me see what you got."

"Yes, ma'am, I love music," you say.

"I know. You did a great job with your solo. And you like grown-up music, too, like 'Moon River,' things like that. I've heard you singing by yourself out on the playground."

You feel your face go red-hot. You never meant for anyone to hear you; when did she hear you? Did you get carried away and sing too loudly, forgetting for a moment that you were on the playground and not the *Lawrence Welk* program? You suddenly feel like diving into the Dempster Dumpster and never, ever coming out, a crazy, misguided child who died in the discarded remains of the lunch food from the Linden Hills Elementary cafe-

torium, food that went unchosen and unconsumed by other children, a perfect metaphor.

"Yes ma'am. My grandmother and . . . uh . . . my parents . . .
and I watch the *Lawrence Welk* program."

"Well, I think it's wonderful," she says, and puts her hand on
your shoulder, setting off instant shooting firecrackers in your
chest. "I bet I know something you'd like. Have you ever listened
to the Music of Your Life station on the radio? The one that plays
the *Saturday Night Ballroom?*"

"No ma'am."

"Oh, it's great, you'd love it. It's broadcast out of New York
City every Saturday night. They play all the wonderful old songs . . .
it's so romantic . . ." Miss Kenan suddenly touches her hand to her
cheek, averting her eyes from yours and gazing off into the distance, and instantly you know—because you understand her—
that she's recalling a lost love, enjoying a brief reverie about a
man that got away. Of course. You were right all along: Miss
Kenan *has* been damaged by love, victimized by romance. Someone from her circus days, no doubt. A heartless ringmaster? An
indifferent elephant trainer?

On a sheet of your tablet paper, she writes down the radio dial
number for The Music of Your Life, and you place it between the
pages of your MacMillan level-five reader, keeping it crisp, pris-
tine. You hurry home, full of anticipation and purpose, brimming
with the thrill of a new discovery, the reader in one hand, and the
hopelessly uncreased baseball glove in the other.

Imagine for a moment that you're not you, that who you are is
Ray. Ray: a good-looking, strong-jawed man nearing forty, with a
pretty, attentive wife—your college sweetheart no less!—an
excellent job as an insurance executive in a warm, friendly, big-
enough town in the home state you love, and have always loved.
You've got good friends and golfing buddies, all of whom remem-

ber you in your college days, when you reigned on campus in your flashy four-year career as an All-American baseball player, and you've just, as of this week, been named chairman of the North Carolina chapter of the UNC Alumni Association, a prestigious honor, and an opportunity for statewide social advancement so vast and far-reaching it's practically obscene. You have a lovely, well-kept home, the trim of which you must now paint Carolina Blue and white in keeping with the tradition of becoming alumni chairman.

And you have a recently divorced mother, a loving but irresponsible woman who, at last, has finally given the whisky bottle a rest, despite your suspicions that she has a lapse every now and then. And, of course, you have a child, an earnest and intelligent little boy who you know loves you, a fact you try to brush off, not dwell on, because you'd rather not be loved by a child you don't understand. Or: maybe you do understand him, and wish perhaps you didn't. Which makes you not want to deal with him at all, even though you recognize that he is what teachers and other parents have labeled as *special, bright, social, a little grown-up*. You grudgingly acknowledge that he possesses unique talents other children probably can't even begin to comprehend; you think perhaps he may even do something on a grand scale someday, find some degree of fame, some kind of acclaim. And you know these are things that you, as his father, should be proud of. But you usually manage to seem busy and preoccupied when he tries to talk to you, even if you're not, and you make only the most cursory, duty-bound attempts to share activities and time with him.

But then: you buy him a baseball glove which he seems completely indifferent to, so . . . well, you do try, don't you? You even went to the store alone to buy it, rather than asking him to go with you, because you knew—somehow you knew—how much he'd hate being forced to go to a sporting goods store. So you stood in the store and watched other fathers and sons there together—and together they were picking out gloves, baseballs, footballs, every-

thing. Alone, you bought him the best baseball glove you could
buy, the one that reminded you of the one your father bought you
when you were ten years old. God, how you loved that glove. How
you loved him for buying it for you. And, well . . . well, you failed
again, didn't you?

You sometimes think: How can he be mine? How can he be
my child? Because your child—yes, Ray, *your* child—does and
says things in a way that you despise in boys, in any male of any
age; he hints at behavior you want no part of, nor want to see
exhibited. He keeps you awake at night, this problem son, and you
bite your lip and shut your eyes and regret bitterly that you even
feel this way, because you see that other people, other relatives,
strangers even, appreciate things about him that you can't/
won't/don't. And you're aware that this makes you a villain, perhaps, because what you want to do is to slap the specialness out of
him, get rid of this . . . *otherness,* knock it out of his little body, by
force if you could, knowing still—and this is the worst—that he
would keep loving you even if you did. You wonder: Does he
know you have these thoughts? Does he sense it? Is that knowledge the thing you see reflected back at you in his little blue eyes
that stare intensely at you from across the dinner table, and then
dart away? Or, while watching television, when he tries to catch
quick looks at you when he thinks your head is turned? What
about when he says good night to you, when he tries to hug you—
God, that's always so awkward! Why does he wrap his arms
around your waist like that and hold on? What does he want? *A
dance?*

Maybe that's just your imagination, though.

But the eyes . . . God, the eyes. Those eyes that everyone says
he got from you—"He has your eyes, Ray," people say. "Have
you ever seen a little boy look more like his daddy?"

And his eyes carry *your* secret, don't they, Ray?

Because what he sees is that you don't love him. And that's like
a refrain from some sad old standard, a duet, maybe, playing over

and over on an ancient, broken turntable that only the two of you can hear:

You don't love him.
You don't love him.
You don't love him.

And you, Ray, are haunted. You are haunted in the way someone who has gotten away with a crime is haunted, haunted like someone who fears a certain diagnosis is haunted. Daily, hourly. It chases you. It hunts you down. *You are haunted.*
And so you should be . . .
That seems fair, doesn't it?

You, being you, have resigned yourself to the fact that on Saturday night you are the only one interested in listening to the Music of Your Life station. Oh, Connie and Ray might have listened, but today is Ray's big alumni association day, and officials from Chapel Hill have come to visit your house, to photograph Ray and Connie and even you for the newsletter (putting you in a "Carolina Baseball" sweatshirt and making you hold your glove up high, as if to catch an oncoming ball) and bestowing gifts upon your home and family. Cans of light blue paint sit in the carport; Ray looks so proud and, you must admit, handsome, in his Carolina Blue blazer with a navy pocket patch bearing the university insignia and the lettering: N. C. ALUMNI CHAIRMAN. Connie has proudly placed in the middle of the kitchen table one of the alumni association's gifts, a new lazy Susan in the shape of a large foot—the Tar Heel symbol of the university—in which the indentations for the toes and heel are designed to hold condiments like relish and ketchup.

Perky is out on a date (Ray: "Just hope she doesn't get knocked up." Connie: *"Ray!"*). So while Connie and Ray busy themselves with the alumni people, you actually get the chance to watch *Batman* by yourself on the small new TV in the family room, another gift of the alumni association. Nothing much has changed since the last episode: the Caped Crusaders triumph, as always, over evil, flattening the villains and knocking their henchmen out cold. *THWACKKKK! POW! BAMMMMM!* At the end of tonight's episode, Batman and Robin aren't tied to a plank or anything like it. They have landed the villain behind bars; they have won; they are free. Free to go. Free to go back and live together as best friends in their beautiful, well-appointed manor house.

But soon it's time for you to head into the living room and turn your attention to the stereo console. You're so excited about the Music of Your Life that you don't even mind that you'll be listening to it by yourself. You like being alone in the room of the house most often used for parties and entertaining, a formal, hushed, and quiet place now, isolated from the everyday activity of the other rooms. And you do so admire the way Connie has decorated: plush couches, deep-pile blue-and-green wool carpeting, flattering, low-level lamp lighting. You, in striped flannel pajamas, roll the red and yellow light dial on the radio console until you find what you're looking for. A man's sexy baritone voice says:

"You're tuned to the *Saturday Night Ballroom* and The Music of Your Life. Yesterday's standards by the great singers of today and yesterday, coming to you live from the King and Queen Room of the beautiful Hotel Astor in midtown Manhattan. Tonight's sponsor is Consolidated Edison, and the good folks over there want us to remind you that they're the ones who 'keep the lights on in the city that never sleeps.' And we do thank them for that. I'm your host, Eddie Edwards, you're in the Saturday Night Ballroom and this is . . . the music of your life."

You lean your small head against the console and close your eyes, and imagine the ballroom in all its splendor. Just the thought of such a place makes you happy, and not just happy, but *relieved*, relieved that it actually exists. That is where you want to be, in the King and Queen Room of the Hotel Astor, in the center of Manhattan, and, thanks to the lavish illustrations of the World Book Encyclopedia, volume N, you know exactly what the center of Manhattan looks like. You wish only that you were decked out in a child's-size tuxedo, instead of new flannel North Carolina Tar Heel blue-and-white-striped pajamas. You picture in your head the photographs of New York City that you've so lovingly memorized from World Book. Beside you on the floor sits one of Connie's silver serving trays on which you have placed canapés: Ritz crackers with little dots of peanut butter on top, and the magic champagne flute filled to the top with fizzy ginger ale. How you wish someone, your grandmother, perhaps Miss Kenan in a glittery evening gown, or—yes—Doris Day, were sitting beside you, whispering throatily: "Darling, will you pass me one of those divine hors d'oeuvres?"

The host says: "Tonight we begin with the wonderful sounds of the great Miss Peggy Lee. But first, I just have to tell you . . . the King and Queen Room looks particularly soignée tonight, folks. Mr. and Mrs. Astor have stopped by this evening, some of the Rockefellers, Mr. Sinatra . . . Just another Saturday night in New York City, and isn't that a grand place to be? And believe me when I tell you that Mr. Sinatra personally gave me special permission to play anything of his I wanted to this evening. Oh, folks, I gotta tell you . . . what a nice guy, and what a great artist, the one and only Frank Sinatra. A living legend, folks, a real living legend. But now here's another one of our great treasured artists, Miss Peggy Lee, singing the Rodgers and Hart classic "The Lady Is a Tramp." You're in the Saturday Night Ballroom, I'm Eddie Edwards, and this is the music of your life. Miss Peggy Lee!"

There is nothing for you to do but listen as Miss Peggy Lee, after a great, lush symphonic fanfare (no vamping) sings about some kind of stew, something about dining on turkey, something about traveling around by hitchhiking. Then she sings:

The Music of Your Life

"Alas, I missed the Beaux Arts Ball,
And what is twice as sad,
I was never at a party
Where they honored Noël Ca'ad. "

You open your eyes. "Noël Ca'ad" you recognize as Noël Coward, whom you recently saw being interviewed on the *Mike Douglas* program. He smoked from a cigarette holder, and said things like "Simply dashing!" and "Can you imagine?" and kept Mike in stitches. You were fascinated, but Ray didn't seem to care for him, so you didn't say anything. You wish you knew what the "Bo Zarts Ball" was, because you're sure it sounds like something you'd enjoy being invited to.

Peggy Lee starts to really swing her big number, and, knowing you're alone in the living room, alone in your own Saturday Night Ballroom, you get up and start to dance around the furniture, champagne glass held as high aloft as your little arm can hold it. You swipe a candle from the candelabra on the piano and pretend to smoke from a cigarette holder. Everyone around you in your Saturday Night Ballroom is *simply dashing* and clearly having a wonderful time. Even Connie and Ray are there, waving to you, happy, dancing, Ray looking Arrow-shirt handsome in his college white dinner jacket, and Connie resplendent in a blue-green taffeta party dress and matching high-heel *peau de soie* pumps. Satisfied that your guests are enjoying themselves, you wander over to the window of the King and Queen Room of the Hotel Astor and peer out on to the twinkly, glittery lights of New York that have been brought to you tonight by the good folks at Consolidated Edison, whatever that is, and from the console Peggy Lee belts out the line: *"I'm all alone when I lower my lamp. That's why the lady is a tramp!"* It doesn't matter that it's only Connie's gauzy, silky sheer curtains hanging in the window; in the absence of a tuxedo, the sheers turn into something even better, they make a decidedly *stunning* evening gown for you, as you twist your little body a couple of times so the material wraps around you and drapes, hanging, leaving your shoulders exposed, a fashionable gown, strapless and backless. You hold the curtain/evening gown in place, feeling very sophisticated, feeling like both Cinderella *and* the prince, and Miss Peggy Lee repeats one more time: *"That's why the lady is a tramp!"*

And through the clear champagne glass, brandished aloft, still wet and fizzy with ginger ale, you see the dark, backlit, silhouetted figure of your father standing in the doorway, watching you, only watching you, watching only *you*, and saying nothing. Just watching, his arms folded across his chest. You want to suddenly throw your champagne flute at him, and scream out that he doesn't *belong* in the Saturday Night Ballroom, that in his tacky UNC alumni jacket he isn't dressed for it, and who in New York café society would want a local yokel like him at their swank parties anyway?

But the two of you just stare at each other. And you say nothing. And he says nothing.

He just turns and walks away.

You drop the sheers and stand there in your pajamas. You're Cinderella and it's the stroke of midnight, and your beautiful dress is only ragged curtains again. And your champagne is only ginger ale, after all.

And from the console, the orchestra swells, the song ends, and the audience in the Saturday Night Ballroom bursts into wild applause.

Though it is deep into autumn, winter almost, in the Mid-Atlantic states it is still warm enough for children to have recess outside during the middle of the school day, so the girls go off together to play hopscotch, and the boys are sent out to the baseball field to play softball. This means, to ward off even more ostracism, you still have to carry the hateful baseball glove to school every day. You've been sitting on it while watching TV to give it the more acceptable folds and creases you've noticed in the other boys' gloves. It was the only way you could think of to break it in. ("Oh yeah," you even once heard yourself say to one of the bullies who questioned the suddenly used-looking glove, "my dad and I play every Saturday. He pitched for Carolina, you know.")

But now you're deep in the outfield, way out, where you always go. A few weeks ago, Eric Tuthill was out there with you too, but recently the other boys have caught on to his athletic prowess and he is now playing second base. They recruited him away from you; he seems happier. Sports skills are so much more important to other ten-year-old boys than the kind, welcoming ambassadorial skills you have, which only adults seem to appreciate. Besides, Eric told you recently that the other guys thought you were a sissy for singing the stupid "Long John" solo in the assembly program. You knew that already, of course; you wanted to tell Eric he was behind the times, the bearer of yesterday's news, but you said nothing. He liked you for a while, after all. Instead of responding, you merely went blank and walked away.

But none of this really matters, because you're just happy to be way out in the outfield by yourself, away from the immediate softball activity and the all-consuming, nothing-matters-but-this-game aggression with which the boys play. Quietly, and with a minimum of what would surely rate as telltale movement if they could see it up close, you pretend you're in the Saturday Night Ballroom with Eddie Edwards and assorted Rockefellers and Astors and Sinatras. You are into a second chorus of "When the Red Red Robin Comes Bob-Bob-Bobbin' Along," in fact, when something as foreign and unknown as a softball comes crashing through the roof of the King and Queen Room, landing at your feet.

"Oh my," says Noël Coward, with whom you've been hobnobbing. "What is that?" He peers quizzically down at the ground
through his monocle.

"Perhaps it's time for a word from our sponsors," says Eddie
Edwards, still dulcet, still *soignée*, but suddenly uncharacteristi-
cally nervous. And then he is gone.

You pick up the foreign object, and look about you at other
schoolchildren. What are they doing in the Saturday Night Ballroom?

Three boys are running gleefully around the field, shouting,
cheering, clearly winning at something, but what?

Other boys, non-cheerful ones, start to walk toward you, throwing down their gloves: *angry.* Immediately, you sense that you've
held the ball too long, and you throw it to them, but it doesn't go
far, it just kind of plunks on the ground like a thudding piano
chord in the lower keys. It doesn't seem to make any difference
anyway; they are close now, a mob.

"Oh, dear," says Noël Coward, and disappears.

"You stupid little pussy!" says Bully Number One, close upon
you now, in your face.

"You stupid asshole!" says Bully Number Two. "What the
hell do you think you're doing out here, faggot?"

And it's a silent but menacing Bully Number Three who
throws the first punch, directly into your arm. *THWACKK!!!!*

"Can you fight back, faggot?" asks Number One, rhetorically.
"Huh? Can you fight back?" And he shoves you down to the
ground and kicks your leg, hard.

You struggle back up, but Number Two is there with a blow to
your chest. *POW!!!!!*

You feel the tears heat up in your eyes, stinging, full, overflow-
ing. You wish someone would come help: Perky, your savior Miss
Kenan—*Where is she???*—maybe Eric, but you see him hanging
guiltily back, not really joining in but not doing anything to stop
it, either. Or Ray. You wish Ray were here! He would push aside

these bullies, Mr. All American Baseball Player of 1957, he would make hash of these uncultured, alien children, these ingrates who don't even know what standards or ballrooms are, who don't know where Manhattan is—they can't even spell it. But they can kick, and kick hard *BAMMMM!!!!!!!!*, and you need Ray to save you. And he *would* save you, you tell yourself, he would scoop you up in his arms, and wipe away your tears and protect and hold you and love you like all fathers do their sons. He would, you know he would.

The kicks and the punches are almost rhythmic now—perhaps the Bully Orchestra was merely vamping—and you're down on the ground and then up, and then down again, and then up, and the kicks and punches are like rhythm, they are like percussion, a different kind of "hit parade." *THWACKK! POW! BAMMM!*

And *this* . . . is the music of your life.

"You gonna lose another game for us, pussy? Huh, sissy? You gonna lose another game for us?"

And somewhere, in the distance, a bell rings. A bell . . . does . . . finally . . . ring.

A bell. A tone. It's music!

B flat . . .

Or C sharp?

THE MOTHER-OF-THE-GROOM
AND I

Mother steps out into our carport from the side door of our house and jangles her big ring of keys to get my attention.

"Hampton, do you want to drive?" she calls out to me.

Do I want to *drive?* I'm already in the passenger seat, with my seat belt and shoulder strap fastened and the door locked, holding a full-to-the-brim traveler's mug of hot coffee in my left hand, and an open copy of the current issue of *Movieline* magazine in my right. Would that suggest the appearance of someone who wants to drive?

I am forced to balance the sloshing mug between my knees so I can roll down the window.

"No, Mother, I do not," I say.

"Well, OK then," she says, and locks the house door and gets into the car.

"Mother, you know I haven't driven you anywhere since I was sixteen and you kept slamming down imaginary brakes on the passenger side," I tell her. "It was severely traumatizing."

"Oh, Hampton. I've never seen anybody hang on to things as long as you do. That was so many years ago."

So many years ago? Mother's unexpected reference to my age makes me bristle, even though I know she probably didn't intend it as a dig.

"It wasn't that long ago, Mother. I'm only thirty-three."

"I know," she says, buckling up. "As old as Jesus when he died."

"Yes," I say, "as old as Jesus, but not nearly as accomplished."

"Well, my heavens," she says. "Who is?"

And we pull out of the driveway.

All right, all right, I know how this looks. I don't lead the unexamined life, after all. It's pretty damn silly for a guy like me to be going out shopping with his mother on a weekday morning in the middle of October; I know that. However, in my defense, this is not just any old shopping day: we are, after all, searching for a mother-of-the-groom dress that she can wear to my younger brother's upcoming wedding. And since I am, shall we say, *unmoored* at present back in New York, where I so-to-speak *live*, I have volunteered to come down and spend a few weeks with my parents getting things ready for Topher and Mary Beth's big event. It is to be the social event of the season, which, in our town of Mullens, isn't very difficult to achieve. Anything a cut above, say, an old bank executive's retirement party or the Mullens Junior High Sadie Hawkins Dance would register as the social event of the season around here. True, the reception is taking place at the nearby Carolina Pines Country Club, which the locals refer to exclusively as "the CPCC," as in "Are y'all going to the CPCC for dinner?" or "Weren't the debs pretty this year at the CPCC?"

"I hope we find something for me to wear so I don't have to walk down the aisle in a potato sack," Mother says, navigating with Richard Petty–like skills onto the interstate, pointing us out of town, heading north.

"Where are we going again, Mother?" I ask.

"We'll end up in Raleigh, I'm sure, but there are a couple of places on the way that Sybil Scruggs told me about. She found a perfectly beautiful dress at one of these places for her daughter's wedding last May. Perfectly beautiful. But I'm sure I won't find anything. I'm sure I'll end up in a potato sack."

"Will you please stop talking about a potato sack, Mother?" I say, somewhat harshly, because with her you must. "Nobody is going to wear a potato sack to Topher's wedding, you least of all. Now, please."

"Well, I don't know," she says, and I can tell she's about to be ominous. "Nothing I've tried on in any store does anything for me whatsoever, so . . ."

"Well, Mother, why do you think I'm here? I mean, this is the reason I'm here, isn't it? To help you and Daddy with all of this?"

"I guess . . ."

"You forget I was a waiter at Caroline Kennedy's wedding, and I took notes. Everything is going to be great. We will find you a dress."

"Well, I don't know," she says. "We'll see . . . I just hope everything we look at isn't tacky. I would just hate to look tacky at my child's wedding."

"Mother . . . *tacky*. Good Lord . . . Can we please get a sausage biscuit at the next Hardee's? Or a gigantic Bloody Mary?"

"Oh, Hampton," she says, passing a slow-moving car on the right. "You don't want to put on weight before your brother's wedding."

I get the biscuit, of course. Actually, I get two. I live for them; I find you can't get good sausage biscuits in New York. I would move back down here for those alone except I would end up looking, as Mother always says, "as big as the side of a house." Fortunately I'll only be here for two weeks, and being with my family will raise my stress level, and thus my metabolism, so I'm sure to burn up the extra calories I accumulate from assorted southern foods. Last summer, I had Mother send up biscuits and pimento cheese, and barbeque and Brunswick stew from the Pretty Pig Bar-B-Q restaurant in Mullens, and I hosted a North Carolina–themed evening for my friends in New York. And it turned out to be an unmitigated disaster, a true Mary Richards party. Can you imagine how disappointing it was to see a bunch of Chelsea gym bunnies standing around trying desperately to pick the fat out of the pork and refusing outright my carefully prepared platters and bowls of coleslaw and Brunswick stew? I ate that pimento cheese, ordered for twenty-five people, completely by myself every day for almost three weeks.

My brother, Topher (derived from Christopher because I, as an apparently verbally challenged three-year-old—imagine!—was only able to say the last part of his name), lives in Atlanta with my soon-to-be sister-in-law Mary Beth, but my parents haven't quite figured that out. They think Topher lives in his little apartment, and Mary Beth lives in her little apartment, and that the two of them meet for chaste dinners and movie dates on Peachtree Street. Mother and Daddy, even though they are forward-thinking Presbyterians and moderately liberal Democrats, just never quite assimilated the deeper meanings of the sexual revolution. I could help, I suppose. I could reveal to them the inner workings of my sexual orientation, or at least the Cliffs Notes version, but I haven't—yet. To my credit though, I don't make up girlfriend stories or talk about pretend dates. To their credit, they don't ask, though I'm anticipating some "And when are *you* getting married, Hampton?" questions during the next two weeks. Not from Mother and Daddy, necessarily, but from "well-intentioned" family friends and relatives. It's bad enough I've had to lay my job woes at my parents' feet in the last couple of months and, on top of that, borrow money from them. (Of course I'm hoping "borrow" ends up being a loose term.) Insult to injury: to be fired from your eight-year job as a leading actor in a children's theater company because one day the producer happened to overhear some grubby little brat in the first row say something to the effect that you looked too old to be the young prince. The nerve! Who knew they were breeding pint-sized Addison DeWitts in rural upstate New York? In my defense, I ask if you know how unflattering and primitive the stage lights are in an elementary school cafetorium? My God, Brad Pitt wouldn't look good in those conditions! I still burn when I think about it. When I stop to think about all the sad productions of *Toby Tyler*, *Rumpelstiltskin*, *Goldilocks*, whatever, that I played in up and down the East Coast for what amounted to practically chicken feed . . . Do people have any idea how unglamorous it is to have to struggle into a ratty old bear costume in a middle school band room in Scranton, Pennsylvania, and wait to make your entrance from the "wings" of a stamp-sized stage at one end of an acoustically challenged gymnasium by shouting out: "Who's been eating our porridge?" When I think of the disgrace, when I think how I should be acting in Coward and Wilde and—

Oh, God. I'm starting to sound like Norma Desmond. In fact, I believe I *am* the Norma Desmond of children's theater.

"Now help me look for Berean Street, Hampton," Mother says, slowing the car down. "That's where this first place is."

"Where are we?"

"Fuquay Varina."

"Mother, how do you expect to find something fashionable in Fuquay Varina? Why don't we just go on to Raleigh?" I have ulterior motives; in Raleigh, I am sure I will be able to get her to buy me a smart sweater or jacket in one of the preppy collegiate stores in Crabtree Valley Mall that I practically *lived* in when I was in college here.

"Well," she says, "Sybil Scruggs's dress was perfectly beautiful. And she got it here."

"What's the name of the place?" I ask, testily.

"The Bridal Barn."

"Well, that sounds exciting."

"Hampton, you're so . . . I don't know what. Oh, there it is. Berean Street."

Mother turns the car onto a side street and sure enough, there a little ways down is a store shaped and painted like a faux barn in cherry red with a little white silo on the side. A small, marquee-like electric sign, the kind usually more associated with fast food and quick-mart–type establishments, reads: THE BRIDAL BARN. *For all your wedding and formal needs. Serving the Heart of Carolina since 1967.*

Mother checks her hair in the rearview mirror before getting out of the car.

"I need a permanent," she says. "I look like the Wreck of the Hesperus."

"Mother, you look fine. I don't think we have to worry about how we look in this place." I steal a quick glance in the mirror myself.

And we get out of Mother's tasteful gray Chrysler Cordoba and walk across a loose gravel driveway into the Bridal Barn.

"How're y'all doing today?" asks a pert, plump, white-haired woman seated on a swivel stool behind the cash register. Her nametag reads: BRIDAL BARN: Evelyn Boals. A yellow tape measure hangs around her neck.

"Fine, how are you?" Mother answers, still touching up her hair.

"Doing just fine," says Evelyn. "What can we help you all with today?"

"I'm looking for a mother-of-the-groom dress."

"I see. Are you the one getting married?" Evelyn says to me. I'm sure she's certain I will answer in the affirmative.

Well, no, Evelyn, you see I'm—

"It's his brother," Mother offers. "His younger brother is the one getting married."

"I see. Well, I'm sure we can find you something. Let me go get Mavis. It's her turn."

She leaves the cash register and heads toward the back of the store, where a frowsy, gray-haired woman, stick-thin in a royal blue dress, stands smoking a cigarette in the frame of an open doorway, outside of which appears to be a tobacco field. Mother and I start to peruse some of the racks of dresses that are mostly encased in clear plastic zip-up bags. The two women return from the back. Their differing sizes make them look like a female Abbott and Costello.

"This is Mavis," says Evelyn, heading over to another customer, whose arrival in the store has just been heralded by a jingle bell on the inside of the door.

The thin saleswoman's nametag reads: BRIDAL BARN: Mavis Bunce.

"Hi, how are you?" says Mother.

"Oh, well, I'm doing pretty good I guess, considering," says Mavis. "My bursitis has been acting up a little bit lately, you know, and I had a bout with that Chinese flu that was going around a while back, which like to have killed me, but other than that, I'm doing about as good as I can do." She makes a little clucking sound out of one side of her mouth, a gesture, I guess, to indicate that she's finished. And Mother is nodding her head in sympathetic understanding, listening attentively to Mavis's litany of illnesses, while I, on the other hand, am standing there thinking: Do we know this woman? Are we related to her? Should we have brought her a casserole?

"Oh, I'm sorry to hear about all that," says Mother, still looking genuinely concerned. "I'm glad you're better."

"Well, thank you, honey, I 'preciate that. Now what can we do you for today?"

"I'm looking for a mother-of-the-groom dress."

"Gotcha. And you're the groom," Mavis says, not even bothering to phrase it as a question and pointing a long bony finger at me, which, I can't help but say, makes me think of the witch beckoning Hansel into the gingerbread house.

"No, it's his younger brother's wedding," Mother says.

"Oh, all righty. Now is this a fall wedding?"

"Yes," says Mother. "Can you believe it? I haven't been able to find a thing, and it's only two weeks away. I've recruited my older son here to help me."

I feel my cheeks flush. I smile weakly and feel myself straighten up and adopt something like a cocky, frat-boy stance to up my masculinity quotient. OK, so it's a knee-jerk reaction of slight panic, more to reassure myself than anyone else. I'm wearing jeans, a North Carolina Tar Heels sweatshirt under a khaki windbreaker and Sperry deck sneakers, so it's not as though I look like I'm in the road company of *La Cage* or something, but, frankly, I'm standing in a women's formal dress shop in Fuquay Varina on a weekday morning. Also, I'm unemployed and unloved, so I'm not exactly at full mast of the masculine ideal I try to project to the world at large. Fortunately, I'm six one, which, in North Carolina, often prompts people to say, "Hey, I bet you played basketball!"; in New York, they just think, "God, I hope he doesn't sit in front of me at the theater."

"Now what did you have in mind, honey?" Mavis Bunce asks Mother.

"Well, to tell you the truth, I just don't know. I've been looking and just can't seem to find anything . . ."

"What color are the bridesmaids' dresses?" Mavis asks, clearly in sales mode, a seasoned pro.

"Midnight blue with black piping."

"OK. And do you know what the mother of the bride is wearing?"

"Purple. Which is good, because purple is not my color."

"OK. I've got something real pretty in a teal green color, just come in yesterday. Be real pretty with your dark hair and your peachy coloring and your blue eyes."

"Well, I have never worn greens well at all," Mother says, in the tone of dread normally used for saying something like "I'm so sick, I believe I might die tonight."

"Mother, just look at it," I say. "You won't know until you see it."

Now Mavis Bunce will see that I am a player in this decision, and from here on out will have to allow for my input and comments. I was not meant to stand on the sidelines where fashion is concerned, particularly as it relates to my mother.

"It's real pretty, honey," Mavis says, her tone encouraging.

"Well, I'll have a look, but I don't know about green . . ."

Suddenly, I realize what my mother's internal conflict behind this inability to find a mother-of-the-groom dress actually is: her three favorite colors, the only colors she feels look good on her, are black, white, and red. I feel the proverbial cartoon lightbulb pop on over my sandy-blond head: I get it now. Black is out for a day wedding; white is out also, of course, and, knowing her, she would think red is too flashy. OK, I'm ready to work.

Mavis produces the teal-colored dress she was championing, draping it flat over her skinny arms. It is very . . . well, it is just so *teal*. It would be a good color on me, I think, though not in an evening gown.

"I don't really think that's right for me," Mother says, feeling the fabric.

"Let me go check on some things in the back for you, honey. You just look around and see if anything strikes you." Mavis scurries like a tough little scrub hen to the back of the store.

"That dress looked like Grand Ole Opry to me," Mother whispers. "Your daddy would say it was something Dolly Parton would wear, I can just hear him."

"I wish you had come up to New York to do this, Mother," I say. "We could have gone to Bergdorf's." I stop short of saying how *fabulous* I think that would have been.

"Which would have cost as much as the entire wedding, probably," Mother says, and I'm not sure if she is talking about a trip to New York or a dress we might have been able to find for her at Bergdorf's. Suddenly, I think about Fifth Avenue, and get a little pang of homesickness for the big city. Of course, sometimes when I'm on Fifth Avenue, I get a little pang of homesickness for North

Carolina, too, especially when I'm walking along, minding my own business, window-shopping at Brooks Brothers or the Gap, and some harried businessfreak bumps into me and continues walking, without even acknowledging the collision, maybe even shooting me a surly, irritated look. That would never happen here. If someone bumps into you at the mall at home, they say, "Oh, I'm so sorry, excuse me, I didn't see you!" and then they might open up their purse to fish you out a dollar or a peppermint because they feel so ashamed and contrite.

"Y'all finding everything OK?" asks Evelyn, brushing by.

"Yes, just fine," Mother says.

"Now when's that weddin'?" she asks, her eyes narrowing in thoughtful concern.

"I'm ashamed to tell you it's in two weeks!" Mother says, full of apology, mournful even, as though she had broken some kind of female point of honor to wait this late to buy her mother-of-the-groom dress. So much shame! You'd think she was Hester Prynne sporting the Big A.

"Oh, goodness," says Evelyn. "I hope you find something. I know a darlin' purple dress that would be good on you."

"Can't wear purple," says Mavis, coming up with a slew of formals draped over her scrawny arm. "Bride's mother is in purple."

"Then you sure can't," says Evelyn, as she goes into the back.

"Now these just come in this morning," exhales Mavis. "I hadn't even looked 'em over good, but there might be something. What size are you, honey?"

"A twelve."

"OK. Now here's something I think is real pretty . . ."

Mavis lifts out a long beige gown that would be all right except it has multiple little yarn balls hanging off at the waist, kind of like what's on the end of an elf's cap, but about a hundred of them.

"These are a little odd," says Mother, fingering the yarn balls.

Mavis continues to sift through formals, and Mother and I mostly veto them. Some of this stuff, I swear to God. Not since the

Captain and Tennille had a TV variety show, or perhaps not since
the heyday of the Gabor sisters, has this much fringe and this
many sequins shared the same surface.

Mother and I finally agree on something, a rather tasteful,
ankle-length pearl gray muted satin. It's actually in her size and
everything. She goes to try it on, leaving me alone with Mavis
Bunce.

"Well, I don't know about deep gray for her. With her dark
hair, she might need something a little brighter," Mavis says,
sotto voce, almost as if it were private information between us.
Mavis Bunce, the Deep Throat of Fuquay Varina.

"Actually, I think she looks good in gray. Good with her blue
eyes." Mavis and I are going point to counterpoint.

"Well," she volleys back, "I'm not too sure that particular
shade doesn't look a mite too funeralish for a wedding. But we'll
see, won't we?"

Mother returns in the dress, having traded her Laura Ashley
floral print skirt and mid-sleeved white cotton sweater for this
formal. I can tell by the expression on her face that it won't do.

"It doesn't really do," says Mother.

Mavis studies her, touching fabric here and there. She
absently makes the clucking sound again. "I think it's a mite dark,
honey. You need a pretty red, or a pink, or something brighter."

And what I think is that Mavis has done this Bridal Barn thing
a *mite* too long. Besides, she looks like she's just dying to get back
out to that tobacco field and suck on another cigarette, illnesses be
damned. But of course, there's no reason to be impolite. In her
way, she has been helpful. I almost feel bad we haven't found
something here at the Bridal Barn. But now I'm moving into
Aggressive Shopping Mode: we have got to find Mother the right
wedding frock! She is going to look good if I have to turn an entire
mall upside down to make it happen.

While I wait for Mother to change out of the gray dress, the
mailman comes in to deliver the mail to Evelyn. He trades pleas-

antries with her, leaning on the counter, chitchatting. Then he looks over at me: the lone man in this women's dress shop. He stares at me for several seconds. I figure he's probably not used to seeing any males in here on any day. He nods, and I nod back, John Wayne—style. He's probably thinking, *What the hell is that boy doing in the Bridal Barn.* Oh, for God's sake, why am I worried? It's Fuquay Varina. Fuquay Fucking Varina. What do I care what Joe the Mailman thinks of me? He's not even cute.

"I'm sorry we didn't find you anything," says Mavis, ushering us to the door.

"Well, so am I," says Mother, with a good-natured laugh. "I hope I don't have to wear a potato sack to my child's wedding."

"Where are you all from?" asks Evelyn, back on the swivel stool.

"We're from over in Mullens. Well, I am. This is my older son, Hampton, and he lives in New York."

"Well, aren't you nice to come all the way down here to help your mama pick out a dress?" she says, in a tone completely free of sarcasm.

"Thank you," I say, weakly.

"Is the reception in Mullens, too?" Mavis asks.

"Yes," says Mother. "At the CPCC."

"Oooh," says Mavis, adding her signature cluck at the end.

"Y'all come back to see us now," says Evelyn, as the jingle bell announces our departure.

I convince Mother to drive straight on to Raleigh, and to ignore Sybil Scruggs's advice to seek out something called Betty's Wedding Emporium in nearby Garner. Garner is simply not on the way to Crabtree Valley Mall.

"Mother," I say, as I eject her *Ferrante and Teicher Play Songs of Love* tape out of the tape deck and try to locate my favorite old high school Top 40 radio station on the dial, "there are so many stores at Crabtree. Belk's, Montaldo's. Dominique's of Raleigh. We'll find something."

She picks up the cell phone.

"Dial Daddy at the office for me, Hampton," she says. "I just want to check in."

Since my father's heart attack three years ago, my mother checks in on him a lot more than she might have otherwise. She is rarely far away from him; today is an exception.

"Brown Landscaping," says my father's voice on the other end.

"Hey, Daddy, it's Hampton."

"Hey, son. Having any luck?"

"Not yet."

He laughs. "Well. Better you than me, that's all I've got to say. I would be of no use whatsoever."

I hand the phone to Mother, and lean back in my seat. Looking out the window behind my Ray-Bans, I watch the signs to Greater Raleigh come into view. It is a shining, technicolor fall day; blue-bright and fresh-aired, and as we go farther north the trees become gradually deeper with color: reds, golds, and oranges. I can't help but think that had I not been replaced as the resident Prince Charming with New York's famed Ragamuffin Theater Company I would probably also be traveling today, somewhere in Pennsylvania, maybe, or Connecticut, on the way to some elementary school to put on tights and apply Leading Man #2 pancake while standing in front of a dimly fluorescent-lit mirror in—God help me—a teachers' lounge men's room.

Which makes me think of Robbie . . . Robbie was a part-time member of the company who played the Scarecrow to my Tin Man in Ragamuffin's production of *The Wizard of Oz*. I happen to know that he has now taken over my prince roles in all the other shows, which really irks me. But, hey, I can acknowledge that boyish little Robbie is younger, cuter, and, yes, more *princelike* than I. I can also acknowledge that I developed a mad crush on him while we were traveling around performing together. I failed, however, to attract his mutual romantic attentions, a sad fact that was brought home to me one day when, while waiting to make an entrance, I inadvertently came upon Robbie with Chad, the diminutive, talent-challenged actor who played Toto, making out near the backstage area of the high school in which we were performing. At that moment, I felt a horrible chill, I felt an ill wind blowing right up through the bottom of my tin suit, up through my heartless chest and all the way out the hole at the top of my upside-down funnel hat. It was devastating. And I must say, you haven't lived until you've witnessed firsthand a scarecrow trying to hump a Scottie dog in a scene shop.

Damn Robbie! Why do I keep thinking about him? It's true about idle hands and idle brains, because the less I have to do, the more he keeps coming up in my mind. I even trained him for most of his roles! Talk about Eve Harrington. But we did have fun during those rehearsals . . . we made each other laugh, we were always sharing jokes, always talking about movies and New York. I thought we had so much in common. But . . . if only this particular Scarecrow had actually *had* a brain, he would have seen that *I*, and not that effeminate little canine, was the perfect guy for him. But he didn't. Or hasn't. So, I guess, the old ending remains the same, in life as upon the stage: the Tin Man's heart gets broken after all, and in a world where scarecrows and dogs run off together, the only available candidates left waiting to grant your wishes are fussy, twittering old men wearing bow ties and peeking out from behind draperies.

Crabtree Valley Mall—"*The Center of It All*"—is busy for a Tuesday. I notice lots of young Raleigh mothers out shopping, their preschool-aged children sweetly in tow, which comforts me somehow, and I think that's not so unlike Mother and me today really, except Mother is in her late fifties and I'm more the age of someone who by now should have had time to accumulate several advanced degrees, perhaps even complete a doctoral dissertation, but I realize other people don't think about things like that as much as I do; at least not in North Raleigh.

At Montaldo's, the salesclerks are mostly college girls from the area. The carpeted, softly lit shop is more elegant than the Bridal Barn, obviously, and I can see Mother looks more encouraged already.

"Hi, how are y'all doing today?" asks a tall blond girl dressed in a wraparound plaid skirt, light blue Oxford button-down shirt, and add-a-bead gold necklace. I instantly recognize her as the kind of girl I always felt like I should try to date when I was in college; she's pretty, she's preppy, she screams Tri Delt. Since the Montaldo's clerks don't wear nametags, she tells us her name is Kimber.

"Mother of the bride?" Kimber asks.

"The groom," I volunteer, cutting to the chase. "My brother."

Kimber steps back to survey Mother. "I'd say you were a winter, is that right, ma'am?"

"Yes, I believe that's right," Mother answers, but sounding none too certain. She quickly looks at me for help.

"Yes, Mother, you're a winter," I say, trying to keep it under my breath.

Kimber smiles. "Great. I'm thinking some kind of a nice, deep blue, or a light gray," she says.

"Well, OK, that sounds fine," says Mother. "But if I don't find something soon, I believe I'll just have to wear a potato sack."

Kimber laughs politely; I'm thinking she's probably heard that one before. She leads Mother over to a rack of formals in the back part of the shop. I would follow, of course, but outside the store, in the mall, I have noticed a very attractive guy, about my age, sitting by himself on a bench. I don't think it was my imagination that I saw him smile at me as Mother and I walked in, and I have kept a watch out of the corner of my eye ever since.

He's still there as I drift, ever so subtly, back over to the front of the shop. Of course, for the sake of appearances, I have to pretend to be doing something, and, unfortunately, the only thing I can do is to look interested in a display of large, crushy velveteen belts. I keep my attention divided between Mother and the salesclerk, the cute boy, and the crushy belts. I can't help but notice that the mall's Muzak machine is currently playing "How Deep Is Your Love."

I pick up a gold belt. The guy uncrosses his legs and leans over on the bench, forward, hunched, looking at me looking at the belts. Oh, this is great, he'll probably think I want one of them for myself, a big, crushy velveteen belt. Jesus. In the back, I can see Mother holding up a sparkly peach-colored gown. I pick up an orange belt and pretend to have an internal opinion about it. The guy gets up from the bench. Is he coming over? Oh God. Mother holds the dress up in front of her, modeling in the three-way mirror while I divert my attention from the orange belt to a skinny leather turquoise belt; maybe he'll think I'm a boyfriend of some girl and I'm out shopping for her birthday; boyfriends do that, I believe. But then I think: No, wait, if he thinks I'm the boyfriend of some girl, he'll be less likely to make a move on me. But then: What would I do with Mother if he does make a move on me?

The guy is now walking over to me, glancing sideways out into the mall the whole time, in the shifty way someone looks around before committing a crime. But he's smiling, looking expectant, like he's about to speak; oh, but then I think: What if he has me confused with somebody else, that he simply thinks he knows me and here I have been cruising him all this time like a fool, like the Gay Village Idiot who didn't know when to cruise and when not to, and he's probably about to scream out, "Please stop cruising me, you Gay Village Idiot!" But—oh dear Jesus, what is this?—he's almost at the edge of the tasteful Montaldo's carpeting. Oh God—

"Hampton?" Mother suddenly calls out from the back of the store.

The guy is almost inside. He's about to make a gesture toward me—is he going to speak to me or hit me?

"Hamp?" Mother calls, now turning in my direction to see where I've gone to.

And like a Three Stooge, I wheel around and knock over the entire standing rack of crushy belts. Oh, this is a disaster. Because what if I'm wrong and what if he actually was going to come over to talk to me because he was interested, what if he was an unmoored person like myself, looking for someone to share his life with, to set up house with, to love forever, to have and to hold till death do us part? And now, like a circus clown, I have knocked over a display rack and he's thinking: "Oh, he's cute, but klutzy— better not," and there goes an entire lifetime of love and romance down the drain because I couldn't control my own motor skills when faced with the unbeatable combination of having to feign interest in a rack of ladies' crushy belts while playing hard to get with a potentially desirable suitor. So I drop to my knees as if overcome by the Catholic need to pay penance, which makes no sense as I am a dyed-in-the-cashmere Presbyterian, but I know I have blown it anyway, and I have to pick up these goddamn crushy belts before the salesclerks uniformly decide to kick my mother and me out of Montaldo's because I'm a liability to the merchandise, and then Mother really will have to wear a potato sack to Topher's wedding, just as she feared all along, and it will be all my fault because I couldn't handle myself with decorum in a women's dress shop in Crabtree Valley Mall when I saw a cute boy who might be interested in me and—OH GOD!!!!

The guy stands at the entrance of the store for a moment as I hurry to replace the belts on the rack. I deliberately don't look at him, because if I did, I know I would be forced to scream out: "No, go away, save yourself! You don't want to date a Three Stooge! Run!" And when I right the rack, I see sideways that he has turned his back on me at the edge of the store and gone back out into the mall, presumably—now that it is clear our relationship will never work out—to trawl again among the great milling masses of the unloved. I want to call out after him: "Good luck! He's out there! You'll find him!" and then just hang myself from the Montaldo's ceiling with the orange velveteen crushy belt.

Mother walks over to me as I stand holding the rack, gazing out into the mall, lost in thought and staring like a hypnotized person into the gleaming red and white lighting of the Chick-fil-A.

"Hampton, what do you think of this, honey?" She has traded the peach dress (which, even in my panic state I knew was the wrong color) for a light silver-gray, knee-length satin brocade dress with a low round neckline encrusted ever so subtly with faux mini-pearls. This one has potential.

"Oh, I'm so glad you picked that one, that's one of my favorites," gushes Kimber, coming up beside us. "Don't you think so?" This is directed at me, though I'm sure she hasn't got the foggiest clue as to the dynamic of my being here in this store. She's probably just glad she didn't have to pick up the belts.

"It's beautiful, Mother," I tell her. "You should definitely try it on."

"There's a fitting room right here," says Kimber, taking the dress from Mother and leading the way.

So now I have, what, four, five minutes of free time? Mother has to take off her sweater, her skirt, and get zipped into the dress. And then she will quickly fluff her hair, say "I look like the Wreck of the Hesperus" to the mirror before walking back out onto the floor to model the dress for the salesclerk and me. Maybe it's not too late to find My Hero again, and convince him that I'm really worth it, after all . . .

I have five minutes.

I dash out into the mall. I look quickly into Spencer Gifts, then World Bazaar, then Baskin-Robbins. No sign. A quick glance into The Hub menswear. Zip.

Oh, what did I expect anyway? This is stupid, infantile behavior; I clearly have lost my mind. And that's when I see him—

about three yards ahead of me, walking hand in hand with some girl. A *girl!* Aha. Well, isn't that interesting. I gain on them, then slow down, then deliberately walk past them. I turn around to catch his eye, and our gazes do lock in a boy-to-boy stare for something like a quick second. But then his eyes glaze over—reflexively? intentionally? both?—under the intensity of my high beams. His look and his message are clear: *Now's not the time.* I smile at him, of course; I may be the Gay Village Idiot, but I'm a gentleman, too, and really—isn't a simple smile the least of kindnesses one can offer when an affair comes to an end? I pause at the window of Crate & Barrel, pretending to gaze at the gleaming display of new copper cookware, and allow the couple to pass me.

I walk back into Montaldo's just as Mother is coming out of the dressing room. Suddenly, in this instant when I catch sight of her, I forget about the guy in the mall, about Robbie, about New York, about all the minutiae of my life, about everything. Because I see Mother emerging from the dressing room with the regal bearing and immaculate glamour of a '50s movie queen, and for a moment, casting aside family bonds, ages, and sexual orientation, I feel like nothing more than just a guy gazing at a beautiful woman in a gorgeous dress. The silver-gray color offsets her dark hair and blue eyes perfectly, the neckline is exactly right for her graceful, feminine neck, the length of the skirt shows off her still-shapely legs to great advantage. All my childhood fantasies of having a mother who looked and dressed like a combination of Grace Kelly, Jackie Kennedy, and Marlo Thomas, with a little June Cleaver thrown in for reality, suddenly come rushing back to me. I'm so proud of her. I'm so proud she's mine.

"Hey," I say, finally.

"What do you think?" she asks, expectant, clearly hoping I will say yes. I would, even if I didn't like it, because for her, it is already yes.

"Mother, it's gorgeous. You look . . . fabulous."

"I told you he'd like it," says Kimber to Mother, then back to me: "We were hoping you would."

"Do you think Daddy will like it?" Mother asks, turning away to make slight adjustments in the mirror.

"Of course."

"What about Topher? Think he'll like it?"

"I'm sure he will. Especially when he finds out how close you were to a potato sack."

"Oh, Hampton. Well . . . I guess . . ."

"Definitely get it, Mother. It's the best one we've seen all day."

I move up into the mirror and stand next to her, and we look back at our reflections. For a second, her sudden glamour casts its glow on me, too, and I get to be Tyrone Power or Cary Grant taking her arm. And then what I think is: Has Mother, at any time today, wondered if this is her only chance to ever be the mother of a groom?

After Mother and I do a late lunch at the mall's food court—I at the Chick-fil-A, she at Salads 'n Such—we stop into Grant's of the Hill, which is Crabtree's best men's clothing store. She buys me a sweater and tells me how grateful she is that I was here to help her today. I feel a little guilty, because of course I had wanted something for myself all along, but I can tell that buying this for me is something she wants to do, and she knows, anyway, that I always have a good time shopping in a mall, no matter what I'm looking for. It's always been this way between us, thirty-three years of small, silent understandings. Besides, it's a great sweater: it's teal! Maybe I'll have at least one date this winter where I can wear it. I almost say this to her, too. Almost, almost, almost. *A date, Mother. I'll wear this on a date. Maybe he'll like it as much as we do. Maybe he'll like me—almost—as much as you do. Maybe, if he stays, you'll like him—almost—as much as you like me. Maybe, if he really stays, I'll love him, Mother. And he'll love me—almost—as much as you love me.* Almost, almost, almost I say this. And I almost see her looking at me with a clear-eyed look of expectancy, as if she knows what I'm going to say. Is it too obvious for me to even proclaim it? Is it too obvious for her to even acknowledge it?

"This is a beautiful sweater, Mother," I say, slowly, my breath coming in choppy waves, though maybe only I can hear that. "Thank you."

"Oh, you're welcome, honey."

"Mother . . . it's so beautiful . . . that maybe I could . . . even wear it . . . on a date."

I'm afraid I might just fall to the floor of Crabtree Valley Mall right at this moment and conk my head on the hard surface and pass out for eternity, clutching a teal sweater to my chest and dreaming of Prince Charming.

She looks at me, right in the eyes. I'm still standing. So is she.

"Well, yes, Hampton," she says, also slowly. "Maybe you could. And wouldn't that . . . person . . . be lucky to be on a date with you? With you and your sweater."

And we both turn away from each other, as if cued, keeping our gazes fixed at the exit sign, but walking side by side for as long as it takes to reach the doors.

Outside, it has grown almost dark, and the tall, fluorescent lights of the parking lot are starting to flicker against the navy blue sky. Mother looks suddenly panicked.

"Oh, I wanted to be home before dark," she says, fumbling in her purse for her keys. "I wanted to get home before Daddy does." And I know what's coming next, because I have heard it many times before:

"So he doesn't have to walk into an empty house while I'm still alive."

"Oh, Mother," I say impatiently, as she starts up the car and begins to navigate us out of the Crabtree parking lot. "It's one day. I think finding your dress was a little more important than making sure Daddy gets dinner on time."

And after a moment, or two, she says, quietly: "Nothing is more important than Daddy, Hampton."

That stops me; I don't say anything after that. At least not for about five hurt, brooding, selfish minutes. But then I realize that she includes me and my brother in that remark too, and Mary Beth; nothing is more important than *us*. I lean my head back against the headrest, and we ride in silence for a while. But soon after we turn onto the Beltline, I pop the Ferrante and Teicher tape back into the tape deck, and the car reverberates with their instrumental piano "stylings" of "Moon River."

"This was popular when you were born," Mother says.

At the stoplight, she all of a sudden reaches over and takes my hand and squeezes it. I squeeze back, and we hold hands until the light changes. "But you knew that already, didn't you?" she asks.

I hum *uh-huh.* I'm hearing the lyrics to the song in my head, over the instrumentals, and I'm thinking of that line about the Moon River being wider than a mile. And I think it's funny how people are always saying something is a mile wide, when what miles are, really, when you think about it, are long. Rivers are wide, miles are long. But maybe it's just the way different people have of seeing the same exact thing; one person's mile is wide, another person's river is long.

"Let's sing with the music, Hampton, like it's karaoke," says Mother.

And that's what we do—we sing, as the mother of the groom steers us, all of us, south, toward home.

WHO LOVES YOU?

CALIFORNIA, 1954

The only person here who knows I'm a boy is Lucille Ball.

A boy. I have to keep adjusting under this dress I've got on so I can feel myself down there, just to remind my*self.* I've never worn an evening gown before, and it's the oddest thing. Not to mention that I can barely see out of these stupid false eyelashes. Why on earth I ever agreed to be a showgirl, I'll never know . . .

I met Miss Ball at a party in Bel Air a few weeks ago, a real fancy type affair, with waiters and valet parking, cocktails, canapés— things like that, things I'd never even heard of till I came out to California. My friend Arthur, who works as an Assistant Director on a lot of movies out here, took me along; he has acquaintances with a lot of showbiz people, and gets invited to lots of important parties. He knows Miss Ball and Mr. Arnaz from when he AD'd a movie they made together a few years ago, and got to know them a little bit, at least enough to speak to. Once he even baby-sat for their kids, and worked in their garden a few times, when assistant work was hard to find.

So we got to this party. And there was Lucy, wearing a bright green party dress, smoking, drinking, standing in the middle of a group of about five or so people, laughing and carrying on. All I could think was *Damn, it's Lucy in the flesh.* And then Arthur just

up and waves to her, all familiar and everything. And she sees him
and waves back and motions for him to come over.

"Do you want to meet Miss Ball?" he whispers to me.

"Yeah . . . I mean, do you think that'd be OK?"

"Of course. Stick with me, 'Bama Boy." Ever since Arthur
found out I was from Alabama—Hollinsville, to be exact, about
forty miles outside of Montgomery—he's called me 'Bama Boy,
though my real birth name is William Abernathy Ford, Jr. "Will"
if you just met me here in Hollywood, "Willie" if you know me
from Hollinsville, "Willie-Bud" if you're a member of my immediate family or one of my thirty-four aunts, uncles, and cousins,
accounting for both the Ford and Abernathy sides. Mama was an
Abernathy, of the Biloxi Abernathys.

"Hello, Miss Ball," Arthur says. "Nice to see you again." He
takes her hand and kisses it, real gallant, like something Errol
Flynn would do in one of his pictures. The people who have been
hovering around her kind of move away, seeing as how she has
made room to talk to us. They were probably, in the language of
Hollywood that I'm finally starting to figure out, "hangers-on."

"Hello, darling," Miss Ball says. "How's business? What are
you up to?"

She has an unfiltered cigarette going in one hand—a Philip
Morris, I'm sure, since that's who sponsors her show—and some
big goblet kind of drink in the other: tea colored, probably some
kind of hooch. Everybody drinks liquor at parties out here; nobody
I knew back home ever drank, and I still can't quite get used to the
taste of it myself.

"Oh, I can't complain," he says, though I know he really could.
"Just finished the new Rock Hudson picture." He runs his hands
through his wiry black hair and pushes his tortoise-shell glasses
up on his nose. He does that when he's nervous. He probably
doesn't want Miss Ball to know he was just an assistant to the
assistant this time.

"Oh yeah," Miss Ball says. "Over at Universal."

"That's right."

"I ran into Rock last week. He's got high hopes for it, but who the hell knows. How'd they treat you over there, Artie?" Her huge, turquoise eyes with the big lashes narrow in at him as she sucks in a vampy drag of her cigarette, like I've mostly only seen in the movies, and then mostly from Bette Davis. The end of the cigarette, I notice, has turned scarlet, from her lipstick, and so has the side of her glass that she's drunk from. Maybe when she's done I can steal the cigarette butt from the ashtray, with a Lucy lip print on it. I could send it back home to my cousin Starla Scott, who claims to be Lucy's biggest fan and is always going on and on about her, mimicking her faces and such from the show. Of course Starla's pretty mad at me for coming out here to be a movie star before she did. Maybe I'll just steal that cigarette butt for myself.

"Everything went well," Arthur tells Miss Ball. "I think it'll be a good picture, but you never know how it'll play in the valley." This makes everybody in Lucy's little circle break out laughing, and Lucy just rolls her eyes, like to say, *That's for sure.* I have no idea what all that means, but it's fun to watch Arthur hobnobbing and being real Hollywoodish. He sure is smooth and familiar, and really knows what he's talking about, and that makes me like him even more than I already do, but I still don't see how he can be so nonchalant about all this. (He calls it a French word: *blasé.* "You have to learn to be more blasé around movie people, 'Bama Boy, or they'll think you're too desperate.")

"Who's your friend here, Artie?" Miss Ball asks, narrowing those eyes and looking in my direction now.

I've never seen hair even close to her shade of red before—it's not really red, it's orange, like a Halloween pumpkin. And with her blue eyes and orange hair and white skin, what I keep thinking is she looks like the colors on the outside of the Howard Johnson's hotel in downtown Biloxi. Arthur says her coloring is so perfect for the camera that here in Hollywood they call her "Technicolor Tessie."

Arthur puts his hand on my back and pushes me gently forward, probably thinking that I'm a little scared, since I'm hanging back a little. He's right.

"Lucy, this is Will Ford. He just got into town a couple of months ago. Will, Lucille Ball."

"How do you do, Miss Ball?" I say, allowing Arthur's hand to move me forward a little more. I'm remembering the way my Aunt Eugenia taught us children how to always greet somebody new, though when you finally say "how do you do" out loud like that, it sounds like you're meeting the Queen of England or something. "I'm pleased to meet you," I tell her. I offer to shake hands, but she doesn't accept. Suddenly I wonder if I've done the wrong thing, and I feel my face flush.

"Hoo-wee! Where's that accent from?" she asks, blowing smoke.

Now I'm *positive* my face is as red as Miss Ball's lipstick.

"Alabama, ma'am. Near Montgomery."

"Good God, child, what are you, all of fourteen? Does your mama know you're here?"

I look to Arthur for help. Since he's twenty-nine, which seems pretty old to me, I figure he's smarter about things than I am, and always knows what to say. But now he just looks at me like: *You're on your own here, buddy.*

"I'm eighteen, ma'am. Almost nineteen," I say, though I feel my hands start to tremble where they're hanging down by my sides. I've never met a real star before; it's a whole lot different than meeting regular people.

"Well, that's legal in some states, I guess," she says, winking at Arthur, and the two of them have a good little laugh. I just smile, trying to be polite. I quickly reach up and touch my cheek to see if it's as hot as it feels.

"So . . . you want to be in show business, Will Ford?" she says. "Is that what you're here in the big city to do?" Boy, she sure is direct.

"Yes ma'am, that's right. I wanna be an actor." And then I add: "More than anything."

"More than anything? Good God Almighty! Can you vouch for this kid, Artie?" She starts waving her cigarette in the air and looking around like she needs an ashtray. Immediately, some guy standing in back of her holds one out. She stubs out her cigarette then waves his hand away. She squints her eyes a little and looks at me up and down, sizing me up, like she's trying to decide if she's gonna buy me.

"Oh, sure. The kid's a natural," Arthur says, lighting up his own cigarette. Arthur is from Illinois originally, but he's good at talking in Hollywood phrases. He's been teaching me to always say things like: *The Business. Pictures. Metro. Box Office. Hangers-on.* Arthur's fond of calling me " 'Bama Boy, Who Likes the Pitcher Shows."

"Artie, would you excuse us a minute?" Miss Ball says, draining the last of her drink and handing it off to the same guy who offered the ashtray. "I wanna talk to your little friend here. Alone, if you don't mind."

"Oh . . ." Arthur suddenly looks very surprised. When he hesitates for a second, Miss Ball says, "Don't worry, I'll give him back to you."

This makes Arthur let out a nervous laugh, and he runs his hand through his hair again and readjusts his glasses. "Oh. Of course, of course. No problem," he says. "Nice to see you again, Miss Ball. As always."

"And you, Arthur," she says, but it's me she's looking at now. She waves at Arthur, but she's really waving him away. She's staring right at me; I don't know what to do. Arthur moves off to another corner of the room, but I can still feel him watching me, which, I realize suddenly, is not the same as watching out *for* me.

"You're a real pretty boy, kid," Miss Ball says, after a second or two of looking me over. "I guess people have told you that before."

"Well, I don't know really, ma'am," I say back to her. I pray I won't start to stutter.

"You know, I could give you a shot on my show, if you'd be willing to do something a little . . . well . . . let's just say, a little out of the ordinary."

I stare at her for a second; then when I realize what she's said, my mouth flies open and hangs there, like I'm some goofy cartoon character. I'm sure my mama would say, "Close your mouth, Willie-Bud. You tryin' to catch flies?"

"Um . . . well, yes ma'am" is all I can come up with. I'm thinking I must be experiencing some kind of fever dream, like when I was five and had measles.

"God, that accent. Jesus. What they couldn't do for you at MGM, honey. Well, anyhow, for what I have in mind, you won't have to talk much. Here's the deal. I sometimes like to play little tricks on my husband, Desi," she says, taking another Philip Morris, which has been handed up to her from the same guy, who then produces a lighter. He must be somebody Miss Ball pays to hand her things.

It sounds funny to me the way she pronounces Mr. Arnaz's name so that it rhymes with "messy," rather than the way I've always said it, which is more like "Dezzy."

"And I think," she continues, "that you could probably help me out. This thing'd kill him, if I pull it off right. Oh boy." And she laughs, a real raspy laugh that sounds more like coughing than laughing.

I can tell Miss Ball is a tough dealmaker, like my Uncle James who sells cars at Hollinsville New and Used Pontiac.

"We have a script coming up in a few weeks where we need about eight showgirls. You ever put on one of your mama's dresses, kid?" She stares me down hard; I look around for Arthur, but he's gone. It's just her and me; the people around us have turned their backs completely now, and are talking among themselves.

"Dresses?" I say.

"That's right, dresses. Don't be coy. I've got a little scene I want you to do. If you're interested, of course. But you'll have to be in a dress. That's the deal. So." She turns around to the guy behind her: "Hey, Bunny, where's the damn ashtray? And can I get a fresh drink? Please?" She turns back to me. "Jesus Christ, you'd think we were in church." She notices I'm empty-handed also. "And get this kid here something, too."

The guy she calls Bunny looks at me. "And what kind of drink would that be? A Shirley Temple?"

Miss Ball laughs again, hoarsely. "Yeah, right, a Shirley Temple. A Shirley Temple with a big splash of vodka. Do you know what we call that, kid?"

"No ma'am."

"A Deanna Durbin. Hop to it, Bunny." And he does.

Instantly, she's back to business again, fixing her eyes on me. "So, kid . . . about my little proposition. What'll it be?"

She blows so much smoke waiting for me to answer that I start to feel all those vapory gray swirls going right into my own lungs, filling them up like a dark balloon. I cough a little, then smile. She watches me think . . . boy, does she ever watch me think . . .

And what I think is: *You don't say no to Lucy.*

So here I am on this soundstage making my debut in show business, which is great, though it's not exactly like I'll be able to tell everybody back home to watch me on the show when it comes on. Just to make fun of me, Arthur said: "*Hey, Mama? Daddy? This is your boy, Willie-Bud. I've got some good news, and I've got some bad news . . .*" He thought that was just real ha-ha funny. I didn't even crack a smile. But they're paying me a lot of money, or at least it's more than I've ever made before, and Mr. Trent was real good about letting me off work at the flower shop where I have my part-time job, so I could have the day at the studio to rehearse and film the show. Miss Ball had one of her assistants work with me alone late one afternoon, so I wouldn't have to come to regular rehearsal with everyone else. This morning, he also sneaked me into hair and makeup early, before anyone else got to the studio.

Now I'm standing here in six-inch white heels, a white, feathery ball gown that looks like something out of the Ziegfeld Follies, and a big blond wig, topped with a huge ostrich-plumed show hat. Makeup, of course, and lots of it: pancake, heavy rouge, even a beauty mark on my lower right cheek. Nobody would recognize me in a million years, except maybe my Aunt Eugenia, since I thought when I saw myself all done up like this in my dressing room that I kind of looked like Starla Scott when she placed fourth runner-up last year in the Miss Delta Flats beauty contest, though I have to admit one thing: I'm prettier.

Miss Ball recognizes me, of course. She's been real nice, real friendly, personally handling everything with the casting people and the wardrobe and makeup people and the people who sign the checks and stuff like that. She made sure I got my own dressing room, away from the other girls in the scene, all of whom seem to be real genuine girls, at least as far as I can make out. Of course, they haven't all been cordial to me, since it looks like I'm getting special treatment from the star, but that's OK; nobody in our high school production of *Romeo and Juliet* liked me either, once I got all the best reviews in the *Hollinsville Daily Dispatch.* I was Romeo, of course, but now I'm thinking that since I look so good as a girl I probably could have played Juliet just as well, too; I know I woulda been better than that no-talent Linda Beth Creech.

"All right, girls, take your places, please," the director tells us. "This is our final dress rehearsal before we bring in the audience, so look snappy!" In this episode, Lucy Ricardo, who wants to get into movies real bad (like me—ha-ha) has gotten herself a job as a showgirl in a big Hollywood musical. And they give her a huge headdress to wear and a specialty walk down the staircase, but in the scene she keeps falling over because the headdress is too heavy, and the director of the movie keeps threatening to replace her. It's amazing to watch Miss Ball work out all her "comic business" (another professional saying Arthur taught me), snapping in and out of character just like that, like on a dime. One minute she's Miss Ball, and I have to say she's real professional and businesslike; she doesn't suffer foolishness and she's not very hobnobby. Then as soon as the director yells "Action!" she becomes Lucy Ricardo and does all those falls and faces and stuff, and it's so hard for me to keep from laughing just watching her, but I can't, because I'm in the scene—I have to keep reminding myself of that. If I'm going to make it in show business, I can't be breaking up like an ignoramus, gawking at the stars the way I would if I was just at home watching them on television.

Miss Ball gets into position with her giant headdress at the top of the stairs. Of course, in real life the headdress isn't heavy at all, and Miss Ball walks around with it real easy, talking to the director, to the script girl, getting makeup touches. But, oh boy, as soon as she becomes Lucy, she staggers and falls and trips down those stairs from the "weight" of the thing. Mr. Arnaz doesn't appear in this scene, but he's always somewhere on the set, dressed in a tuxedo and wearing makeup, with a handkerchief tied around his front to keep the pancake from getting on his costume. He and Miss Ball don't talk to each other much, but since he's the producer, he oversees everything. He mostly stands in the corner by himself, smoking, and every now and then goes over to the director or the cameraman, whispers a few things to them, and looks through the camera viewfinder to check out the shot—at least I guess that's what he's doing, since I've never been on a set before today.

I'm on Miss Ball's right, and as she walks up the stairs to start the scene, she winks at me. "How you doing, kid?" she whispers, hoarsely, handing off her half-smoked cigarette to an assistant girl, who scurries up with an ashtray, then dashes away. I nod and smile; she told me not to speak much, since somebody might hear my voice and figure things out.

"We ready? Action!" says the director.

Almost instantly, the actor playing the director in the scene says the same thing: "Is everybody ready? Ac-tion!"

The music starts, and Miss Ball—I mean, Lucy Ricardo—starts her walk, and then her side-to-side tumble down the stairs, as the rest of us follow like well-mannered ladies-in-waiting behind a fairy-tale queen. I think to myself, hell, if Starla ever gets married, I can just be one of her bridesmaids. I'll even keep the beauty mark.

"Cut! Miss Ricardo, what are you *doing?*" asks the actor playing the director.

"All right, cut!" says the real director. "We need to adjust Lucy's key light. We're getting shadow. Herbie?"

"Oh for God's sake," says Miss Ball to nobody in particular, looking peeved, as the assistant girl comes rushing up with the burning cigarette in the ashtray, just as if she'd been cued.

"Fix it, and let's get going, fellas," says Miss Ball, in a voice different and louder than the one she speaks with as Lucy Ricardo. "We haven't got all day here. And this headdress is goddamn hot. Hurry it up." She goes to sit and smoke in her high-backed director's chair, which is red and has *Lucille Ball* written on the back of it. The assistant girl hovers next to her, holding the ashtray and looking all rabbity and jumpy.

The rest of us stay on the set, under the burning lights, waiting. I notice one of the other—I mean, one of the *girls*—looking over at me. She's a brunette—real pretty, it seems like, though who can tell under all this paint. She smiles at me, but she also looks at me kind of funny, like she knows something is up. I make a mental note to avoid her.

"All right, everybody, places please!" yells out the floor manager after a couple of minutes. The assistant helps Miss Ball out of her chair and over the lengths and lengths of cables on the floor, back onto the set. "Listen up, folks," he says. "We've got exactly an hour and a half before the studio audience comes in, so please let's try and get this done so we can move on."

And we pick up where we left off, which is to say, we start all over again.

"You're the quiet type, aren't you?" asks the showgirl who had been eyeing me on the set. We're hanging out in the back of the studio after the filming in front of the live audience, still in costume and waiting to get clearance that everything "made print." She seems to be zeroing in on me, which makes me jumpy. Her demeanor is a little tough, like someone my daddy would call "from the wrong side of the tracks."

"No," I say, and I'm so nervous my voice actually sounds high enough to be a girl's.

"The other ladies thought you might be one of Miss Ball's relatives or something, since you had your own dressing room."

Immediately, I decide that's as good an excuse as any, and take her up on it. "Yes. I'm . . . Lucille is my cousin."

"Oh yeah? Well, how 'bout that. One of her southern cousins, obviously. Well, that's just bitchin'. My name's Lena." She sticks her hand out, very confident, almost like a man. "Pleased to know you."

"Thank you." I shake her hand, and make sure I give her the fish hand, the opposite of what Daddy always taught me to do. Hey, I figure it's just acting. But what would I do if she found out? Her grip, I notice, is pretty strong.

"And your name is?" she says, looking me in the eyes, real direct.

"Wilma," I say. Miss Ball cooked that up for me, in case anybody asked.

"Wilma. I see. Been in Hollywood long, Wilma?" The more she talks, the tougher she seems. It's kind of strange to see someone looking so feminine, wearing ostrich feathers and fake eyelashes and red lips and rouge and a showgirl hat, but talking like Jack Webb on *Dragnet.* Or at the very least, like Miss Ida Lupino in one of those women's penitentiary pictures.

"No. I was just visiting Lucille, and she offered to give me a chance."

"Ah. I thought so. Nepotism—works every time." She looks away. "You probably put one of my friends out of a job, you know, just 'cause you're lucky enough to be a star's relative."

"Oh. I'm sorry, I didn't mean—"

"Yeah, yeah, I know. There's never enough work to go around, luck of the draw, knowing all the right people, all that shit. Hey, I don't care, it happens all the time; I'm just razzin' you." And she smiles at me real big, but I don't smile back.

"Oh," I say.

"Sorry, I don't mean to shock you. It's just my sense of humor. Say, listen, Wil—"

My heart just about stops when she says that. But then I realize she's just shortening Wilma. She looks at me kinda curious-like, and moves in a little too close.

"Listen, if you're not busy after the wrap, after we get out of all this shit, how'd you like to go out and get a drink with me? Maybe with one or two of my buds?"

"Oh, well, I can't, really, but—"

"Aw, come on. There's a little bar a few of us go to, over on Sunset. Very quiet, private. Everybody's cool. No industry types lurking around, taking mental notes. You know."

"I'm sorry, I can't. I just can't. I have to—um . . . but thank you, anyway."

She pulls away, and I hear myself exhale.

"Sure, Wil," Lena says after a second, studying me, and beneath all the makeup, I can see she looks a little hurt. She's probably a lot older than me, probably close to thirty. "Sorry. Jeez, I didn't mean to make you uncomfortable or anything."

"No, no, that's OK. You didn't."

"OK then, Wil. Nice working with you. We'll see you around."
She shakes my hand again, and heads over to another part of the
backstage area. I see her bum a cigarette from the stagehand.
Then she looks back at me from across the floor and salutes, like a
WAC in a wartime newsreel. A WAC in a three-foot headdress. I
smile back at her—weakly, I'm sure.

Over the PA system comes the announcement that we made
print, that we're now free to go. As I start for my dressing room,
Miss Ball's assistant girl comes running after me with a note.

"Miss Ball said to give this to you," she says, all distracted and
out of breath, shoving a note into my hand. Before I can even say
thank you, she scurries off down the hall.

I open the note: *Come to my dressing room in five minutes. In
costume. L. B.*

There's a real gold star on the door, just like in all the movies I've
ever seen about Hollywood. I knock.

"It's open."

I walk in and shut the door behind me. She's sitting at her
makeup mirror, taking off her false eyelashes. I notice she has two
cigarettes burning in two separate ashtrays.

"Well, well . . . how you doing there, kid?" she asks me,
unhooking the lashes, looking in her mirror and not at me.

"Fine, Miss Ball. Thank you."

"So did you have a good time? It's a helluva business, isn't it?"

"Yes ma'am. I really . . . I did have a good time."

"Yeah? That's nice. Well, you did a damn good job. Looked
real pretty up there, too. But then I knew you would." She laughs
and takes a drag off of one of her cigarettes. "I'd tell you to sit
down, but that's probably not so easy to do in that get-up, is it?"

"Yes ma'am. I mean—no ma'am."

"So," she says, finally turning around to look at me. "You
gonna tell the folks back home about this?"

I swallow hard. I don't want to offend her. "Uh . . . well . . . I'm not too sure that I . . ."

"Yeah, that's what I thought." And then she laughs, but it's really more of a snort. "Well, don't sweat it, Bill. I probably wouldn't either, if I were you. Maybe we'll have you back again, and next time you can be a boy. I consider this one just doing me a goddamn favor."

"Yes ma'am. You know, I thought you were wonderful in the—"

But a rap on the door stops me. She shoots me a quick look as if to say: *Get back in character, kid. You're still working here.*

Mr. Arnaz pokes his head in.

"Hi'ya sweetie," he says to Miss Ball, and goes over to kiss her.

"Desi," she says, offering her right cheek to be pecked, but not getting up from the table. "A damn good show, didn't you think?"

"Yeah, no problems. Everything looks good."

"Desi, this is one of the showgirls. Wilma. I'm sure you noticed her. The prettiest one out there today, if you ask me. Did you get to meet her?"

He looks at me and smiles. "Well, no, I didn't. How do you do, Wilma?"

And I give him the fish hand. This is getting easier.

"That's funny," Lucy says. "I could've sworn I saw you giving her the eye while I was talking to Herbie. Coulda sworn it."

Mr. Arnaz feigns a little shock, and then says to her, all sincere: "Come on, sweetie, you know me better than that." But that has to be a lie, because the way he's giving me the once-over now, it's like I'm the hog and he's thinking about bacon for breakfast. He straightens his tie and grins.

"No, I don't think I saw you before, dear," he says to me, "but I'm glad to meet you now. Say, Lucy, is this the girl you met at the party? The one you told me about?"

"Yeah, that's right, this is the one. I don't even know why we pay the casting people. I find all the best ones myself. If my television career doesn't work out, I'm gonna become a talent scout." She exhales a big puff in the direction of the ceiling, not taking her eyes off our little scene for a minute.

"You do know how to pick 'em, sweetie," he says, grinning at me even bigger now. I can't believe how he's staring me up and down, with a big old gleam in his eye like the men at the barbershop back home get when they paw all over the new girlie calendar. And right here in front of Miss Ball, too! I guess I shouldn't be too surprised, though—I read in *Modern Screen* that Mr. Arnaz is known all over town as a womanizer and that he's been known to cheat on Lucy. He sure is charming, though, and real handsome, I gotta admit that. I didn't know too many Latins back in Alabama. My heart skips a little beat just knowing he's looking at me, even though, for the moment, I'm a girl, and a pretty one, and I know that's the reason he's looking.

"Yeah, well," Miss Ball finally says, real sarcastic-like.

And she gets up from her makeup table and looks us over—or, she looks at him looking me over. My heart is beating so fast now that all I can think is I wish I were home in Hollinsville, sweeping up for my uncle at New and Used Pontiac. Anything but this.

"Will you two excuse me a minute?" she says, and starts out of the dressing room. "I won't be long."

"Sure, sweetie," he says. His back is to the door, and I'm facing it—and him—and I can see Miss Ball leave. She doesn't shut the door completely, though, just leaves it cracked against the frame, which I notice, but Mr. Arnaz doesn't. He doesn't even turn around to look. I wonder if I should tell him.

"Wilma," he says, touching me lightly on the arm. "That's a pretty name."

"Thank you," I say. What else would I say?

"A pretty name for a pretty girl. We like having pretty girls on the show, you know. Helps with the ratings." His hand starts to stroke my arm a little, up and down, while he grins. Of course he's still in makeup too, and, up close, he looks older than he does on

TV. But handsome, definitely handsome. I hope he won't notice my breathing.

"You're kind of excited, aren't you, Wilma?" he says. "You're . . . you're breathing very fast."

"Yes sir. Well . . . I've never met a movie star before, I guess."

He chuckles, and grips my arm even more tightly. "Television star, dear," he says, and he pronounces it *tale-a-visshun.* "Television is everything now."

"Yes sir."

"Wilma . . ." he says, moving in closer. "I'll bet a pretty thing like you has lots of dates. Do you? Maybe you even have a boyfriend. Do you have a boyfriend, Wilma?"

I figure I'm not lying if I say yes.

I say no.

"Well . . . someday, I think, some guy will be lucky to have you, my dear. Very lucky." And he leans in to me, and smiles, then closes his eyes. His hand moves from my arm around to my back, and he pulls me into him. Ohhhhhh . . .

And after what must be the longest kiss I've ever had with anyone, I finally see, over Mr. Arnaz's black, brilliantined hair, the door opening slowly, and, of course, Ol' Red standing there, smoking a cigarette and smirking. I'm almost sorry she's back so soon.

"Well, whaddya know?" she says.

Instantly, Mr. Arnaz pulls back. He doesn't even turn around to look at her, doesn't even say anything. He just looks at me with an *oh well, I tried* smile on his face.

"Hi'ya, sweetie," he says, and I don't know if he's talking to her or to me.

"Can't leave you alone for a minute, can I?" she says, coming in and shutting the door behind her.

"Now, Lucy," he says. "Wilma and I were just having a little chat."

Mr. Arnaz doesn't seem to be at all upset that he got caught, which seems real odd to me. In Hollinsville, when this sort of thing happens, when a wife catches her husband with a floozy, somebody usually ends up hauling out a gun. It's true, I guess, what everybody back home is always saying about the "wicked ways" of Hollywood.

"A little chat," she says. "Gee, I guess I should be surprised, but I'm not."

"Come on, Lucy," he says. "It's just a kid here."

She smirks. "You can say that again."

He goes to kiss her now, but she pulls her cheek away.

"Don' be mad, sweetie," he says, then winks at me.

"Oh, no," she says. "I'm not mad." She turns to me. "Do you think I should be mad, Bill?" I don't know what to say, I'm just trying to keep all this straight: I'm Will, but Miss Ball thinks it's Bill, and Mr. Arnaz thinks it's Wilma. I have no idea which one I'm supposed to be now.

"Bill?" Mr. Arnaz says.

She laughs. "That's right. Didja ever know any showgirls named Bill, Desi?"

"Huh?"

"I didn't think so. All right, kid. Well done. You can take off the wig now."

I look at Miss Ball. Then I look at Mr. Arnaz, who has definitely lost his big grin from a minute ago.

"Go on," she says, more forcefully.

And right there in front of them, I take off my showgirl hat and wig, and peel off my eyelashes. I feel like somebody having to strip so he can be examined.

"Holy fuck!" Mr. Arnaz shouts. "What the hell—"

"Desi!" says Lucy, clapping her hands. "Isn't it wild? We had us a genuine transvestite showgirl! How about that, sweetie? And you thought she was the bees knees! Didn't you, hon? So tell me, darling," and she puts her arm around me, around my bare shoulders, like a mother would her son, or her daughter, "is the boy here a good kisser? Is he? Jesus, he's so pretty, I ought to kiss him myself, come to think of it."

And Miss Ball breaks up in big guffaws, laughing and smoking and coughing, laughing and smoking and coughing, all at the same time. Mr. Arnaz can only stare at me and shake his head and say "Jesus Christ!" in his Cuban accent, and it's just like on the show when Ricky gets furious at Lucy for spending too much money on a hat or a dress or some such thing. I feel like the room is starting to spin, and I look from her back to him back to her and then finally down, staring at the floor because seeing my reflection in Miss Ball's mirror, half in makeup and half out of it, is starting to make me feel sick to my stomach.

Mr. Arnaz is real angry now, and he's muttering practically a chorus of angry Cuban-sounding words. He gives me one more hot, mad look before turning to leave. He slams the door hard, and he's gone, like that, without saying good-bye or anything.

Miss Ball is still laughing.

"Hey, thanks, kid. Thanks for everything," she chokes out, smoking the last of her cigarette.

And I realize that's my cue . . .

And I exit.

Back home in Hollinsville, I used to get beaten up a lot. No surprise there, I guess. For screwing up some stupid football thing in gym class, for refusing to take off my underwear in the gym showers. For being caught buying *Photoplay* and *Modern Screen* at the drugstore. At least I always had Mama and Daddy to go home to; they always listened to me, always made me feel safe, even if they didn't really understand me either. Just being at home made me feel like I was a long way from the ugly schoolyard and the dirty locker room.

Of course home is a long way from Hollywood, too. Sometimes I can't believe I'm here, and sometimes I think I should never have come, because I'm so far away from my family, and Hollywood just seems to get stranger by the day. But I also wasn't gonna miss that bus to Los Angeles when it came my way, either . . . I couldn't stay in Alabama for the rest of my life and never take a chance on being a movie star, I just couldn't.

At least Arthur is here, even if my folks are not, and while it's different, it still means having someone to go home to, somebody I can feel safe telling stuff to, even crying in front of. When I'm away from him during the day, I think about him all the time . . . soon after I met him, he started coming into the flower shop where I had just gotten a job—he would pretend he was on some business errand—and at the time he was working for Milton Berle as one of his personal assistants. A gopher, he called it. He started asking me to go out for Coca-Colas with him after work, and then we started going for drinks at clubs, and then, later . . .

I never thought I'd be in this position, to have another boy in my life like this, another boy to be with all the time, day and night. I love seeing Arthur's naked body next to mine in bed at night, or in the shower in the morning. I want to be with him all the time, and I know he wants to be with me, too, even if I know sometimes he thinks I'm just a stupid, backwoods kid. And even though I want to be a movie star more than anything, I want to be with Arthur almost more than that. He laughs at me when I tell him these things. He says: "You're in love with me, 'Bama Boy." And I think that's true; I think this might be what love is, I think this might be like what Mama and Daddy feel about each other, like what Aunt Eugenia and Uncle James feel. It just takes some getting used to . . .

In school, I got called names like "mama's boy," "queer," "fag". . . Is this what they meant? Because if it is, well, I guess they were right. I always figured I probably *could* feel this way about another boy; I just never figured another boy would ever feel this way about me. And Arthur does; Arthur says to me:

"You're in love with me, 'Bama Boy. And I'm in love with you, too. Who loves you, 'Bama Boy? Who loves you?"

After I tell Arthur about my day on the *I Love Lucy* set, he says to me, "You mean he didn't say 'Ay yi yi yi yi' and slap his face?" We're in his bed, or *our* bed since I mostly live here, in his small apartment in West Hollywood, instead of my room at the downtown YMCA which I rented when I first got here. We're in our usual position: me in his arms, my head resting on his shoulder; as I stare down at his hairy chest, he keeps his hand on my head, twirling my hair.

"No," I say. "I don't think he does that in real life." I'm a little tired of talking about this, but Arthur can't seem to get enough of it. At first, I thought he was jealous of Miss Ball's attention toward me, but now he seems to be enjoying the joke part of it, which kind of galls me. Truth to tell, the more I've thought about it, the more I'm not too happy about being on the short end of Lucille Ball's joke either, but I figure I did get a few things out of it: some money, a chance to be on TV, and a big, wet kiss from a handsome movie star. No—a television star. I didn't tell Arthur too much about the kiss.

"And that dyke, that dyke put the moves on you!" he says. "That's the funniest fucking thing." And he starts guffawing all over again. "A dyke thought you were pret-ty," he says, in like a child's singsong, and he laughs so hard he starts to cough. *God*, I think, *he sounds like Lucy.*

I wriggle out of his arms and turn over on my side, facing the nightstand. I reach for a cigarette; after today, I've finally decided to take up smoking.

"Can we just stop talking about this now?" I say as I light up, and I know how ticked off I probably sound. "I have to go back to the flower shop in the morning, and I'm tired."

"Oh, OK, I know . . . I'm sorry, Willie," he says after a second or two, and leans over on top of me. "Hey, 'Bama Boy. I'm sorry, buddy." He kisses me, on the cheek. "I didn't mean anything by it. I just thought it was funny, that's all."

"Funny. OK."

"Hey, look, I'm proud of you. You got a real job in show business. On the number one television show in the country. That's really something, you know."

"Yeah, I know, only I can't tell anybody about it, so big deal." I'm smoking, but not inhaling. That way I don't cough like an amateur, or like a kid.

"But *you'll* always know. You'll always know Lucille Ball personally picked you to be on her show. How many people can say that?" And he kisses me, and la-las the *I Love Lucy* theme song quietly in my ear.

"Shut *up*," I say. But then he slides his hand down to my chest and begins stroking it lightly. "I'm sorry," he whispers. He kisses me, right over my heart. "God, you're so smooth," he says, with a hoarse catch in his voice.

I accidentally inhale a puff of cigarette and start to choke.

He looks up at me, then reaches over to the nightstand for his glasses, so he can see me better. "What are you doing? Since when do you smoke?"

"I don't know," I say, still coughing. "I picked it up . . . on the set."

He lifts his fingers up to my mouth and takes the cigarette away, and stubs it out in the ashtray.

"Jeez . . . look at you . . . you're getting so tough. 'Bama Boy is growing up."

"Yeah, that's right, he is," I say back. " 'Bama Boy is growing up. What's it to you?"

"Oh, Christ, you're too much," he says, sliding over to his side of the bed. "Go to sleep."

"Maybe I will, maybe I won't. Good night to you too."

He turns over and looks at me. "Hey, Willie . . . who loves you?" he whispers, and it always makes me smile when he says that, even if I'm ticked off. Usually, I don't answer him, I just let the words hang there in the air for a second or two. He probably doesn't think I appreciate it enough, that he says that to me, and maybe I don't, or maybe I just don't show it, but inside I really am glad he keeps saying it. I'm more glad for this than for anything else, if I'm being honest. And then he sings his own words to the *Lucy* tune, which is *so* corny, even I can see that, and I'm from the damn sticks.

"I love Willie, and he loves me, we're as happy as we can be . . ." he sings in my ear.

"Don't quit your day job," I say, rolling my eyes.

But then he can't resist la-la'ing one more chorus of the *Lucy* song into my ear, real quiet and hushed, like a lullaby—a Hollywood lullaby: "I love Willie, and he loves me . . ."

And just before I drift off, I whisper to him: "That'll never play in the valley," and then I'm all the way out, on the way to dreaming, as I do every night, about the movies.

CONNECTICUT, *1993*

The phone rings in the back of the shop, right in the middle of my increasingly futile attempt to persuade Claire Tillinghast and her daughter Marcy to choose coneflowers and freesia instead of daffodils and asters for Marcy's bridesmaids' bouquets. Already, they are in the throes of High Panic, and the wedding is nine months away. I should be used to brides and their mothers by now; but, then, how do you ever get used to the sight of silly rich people working themselves into a frenzy over an altar arrangement? The phone rings again.

"Excuse me, ladies."

They continue to sort through the catalogs, and I close my office door.

"Old Lyme Flower and Foliage," I say into the receiver, a phrase that comes as natural to me as breathing.

"Uncle Will?"

"Well, well, Mr. Toby. How are you?"

"I'm good. Is this a bad time?"

"No. As a matter of fact, it's the perfect time. I was in bride and mother-of-the-bride hell, and here you are, come along to rescue me. You've heard me rant about the Tillinghasts."

"Oh yeah," he says. "You and those crazy Connecticut WASPs. Listen, I was wondering if . . . if it's convenient and you're not busy, if I could come up this weekend? I really need to get out of the city, and I . . . well, actually I have a new . . . I've been kind of seeing this guy, you know, kind of a new guy and all, and . . ."

"Oh. And?" My nephew is the most lovable boy in the world, and the most transparent.

"And . . . I kind of told him about the Lucy thing. And he'd like to see it. Don't hate me."

I close my eyes and suppress an exasperated sigh. "Oh, Toby. I'd love to have you, but must we do that? You've seen it a million times. Tell your friend he can rent it in any video store in Manhattan."

In the other room, I hear Marcy shriek: "Oh God, Mother! *Orchids?!*"

"Gee, thanks," Toby says quietly, and immediately I realize what a jerk I've been. *Jerk!* I'd forgotten how much of a kick he gets out of that damn thing. As I start to formulate some kind of apology, Toby graciously picks up the slack. "I want him to meet you," he says. "It isn't just about the video."

"Oh, Toby, I'm sorry. I didn't mean it like that. Forgive me? Please?"

"Of course. So can we come?"

"Yes, and I'll cook. Pasta, lamb, sun-dried anything, whatever you want." He starts to protest, politely, so I cut him off. "No, no, I was an ass, so now I have to make amends." I know this child so well, I can actually *hear* him smiling on the other end. "How's Saturday?"

"Brett *hates* pink, Mother!" moans Marcy in the other room.

"William, *please* help!" Claire calls out to me. "You have to help me with my im*poss*ible child!"

"Saturday's perfect. His name is Ethan, by the way."

"I'll look forward to it. Come up anytime in the afternoon."

"Thank you, Auntie Mame," he says, and then adds: "Your little Patrick loves you, you know."

After dinner—a Southern meal of ham, potatoes, and black-eyed peas, Toby's suggestion—the three of us retire to my combination glassed-in sunporch and TV room for our mini film festival.

With Toby's and my permission, Ethan, the dear boy, has been given the right to commandeer the VCR's remote control for the evening. Toby and I don't need to stop the tape over and over to look for me, to try and figure out if it's really me, to try and see how I've aged, or depreciated, or whatever forty years has done to me. We both know. The fun, I suppose, is in seeing a new person get clued in to the old joke. That's the subtitle to tonight's screening: *Old Lyme, Old Joke, New Face.*

And, oh, what a nice new face it is. Toby hadn't elaborated; either he didn't want to boast, or he didn't want his old uncle to get too excited at the prospect of his handsome new boyfriend coming to spend the weekend in Connecticut. The boys—I say boys, my God, Toby's getting near to thirty, though I surmise Ethan is somewhat younger—are sitting close together on the couch; Toby holds the hand Ethan isn't using to freeze-frame. I'm watching from my recliner (a very un-gay-like piece of furniture, I'm told by my *au courant* friends who know these things, but I say: I'm old, it's comfortable, fuck 'em).

Just as in any proper screening room, the only light comes from the screen itself. The black-and-white illumination from my big Trinitron set flickers across their faces in the darkness. I confess that I no longer enjoy watching these old things—it makes me feel a little like Norma Desmond holed up on Sunset Boulevard—but I never seem able to say no to Toby when he calls up with a new reason for wanting to watch it again in my presence. I believe he uses the fact of my years in Hollywood, especially the Lucy episode, as a little cachet to impress new or potentially new boyfriends, which I actually find rather sweet, though he certainly doesn't need me to impress or attract other people. This is the third boyfriend for whom the two of us have screened "Lucy Gets in Pictures," always here on the sunporch, always in the same configuration: the two of them sitting together on the couch, me sitting alone in my chair, watching them watch the TV. Oh, I worry about Toby; God bless him, he's had trouble keeping the beaux. It runs in the family, I suppose.

He keeps looking over at me to see if I'm OK with this. All we have to do is meet each other's glance to understand what the other wants to communicate. It's been that way with us ever since he was a child. I should have known then that he would turn out to be gay. Actually, I must have known instinctually all along; I was giving him books of poetry when he was five and six, *A Child's Walt Whitman, A Garden Verse of Emily Dickinson*, which he loved, and then later, for Christmas, bestowing him with signed 8 x 10 glossies of stars I knew, or had known briefly—he would always frame them meticulously for the wall of his room. I finally got it, slowpoke that I am, when, for his twelfth birthday, he asked me for the cast albums of *Company* and *Follies*.

While he was in college, he finally confessed his sexual preference to me, and I, of course, in turn told him all about myself.

Toby was the first person in my family I ever confided in, face to face, though I'm sure most of them had figured things out by then, whether they accepted me or not. And Toby had made it easy for me; he was the brave one, he said it first. All I had to do was say back to him: "Me too." We cried, hugged, laughed; then we traded stories about Cousin Starla Scott and what Toby called her "Legacy of Tackiness."

"Oh . . . My . . . God," Ethan says very deliberately, sounding almost as though he has rehearsed the response. He is transfixed by what he's watching: a bunch of leggy showgirls on a set of stairs, and one funny redhead falling all over them. Toby pointed me out immediately to Ethan as soon as the scene began—second girl from the top, upper right-hand corner. "This is so awesome. I can't believe it."

"Yeah, well," I say, because after the scads of gay men who have been let in on this little secret and have watched this episode in my presence, I can no longer muster up the energy to voice even the old standby responses. "There you have it."

"You were a great-looking showgirl, Mr. Ford," Ethan continues, and I see Toby looking at him, expectantly. I understand the difficult position Toby's in: He wants me to like Ethan, he wants Ethan to like me, and he knows there's a chance that might not happen in either direction. The Auntie Mame curse!

Ethan turns to study me. He has intense blue eyes and a blond buzz cut, and three small gold studs in his right ear—probably a tiny little revolt against his über-WASP Greenwich upbringing. (We even discovered over dinner that he went to college in Hartford with Marcy Tillinghast. "Connecticut is *such* a small state," he offered, as though he were saying something original; his forced "acid" tones sounded more rehearsed than spontaneous. He seemed more honest when he added: "And Marcy—what a Neanderthal bitch!" which, though it's true, I still found rather unmannerly, and not, I surmise, the type of dinner conversation his Greenwich parents would approve of.)

Toby eyes our exchange tightly, though he knows I'd never be less than gentlemanly to his friend. It's probably Ethan being ungentlemanlike to me that he's more worried about. *Relax, Toby.*

"I'm thinking . . ." Ethan says, in a faux-scholarly tone that I'm sure he doesn't think is faux at all, "that you were probably a very, very attractive man when you were that age." I throw Ethan an unchecked look of daggers, which Toby also happens to catch. There's a palpable moment of frozen silence, so Ethan immediately begins to sputter: "I mean," he says quickly, in what is decidedly not the scholarly tone, "that you probably had your pick of any man in Hollywood. I mean, not that you still wouldn't, you know . . . um . . ."

It's like watching someone drowning, and you choose not to save them.

"Ethan," Toby says in a low and embarrassed voice. What I feel most keenly is not the pinprick from Ethan's implication that I'm a has-been in the looks department, but Toby's disappointment in Ethan's own pompous lack of manners.

"Well, I think I did all right in my time, as I recall," I say.

I'm pretty sure I see Toby kick Ethan's foot. But then they giggle together, and Ethan gives Toby a spontaneous kiss, and then suddenly, the room becomes their room; they have seized a private moment, forgetting that I'm still here. I glance away, feeling like an onlooker in my own home.

"Well, I think you're still very attractive, Mr. Ford," Ethan says, after they break, words tumbling unmonitored from his dimpled mouth, "it's just that you made such a . . . well, pretty woman."

"Thank you, Ethan. I think."

"He went out with Rock Hudson," says Toby, and I wince inwardly when he brings this up, though I realize he's probably said it to come to my defense.

"Oh . . . My . . . God. Is that actually true?" says Ethan, back in his studied manner again.

"It was one date. Well, two. Really, Toby, you know it wasn't that big of a deal, and it was . . . please, it was thirty years ago."

"I'm *extremely* curious about that, Mr. Ford," Ethan says.

"I'm sure you are," says Toby, a hint of warning in his voice. "And you can call him Will."

"Yes, please do, Ethan. I really don't want to play the chaperone."

Ethan rewinds the tape so that we can watch Lucy falling down for the one hundred millionth time.

"What a genius she was," Ethan says, and I suppress an urge to roll my eyes upward. "I really believe she was, like, the Sarah Bernhardt of American television."

"What exactly is it that you do again, Ethan?" I say, though my hunger for this particular piece of knowledge isn't exactly overwhelming.

"Well," he says. "I'm in film school at NYU. Second year. I thought I had mentioned that. Anyway, you can see why I'm so interested in all of this."

"Film school. Of course."

"That's funny," says Toby in a tone that sounds only half kidding. "I thought you were interested in this because it had something to do with me." And he playfully takes a swipe at Ethan's blond head, which, now that I look at it, I realize is kind of bullet shaped, not traditionally pretty-boy perfect. Good. He needed humanizing.

"Ouch. That. Hurt," Ethan says, in what sounds like the deliberate flat tone of a robot in old '50s sci-fi films. "Please. Don't. Do. That. Again."

"You're an asshole," whispers Toby, and leans down and kisses the place he just swatted. "Can I get anybody another drink?"

"Merlot?" says Ethan, back in rewind phase.

"Uncle Will?"

"Nothing for me, Toby."

He goes off, and Ethan and I sit in silence as Desi (Dessie) enters the scene.

"Lu-cy! What do you think you're doing?" he bellows from the screen, and the studio audience emits an unseen cloud of laughter. The showgirls look at each other in the background and titter mildly. I notice what's-her-name . . . God, what *was* her name, the lesbian? Oh well. She keeps glancing my way in the scene, trying, I guess, to make some sort of eye contact, something I certainly hadn't noticed at the time. She really must have been into me from the get-go. God. Where on earth would she be now? Oh, if I had only been able to tell her right then and there what the deal was. I've thought about that many times over the years. She might have gotten a big kick out of it. Or not.

"Will," Ethan says, Toby-less from the sofa. "Tobias said you can also be seen in a film with John Wayne, is that true?"

"Yes, that's true, believe it or not. John Wayne, of all people. *The Searchers.*"

"Directed by John Ford. Very impressive. Any relation?"

"Yes. He was my grandfather."

"Oh my God," he says, and this little tidbit seems to get him in a tizzy. "I can't believe Toby didn't mention——"

"I'm kidding, Ethan."

And his mouth opens slightly, then closes again, trying to figure me out. Then he smiles wanly, though rather condescendingly; it's clear he realizes that, well, yes, I've kind of gotten him back, and he turns his pretty, self-involved gaze back to the television.

"I'm very interested in traditional Hollywood portrayals of masculinity," he says, composed and scholarly once more. "I'm actually writing my thesis on it. I don't know if Tobias told you that. And, of course, Wayne is a huge benchmark in this particular area."

Toby returns with a tray of three drinks. He carries it beautifully, like the Manhattan cater-waiter he sometimes has to be when his freelance magazine assignments get scarce.

"Brought you a vodka soda anyway," he says, and as he hands

me the drink, he leans down and kisses me on the forehead. "Thanks for being patient," he whispers. I wink *no problem,* and he rejoins Ethan on the couch, scooting in, I notice, even closer this time.

"You wouldn't happen to have a copy of *The Searchers* around, would you, Will?" Ethan asks. "I'd really like to see you in it. Of course, I've studied the film several times, but that was before I met you."

"Yes, Ethan, I do, as a matter of fact, being such a huge fan of John Wayne's. He was my all-time favorite actor, you know, he was so brilliant, such a consummate interpreter of text, really, and, of course, politically, he represented everything I stand for."

Ethan is clearly not quite sure how to take anything I say at this point. Toby glances nervously at me with his *What the hell are you doing, Uncle Will?* look.

"I'm kidding, Ethan. Again." For all their supposed sophistication, sometimes the younger generation just doesn't seem to grasp irony. Or maybe what they understand is post-irony, and I'm still stuck in irony. Or sarcasm. "Yes, I have the damn *Searchers,*" I say, suddenly feeling testy and—*mildewed.* "I'm in three very minor scenes, and Toby knows exactly where they are."

Toby goes over to the video cabinet and finds *The Searchers,* and begins to switch the tapes in the VCR.

"John Ford mastered quite a few genres, didn't he?" Ethan begins, as if giving a lecture. "There was the western, of course, of which I believe he was the undisputed master. Then, the war films, *What Price Glory, Mister Roberts . . .*"

CALIFORNIA, 1955

"Why can't they get this stupid shot set up, anyway?" I say to Luke, who's definitely become my best friend on the set of this picture. We're on location, in the desert, near Baja. "We've been waiting forever." I've done enough extra work by now to talk shop, the way I used to hear other extras carrying on when I was just starting out. I was always too intimidated to say anything myself back then.

"Sure seems like it," says Luke. He and I have gotten along real well since we met a couple of weeks ago, when we got hired as extras in the new John Wayne picture. He's a southern boy too, from South Carolina. Told me nobody in his family has had anything to do with him since he left the farm two years ago to come to Hollywood. "They didn't have too much to do with me before that, anyhow," he said, "so it don't make all that much of a difference."

Luke's just about everything I like in another guy: he's handsome, looks kind of like a young Clark Gable, but in a down-home sort of way, big ol' movie-star grin and these wide-set brown eyes that are just perfect for staring off onto the prairie in the final shot of a western—no wonder he got hired! I told him I thought he had what it took to be a big star, and he smiled at me sheepishly and chucked me under the chin, then slapped me on the back. Much as I hate to admit it, that little gesture sent a hot rush all the way through me, and endeared him to me like crazy, and I haven't been able to stop thinking about him since, even in bed at night with Arthur. I feel pretty guilty about that, so I've been trying to make myself not think so much about Luke. At least at night.

The things I don't tell Luke are: that I was a showgirl on *I Love Lucy* last year, and that Arthur is my special friend. (Arthur says we're "lovers," but somehow I can't learn to use that word.) Arthur is the second assistant director on this movie—he helped me get the job; out here, it's always who you know—and he's also personally in charge of handling Mr. Wayne. This means the two of us have to be real, real careful about the way we act around each other on the set. Arthur has basically said we should behave kind of like we don't even know each other, or like we're just friendly, working acquaintances. ("But you know I love you, Willie. You

know that, right? Who loves you, Willie? Huh? Who loves you?")
Fine with me, I guess—it gives me more freedom to spend time
with Luke. Besides, Arthur's been real edgy on this picture. He's
afraid that big he-man types like Mr. Wayne and John Ford will
think he's "light in the loafers" (that's how he put it) if he's not
careful. But I guess I shouldn't be too hard on him; he's promised
me he'll get Mr. Wayne to autograph a picture to my brother
Aaron, who loves the "Duke" more than anything. I would have
asked Mr. Wayne myself, but on this picture word has come down
that no extras are allowed to approach the stars unless approached
or spoken to first.

"That Natalie Wood sure is growing up to be a pretty girl,"
Luke whispers to me, as Natalie walks past us—friendly but
shy—with her on-set tutor on the way to her trailer. We're still in
our cowboy outfits, and hanging out in the little coffee and
doughnut tent that the production people have set up for day
players and bit-part players. Luke and I both got upgraded yesterday when one of the AD's made us part of a posse of five. This
means that I've graduated from the extras tent, which is nice,
because the extras tent is usually a much farther walk from the
set. I should know; that's where I've been on my last two pictures.

"Yeah, she's pretty, all right," I say. "But lots of girls in Hollywood are pretty. Besides, she's too young for you, Luke. She's
jailbait."

"Shit, in Hollywood there ain't no such thing as jailbait," he
says, and we both laugh hard at this. "If she's jailbait, then you are
too, Pretty Boy." *Pretty Boy.* Those words just kind of hang there
for a few moments; they ring in my ear.

"Well, still," I say back, finally. "You better keep your distance there, pardner." I mean from Natalie Wood, of course; I
hope he doesn't think I mean from me. I wouldn't want Luke to
be distant at all, even though I know I should.

And he grins up at me, then laughs and claps me hard on the
back, which sends another hot little shiver running all the way

through my body. I don't know why he makes me feel like this; sometimes I can't even look at him, and sometimes I can't *stop* looking at him.

In the distance, we can see all the cables, the riggings, the light poles, the crew running around, fixing things, the extras hovering all around. Mr. Ford confers with the first AD, who then barks something at Arthur, who then runs around and barks at everybody else. Arthur is not a barker most of the time; I guess he thinks that being gruff and loud makes him look more manly in the presence of Mr. Ford and Mr. Wayne. Maybe so, but it sure doesn't make him more likable. At least not to me.

"Do you date many girls out here, Will?" Luke asks, in his deep, country-boy voice, but wearing a puppyish expression on his face.

"Nah, I don't have much time. I have a job at a flower shop, too, when I'm not working in the movies."

He studies me a bit, but says nothing.

From the PA system: "THE SHOT IS NOW SET. WILL ALL PRINCIPALS, KEY PLAYERS, AND BACKGROUND REPORT TO THE SET AT THIS TIME?"

It's Arthur on the loudspeaker, of course. I can tell he tries to make his voice more manly when he speaks on that thing.

Luke and I go to mount our horses, although we won't be riding them. In this scene, Mr. Wayne and his men receive instructions from a "friendly posse" (that's us, that's how they call us in the shooting script—Luke kept calling it "friendly pussy") on how to reach the next town beyond the mountain range, so the shot here is all talk, no riding. Luke and I are side by side on horseback in the shot, and all we have to do is pay attention to the principals; one of the other posse guys has the lines. Mr. Wayne emerges from his trailer, in full makeup and with a white protective cloth tied under his chin. He is helped onto his horse by two assistants. It's Arthur, in fact, who runs up to untie Mr. Wayne's makeup cloth, and I try to catch his eye, but he doesn't look over at me, just attends to Mr. Wayne and rushes off. I decide to not feel guilty about paying so much attention to Luke after all.

"OK, let's nail this sonofabitch before we lose the light, everybody," Mr. Wayne says.

And the shot, which lasts all of thirty seconds, gets a take. Mr. Wayne doesn't fuss around, and usually gets a scene in one or two takes.

"Cut!" More talking among Mr. Ford, camera people, and ADs. All of us, even Mr. Wayne, stay in place.

"Anybody got a cigarette?" he asks, to nobody in particular, and several starstruck extras reach like lightning into their prairie purses, saddlebags, and costume pockets hoping to find one. Anything to do something nice for the star, hoping he'll remember them for it later. While we wait, I feel Luke kind of shuck his horse over closer to mine, but real subtle-like, so that no one, including Arthur, will yell at him for disturbing the shot composition. He smiles at me, that old country-boy way that I know so well from guys back home. Then suddenly I sense something that makes me sit up a little straighter. I'm not sure, but it feels like Luke's leg is rubbing up against mine, blue jean calf to blue jean calf, cowboy boot to cowboy boot. I look over at him; he doesn't look back at me this time, but he doesn't move his leg either. I look at Mr. Wayne and hope he won't notice. The same goes for Mr. Ford. That wouldn't be good; I'm counting on my folks being able to see me in this one, but not with a boy's leg rubbing up against mine. Damn. But I figure they probably won't notice that. Especially if pros like Mr. Ford and Mr. Wayne don't. I keep my calf and boot right where they are, and so does Luke.

The shot gets tried again. "Action!"

"Cut!"

And again. Finally, another time. We hold for clearance.

Arthur on the PA: "BACKGROUND STAY IN PLACE, PLEASE. WAITING."

Then: "SHOT IS GOOD. THANK YOU."

Luke's leg stays on mine the whole time we're waiting for clearance. Finally we break, and I breathe again.

On our way back to the trailer, I wave bye at Arthur, but he gives me only a small flick of his hand, then looks around to see if anybody noticed. It's funny about Arthur; he's acting so different on this picture from the way he usually does, which is usually friendly, laughing with everybody, real relaxed. And away from movie sets, he gets even more relaxed than that, and sometimes even acts nellie at parties, especially those that we've been to in West Hollywood, and at George Cukor's house. But being around "men's men" seems to make him jumpy and scared. I'm sure he's probably none too happy to see how much time I'm spending with Luke, either, although he may not have even noticed. I'm starting to think I have more in common with Luke anyhow, both of us being actors and all.

"Hey, come over here with me, Will," Luke says. "I've got a picture in my suit pants of my girlfriend back home that I wanna show you. I think she looks like Natalie Wood, if you wanna know the truth."

Luke and I follow the other friendly posse actors, three other guys, into the trailer they've put us all in. I take my time changing out of my costume, giving Luke plenty of opportunity to look at my chest and arms and legs and stuff, if he wants to. My heart is kind of racing, since I'm hoping he'll look me over, but he doesn't, not really. I try not to feel too disappointed.

The other posse guys are nice, but standoffish, and kinda tough-looking. Since Luke and I are always off together somewhere, I guess they feel like we're not real friendly. In the trailer, they change quickly and, with a lot of gruff good-byes and see ya tomorrow's, leave in a hurry. Luke and I are by ourselves now. I look at the door to make sure the last guy shut it all the way.

Luke is hanging out in his boxer shorts, with his shirt off. He's better developed than Arthur, and smooth-chested, like me. Luke isn't looking my way, exactly, but he isn't rushing to put on his shirt or pants, either. All I can think is we're alone together in this warm, sticky trailer getting out of our clothes, one piece at a time and . . . Luke finally glances over at me, then quickly looks away. My head starts to swim . . .

"I know that picture is here someplace," he says, fishing around in the pockets of his street pants. "I carry it with me all the time."

"What's her name?" I ask, though I really couldn't care less. I make it sound as if I care, though.

"Shirley. Here it is." And he sits down next to me on the bench, real close, our bare shoulders and bare legs touching. "Told you she was pretty."

Actually, what I think, looking at the photo, is that Shirley looks kind of dishwater blond and sleepy-eyed, like a bunch of my female cousins on the Abernathy side, the side that didn't enter too many beauty contests. I wouldn't tell him this, but to my eyes Shirley is about as far from Natalie Wood as a girl could possibly get.

"She's nice. Right, Will?" Luke says.

"Real nice. I bet she misses you too."

"Damn, I sure do miss her. Sometimes I look at this picture, and I just turn into an old horndog—just from lookin' at it." And he slaps my thigh kinda hard, which makes me flinch, and then he laughs real big. But then when I don't laugh back he stops and just looks at me, and just kind of hangs his head down close to mine.

"You turn into a horndog?" I say, after a second. My breath is coming real fast and shallow now.

"I sure do," he whispers. "A big ol' damn horndog, buddy." We're sitting side by side, our hips against each other, and all our sweaty limbs are brushing up, back and forth and up and down. Our faces are turned toward each other, and our eyes are blazing. It's almost like . . . we're about to play a love scene. Good thing for me nobody's around to yell "Cut!"

Luke smiles, but it's kind of scared-like.

"A horndog?" I whisper, and I can barely speak, my heart is racing so damn fast.

"Yeah," he croaks, and the palm of his hand starts to rub my leg. Shirley's picture drops to the floor, just falls out of his hand, as our mouths get closer and closer until we start to kiss, just like Clark Gable and Carole Lombard or something. Or like Clark Gable and . . . Rock Hudson.

But what happens then is not like in any movie I've ever seen. Luke's hands start to roam all over me, and he's getting all heated up, and he's touching me everywhere. *Everywhere.*

"Are you my buddy, Will?" he groans, all hoarse and breathing heavy, mauling me like a big grizzly bear, though I don't mind it. "Are you my buddy, man?"

"Yeah, Luke, yeah . . . hell yeah, I'm your buddy." And then we're kissing and sliding off the bench and rolling around on top of each other, and that's when I hear voices outside the trailer.

One of them is Arthur's.

"Will you wait here, Mr. Wayne?" I hear him say. "The kid just wanted an autographed picture for the folks back home, you know how it is. It'll give him a thrill."

Luke and I jump off of each other like two frogs buckshot off a lily pad. We're scrambling to pull up our underwear, but it's too—

Arthur opens the door. He catches us, and freezes. I can see Mr. Wayne down below the steps; the trailer sits way up high, on cinder blocks, so he's not looking at us, just turned around smoking, not paying any attention. Thank you, Lord.

But it's Arthur who looks like he's been shot.

He and I just stare at each other for what seems like eternity, though it's probably just a few seconds.

He turns around and closes the door tightly behind him.

"I think we have the wrong trailer here, Mr. Wayne," I hear him say, all business and put back together, and we hear them walking away.

"Fuck, man. That was that AD guy!" Luke says, suddenly looking all terrified.

"Don't worry about it, Luke," I say, because the right words to say—whatever they are—are nowhere in my head. "I know him. He won't tell anybody. I know him."

And I bite my lower lip and look down at the floor. I don't even want to see Luke naked anymore. I wish it was just me and Arthur in the trailer now. Just me and him, like the way it is at home. Our home.

Luke is hurrying to get dressed now, and he keeps saying "Just my damn luck" under his breath. I just sit there. What I want is to run after Arthur and say "Hey . . . come on . . . it's me . . . it's 'Bama Boy. Who loves you, Arthur? Who loves you? I do! Come on, Arthur! *Come on!*"

And then, if he did turn back and listen to me, I'd say: "It wasn't like it was real or, or anything like that. It was just . . . we were just . . . acting."

CONNECTICUT, 1993

Ethan is up close to the TV screen, studying it. He has frozen the scene, so that it holds still and flickers on the monitor at the same time.

"Oh, yes. I see. Your legs are definitely rubbing together. That's unbelievably fucking great, you know. You must be the only actor ever who managed to inject inadvertent homosexual activity into a John Wayne film. My God. You're some kind of unsung gay film pioneer."

"Must you always talk in thesis statements?" Toby says, sounding peeved, but Ethan is suddenly having the opposite effect on me; he's making me smile. Poor Ethan is so damn earnest in his own pretentiousness that it almost seems beside the point to mock him.

Ethan looks back at Toby, clearly having registered the dig. I can see him trying to decide if he should deflect or shoot back. "Do you have a problem, Tobias?" he says, lowering his tone.

"Please, for fuck's sake, stop calling me that!" Toby says, giving Ethan a shove that isn't exactly playful.

It's my house. I'm going to intercede. "Well, thank you, Ethan. I never thought of it that way, but I think a new perspective is always welcome. Unfortunately, they don't give out Oscars for things like that, do they?"

Ethan stares at Toby, clearly stunned that his new boyfriend would actually shove him. Then, recovering, he turns to me. "Oh, the *Oscars* . . ." he begins, practically sneering. "What a hollow, bourgeois ceremony that is."

"I'm going to bed," Toby says, jumping up. "Good night, Uncle Will."

He exits the room abruptly, and I hear his clunky Doc Martens stomping down the hallway into the guest bedroom. I—or we— hear the sound of the bedroom door creaking open, then slamming shut—like sound effects in a horror film. Ethan and I both glance casually around the room, pretending not to have noticed.

"Well," Ethan says, after a couple of moments, "I guess that . . . I should go too," and suddenly, he looks a little vulnerable, and not quite so . . . *armed.* I feel the oddest unexpected urge to comfort him, but I resist it. I'm old and smart enough to know that they'll work everything out on their own, or they won't. And is it jealousy or protectiveness that makes me secretly hope they don't?

"Well . . . good night, Will," Ethan says, rising, and clearly making an attempt to gloss over the last few awkward minutes. "This has been a very instructive, quite fascinating evening."

I get up to see him down the hall. But then he does a surprising thing: he throws his arms around me, and gives me an awkward, boyish hug. I'm so stunned by the sudden proximity of a male body to mine that I actually gasp.

"Did you love him?" he whispers. "That cowboy, did you . . . were you ever . . . did you ever become lovers?"

The question takes me aback, and, breaking the hug, I stare into his eyes, as if caught in the glare of headlights. Very young headlights, like my own used to be.

"Oh . . . no. No, I . . . I loved someone else. I was . . . with someone else at the time. I loved someone else then," I tell him. Instantly, I feel foolish, afraid that I sound like a doddering old man. I hope Ethan doesn't think so. I hope Toby doesn't think so.

"Oh," Ethan says. "I see. Well, thank you again. I really had a good time tonight," he says, in a normal tone at last. He turns away from me to go into the bedroom, though I notice that he hesitates a second or two before opening the door and then quietly shutting it behind him.

I have a shelf where I keep these things, this comparatively small collection of my appearances in Hollywood. As I look at the *Lucy* box in my hands, it makes me smile, holding it, because, all silliness aside, it was a one-of-a-kind experience, a Big Star encounter, a real adventure, no matter how embarrassing it seemed at the time. Of course, to this day, Toby is the only member of my family who has ever known about it. I place it back on the shelf. Holding the *Searchers* box feels different in my hands, somehow; I haven't screened the lamentable "friendly posse" scenes for friends nearly as often as I have the Lucy episode. It's a memory I haven't talked about as much, either.

I saw Luke only a few times after that; eventually, he went home to South Carolina, no doubt to marry that poor homely girl who he thought looked so much like Natalie Wood. And Arthur . . . I lost Arthur, of course. I deserved to. A few days after catching me in the trailer with Luke, he asked me to find another place to live; I expected that, actually, I just hoped it wouldn't happen. I moved in with a couple of friends who had a house in the valley. After that, I ran into Arthur a couple of times here and there, at parties, but he would never really talk to me again. Eventually, I lost track of him. I heard through the grapevine that he moved to New York to work in the theater, but when I visited the city a few years later, and called information, his name didn't come up. I never saw him again; obviously, he never became a famous director. And, of course, God knows, I didn't become famous either. Eventually, I followed a terminally ill friend back to his family home in Connecticut, and after he died I decided to stay. I found it peaceful in Old Lyme; I still do. I get to work around flowers and plants all day, and deal with mostly unhurried, unambitious people, sort of like the people I grew up with, though more open-minded. It suits me here.

In my more shamelessly sentimental moments, usually during some idle hour at the shop, I do still think about Arthur. I'll often wonder what he went on to do, who he went on to love, if he's living or dead. I fantasize that one day, by pure happenstance, Arthur will be in the area for a wedding or a party and find himself in need of some last-minute flowers, and he'll walk into my shop. And I'll recognize him, of course, and perhaps apologize to him in a way I was never able to when I was young, green, and stupid in the ways of love—and of Hollywood. I think maybe he'll wink at me, and sing a few bars of "I love Willie, and he loves me," and then he'll give me a sweet peck on the cheek, when no one is looking, and he'll walk back out of the shop as quickly as he came in, and wave as he drives off in his car.

Arthur, wait! We were just . . . acting.

As I drain the last of my vodka and soda, I hear the back bedroom door open. I'm not surprised to see Toby creeping silently back down the hall to see me. He's in a tank top and boxer shorts.

"Hey," I whisper. "You OK?"

"I was just about to ask you the same thing."

"Oh, yes. God, yes. Just having a silly old boy's reverie out here on memory lane. Really, not a good thing to do." I move back over to the couch, and sit.

"Oh . . ."

"And what about you, kid? Did you straighten everything out?"

"I guess. Whatever. God, he can be *such* an asshole."

Toby sits down next to me on the sofa with a boyish plop. With the moonlight streaming in through the pine trees over the sunroom's glass roof, I can see all the Abernathy and Ford features intermingling on his fine, strong face: my father's furrowed brow, my mother's pug nose, my own once-dark hair and blue eyes. It's a serious face, always has been, but handsome and striking. As they say in Hollywood, he'll age well.

"It's so fucking hard, isn't it?" he says, finally.

"What, Toby?"

"Oh . . . you know. Just trying to figure out who loves you, if you love them back, if they love you *enough*, if you love them too much, if the percentages add up and equal out on both sides, all that shit."

I burst out laughing, though I know I probably shouldn't; he's so earnest! "Yes, I would say you've got that right. It is . . . um . . . *fucking* hard, as you put it. But you get a lot of points for hanging in there, kid. I mean, you don't see me out there dating, God knows."

"But you know you could if——"

"Shhh, little one. I'm just fine without. Don't worry about me."

He laughs and rolls his eyes to say *whatever.* Which I appreciate.

"And by the way," I continue. "I know what you want to ask me, so let me just go ahead and answer it for you. I——"

"Wait. Auntie Mame? Patrick?"

"Ah, ahead of me as usual."

"I know. So?"

"So . . . I did *not* feel like Auntie Mame trying to get rid of Gloria Upson for little Patrick tonight."

He grins. "Really? So . . . you like him?"

"Well, I think he has potential, if he could learn to just . . . loosen up a little bit. Maybe you can help him with that."

"We'll see," he says. "It's like, he can be a total asshole, but then . . . he can be cool, too."

"Toby, there's something here I wanted to show you." I get up and go back to the video shelf, and select a box marked *Family, Late '6os–Late '7os.* "Do you remember your twelfth birthday party? I have it on tape now."

"No way! You had all those old sixteen-millimeter home movies put on video?"

"Yep. The Fords and Abernathys in all their glory. A family saga to rival the O'Haras, Minivers, and Ambersons combined. I was thinking this was not something we wanted to screen for Ethan."

"*Excellent* call."

I push the button on the remote, and after scattershot jump cuts of old relatives, church socials, Christmas gift giving, and various weddings and baptisms, we get to Toby's twelfth birthday party.

"Look at that," I say, and he does; he's instantly rapt. On the screen, younger Toby is opening up two packages, both record albums, one of them *Company*, the other one *Follies*. I am in the background; Starla Scott, who, of course, never got to Hollywood, and who by this time is permanently fat and sloppy, has to pull me forward to get to Toby. The expression on his twelve-year-old face is one of unmitigated joy, and he jumps up and hugs me, while everyone else looks bored, and more than a little confused.

"God, look at my hair," I say, wincing. "And what is that, an ascot? Ohhh . . ."

He giggles. "And what's that other thing, hanging around your neck?"

"Unfortunately, that's an ankh. They were very big then. Christ. So awful. Definitely my Paul Lynde phase."

"You're not the only one who should be embarrassed. Look at the cousins! This is, like, torture."

But of course we can't tear ourselves away from it—it's our family, for God's sake. Later, in the film, I'm balancing a drink and cigarette in one hand, and another gift in the other, which I hand to him: he tears it open, stares wide-eyed at the three glossy photographs, and clutches them to his little chest, making silly kissing sounds. Everyone laughs, except my brother, who I'm sure wished it had been a football.

"Who were they?" I ask. "Do you remember?"

He doesn't miss a beat: "Of course. Patty Duke, Barbra Streisand, Ginger from *Gilligan's Island.* I had a crush on her, but I realize now it was her evening gown I was in love with."

"Look at your dad disapproving," I say. Aaron sits at the kitchen table, looking surly and drinking a can of Pabst Blue Ribbon. He had already lost his looks by then.

"What else is new?" Toby says. And then the video goes blank.

"Wow. That's wild," he says, leaning his head against the cushion. "A Sondheim freak, even then. I'd forgotten all of that. What kind of uncle gives *Company* and *Follies* to a twelve-year-old?"

"Sounds like a joke," I say. "Let me guess. A gay one?"

He laughs. "You're responsible for all my damage, Uncle Will, and that video proves it."

"Well . . . homosexual rites of passage have always been my specialty."

And then we sit in the moonlight for a while, quiet, listening to the summer night sounds from outside, two generations of one family, lounging around in Connecticut and ruminating. Very *Long Day's Journey.*

"I read something interesting the other day," Toby says,

JOHN ROWELL

finally, exhaling. "Did you know *I Love Lucy* is always playing somewhere in the world? At every second of the day, it's playing somewhere. So chances are, you're walking down that staircase on somebody's TV screen somewhere right at this very minute."

"Ah. Well, that's a comforting thought, I suppose."

"I think so."

"Hey, Toby . . . it's late. Don't leave poor young Ethan in there to fend for himself. We Fords are gracious hosts, after all, aren't we? I think we should all turn in."

He stands and forehead-kisses me good night, then heads down the hall to join his . . . what—boyfriend? lover? squeeze? Before I head to my own room, I remember to rewind the video and as I sit there, I'm lit by both the moon, shining in through the glass ceiling, and the flickering, yellowish light of my family rewinding itself on the screen, hurtling backwards, from 1978 to 1965, getting younger, bigger-haired, less fashionable with each spinning-back frame.

And it's odd, but what comes to mind all of a sudden is Jimmy Durante's phrase, "Good night, Mrs. Calabash, wherever you are"—his hallmark, and his exit line of every show. Arthur worked for a time as Mr. Durante's floor manager, when Mr. Durante was the host of his own radio program in Hollywood, and it was in that tiny little recording studio off of Vine where I first met Arthur one night, through a mutual friend. When was it? Nineteen fifty-two? Fifty-three? The friend and I were picking Arthur up to go have drinks and to meet Mr. Durante.

Good night, Mrs. Calabash, wherever you are!

What did that mean, anyway?

Durante, wearing a hat and shirt and tie, was wrapping up the show, speaking into an old Philco microphone behind a glass booth. I watched from the outer area, as our friend brought Arthur forward to meet me.

From the inside of another glass booth, Durante's announcer said: "That concludes tonight's broadcast of *The Jimmy Durante*

Hour, live from the CBS Studios in Hollywood. Tonight's program has been sponsored by Lustre-Creme Shampoo—'*It Never Dries, It Beautifies.*' Join us next week when Jimmy's guests will be—"

And at that moment Arthur and I shook hands, both of us in suits and ties and pocket handkerchiefs—menswear, like our fathers probably would have been wearing back home at exactly the same time—but the charge that passed between us was naked and hot and electric, giving the lie to the fuddy-duddy men's clothing we sported: we were only boys.

Our eyes locked as our hands clasped. ("Firmly, son, no fish hands," Daddy always said.)

"Arthur, this is Will Ford, he's new to Hollywood . . ."

And in the booth Jimmy Durante said: "Good night, Mrs. Calabash! Where-evah you are!"

Mrs. Calabash. Mrs. Calabash. What an odd name. Who was she?

"Arthur, Will . . . Will, Arthur . . ."

Wherever you are. Whoever you are. Are. Was. Were . . .
Good night.

SAVIORS

Burton punches in the numbers of Kent's private line at the Colesville United Methodist Church almost without looking at the keypad; he has had the sequence memorized for years, though he wouldn't necessarily want Kent to know that. Burton calls Kent once a week to commiserate and share *Wait till you hear what they did this week* stories about their respective church choirs: those well-meaning, good-hearted, mostly middle-aged and Social Security–eligible people who bring to choir practice "the joy of singing," but nothing like the passion for Brahms, Ives, Vaughan Williams—secular, nonsecular, *anything*—that Kent and Burton have clung to since joining Junior Choir at age eleven or twelve. It's the music they have spent all of their teenage and adult years studying, playing, practicing, and practicing again—a "calling" that goes far beyond the mere *joy of singing*. At least this is what Burton tells himself, and he is grateful that Kent agrees . . .

Or says he does.

Burton and Kent are friends from their conservatory days, from when they were both organ students at Kensington Choir College, but now they mostly just see each other at yearly statewide meetings of church organists and choir conventions—"sing-offs," as Burton likes to say. Burton only calls Kent at the office, not wanting to bother him at home, where Kent lives with his wife and two children.

"Kent Willis," says the familiar voice on the other end of the line after two and a half rings. Burton is relieved that Kent has picked up—he knows three rings means voicemail, and voicemail always trips him up, makes him stutter, makes him sound, he thinks, too . . . too friendly? No: too eager.

"Do you think God forgives church organists for hating Easter?" Burton says into the mouthpiece, skipping "hellos" and "how are yous"; he believes this makes their conversations more like those of close buddies who speak once or twice a day, friends so tight they don't have to bother with formalities. Burton doesn't so much ask the question as "lead off" with it, for he has thought about what he would say to Kent all morning. It is Wednesday, the day he always calls, because Wednesday is equidistant from Sunday on either end, the least pressured day, theoretically, for church workers.

"You don't hate Easter, Burton," replies Kent. "You just hate all the work that comes with it. You resent having four choir rehearsals a week instead of two."

"Christ Almighty, that's it," Burton says, though he's aware of how unseemly it sounds for someone in his profession to take The Name in vain. Even, perhaps, to Kent. He continues anyway, barely bothering to breathe: "OK, well, how's this? I hate the *Messiah*. I hate the 'Alleluia Chorus.' There, I said it. I *voiced* it. I almost even sang it."

Kent laughs on the other end, which gives Burton a small stab of pleasure.

"I know," Kent continues. "I hear you. But you know as well as I do if we didn't give 'em the *Messiah* at Easter, they'd call us heathens and kick us right out of the choir loft."

Burton sighs. He is grateful Kent agrees with him about the Handel; he searches out commonality between them. He knows being snide about the *Messiah* at Easter is a popular sentiment among choirmasters, but still it feels as if Kent is siding with him specifically.

"Please," Burton says, taking pains to sound casual. "I get so tired of trying to please everyone. I mean, it's really just the Lily and Poinsettia Christians who make a fuss about the *Messiah*."

There is a pause. Then Kent asks: "So how are your sopranos and altos *this* week?"

"Oh . . . the same, of course. They're always the same. I said to Louise Eller on the phone this morning, 'How can you be in my hair all the time, Louise, when the fact is you've already caused me to pull most of it out?'"

Burton has used this line before, but Kent laughs politely anyway, then tells Burton he has to get to a meeting.

"Talk to you next week, Burt," Kent says.

"Yeah . . . sure . . . have a good one, buddy." Burton tries not to let his disappointment translate to his voice.

"Happy Easter, Kent," he adds suddenly, then instantly wishes he hadn't.

"OK, you too."

Burton returns the phone to its cradle. On his desk blotter, he looks down at his calendar for April. On each successive Wednesday, he has written, though he hardly needs to remind himself: "Call Kent."

Jean Nimocks Sloop is a woman on a mission. Ever since she found out the news about her niece Bitsy Nimocks Evans, that Bitsy had just "up and walked out" on her seventeen-year marriage to Riley Evans, a prominent North Raleigh lawyer, she has been working round the clock to salvage Bitsy's life. Jean believes— no, Jean *knows*—that the only thing to heal the loss of a man is to acquire a new one. Jean feels it is her duty as both aunt and empathetic fellow divorcée to find her niece a new man, and pronto.

It was last week, on Thursday afternoon, when the proverbial lightbulb finally flashed over Jean's head. She was driving herself and Norma Davenport to choir practice; Norma's car was in the shop and Jean was only too happy to swing by in her Camry to give Norma a lift to First Church, since, as Jean said, "It's no trouble a bit, Norma. Not one bit. I won't even hit you up for the gas money, honey." Jean is always happy to have someone to talk to, especially lately, as she has particularly enjoyed unloading the Ballad of Bitsy in full detailia to her friends. Jean was particularly happy to see Norma, in fact, for she was fairly certain that Norma, being both a homebody and a quiet type, wouldn't have heard the story from other people. Jean relished the chance for a fresh telling.

"To tell you the truth, Norma," Jean said, as she drove them down Wilmot Avenue, "and I've never said this to anyone before, honestly I haven't, but I never liked Riley Evans, despite all his good looks and money. I didn't like him when he and Bitsy were dating, and I didn't like him when they got married, and I sure don't like him now. And, oh, I have tried to be Christian about him, I swear I have, Norma. But you know how that goes. I just don't have the gift for faking my feelings! So now I can just come clean and say that I never liked the man, and not even feel guilty about saying it, because look what happened! I hate to say it, I hate to even put it out into the air, but I believe in this case, I was right all along. Poor Bitsy. You know, she's wasted all her good years . . ." And then Jean breathed out a very large and dramatic sigh, a sigh Jean knew would be recognized by women the world over who had made a wrong turn in romance somewhere along the way. Jean is fond of saying that sighs, not smiles, are the real universal language.

Norma did, in fact, recognize that sigh for what it was, and assumed it signaled the end of Jean's discourse, whereupon she started to add something of her own—she felt she was entitled to join in a two-party conversation when she happened to be one of the two parties. Besides, she had her own opinions on the subject, and desired to air them, but Jean, a quicksilver talker, returned post-sigh with lightning speed to add: "Well, anyway, Norma, here is the one thing that I think is just clear as day: it is up to me to help that poor child out. Whatever I can do. I mean, *whatever is in my power to do* I have just got to do it. Oh, Norma, Bitsy is so pitiful, you have no idea."

"Is she?" asked Norma weakly, having given up on whatever it was she had planned to say mere moments before. In thirty years of knowing Jean Sloop, Norma has fought the good fight of trying to get a word in edgewise, and has mostly lost that sorry battle, since Jean talks almost as fast as she drives. Jean's driving, in fact, constitutes a whole other issue for Norma, since her already problematic and pacemakered heart remains constantly in her throat every time Jean chauffeurs the two of them to choir practice.

"Well, yes, she is pitiful," Jean continued, "and I don't believe that's just my opinion, I believe that is cold, hard fact. I mean, look: she's staring at seventeen years of a childless marriage down the drain. Wouldn't you be pitiful? And, you know, getting older by the day. Oh, Lord, it is just so obvious: that girl has got to have a new man!"

And that is when it hit Jean, right there at the Hawkins Street exit off the Beltline: *Burton.* Burton and Bitsy would be *perfect* for each other.

So that afternoon at choir practice, as she sat there among the altos, warbling through the descant of the "Alleluia Chorus" ("We'd be sopranos, honey, but we smoked" is a line Jean tosses off to a crowd of new people every year at the state choir convention), she studied Burton as she never had before, in all the fifteen years that she's known him. *Burton and Bitsy, Bitsy and Burton . . .* their names linked together like that just seemed right to her all of a sudden, and the combination kept repeating itself like a singsong rhyme in her head, *Bitsy and Burton, Burton and Bitsy,* which managed to put her off rhythm in the sheet music she was supposed to be paying attention to.

"Concentrate please, altos!" Burton said from the piano, glaring right at her.

But as Jean continued to study Burton, the names together

began to form an image, which then created a Scenario, which morphed into a PLAN that, Jean realized, with a self-satisfied sigh, only she could see into fruition. Yes. Burton and Bitsy. *Neither one is getting younger and neither one is winning beauty contests, either, per se,* she thought, as she watched Burton conduct their little choir with one rapidly waving hand from his perch behind the old upright in the corner of the practice room, *but they're good Christian people, and single—and lonely . . .*

And Jean Sloop, one of the most glamorous women in her community and church, dressed in a Talbots pants suit of the color she calls "New York black," her frosted blond-gray hair cut in a stylish bob, big diamonds on two fingers, and Pappagallo patent leather flats on her feet, Jean Sloop, a divorcée herself, a forty-three-year member of First Church and a second alto for twenty-two, silently patted herself on the back for being such an amazing judge of people's character, and more than that: *a person who unites others in joy and in love.*

Bitsy stares in a mirror and wonders what became of the life that only six months ago she felt she had under control. *What happened to my life?* she asks herself over and over, and she hates the generic, TV talk-show blandness of that silly phrase, but that's it, that's the question, she can't be more specific than that. Oh, she knows all the details, the reasons, the explanations, the whys and hows of leaving Riley—or did Riley leave her? She can't really remember now. She shuffles those questions around in her mind like a shell game—*he left me,* or *I left him,* or *we both left each other,* and no answer is correct, no answer is helpful, no answer wins any prizes. One day, Bitsy is sure, she will sort it all out, *see the big picture,* as well-intentioned people are so nauseatingly fond of saying. Finally, one day, she will be able to talk about it, to tell the story of it without becoming emotional, relay it as nothing but *fact* to those concerned and sympathetic faces she's so desperately tired of seeing every time she opens her door. This is what she will strive for: a clean narrative with a chronological sequence of events resulting in a final outcome that will show them how—despite what happened—Bitsy has moved on, gotten it all together, *picked up the pieces.*

But the pieces aren't coming together yet; no, not yet. They're still just fragments of explanation, hovering and disconnected in her mind, and Bitsy simply looks in a mirror and thinks it again: *What happened?*

So when her Aunt Jean called and said she had a man she wanted Bitsy to meet, Bitsy couldn't come up with any good reason to say no. It seemed like the thing to do, or: it just seemed like *a* thing to do.

Today's the day, for what it's worth.

Bitsy gets ready. She brushes her hair *He's your age, never been married* then rubs on a new shade of foundation the cosmetics girl at Belk's convinced her to buy and *He's so talented, and so nice* she applies lipstick named "A Night in Havana" *and a good Christian, to boot* which she hates immediately but doesn't bother to take off, *A gentleman, you can rest assured about that* then puts on a light blue oxford shirt dress she swore she'd never wear again after she resigned from the Junior League *All the women just adore him, Bitsy, you'd be lucky to nab him, hon* and she hates that too, but stays in it, what the hell *He has nice blue eyes, though not much hair, but Riley had hair, and look what happened with that, so . . .* and she's out the door on her first blind date in nineteen years.

Sometimes Burton thinks Dr. Lundy doesn't listen to him, which is not, he feels, a commendable characteristic in a therapist. It's bad enough that he has to drive the fifteen miles out of Colesville to get to the far side of North Raleigh, but then not to be listened to . . . Often, Burton has caught Dr. Lundy glancing out the window during a session, usually when Burton hit an embarrassing crying jag there on the couch. Once, as Burton was discussing one of his phone calls to Kent, Dr. Lundy even began to nod off. Burton keeps thinking he should change therapists, but it's difficult to do that after fourteen years with the same one. He's bad at breaking patterns, which is one of the topics he and Dr. Lundy have dealt with in their work together. But it has also occurred to him to find a second therapist simply for the sake of discussing the issues he has with Dr. Lundy. However, Blue Cross will not cover two therapists—he has checked.

The questions Dr. Lundy asks today are: 1) "And how did you feel after the last conversation you had with Kent—different or the same?" 2) "Did you continue to feel the same rage about conducting the *Messiah* at this week's choir practice that you felt last week?" 3) "Do you feel you're getting closer to telling the church people, specifically the ladies, the truth about your preferences?" 4) "How does the possibility that Mrs. Sloop may be trying to fix you up with a woman make you feel?"

The answers Burton gives are: 1) "The same." 2) "I decided I don't hate the *Messiah*, just the 'Alleluia Chorus.' And I *do* hate them for insisting on singing it every year." 3) "Maybe a little. But I still feel it would jeopardize my job security." 4) "Like I'd like to just about kill her, maybe beat her to death with the back of one of her Pappagallos, or choke her to death with her web belt."

Then silence.

And after a few moments, Dr. Lundy gently offers Burton the Kleenex box, which Burton thinks is odd since he hasn't done any crying today. He takes one anyway, and blows, just to be polite, while Dr. Lundy looks down at his notes.

Silence.

Silence.

Clock ticking.

Burton wadding up the dry Kleenex and clenching it in his fist. Waiting.

Cars passing out on the highway.

Silence.

Finally Dr. Lundy saying in a voice of practiced calm, "Our time's up for today."

Burton thanks him, then walks out of the office, nodding a discreet hello to the teenage girl sitting alone in the tiny waiting area. In the parking lot, he gets in his car and sits there for a very long minute and a half without starting the ignition. He keeps hearing the *Messiah* phrase "Lord God Omnipotent" repeating in his head. He thinks back to one late November afternoon in choir college when he and Kent sat side by side at *Messiah* rehearsal, and Kent kept singing the phrase "Lord God is Impotent" instead. He remembers how they giggled under their breath, like schoolboys half their age, and how Kent kept knocking his knee against Burton's for emphasis, to keep Burton in the giggling game. He can still see the stern, prune-faced looks of the dreaded old choirmaster, Dr. Otis, the one they imitated and made such mocking fun of, back in the safety of their dorm rooms late at night.

"Lord God is Impotent," Burton half sings, half whispers in his car.

And then he begins to cry.

Jean Sloop is proud that she has a home where people are allowed to smoke, which accounts for many afternoons spent with other middle- and late-aged church choir altos. She smokes now, aware nonetheless that any minute she will be hosting Burton and Bitsy, two nonsmokers, in her home. She wonders if perhaps she should not smoke for their sakes, but then she thinks: *No, it's my home. And I'm a smoker.* Besides, Jean has gone to all this trouble today for the two of them, so they shouldn't mind a little nicotine in the air. In Jean's air. Oh, but there will be nothing negative here today, she thinks, because bringing Bitsy and Burton together like this is going to be wonderful for everybody; Jean even feels a palpable glimmer of pride when she thinks of how there may soon come a day when she'll be taking a little trip to New York to buy a smart new outfit to wear at a party for Burton and Bitsy. Images of the ladies' departments and the couture collections of Saks and Bergdorf Goodman swirl in Jean's head for a few dazzling minutes . . . *"So nice to see you again, Mrs. Sloop . . ." "Yes, and you too, Patrice . . . Ooh! I love these shoes, and . . . oh Lord, that's a fabulous blouse!" "It looks divine on you, Mrs. Sloop." "These shoes . . . Oh my Lord, do I dare buy these shoes?" "Right this way. May I show you a new Christian Lacroix in your size?" "Have you seen the fall Versace line?" "Will you be putting this on your store charge?"*

. . . But then she returns to her living room, her wonderfully appointed room where it all begins today for Burton and Bitsy, and Jean knows that is the most important thing. Today marks the realization of a plan in which Jean, clearly, has utmost faith. Faith—that is what it's all about. That is what it is always all about.

Jean has laid out tumblers, ice, bourbon, soda, on her heirloom Confederate silver serving trays. Jean's housekeeper (Jean is constantly reminding herself not to say "maid"), Darcy, fixed finger sandwiches this afternoon: fresh chicken salad, cucumber, watercress, the kinds Jean favors at the country club after golfing. They have been arranged in dainty circles on medium-sized blue and white Limoges china plates, on which pretty milkmaids in pigtails and even prettier Dutch boys in wooden shoes flirt innocently with each other all around the edges.

Jean's eighteenth-century cuckoo clock ticks away minutes in the otherwise silent room, on an otherwise sleepy spring afternoon, and Jean sits in her favorite fancy brocade occasional chair, languidly smoking a cigarette, and waiting.

Burton pulls up to Jean Sloop's house and sees the stranger's car parked in the driveway, behind Jean's Camry. It is a nondescript vehicle, really, just tannish and dusty, but at least there aren't any bumper stickers that say "Proud Parent of an Honor Student" or "Have You Hugged Your Child Today?" He waits in his own Jetta for a minute, wondering if he should just leave and call by cell phone with an excuse.

Bitsy wishes she were anywhere but here, sitting on her Aunt Jean's immaculately upholstered Colonial Williamsburg–inspired love seat. ("Sit on the *love* seat, Bits," Aunt Jean had said, rather too emphatically, Bitsy thought.) Why, Bitsy wonders, is there such a thing as a love seat, but no such thing as a hate seat? Or an indifference seat? Or an *I'm bored, fuck this* seat? When her divorce is final, she will buy a new home, she decides. That is, when Riley comes through with the Big Bucks her lawyer has said she will get. She will also purchase all new furniture. And she will name it, every stick of it, after a recognizable human emotion. "Love seat" will sound mighty quaint after guests get a load of an "irritation ottoman" and a "pissed-off chest of drawers."

Bitsy loathes the torturous ticking of a cuckoo clock. She will never have one. Aunt Jean keeps smiling and making small talk, but Bitsy can't concentrate on what she is saying. Outwardly, she remains calm, but inside, she feels like a substitute teacher about to face a particularly mean fifth grade. She would love to locate a fourteenth-century chalkboard somewhere in Jean's house and scrawl upon it this message: "Mrs. Evans. Recently separated. Facing divorce. Not young. Please be nice to me."

Then she would run out the back door.

Burton stands on the porch. He is a gentleman, after all. He rings the bell.

Jean Nimocks Sloop, alto, is prepared with something when she opens the door:

"Alleluia!" she sings. "Alleluia! Alleluia! A-lay-ay-ay-loo-ya!" She grins proudly and takes a big puff from her Merit Light.

And Burton, for lack of anything else he can come up with, standing on a rough, horsehair mat that spells out, in Olde English script, ALL YE WOLCUM HERE, gives Jean a polite round of applause, whereupon she invites him in, as though he's just whispered the secret password to the castle gate.

Burton enters Jean's living room and instantly feels smothered by the antiqueness of it, the overwhelming Old Confederacy–ness occupying every viewable inch. He considers the myriad of available objects with which he could bludgeon Jean: a silver salver, bronzed baby shoes, a heavy family Bible, opened, as always, to First Corinthians 13. Would he be relieved of his duties at First Church, he wonders, if he commenced to beating Jean Sloop over the head with her oversized King James version?

"Burton, this is my niece, Bitsy Nimocks," Jean says, full of hostess bravura and deliberately leaving off the "Evans" part of Bitsy's name. "Bitsy, Burton Warren."

Burton and Bitsy shake hands, exchange perfunctory pleasantries, and sit together on the love seat.

Minutes pass. Sandwiches are politely eaten, corners of mouths are gingerly daubed with crinkly linen cocktail napkins. At five o'clock, the cuckoo finally makes an appearance, startling Bitsy and Burton, but not Jean. Jean regales them with memories of past church choir days, such as when she and Burton were at a choir convention in Nashville and ended up locked out of their rooms at three o'clock in the morning, drunk as lords (meant to show Bitsy how much fun Burton can be). She then shares funny stories about Bitsy as a child, such as when, in the seventh grade, Bitsy wanted to go to the school Halloween carnival dressed as Cher, but switched to Mother Goose at the last minute after her mother burst into tears upon the sight of twelve-year-old Bitsy in long black wig, a bikini top, and gold hoop earrings (meant to show Burton what a good, sensitive girl Bitsy has always been). Jean is having a grand time in her own home and believes her guests are as well.

Bitsy watches and listens to Jean, and nods, and laughs dutifully, but soon Bitsy begins to check out, and in her vision Jean becomes a talking head from a TV screen on which someone has pressed the mute button. Bitsy steals glances at Burton, who steals them back at her. They smile at each other, and when Jean's head is turned, to readjust a grouping of marble Easter eggs on a side table, they trade a very long, knowing look, eyeball to eyeball, and they nearly begin to giggle simultaneously, but as soon as Jean turns back, they suppress it—in sync, like acting partners.

Smiling graciously at Jean, Bitsy drinks bourbon. She knows now, she gets it. Bitsy has been around a block or two in North Raleigh. She can clearly see that Burton is a lovely man—*anyone* could see that. But he will never, ever want her. At least not in the way she believes her aunt intends. And this, she can't help but feel, is a gigantic relief. Bitsy relaxes considerably.

Burton also listens attentively to the stories, but he too is accustomed to tuning Jean out, and does. He also drinks bourbon, and after a while, he is pretty sure Bitsy knows. Her eyes radiate intelligence and perception. He is almost certain they have shared the same unspoken thoughts in this antique-infested room. Bitsy is not at all like her aunt. She is modern, after all. She is going through a divorce. She'll grasp certain situations, things having to do with relationships. She'll *get* him. He wants, needs someone around here to get him—a man, a woman, anyone—someone he can talk to in person about anything, at any time, with no restrictions, someone who wouldn't expect to be paid to listen to him, someone who wouldn't say "time's up for today." Burton finds himself hoping that he and Bitsy will become friends. He relaxes considerably. And he will not bludgeon Jean in her home this afternoon after all, if only because that would leave a serious gap in his alto section this coming Sunday.

"And that is why the good Lord saw fit to give tails to monkeys and not to snakes!" Jean says with a flourish, finishing a long story-joke that neither Burton nor Bitsy has heard one word of. Jean laughs heartily at her own retelling of this tale, a favorite of her first husband's. Suddenly getting the prompt, Burton and Bitsy laugh, too, which pleases Jean, because she knows she is a born raconteur.

And a born matchmaker. Jean Sloop relaxes in her favorite chair, and drinks bourbon, and smokes. She is always relaxed. She takes in the sight of Burton and Bitsy, two lonely about-to-be-middle-aged people sitting side by side on a love seat in the comfort of her beautiful living room, two people whose lives she has changed in the course of a small spring afternoon. She'll have to give Norma Davenport a call later and fill her in. Jean knows Norma will concur and agree that Jean was right about this all along. If Norma were here to see the way Burton and Bitsy are laughing, talking, enjoying each other's company, the way Jean can see it now, she'd know it for herself, without Jean having to tell her. *But:* Jean will tell her.

More bourbon, all around, and Jean, bowing out of conversation for the moment to allow Bitsy and Burton to converse more intimately on the love seat, lifts her tumbler silently to herself as a doer of good deeds, an exemplary Presbyterian, a modern woman. She has brought two people together who need each other. If it works out, and she believes it will, they will not be lonely, they will not be alone. And they will have her to thank.

Thanks be to Her.

She has saved them.

Alleluia.

SPECTATORS IN LOVE

I.

The little boy stands under the dogwood tree in the front yard, holding the *Mary Poppins* record album close against his side. He keeps it with him most of the time, even though he has been told it doesn't do much good to carry around a record, since a record needs a record player in order to be a useful thing. But he loves the illustrations on the front and back of the album and the record jacket's sleeve. He does have a record player, of course, a small one, but when he is not playing the record, he is content to stare at the album cover, with its photos of the stars and the colorful artwork.

The *Mary Poppins* album is the first big record he has ever owned; up until now, his records have mostly been the little red and yellow 78s that play songs like "Turkey in the Straw" and "She'll Be Comin' Round the Mountain," sung by childish, high-pitched voices he doesn't much care for, though he sings along anyway. *Mary Poppins* is a big black record, like grown-ups have, and his father has explained that it is called an LP, for "long playing." He likes that; he seeks out activities that occupy his mind for long periods of time, activities that require his constant and careful attention. The boy plays *Mary Poppins* for its duration, both sides, and when it is over, he lifts the needle and cautiously repositions it at the beginning of the record, as he has learned how to do. Again and again.

The boy has just turned five, and the *Mary Poppins* LP is a birthday present from his mother and father. He thinks of it as perhaps the best gift he has ever received, and he has, in a matter of weeks, learned every song by heart. He sings the words over and over, sometimes loudly for Mama and Daddy, like a performance, and sometimes just softly to himself, as he is walking along the sidewalk in front of his house or climbing the dogwood tree that has turned so green and white-flowery since the spring came.

His name is Hunter. It is 1964. He is dressed in a sailor suit and new Buster Browns, and his short honey-brown hair has been combed wet and parted on the side, the way it is usually groomed for Sunday school, only this is Saturday night, and he is going to the movies with his mother to see *Mary Poppins*—it has finally opened in their town. How long it has taken for this evening to come! He has hardly thought of anything else for weeks, ever since he saw a preview for the movie during a telecast of Walt Disney's *Wonderful World of Color*, which isn't in color on their black-and-white TV, but is still something he watches faithfully every Sunday night. He has seen other movies before, and enjoyed them, but this one promises to be different. It looks bigger and more lavish than any of the other movies he has seen, containing, as its ads promise, both cartoons and live action.

"Mama, look, it's cartoons *and* people!" he had said, when he first saw the two adult characters dancing on dark rooftops and alongside bright, animated penguins.

"Yes, I see that," she said. "We'll have to make a special trip to see it when it comes."

"Is *Mary Poppins* gonna come here? To our town?" Hunter asked, aware of his own heart starting to beat faster with anticipation.

His parents assured him it would, and they promised to take him when it did.

At kindergarten, he made a detailed canvasing of the other children, to see if they had seen the *Mary Poppins* movie preview during the Disney program on the peacock channel. Some of them had, but they didn't seem to share his enormous sense of enthusiasm about it. That didn't surprise him; he was already used to the indifference of other schoolchildren. He fared better with adults; they listened when he talked nonstop about a television show, or a book he had checked out of the library, or the new song he had learned in Sunday school. He liked the way adults paid him attention, the way they included him more readily in their conversations than other children did.

A few days after seeing the movie preview, he was shopping with his mother at Sears and discovered that there was a record version of the *Mary Poppins* movie. Hunter then wanted to own the record as badly as he wanted to see the movie, and he thought if he could just achieve these two goals, he would never ask his mother or father or God for anything ever again. He would promise always to be kind to animals and other children, even the ones who shunned him at kindergarten, and to smile and hand out nickels to the poor people he occasionally spotted on the main street of his town, the ones who slept on the park benches outside the library, near the movie theaters. He vowed never to argue or be disagreeable, to never call anybody "stupid" again, and he would never again step on the red and black anthills in his yard, destroying their homes when they had never done anything to him. He would even stop asking God to send him a baby brother, which, before the appearance of *Mary Poppins*, was something he had hoped for more than anything else.

"I don't think you have to sacrifice all that much just to get a record and see a movie," his mother said, when he told her of his *Mary Poppins* wish and recited the list of things he would no longer do. He didn't know what a "sacrifice" was, but he thought it might have something to do with stepping on the anthills, and he had already promised to stop doing that.

"You have a birthday coming up, Hunter," she had said. "The record might make a good birthday present, what do you think?"

As it turned out, his birthday arrived before the *Mary Poppins* movie opened in town. ("Nothing ever gets here on time," his father said. "Why is that, Grace? Do we live in the boondocks?") So he had gotten the record first, and proceeded to learn all the songs. When his grandmother asked him what his favorite songs from the LP were, he found it impossible to answer. He had no favorites; they were all his favorites, and he could sing the words to every one of them. "I just . . . I just love them all," he told her.

"I love them all," he whispers again, to himself, as he stands under the dogwood tree on this Saturday evening, waiting for his mother to come out of the house, car keys in hand, ready to go. She will be dressed up in a Sunday dress and high heels and carrying a pocketbook. She peers out of the living room window, which is open. "Hunter! Are you ready to go, honey?"

He has been ready for weeks. For years.

"Uh-huh," he says, still staring at the album cover, and then, remembering, says, "Yes ma'am."

"Do you need to go to the bathroom one more time before we go?"

"No ma'am."

"I'll be right out."

His father is also outside, watering the azalea bushes. As it turns out, he is staying home tonight—there is an educational program on TV he doesn't want to miss. Hunter stands under the tree, and his father stands next to the bushes; finally, after a moment, their eyes connect across the small expanse of yard; the father holds a garden hose, the son holds a record album. Hunter's father wipes his brow with his sleeve; it is a warm night, unseasonably warm for late April. "Hunter," he asks, "are you taking the record album to the movie?"

Hunter looks at him warily. "Yes," he answers. Of course yes. Why not? This is his evening. *His* evening. "Yes sir."

"Is that a good idea, son? To carry the record with you to the movie? Why don't you leave it here?"

Hunter says nothing, just stares at him.

"Suit yourself, then," his father says, and returns to watering.

Hunter glances back down at the record jacket. *Julie Andrews. Dick Van Dyke.* He can't read the names, really, but he knows which one is which. He has grown to love them without ever seeing them. Richard M. and Robert B. Sherman. They must be wonderful people to have written something like this. He knows what music is; his mother helped him look up "lyrics" in the Webster's dictionary.

"A song is a poem set to music," the kindergarten teacher has said.

Hunter thinks Julie Andrews is beautiful, and he thinks his mother is beautiful too.

"Look at this. Julie Andrews and I are the same age," she told him, while reading him the liner notes on the album sleeve, which he often chooses as his bedtime story. He looked up at her, wide-eyed. He saw it made his mother happy, too, to know that she was the same age as a famous Walt Disney movie star. He was thrilled.

"I'm almost ready," his mother calls out again from the living room window. "Don't give me up. Ed? Ed, are you still watering?"

Earlier that afternoon, Hunter and his mother had walked up and down Mount Pisgah Avenue collecting for the Heart Fund. Hunter wore pedal pushers and PF Flyers and a Green Hornet T-shirt. His mother wore a light cotton red-and-white-checked dress, with white patent leather high-heeled shoes and matching pocketbook. She wanted to make a good impression for the Heart Fund people. The two of them took turns carrying the collection canister.

"Are you the little Green Hornet?" Mrs. Brinson, at 2601, asked him, bending down to put a quarter in the tin cylinder.

"No ma'am."

"Isn't that a sweet little boy?" she said. "All little boys seem to love those Superman-y things like that, don't they?" she asked his mother, indicating his T-shirt.

"He's just crazy about all kinds of entertainment," said his mother.

At 2610, Mrs. Faircloth hemmed and hawed about giving to the Heart Fund.

"I'm going to see *Mary Poppins* tonight," Hunter offered, aware of the awkward moment.

The older woman looked at him quizzically.

"Who?" she asked.

"It's a Walt Disney movie," he explained. "Julie Andrews is the same age as Mama, and she sings and dances on a roof with a broom and a penguin and she sits on a . . . um . . ."

He looked to his mother for the word.

"Banister," his mother said.

"A bansitter," he continued. "And she slides up it."

"My, what a talkative child," the woman said, after a moment. "And so taken with things. Do you go to Sunday school too?"

"Yes ma'am."

"Here's a dime, then."

At 2102, for a young couple who had just moved into the neighborhood, he sang, in its entirety, the song about a spoonful of medicine going down like sugar.

Clink went a fifty-cent piece into the canister.

"What a talented child I have," said his mother, holding his hand on the way home.

Now, waiting for her, he leans against the dogwood tree and holds *Mary Poppins* against his chest. He shuts his eyes and practices the "Supercalifragilisticexpialidocious" song in his head. It is, by far, the hardest lyric to get right.

"Let's go, honey," says his mother, finally emerging from the door, and fishing in the white patent leather pocketbook for the keys to the Rambler.

He carries the album into the car, somewhat defiantly.

"Have a good time," says his father, sitting on the porch steps and stuffing his pipe with Kentucky Club.

"You could still come with us, you know," she says slowly, standing next to the car, twirling the car keys on her index finger. Hunter fidgets—why is she not getting in? His father made it clear he doesn't want to go—why is she wasting time?

"I can't miss this program, Grace," his father says, lighting the pipe and puffing.

"Oh, what program is it that's so important?"

He looks at her. "The one about the Korean War. I told you that."

"Mama, let's go!" Hunter says, as loudly as he can. "We have to go *now*!"

He cannot miss even one minute of *Mary Poppins*. He cannot allow them to do that to him.

The Miracle Theater—at last. Hunter and his mother join a long line of people waiting to get in—parents with children, some teenagers, a few adults by themselves. Many of them are dressed up, as if for church, as Hunter and his mother are, and the people, the spectators, are talking and laughing—he feels the hubbub in the air; he didn't realize other people would be as excited as he is about *Mary Poppins*.

Suddenly, while standing in line, he realizes that he has left his album in the car.

"Mama, I have to get my record!"

The line begins to move.

"Oh, Hunter, sweetie. You don't need it now. Look, we're going in."

He has no choice but to clutch her hand and walk beside her; he is jostled by other patrons, by other children the same height as he, though they don't really notice or look at him. He notices a little girl carrying a Mary Poppins umbrella—it is bright pink, with a green parrot head for a handle. Before he can get a good look at it, the girl and the parasol disappear in the crowd. The uniformed ushers point the way for the spectators through the auditorium doors on either side of the concession stand, over which a bright neon sign blinks out a message Hunter's mother reads for him: "MIRACLE THEATER: SHOWPLACE OF THE SOUTH."

"This way for the seven o'clock show!" the ushers shout out, cupping their mouths with white-gloved hands. "Through these doors for *Mary Poppins*!"

Hunter and his mother find seats in the center. Seated next to him on his right is a teenage boy, who holds hands with a teenage girl seated on the boy's other side. They nuzzle each other a bit, the way cats do, Hunter thinks. He watches them, fascinated; he stares at their hands, their clutching, interlocking fingers. When the boy catches him staring, he whispers, "Whatcha lookin' at, little boy? Huh?" Hunter quickly turns his head away to face the screen, which is still draped with its massive gold and orange curtain. And in a moment, the lights go down and the curtain lifts, slowly rolling itself up into ornate folds and finally disappearing at the top. Hunter holds his breath as the gray screen suddenly begins to flicker with color and the music from the speakers surrounds the entire auditorium.

And he reaches over, takes his mother's hand, and holds it, interlocking their fingers, staring straight ahead as *Mary Poppins*, finally, begins.

"How was the movie?" his father asks, waking up on the couch at the jangle of keys in the door. The TV is tuned to *The Hollywood Palace,* where Van Johnson and Juliet Prowse are executing a lively song and dance.

Hunter stands in the doorway with a tear-stained face, hiccuping little sobs.

"It was good," he chokes out.

"His record got warped in the car," Mother says. "He left it by accident, and you know how warm it was tonight."

Hunter holds the record up for his father to see; it is clearly misshapen, a curve now, instead of a plane.

"Oh, Hunter," his father says. "I told you, didn't I? I told you to leave it here."

"Ed," his mother says.

"Let me see it," he says. He examines the disc. "Oh . . . this is . . ."

"I know," Hunter sob-hiccups.

"Let's play it and see what it sounds like," says his father, taking it to the stereo console.

And when the needle bobs up and down on the record, what they hear is: "*Just a waaa . . . waaa . . . of suuuuugaaaaaa . . . helllps . . . theee . . . waaaaaa. . . . waaaaaa . . . go downnnnn . . . a waaaaaaa . . . waaaaaaaa . . . go downnnnnnnnnnn . . .*"

"Well, maybe we can get him another one," says his father. "What do you think, Grace?"

"Oh, well, I don't know," says his mother, by which she means: *It's not in the budget.*

Hunter's father lifts the boy up onto his lap. Hunter buries his face in the big, rounded shoulder; his tears instantly dampen the sleeve. His father's lap is a warm, safe place; held tight against his father's chest, he can smell the strong, dark aroma of pipe tobacco. Even as he cries bitterly on his father's shoulder, he breathes in to get more and more of the Kentucky Club, suddenly craving the smell, the scent of his father.

"Why . . . why did it have to happen?" he sobs.

"Hunter," says his father, pulling Hunter's chin off his shoulder with his thumb and forefinger, and smoothing his damp hair off his forehead. "Your mother and I have something to tell you that I think will make you feel better. And now seems like a good time, I guess."

"I think so," his mother says, sitting down next to them on the sofa.

"What? What is it?" Hunter says, still sob-hiccuping.

"Well, sweetie," she says, glancing at his father. "We have a special surprise to tell you about. And what it is . . ." She glances at his father expectantly.

"Go ahead," he whispers.

She smiles. "Well . . . in a few months, you're going to have a little brother or sister."

"What do you think about that?" his father asks, beaming. "How do you feel about that, son?"

"Good, I guess," Hunter says, brightening a little, but suddenly sleepy. He feels overwhelmed; first the movie, then the warped record, and now . . . a new brother or sister. Being responsible for so many things makes him tired.

"Let's get you to bed, little man," says his father, and he carries him off to his room on his shoulder, lifted high, like a hero.

Under his Mighty Mouse sheets, Hunter lies awake in the dark room lit only by the tall streetlamp outside his window. There is so much to think about before going to sleep . . . Perhaps he is starting to see things more clearly. Maybe if he can persuade his parents to get him a *Mary Poppins* umbrella, like the one he saw the little girl holding at the theater, he won't mind so much not getting a new record. He knows all the songs by now anyway. He wonders if they make the umbrellas in other colors besides pink—pink, he knows, is for girls. Perhaps he can convince his parents to buy him a yellow one. Or maybe he could get it himself . . . The people in the neighborhood seemed to enjoy hearing him sing on their front porches today when he collected for the Heart Fund. He could walk up and down Mount Pisgah Avenue tomorrow with a can and collect money to buy his umbrella. A door-to-door entertainer: he could sing songs from the movie, he could tell them all about Julie Andrews. He will tell them he has to buy the *Mary Poppins* umbrella before the new baby comes, because he'll use it to shelter the baby from the rain, and the parrot-head handle will talk to the baby just as it talked to Mary Poppins, and will stop him, or her, from crying. The neighbors will smile down on him once again, and his can will clink with shiny fifty-cent pieces. They will recognize him as a smart and resourceful child, a loving, generous, talented child, and they will reward him for that.

Yes . . . they will give generously to the Hunter Fund.

II.

There are lots of things people can say about my best friend Lynette and me, and we know they do, but one thing they can't say is that we're not creative people. They cannot say: "Oh, that Lynette and Hunter . . . *they're just not creative*." No one can utter that phrase and not be known among the entire eighth grade of Stafford Hills Junior High for a bald-faced liar. For instance: last week, our math teacher, Mrs. Wright, who also goes to our church, told our class to come up with our own word problems as a homework assignment. Now some of our friends said they thought that was a lazy thing for her to do, since teachers are the ones who usually give out the problems so students can come up with the answers, but Lynette and I chose to see it as a chance to be creative—the only creative thing, in fact, we can *ever* remember being told to do in a math class in all our eight years of school. So this is what I came up with: "If, in one month's time, Hunter goes to see four movies at the mall and watches forty-six television shows, and his friend Lynette goes to see two movies and watches twenty-nine television shows, between them, how many movie and TV stars will they have seen?" I calculated it and came up with 219, because you don't count the extras and people with small speaking parts, since they aren't famous.

Lynette wrote this one, which I love: "If Lynette buys *Tiger Beat, Fave, 16*, and *Teen Beat* once a month, how many times will she have kissed pictures of David Cassidy, Bobby Sherman, Donny Osmond, and all the Cowsill brothers over a six-month period?" And her answer was: 684, which I thought was just about right. That's probably as many times as I'd kiss them, too, but I wouldn't tell even Lynette that.

So as hard as this is to believe, Mrs. Wright didn't like our word problems! (Though I think it's important to note that the rest of the class did.) She said she thought that perhaps we'd "missed the point of the assignment." We didn't agree, we believed we had brought something extra to the assignment, something to liven it up and make it "fun." She told us to try it again, saying flat out that we were concentrating too much on having fun and not enough on the true meaning of the mathematical task at hand. Lynette and I made faces at each other as soon as Mrs. Wright turned her back. But since we're good Presbyterians, we took the high road, as our minister is always telling us to do, and did not say what everybody else was thinking too, which is that Mrs. Wright is, in fact, the laziest teacher at Stafford Hills Junior High. We also think, however, that Mrs. Wright missed *our* point, which was to turn eighth-grade math from drudgery to entertainment, sort of the way, I reminded Lynette, Mary Poppins turned medicine into candy. So about this, we are right, and Mrs. Wright is wrong.

It's so incredibly cool to have a best friend like Lynette who hates math as much as I do; we don't understand why anybody should have to do math homework in the first place when there are: a) so many cast albums and soundtracks to be played, and b) so many movies to see and TV shows to watch, and c) so many movie-star and teen magazines to buy and read. These are the topics we prefer to multiplication and long division.

Plus, it's the remedial math class! Lynette says we're like the Count of Monte Cristo, being unjustly punished with imprisonment—in this case, in the math class for dummies—even though we both freely admit we can't do math to save our lives. I said I thought this was God's way of holding us back for a couple of really mean things we did to my little brother and Lynette's little sister when we were in the fifth grade, even though I prayed for forgiveness soon afterwards. And I told my parents if I decide that's true, that if God is still punishing me for things I did a long time ago, and already asked forgiveness for, then it just might come to pass that I will have to stop attending Second Presbyterian Church because of it. They said you don't give up being a Presbyterian simply because you can't grasp integers and subsets, that God didn't create mathematics to personally torture me. Lynette said they were blind to the truth! They said she was being dramatic.

Nevertheless, Lynette and I have something much more important to concentrate on: the new movie *Cabaret* starts at the Park Point Mall Cinema 3 on Friday, and we, of course, plan to be there. We've been talking about this for three months, ever since we first saw the previews of the coming attractions. Lynette is even going to leave JV cheerleading practice early on Friday so we can go to the first evening show and then to Farrell's ice-cream parlor afterwards, just the two of us, like a date, although we know it's not since we're best friends. The only problem is that her mother, who at first was just going to drop us off and pick us up later, is now talking about taking us to the movie herself, and we are trying to figure our way out of that. Lynette and I go to movies by ourselves just about all of the time now, but unfortunately for us, Mrs. McKinney has recently started subscribing to *Modern Parent* magazine, which has some kind of a stupid movie guide for parents, and she read that *Cabaret* "contains some material not suitable for teens and preteens." If Mrs. McKinney does actually take us to see *Cabaret*, I will die of embarrassment if she attempts to cover our eyes and ears should any unsuitable material suddenly appear on the screen. I may have to bite her.

On Tuesday afternoon, three days before our *Cabaret* night on Friday, Lynette and I are in my room, pretending to study.

"What is an integer, anyway, Hunt Boy?" she asks me. She's sitting on the floor of my room, on my cool new shag carpeting—checkerboard squares of light blue and orange—which I picked out myself at Sears. Our textbook, *Explorations in Mathematics*, is open in front of her, even though she has this month's *Tiger Beat* right next to it, opened to a full-color photo spread of the Osmonds riding the water slides at Disneyland. She twirls her shoulder-length, bleachy, strawy hair with a pencil, something she has done ever since I've known her, which has been since third grade; it's just a Lynette thing, as far as I'm concerned. But this little habit drives her parents crazy; they're sending her to a psychologist twenty miles away in a bigger town in search of a cure. I wanted to ask Lynette's mother why didn't she just look for the answer to the problem in *Modern Parent* and save all that money, but I don't think Mrs. McKinney likes me much anyway, so I kept that thought to myself.

Since Lynette came to my house directly from JV cheerleading practice, she is still wearing her blue and gold cheerleading uniform and black and white saddle oxfords; her crepe-paper blue and gold pom-poms are tossed onto my bed. It's so sad that we even have to have a conversation about integers; I'd much rather be helping Lynette write new cheers, or planning what we're gonna wear to the movie on Friday. Besides, what does it matter if we know what an integer is, anyway? This is the problem with the world, as I see it, because not only is Lynette a beautiful person on the outside, she is also beautiful inside, whether she can do eighth-grade math or not. What the world should know is that Lynette is a great humanitarian, and here's why: she is the only white person in our class who bought a Flip Wilson as Geraldine ("Shut up, Killa!") lunchbox *and* a *Get Christie Love!* composition book and brought them with her to school, which I thought was the coolest thing I'd ever seen anyone do. She said: "Now that our school is integrated, Hunter, we have to show the black students that we care about them and their culture."

"Who cares what a blankety-blank integer is?" I say. The only thing I have open in front of me is last month's issue of *Photoplay* magazine that I retrieved from the throw-out pile at my mother's beauty shop, and I have it opened to a four-page spread on Liza Minnelli and *Cabaret.* "Integer . . . it sounds like something the doctor sticks in your mouth to look down your throat."

My brother knocks at my door.

"What, Henry? We're doing homework!"

"Hey, Hunter, I can't get the knot out of my shoe."

I open the door, knowing full well Henry just wants to hang out with us, something Lynette and I just cannot allow. I examine the shoelace of his sneaker.

"It isn't knotted, Henry. You can do this," I say, unlacing it for him anyway and tossing it back at him.

"What are y'all doing?" he says, peering into my room like a little thief, all nosey and inquisitive; he doesn't often get such an easy entrance into my private lair.

"Homework," says Lynette.

"Then how come Hunter was looking at a magazine?" he says, pointing to my opened copy of *Photoplay*.

"Because we're taking a break," I say. "It's time for *Speed Racer,* Henry. You better go watch it."

"I'm telling Mama you won't let me in."

"I let you in! Now go watch *Speed Racer.*"

He doesn't move.

"You can play with my pom-poms if you want, Henry," says Lynette. And then she and I both look at each other and break out laughing. I say: "I bet a lot of guys would like to hear you say that, girl."

"Shut *up,* Hunt Boy, you're so *gross,*" she says, but she keeps laughing anyway.

Henry doesn't get it. "Pom-poms are for girls," he says, which I don't like hearing, and I take a swipe at his arm. It still makes me angry that my school once allowed male cheerleaders on the squad and now they don't. I know in my heart I would have been the best male cheerleader Stafford Hills Junior High ever saw; Lynette and I would have made such a great cheerleading team. We tell ourselves we would have been the Fred Astaire and Ginger Rogers of junior high cheerleading.

"Besides, Henry," I say, "we're going to play the *Cabaret* album, and you know how you hate that."

"Gross!" He takes his sneaker and barrels off to the family room.

I shut the door again, and go over to my stereo. I start it up and the turntable starts spinning.

"'Mein Herr,'" Lynette says, as I hold the needle above the whirling record, like a tease. It's her turn to pick. I do wish Lynette could say it in the right German way, instead of making it sound like "Mahn Hay-yur," but I don't want to hurt her feelings by correcting her.

"This is the number with the chairs," I say. I know this, because I pretended to be sick one day last week so I could stay home from school to watch Liza on *The Mike Douglas Show.* They showed scenes from the movie, and I tried to memorize as much of it as I could.

We sing along. We are pretty good, too, having honed our singing voices as well as our ability to "sell" a number last summer, when we played Louisa and Friedrich ("I'm Friedrich and I'm incorrigible") together in the Second Presbyterian Church Chancel Choir's production of *The Sound of Music.* We like *Cabaret* more, we've decided, because it deals with sleazier topics.

"You have to understand the way I am, mein herr . . . a tiger is a tiger, not a lamb, mein herr . . . "

Lynette had to ask her father what "mein herr" meant, but I went to the school library and looked it up in an English-German dictionary. "My man." It means "my man." I know I shouldn't sing that lyric out loud, being a boy, but Lynette doesn't care if I do. I just don't sing it in front of other boys, not even in front of my little brother. Especially not in front of my dad.

Lynette and I dance around together, seriously at first, as if we were actually in the movie, but then we get tickled and start to laugh. But when we pull ourselves back together, we dance even more seriously and when the number is over, we hug each other and collapse onto the floor. Sometimes we kiss each other too, but it's play kissing; we just giggle about it and make jokes. Lynette has a boyfriend anyway, Mark Perkins, who plays center on the JV basketball team. I don't mind so much that she has a boyfriend; I just wish she had a better one than Mark. Mark personally hates me. I know this because Lynette says he's insanely jealous of me because of all the time she and I spend together, and because we can talk about absolutely anything with each other, which to his warped-up, basketball-for-a-brain mind means that we are secretly in love with each other. Mark keeps threatening to beat me up, but he never will, because he knows Lynette won't let him unhook her training bra ever again if he does. So he acts nice around me, and I know it's totally fake.

"You have to understand the way I am, mein herr . . . you'll never turn the vinegar to jam, mein herr . . ."

We close our eyes and keep singing, and all I can think about is how cool it will be to see *Cabaret* at the mall on Friday night, even if Mrs. McKinney *is* sitting there, worrying about non-Presbyterian-like subject matter up on the screen tarnishing our innocent eyes and ears.

Suddenly, I hear my father coming in the house, home from the high school for dinner before going back out to teach his evening community college American history class. I shove the *Cabaret* album cover under my bed. I don't think he cares what I listen to, I just don't want him to see that photograph of Joel Grey wearing red lipstick and rouge on his cheeks. I look over at Lynette, feeling slightly stupid. Of course she has a stupid expression on her face back at me.

"You're so crazy," she says. "Why do you do that? What if it was an Alice Cooper album? He wears lipstick and stuff, and guys listen to Alice Cooper."

"I don't know, it's just different," I say, as I fold up the *Photo-play* and open my own hardly dog-eared copy of *Explorations in Mathematics.*

Daddy just says hello from the hallway, doesn't knock or come in. That's fine, I guess. I didn't have to hide the album cover after all.

"Would you have hidden Joel Grey from your mama?" Lynette whispers, still twirling her hair and making another stupid face at me.

"Shut *up!*" I tell her. "She doesn't care. She's seen it." I feel my face turn red all of a sudden, an old habit from sixth and seventh grades that I'd hoped I'd gotten over.

Lynette is lately starting to ask me dumb questions like that, all nosey about stuff since she started seeing that psychologist. But I can always come back at her with things that I know get her goat—I've learned how to use her own stupid psychology against her. I can shoot her down pretty easily with stuff like "How come you sneak Moon Pies into your room so no one will see you eating them?" or "Did you know that Greg Winston saw you buying Kotex at the Winn-Dixie last week—and *told?*"

But I refuse to let her get to me. "Let's just think about Friday night, OK?"

"OK, don't get all upset."

She throws one of her pom-poms at me and I throw it right back at her.

"Rah-rah," I say.

She just looks at me and rolls her eyes. "You're such a goofball, Hunt Boy," she says.

"Shut *up,* you are too."

The big sound of Liza Minnelli's voice fills my room; we start singing and dancing all over again, and making complicated hand gestures (I make sure my door is locked)—choreography that we think might be close to what Liza does in the movie. The song ends and I get up to reposition the needle, to start it again at the beginning. Looking out my window, I see Daddy and Henry tossing a softball out in the front yard. I watch them for a minute, before starting the song again, wondering why they go out there every afternoon, just to throw that stupid ball around, back and forth, back and forth. Back and forth, over and over. And over again. They don't even ask me to join them anymore, the way they used to. I guess they got tired of me saying no.

I turn back to Lynette and lift the needle. "What'll it be now, girl?" I say. " 'Maybe This Time' or 'Tomorrow Belongs to Me'?"

On Friday afternoon, three hours and thirteen minutes before *Cabaret* begins at Park Point Cinema, the phone rings.

"Hey, Hunt Boy," says Lynette.

"Hey, Lynette Girl," I say. "Are you getting ready? I am."

"Well . . . you're gonna be mad at me," she says, kind of sing-songy, and I don't like the sound of that one bit.

"What?" I say. I feel an ominous sense of dread washing over me. I lay the Pop Tart I was eating on a napkin, suddenly purged of appetite.

"Well . . . I don't know how I coulda done this, but I kind of forgot about this dance at Mark's church that I was supposed to go to with him tonight. I can't believe I just forgot all about it."

"Tonight? Lynette! Have you lost your mind? This is our *Cabaret* night! We've been planning it for two months!"

"I know," she says. "I'm sorry, but he gets all . . . it's a stupid dance, I'd rather go to the movie. But Mama says I promised him, and his father is gonna pick us up and everything, so . . ."

"OK," I say. "I hope you have a great time." I swear, if she were standing in front of me, I would hit her over the head with the phone. Maybe I'll just say: "Lynette McKinney, you're the

biggest bitch at Stafford Hills Junior High, and everybody knows
it!" and hang up real fast in her ear.

"Are you totally angry at me?" she asks, trying to sound pitiful
so as to make me less mad at her. I know her tricks.

"No." I feel a lump in my throat. I just want to hang up. I can't
even call her a bitch.

"You sure?"

"Yeah, I gotta go, my brother's calling me."

"Well . . . OK. I'll see you at church on Sunday."

"OK . . . Bye."

Damn her and her stupid boyfriend, I think, as I slam the phone
down hard into the receiver.

"Hunter, what's the matter?" Mama asks, suddenly in the
kitchen and starting to open up the cabinets and stare into them,
which is what she does when she has no inspiration about what to
make for dinner.

"Nothing."

Daddy comes in from watering the azalea bushes.

"Who slammed the phone down like that?" he says. "What's
wrong, Hunter?"

How lucky, here I am about to cry and my parents descend
upon me from all corners, like disciples rushing after Jesus upon
news of the crucifixion. Can't I ever get any privacy?

"Lynette can't go to the movie, that's what!" I yell. I can't help
it. I have to tell somebody.

"Oh, honey," says Mama. "Well . . . that is a disappointment.
Hmmm . . . well . . ." I can see she is thinking of a way to fix it,
and I just wish she wouldn't.

"What movie, Grace?" Daddy asks, washing his hands with
lye soap in the utility room.

"That *Cabaret* that he's been talking about for weeks."

"Oh," he says, and I can tell he is also trying to fix it. *Oh, please
don't,* I think. *I'll just stay home and watch* Love American Style
with all of y'all and won't that be one hell of a good time.

"Who's in that movie, Hunter?" he asks, drying his hands on a towel.

God, I'm so embarrassed to even have to say it, why is this happening in our kitchen, why do I feel like I'm on a stage with a hot spotlight shining on me?

"You know . . . I don't know . . ." I say.

"Judy Garland's daughter," Mama says. "Lisa something."

"Liza," I mutter. "You always say it wrong, Mama!"

"Well," says Daddy. "I can take you, son, if you still want to go. We can go after supper."

"Can we all go?" I ask. "All of us?"

"Now I don't think that's the kind of movie to take Henry to, is it?" asks Mama, even though she knows it isn't. She subscribes to *Modern Parent* too. "Is it a Walt Disney?"

"No, Mama, you know it's not!" I say, slamming my hand down on top of the phone book, for dramatic emphasis.

"Well . . ." she says, folding her arms and looking at me hard, "maybe somebody with a bad attitude like that shouldn't see any movie of any kind." She turns back to the cabinets, which are mostly empty. "Who would like to pick up dinner from Hardee's tonight?" she asks.

"You and I can go to the movie, son," Daddy says. "I don't mind. Mama and Henry can stay home."

"You won't like it, Daddy," I say. "You never do." *God, anything but this.*

I'm thinking of the previous year's movie debacle. I got Daddy to take me to see *Nicholas and Alexandra*, not because I thought I would like it, particularly, but because I thought he would, being a history teacher. For reasons I still can't figure out, he hated it, and we heard about it for months—the broken record of what a miserable time Daddy had at the *Nicholas and Alexandra* movie.

"Nah, nah," says Daddy. "If it's got Judy Garland's daughter in it, it ought to be good. If she's anything like her mother. Besides, y'all are too hard on me. I don't dislike things."

"Oh, Ed," says Mama. "I still have to listen to how much you hated *The Graduate.*"

"That's because I thought it was gonna be about teachers," he says. "It sure wasn't, not by a long shot."

"Well . . . if you don't like it, I'm telling you now that I don't want to hear about it for a week. And I'm sure Hunter doesn't, either."

"Where is it playing? Down at the Miracle?"

"The Miracle?" Mama says. "Ed, you're just plain out of it. They don't show anything at the Miracle anymore except the Oriental Kung Fu movies. I thought you knew that. There hasn't been a good movie down there for years."

"It's at the Park Point Cinema!" I scream. "Park Point Cinema! *Park Point Cinema!!*"

Daddy sighs. "What time?" he asks.

So that's it, then. Me, Daddy, and Judy Garland's daughter at the Park Point Mall Cinema 3. That's just about perfect.

I could just bag it, I guess, but it does seem like seeing the movie even with Daddy sitting beside me is probably better than not seeing it at all. Maybe he'll just fall asleep anyway, like he often does. I try to decide if I should still wear the outfit I've been planning on, my favorite bell bottoms with the alternating burgundy and cream panels on the legs, and my new two-toned tan and brown ankle boots with side zippers. *Damn Lynette,* is all I can think. I hope Mark Perkins calls her a big fat whore at the dance and tells everybody that she stuffs her training bra on JV basketball game nights.

If he doesn't, I will.

As soon as the lights go down, I start to glance over at Daddy, as slyly as I can, without turning my head, to check for any visible signs of disgust. It doesn't seem like he's gonna fall asleep tonight though, like he did when we saw *Sleuth,* which is too bad, because when he sleeps through a movie, he can't rightfully claim later on that he hated it because he knows I'll say, "Daddy, you can't hate something you didn't see."

The movie starts to deal with some Nazi stuff, which I hope appeals to his love of war things. Now if only they would have some battle scenes or something, instead of so much stuff about trampy-looking women at the nightclub acting trashy, which is, of course, *my* favorite part. Actually, he seems to be enjoying it; I think it helped that when we were out in the lobby getting popcorn there were several friends of ours from Second Presbyterian Church whom he spoke to.

On the screen, Michael York and Liza are hanging out with their German friend, who is blond and really handsome; he looks like he could be in the J. C. Penney catalog modeling suits. The three of them are getting drunk or taking drugs or something, and dancing around, not caring if they knock things over or bump into each other. This is kind of a serious part, because nobody sings any songs. Suddenly, in the scene, the old-fashioned record player stops playing music and the needle scratches and starts to repeat. Michael, Liza, and the German guy are all kind of looking at each other, and they keep moving together, kind of as one—a girl and two boys. And the two boys' faces get real close, and they kind of nuzzle each other, with their noses, the way Lynette and I sometimes do, and I can't explain it, but, watching this, I feel kind of like I'm gonna faint or something, and I feel sweat break out on my upper lip, and my stomach starts to swim around. I shift in my seat, and cross my legs, and lean over on my elbows, for protection, so no one will notice anything. If the two men kiss each other, I know my father and some of the other people in this theater are gonna start heading for the aisles, screaming that this is filth and calling out for the manager. *Please, God, don't let me faint.* Of course I don't shut my eyes or anything like that. I wouldn't miss this for anything, I don't care who's sitting next to me.

I don't dare glance over at Daddy now to see how he's reacting.

In fact, after this, I may never be able to look at him again. Mama was right: this is definitely not Walt Disney. I shift around again, and hope that the action will soon go back to the club where Liza sings, even if that does mean Joel Grey running around in lipstick and rouge. But still . . . this is fantastic. Two boys . . . and a girl.

I'm not ever gonna stop thinking about this.

"You enjoy it, son?" Daddy says. We're in the car on the way home.

On the way out of the theater, I'd already started to think about all his potential questions, and all my potential answers. This was definitely one I had counted on. "I thought it was good, not great," I say, trying to sound as nonchalant as possible. And then, I probably shouldn't add this, but I do: "What did you think?"

He hesitates. "I don't know. I don't know," he says. "Did you . . . was it what you thought it was gonna be, from playing the record so much?"

Is this a trick question? I hadn't figured on this one, so I wait a few seconds before answering.

"Pretty much, I guess. Yeah, I'd say pretty much. So . . . did you like it?"

He pauses a long time, so long I start to feel sweat at my temples. I roll my window down even further, to get a breeze and also to invite street noise and honking sounds into the car so it will be harder to talk.

"It was all right," he says, finally.

I feel the tension start to drop from my shoulders; at least this is better than the anger with which he greeted *Nicholas and Alexandra*. I'm thinking maybe he didn't notice that scene with the two guys nuzzling after all; maybe God did me a favor and caused him to nod off right at that moment. Now I wish I *had* looked over to see if he was watching. Or maybe the scene didn't even happen, maybe I imagined it. So why did I almost faint? I will have to ask Lynette McKinney, Youth Psychiatrist, why she thinks I nearly passed out from seeing two boys dancing with each other. Except . . . wait . . . it's because of Lynette and that stupid basketball player that this whole evening happened to me. This is the thanks I get for helping her write all those cheers and let her claim them for her own and have everybody say what a good cheer writer Lynette is and *isn't she the most valuable addition to this year's JV squad.* I plan to never speak to Lynette again, and hope that some good Christian tells her mother that *Cabaret* is the dirtiest thing to ever come to our town, and that no child of hers should ever even *think* about seeing it. Then she will be all pitiful and want to hear my blow-by-blow description of the movie, and beg me to re-create the "Mein Herr" choreography on a bar stool in her downstairs family rec room, and I will not do it. I will stick to my guns. I will deny her, and she will just have to suffer, suffer, suffer. I might even say, "Why don't you let that stupid, thick-headed caveman boyfriend of yours take you to see it?" I won't even let her listen to my soundtrack album anymore. Lynette and I are through!

"Some of the stuff in that movie, though, son . . ." Daddy says, as we are waiting at a particularly long light, in front of the Hardee's where we got supper earlier, and where the high school kids are now hanging out, like they always do on Friday nights, even in late winter. I stare into the parking lot to see if I recognize anybody from the church Teen Fellowship. If I see someone I know, I will lean my head out the window and scream out, "Hey!" and then Daddy won't remember what he was just about to tell me.

"Some of that stuff," he says again, as the light changes green and he goes, ruining my escape plan, "Good God Almighty, I never thought I'd see—"

"Yeah, I know," I say. "It's outrageous."

"Good Lord," he says, shaking his head. "Good Lord."

Then, after a moment, a moment in which I haven't even *thought* about drawing breath, he says, "But that Liza Minnelli . . ."

"What about her?"

"Well, she's talented. But I don't believe she'll ever be as good as her mother. Now her mother was something."

I'm thinking we've now gotten through the worst of this conversation—maybe I'll be spared what he has to say to Mama after I go off to my room—so I spend the rest of the ride home trying to think of movies that Daddy liked. I can only come up with two or three, most of which are before my time, but he's talked about them since day one. *The Bridge on the River* . . . something, *The Guns of Navarone, Airport.* No, he hated *Airport.* I guess he likes *The Wizard of Oz* OK. He watches it with us every time it comes on TV, even though he always asks, "How many times can you all watch the same movie over and over?"

I wish I could watch *Cabaret* again, that's for sure.

Later, in my room, I reach under my bed and pull out the *Cabaret* album cover; I suddenly remembered that I stuck it under there a few days before. I replace the record in the sleeve and return it to my gold wire record rack, placing it between *The Partridge Family Sound Magazine* and one of Mama's records, *Mantovani Plays the Best of Broadway.* I take that one out and look at it. It's one of my all-time favorite album covers because of its neat photograph of the New York City theater district, with the marquee lights glistening way up in the sky but also reflected down on the ground in neony rain puddles on the sidewalks and at the edges of the streets. In the picture, the women are all in mink stoles, with bouffy hair and diamonds, on the arms of men in tuxedos, and they're all getting out of limousines and taxicabs and hurrying into some Broadway theater lobby. I've always loved this picture, and someday I plan to go to New York to become like the people in the photograph, well-dressed and glamorous, and going to

Broadway shows all the time. That is, if Mama and Daddy will let me. I'll have to start working on them soon.

In the back of the record rack, I spot my old *Mary Poppins* album, the one that got all warped in the hot car when I was a kid. I haven't thought about it in years; Henry must have been playing it. I remember he used to think it was funny how the song went "Super-cali-fragi-waaa . . . waaaa . . . expi . . . waa . . . waa" all over the place. He liked it because he said it sounded like Charlie Brown's teacher. I return the record to the last wire groove and get into bed.

But as I lie there, I keep hearing all the songs from the movie in my head. Liza keeps singing to me, even as I roll over and try to go to sleep. I put the pillow over my head to try and block the music out of my mind.

But I also keep thinking about that scene—that nuzzling scene. It keeps playing in my head, too. I feel suddenly sweaty, and my stomach feels airy. I look to see if my door is closed all the way. My room is totally dark now since they moved the streetlamp that used to shine in my window.

I'm not sure I should do this, this thing I love to do, but I do it anyway. I can't believe anything can feel so good as this. Especially tonight. I keep picturing the scene: the girl and . . . the two guys. It's almost like how I used to picture my old G.I. Joe doll out of his uniform, when I'd be in bed at night, and that would do the trick. And after my cousin brought over her Barbie and Ken dolls, I switched to thinking about Ken naked. I liked Ken even more than G.I. Joe.

I turn over in my bed, and then back over again. I picture Ken and G.I. Joe dancing together like the men in the movie, with Barbie sitting in a Barbie chair, just watching them, not saying anything, and then I see Joe and Ken lying next to each other on the floor, and they are naked. I make them nuzzle each other's faces. I imagine the men in the movie taking their clothes off, so they can be just like Ken and G.I. Joe. Then they could all dance together and nuzzle each other and lie down side by side as I watch.

Gee . . . this is . . . great . . .

I love having secrets only with myself, and this is the best secret I've ever thought up. I wouldn't even tell Lynette about this one, that is if I ever decide to start speaking to her again. Which I won't.

God, this is . . . it's hot under the sheets. I kick them off.

Much better . . . oh . . .

Before I fall asleep, I try to figure out how I can get back to the Park Point Cinema to see *Cabaret* again without my father finding out. Maybe I'll take a bus, or call a taxicab, or even just walk; it's worth it. I want to just go back and see it by myself; it'll be much better that way. Everything always is.

III.

Soon after I start tenth grade, a Broadway director comes to our town and holds a workshop for some of the more talented local student actors—I make sure to get myself chosen. In my private evaluation, he says to me, "You're a gifted young man, Hunter, but you shouldn't always try to be funny onstage. You're good-looking enough to be a leading man someday, someday soon, I might add, but you've got an image of yourself as a comedian. Try lowering your voice—it's too high-pitched. And don't stand onstage with all your weight on one foot, it makes you look like a sissy. Even your weight out and stand up straight. Make direct eye contact with your acting partner, and with the audience. Don't move your hands and arms around so much."

A leading man . . . The phrase rings in my head; I've never considered it before. As I sit there thinking about that, he pats my hand and starts to tell me again how good-looking I am, which makes me feel kind of creepy, but I don't sweat it, or tell anyone. I just slither away from him as politely as I can, thank him for the advice, and walk out.

A leading man . . . My high school is full of them. I start looking around at the popular boys, not just the jocks, but some of the honor students, also, and the school leaders. I begin to study them up close and from far away, too: what they wear, how they carry their books and saunter, maybe even swagger, down the hallways, how they slump in their seats in class, chewing on pencils, long legs outstretched in the aisles . . . I watch the way they smile at girls, then look away, then scoop their bangs off their foreheads only to let them fall back again, pretending to yawn, pretending to be distracted, batting their eyes . . . I want to do all those things, too. And even if inside I still know I'm a "comedian," I'm an actor, too. And if I'm not really a leading man, I can at least play one. I can look, and act, the part.

One thing I learn is that leading men not only know how to stand, stretch their legs, and play with their hair so that everybody notices, they also know how to get elected to office, gain position, run the school. And even though at home I keep reading movie magazines and playing cast albums by myself, at school, in the midst of stretching out my legs, sauntering down the hallway, winking at girls, and scooping my own bangs off my forehead, I am unanimously chosen to be: prom chairman, vice president of the Student Council, and even editor of the school newspaper. I actually go so far as to make myself the paper's first ever movie critic; my friends' parents tell me they always read my reviews before deciding what movies to see.

I have become a leading man.

So now: Chapel Hill. Chapel Hill, the home of the University of North Carolina, is the land of leading men, like a lot of college towns are, I'm sure. And even though I am only one of many leading men here, I imagine that I'm still unique, in my way. Here, leading men practically fall from the branches of the pine and dogwood trees, and when they hit the ground, they travel alone or in packs: they come at you around the corners of buildings; they ascend and descend dormitory stairs day and night, sometimes wearing nothing but running shorts; they sit around in the quad, sunning themselves, or on the library steps, and it's as if invisible spotlights are always aimed to shine directly on them from some unseen lighting grid up above, because they're impossible to miss. Everyone sees them, everyone knows them, everyone wants them. Or wants to be them.

There's a song leading men sing at Chapel Hill: "I'm a Tar Heel born, I'm a Tar Heel bred, and when I die, I'm a Tar Heel dead." My parents now laugh about how they tried to bring me up a Tar Heel, but I resisted what I called, at the time, "all that college crap," content as I was only to play records and read movie magazines, go to movies all the time and act in community theater plays.

Now I'm a leading man both onstage and off, and when the leading men of Chapel Hill come to see the drama department productions, the ones that I'm starring in, they see themselves reflected in my performances. They now want to be what I am, because, in a play, the leading man always gets the girl, always triumphs at the end, always ends up on top. He wins.

I'm a leading man born, I'm a leading man bred, and when I die . . .

Wooley Dorm, a bright Saturday morning in late April. It's not even 6 A.M., five minutes away, in fact, from the hour-on-the-hour chiming from the campus bell tower. I don't need the bells though, since Dalton is next to me, poking me with his fingers.

"Hey, buddy, you awake? Let's play *Chinatown*," he says, now nudging me with his leg, and then more insistently: "Come on, Hunter, let's play." Now his hand is pushing against my rib cage and he's trying to roll me awake, trying to rock me from side to side. I'm already awake, of course; I heard him the first time. I just like his hands on my body like that; and I especially like it when he wants to play the games I invented—games I invented just for us.

"I have to study," I mutter into the pillow.

"Yeah, right. It's six o'clock in the morning. Study me," he says.

And I do, and for this I have no need of Cliffs Notes.

But after a while, he interrupts and says: "Now let's play *Chinatown.*"

"OK, who's Mrs. Mulwray?"

"I'm Mrs. Mulwray. You're Jake."

We sit up in bed and hike up our underwear. We're actors after all, and it is just instinct to want to adjust costumes and hair. Lights. Camera. *Action.*

"Who is she?" I ask, in character, gruff and resonant. "The girl. Who is she?"

Dalton/Mrs. Mulwray demurs, looking far away, somewhere in the corner of the room.

I grab him by the shoulders and shake him. "Who *is* she?"

"She's . . . she's . . . my sister," he says, in a husky stage whisper.

I mock-slap him across the face, and his shock of brown-blond hair does indeed fall over his eyes, as if on cue. He's so incredible to look at, I almost break character. I can't take my eyes off of him. Ever.

I snap back as Jake. *"Who is she?"*

"She's my *daughter!*" he exclaims.

Mock-slap the other cheek. Hair falls to other side.

"She's my sister!"

Slap.

"She's my daughter!"

Slap.

And then, hysterical, in full movie-star breakdown mode: *"She's my sister and my daughter!"*

Great wracking sobs. I hold him. *Cut.*

"You were brilliant," I say, as we collapse back into my iron-frame single bed, of the Early American Institutional variety.

"Faye Dunaway was robbed of that Oscar, man," he says, as though it were his own deep personal regret.

It is one of our favorite movies; we've seen it twice at the Student Union Film Series. I've known Dalton for four semesters, from the fall of our junior year—he had transferred to Carolina from another college. We met at a Student Union screening of *The Seventh Seal* one rainy late September afternoon while practically the whole rest of the student body was at a football game in Kenan Stadium. We were both sitting by ourselves; he was a few seats away from me, and when the film was over, he turned to me with a big smile on his face and said, "Well, that was cheerful!" So we became steady movie "dates," even though his girlfriend Susan sometimes came along, too. The movies mostly seemed to bore her, though; she obviously just liked being with him. Dalton and I took in a lot of classics together: *Citizen Kane, Dog Day Afternoon, Mr. Smith Goes to Washington, The Manchurian Candidate* . . . he even let me talk him into attending a midnight showing of *Whatever Happened to Baby Jane?* This was October, and we were newly seniors; we had spent the whole summer writing and calling each other (his hometown was about two hundred miles away from mine) and comparing notes on the current crop of mostly awful summer movies. After seeing *Baby Jane,* we were walking together through the dark, lamplit campus at two-thirty in the morning, kicking at leaves and pushing each other into the piles, acting like kids.

He said: "Were you scared of Baby Jane, Hunter?"

"No. Why?"

"Yes, you were. You were scared of her."

"Oh, is that so?"

"Yeah. You squealed like a girl a couple of times."

"Screw you, I did not."

"Yes, you did, son. You squealed. And everybody heard you."

We were near the Davie Poplar, which campus lore says is the oldest, biggest tree on campus. When you stand underneath it, the shade of its branches covers you like a giant, leafy umbrella. It was pitch dark; no one was around. We both had on white oxford shirts, which shone in the moonlight, making it easier for us to see each other.

"Asshole, I did not squeal."

"Yes, you did. Like a pig. Like a little pig who's about to be made into barbeque."

I sat down on the small stone bench underneath the tree.

"You're full of shit," I said. "And you make me tired."

"Go back to your room and go to bed, then, little Hunter boy," he said, kicking up leaves and stretching his muscular arms. He yawned.

"I'm gonna sit here for a while," I told him. "*You* go back to *your* room."

"Don't tell me what to do, squealer," he said. "I'll do what I want." After a few seconds, he kicked his way through leaves until he was standing in front of me at the bench; he was very close, closer than he needed to be. In his right hand he held a twig.

"So . . ." he said, in a low voice. "What are you gonna do? You're just gonna sit here?"

"Yeah, I thought I would. What's it to you?" I looked up at him. He had a little smirk on his face, and he was staring at me. I stared back. For a very long minute, neither of us stopped staring at each other, though neither of us said anything; we just looked at each other, smirking and breathing. Then he lifted the twig and guided it softly against my cheek and over the top of my hair and down the other side of my face, and under my chin, keeping his eyes locked with mine the whole time. My heart was pounding so fast I thought it would burst my chest wide open.

"Excuse me," I said, using acting skills to speak in a normal-sounding voice. "Get that twig off of me, please." I made no effort to move away from it myself, though I could have.

"Why?" he whispered, still tracing me with it. "Doesn't it feel good?"

I looked away, finally. "You're nuts, Dalty."

He smirked again. "Maybe."

"OK, well then I need to get going," I whispered, and I hated how hoarse my voice sounded all of a sudden. I started to rise, and his palms glided down onto my shoulders, pushing me back on the bench, but gently. He lowered himself at the same time, crouching on his knees.

"Hey," he whispered. "Don't go, man." He lifted his index finger to my lips and began to trace them. I closed my eyes . . .

Now the alarm clock suddenly jangles madly, wildly, and Dalton reaches over to turn it off with one hand. "OK, quick, first line of dialogue," Dalton says. It's another game we play: recite the first famous line from a movie that pops into your head.

I'm excellent at this. "What can you say about a twenty-four-year-old girl who died?" I say immediately.

He giggles, and strokes my hair. "No, don't do a morbid one. Do a happy one."

"OK. What can you say about a *twenty-one*-year old *boy* who . . . *lived?* That he had hair the color of honey, and, uh . . . Carolina-blue eyes—"

"That's cheating, but keep going."

"That he stood six foot two and weighed a hundred and seventy-five pounds, except in the summer when he ate too much of his mother's cooking, and then he—"

"Fuck you. Revise."

"—That he stayed slim and desirable at all times, and was the envy and unattainable object of desire of everyone and everything on campus, teacher or student, male or female, dog or cat, bush or flower—"

"You're crazy. Keep going."

"—that he was the pride of the metropolis of Rocky Mount. That he loved English, and drama, tennis and basketball, the theater, movies, literature, even his infantile, stupid-ass fraternity, a house of morons known through all of Chapel Hill as—"

And at this point, he hits me, but not hard. "You, son, are *consumed* with jealousy," he says.

"Yeah, right, fuck you too—that he loved beach music, Broadway cast albums, Baskin-Robbins, masturbation—"

"Highly accurate, son. Any others?"

"—and me." And he smiles, but he doesn't say anything, just rests his head on the pillow.

"Is that it?" he asks, finally.

"Well, yeah. I saved the best for last, didn't I? *Didn't I?*"

"Hmm . . . if you're lucky," he says. "On your good days."

But the boy can't lie. I know I fascinate him; he claims I've "unlocked" (his word) things inside of him that he never could have unlocked on his own. He told me this, though he didn't have to; I see it in his eyes, I feel it when he touches me and holds on to me all night long, refusing to let go of me even when I try to pull away from him, which isn't often.

I lean over and kiss him, and run my hand along his tanned chest, smooth and hard as alabaster. Last fall, before Dalton and I got together that first night, I was a determined, focused college senior full of drive and ambition; this spring, I've been nothing but a dopey, dreamy mess—it's a wonder I'm going to graduate at all. I don't remember much about turning in papers in January, or taking midterm exams in March, but I must have passed. I know I've spent time with other friends, played Trofimov in the drama department's production of *The Cherry Orchard*, had front row seats for the Hall and Oates concert at "Spring Thang," even had my little brother Henry come stay with me on two separate weekends. But all of that is a blur; it's the time I've spent with Dalton that plays like a movie in my head—clear, sharp, in brilliant focus—and I can concentrate on nothing else.

Nobody in my dorm knows about us, as far as I know. You can get away with this kind of stuff when you blame it on alcohol, and lots of weekend-drunken guys crash in each other's rooms, too tanked to drive back to an off-campus apartment, or even just to walk a few yards back to their own dorms. Most guys have some sort of couch in their rooms, and nobody knows where anybody sleeps once doors are shut—and locked.

"Gotta go, Hunt," he says suddenly, kissing me on the forehead and tumbling out of bed, pulling on his "Property of UNC Athletic Department" sweatshirt and khaki shorts and Chuck Taylor All-Star high-tops. "Susan's parents are taking us to breakfast. I gotta look decent."

Usually, I deflect these tidbits of Susan information. I've practiced. This one, however, has caught me unaware. It grazes.

"Fuck that," I say, angrily, for once.

He looks at me, a slight expression of bewilderment on his face.

"What's the matter with you?"

"Nothing. I just wish you didn't have to go is all."

He turns away. He's too smart not to see through this, and too unwilling to allow it. I instantly know I've screwed up.

"Hunter," he begins. "Don't get weird about Susan, OK, buddy? I thought we had worked through all that."

I don't want him to get mad at me, so close to graduation, the end of our student life together. We've already made plans to go to New York in the fall, just the two of us; we'll get an apartment and start auditioning for theater. It's all planned, has been since January 21, the night of the year's first snowfall in Chapel Hill, when we held each other all night under the covers, riffing nonstop about our dreams and plans, laughing and kissing until the sun came up on the white-frosted campus.

"No, it's not that, Dalty, come on," I say. "I'm sorry."

He leans in close.

"You're my buddy," he says, nuzzling me nose to nose, lips almost touching. "My special buddy. OK? There's nobody else like you. But Susan is . . . you know . . ."

"Yeah, I know."

You have to understand the way I am, Mein Herr . . .

He kisses me, full, with his tongue, holding the back of my head, pulling me into him. I would gladly fail all my spring semester courses for another year of this.

"Gotta go, bud," he says.

"Hey. Tomorrow night. The new Al Pacino film at the Varsity. Are we still going?"

"Is that the queer one?" he asks, crinkling up his cute nose.

"The queer one? Jeez. Well, yeah, I guess. I mean it's called *Cruising.* But it's a major studio film, it's not like it's gay pornography or anything like that."

He thinks a second.

"We'll talk about it later, OK, bud?"

"OK . . ."

He gets to my door, slowly opens it up, looks out in the hallway to see if anybody's there, and, seeing the coast is clear, turns back to look at me. Whispering, he leaves me with this: "Forget it, Jake. It's Chinatown."

After what we now refer to as the *Baby Jane* night, we accelerated our "special" friendship; or more to the point, our special friendship accelerated on its own. Being in the drama department made us naturally suspect anyway, and some of the majors, mostly those we didn't hang out with or know very well, spread rumors. Some of the male theater majors were openly gay, but they were pretty swishy and didn't live in dorms or belong to fraternities; we were cautiously friendly with them, but didn't seek them out outside of classes and productions. Soon after *Baby Jane,* we both got cast in the winter undergrad production of *A Midsummer Night's Dream;* I played Lysander, and Dalton, rather conveniently, played Demetrius. Of course, in the play, Lysander is in love with Hermia, but then, because of the magic and the spells and the dreams, goes after Helena. We did Shakespeare one better offstage though, because this time Lysander really wanted Demetrius, and Demetrius pursued Lysander, too, and, for all we could have cared, Helena and Hermia could have just gone off and mated with the Rustics.

"Bad, evil, jilted actresses!" we would say in the safety of my dorm room, in the dark and under the sheets. "Mean-spirited evil wood nymphs! Get thee to nunneries, get thee to acting class, thou jealous drama department goons and sorority rejects! You have no power here! Be gone, before someone drops a house on you too!"

And we would laugh and kiss and strip quickly at the drop of a baseball cap, then shush each other when we heard fellow dorm rats in the hallways. We held still, listening to them: nineteen- and twenty-year-old brutes and ruffians, intent on proving their masculinity at all hours of the day and night, breaking beer bottles, playing hall soccer with discarded pizza boxes, mock-slamming each other around those ancient industrial-green corridors in their underwear and gym shorts, roughhousey and mean. Dalton and I tackled each other's bodies too, a few inches away, separated from the guys outside by nothing so much as an old, thick door, made, I'm sure, from pure North Carolina pine.

Later that Saturday, several hours after Dalton's fast exit to meet up with Susan and her parents, I am actually attempting to study for a theater history final when my mother calls.

"Hi, Grace," I say. I've taken to calling my parents by their first names; I saw it in a movie somewhere.

"I remember when 'Mother' was sufficient." She sighs.

"I was a different person then, Grace," I say. "I'm now a new version of my old self. Sleeker, much improved." I figure if I talk in enough code, they'll finally figure me out. I think of myself as an interesting character in a difficult screenplay; you have to pay attention to what I say to really understand me.

"Well, all right," she says. "Far be it from me to try to change that. I just wanted to finalize plans for graduation weekend. I hope you've not become too sophisticated to don a cap and gown for a couple of hours."

"Copy. Can do. Anything to make the mother character happy."

She lays out the plans, which I've already heard about twenty times. Why she wanted to "finalize" them, I have no idea; the whole weekend will follow the same scenario of her graduation weekend, the same one as Daddy's, the same one Henry will have with them a few years from now. It's tradition: Saturday night cocktail party at Olde Campus Hall, dinner at Slug's-at-the-Pines, breakfast on Sunday at the Carolina Inn, the filing in of graduates in Kenan Stadium, "Pomp and Circumstance," blah blah blah. But then she says the strangest thing:

"Do you know what I found the other day, sweetheart?"

"No, please reveal."

"That old *Mary Poppins* record that you loved so much when you were little."

"You mean 'Super-cali-fragi-waa-waa'?" That's what Henry and I eventually dubbed it.

"Yes. You were so upset when that thing got warped in the hot car. So sad. Do you remember that?"

"Yeah . . . sure I do."

My mother narrates stories of my childhood to me so often that I have begun to feel that the little boy she talks about is not actually me, but some role I played. Sometimes, it seems that I had nothing to do with my own early years at all, that instead I am sitting in a dark theater watching some other child actor play *me* up on the screen. I watch him enacting events in my life better than I ever could have, and I seethe with jealousy over his uncanny ability to portray me, to capture me correctly in scene after scene, something I never seem to be able to do. A guy could watch his whole life like that . . . he could start to think of himself as a character portrayed by someone else, as someone he knows only in third person. Sometimes, I actually feel angry that another child actor beat me out for the role of Hunter, a part I very much wanted to play.

"Anyway," Mother continues, "I was going through things to put out for the yard sale, but I just couldn't part with that. Thought you might want to keep it."

"Sure, why not? Good call, Grace."

"But I did put out those old Partridge Family albums. You didn't want to save those, did you, honey?"

On Sunday afternoon, after a morning of studying in which I finally ceased to care whether I could differentiate between Euripides and Aeschylus, I walk across campus to the Pi Kapp house to look for Dalton, since I haven't yet heard from him about the movie. I'm anxious to see *Cruising;* it's apparently gotten quite a controversial reception in the big cities, and on Friday night, when it opened here at the Varsity Theater on Franklin Street, groups of protesters led by the Berean Baptist Church and the Pentecostal Holiness people picketed outside. I was glad to see the Presbyterians stayed home.

I saw on the news that certain homosexual groups also have come out against the movie because of the violence and for what they claim is an inaccurate depiction of gay city life. Since I don't know any New York homosexuals, I won't have much to compare it to. We have a grad student in our theater department—a large guy with a pompous personality—who has a tendency to walk across campus on Saturday nights in this head-to-toe leather get-up—boots, cap, vest—but he always looks kind of foolish walking down Franklin Street by himself dressed like that, huffing and puffing his way through a sea of people in polo shirts, plaid skirts, and Top-Siders. His acting, we've noticed, always seems to be about expressing anger.

When I get to the Pi Kapp house, Dalty is out in the front yard, tossing a football with some of the brothers. It's hot seeing him "act" like a jock—he's very convincing—but I can't help resent that he goes to the trouble to do it, when he could just be alone with me, talking about movies and making love. It's funny to me how we make fun of fraternity boys when we're alone—we call them "fratty baggers"—since, in reality, we can both "pass" for one when we want to, or have to. The difference is that Dalty actually thinks he is one, which is laughable to me, but I don't tell him that. It's his own dream factory. But what do I care, really, as long as I get to watch him playing football with a bunch of real jocks, all of them in sweaty jerseys and tees, gym shorts and sweat-pants. It's all I can do to keep from grabbing Dalty and throwing him down right there on the Pi Kapp yard . . .

"Hey man," he says when he finally looks over and sees me watching him, perhaps not as discreetly as I should. He turns back to them. "Um . . . you guys know Hunter, right?"

Yup, yeah, how's it hanging, Hunt.

"We gotta go study, sons," he says, and I can tell he's trying to figure out how to ditch them for me. "Got a big ol' fuckin' exam tomorrow. Last one, then I'm a FREE MAN!!" They chortle frat-speak back at him, clearly charmed by him, too; yes, even them, leading men themselves. When he snaps, they respond—they are a part of his dream, he is a part of theirs; in his dream, they do as he commands, in their dream, he indulges their every wish. As they head off into the house, the brothers flash clandestine hand and finger gestures at each other, the meanings of which, I guess, only Pi Kapps the world over would know.

He saunters out to the perimeter of the yard, toward the street, and I run to catch up with him.

"You looked great out there, big guy," I say.

He rolls his eyes. "Thanks, Coach."

I punch his arm. "Hey, the movie starts in an hour, I thought we could get a pizza or something first."

"Yeah. Hey listen, Hunt. I can't go to the movie, OK?" He doesn't look at me when he says this.

"Oh . . . OK," I say after a moment. We're standing on the edge of Cameron Street, on the curb, looking out at this little corner of the campus known as Big Fraternity Court, watching students go by on bikes, staring out at the tops of the Franklin Street buildings in the distance. The trees have turned leafy and light green now, and white, flowery dogwoods are out in full bloom. It's like a photo out of my parents' old '50s yearbooks, two young college students in love, in April, standing side by side on a Chapel Hill street: "*Spring and a young man's fancy* . . ."

"Why not?" I ask, finally.

"Well . . . I don't know, man . . . I don't think it's too cool, OK? It's just kind of . . . I don't know, it's a queer movie."

"Al Pacino is your favorite actor, Dalton! You'd bag it because it's about homos? In New York City?"

"I dunno, man. I just don't think it's too cool, you know? I don't think it would be cool for us to go to that together. I mean, I think I might go see it with Susan, I think that'd be OK."

He stares deliberately off into the distance, and then down at his feet, pretending to be distracted by something on his basketball sneakers. I try to deflect that last comment, but this one does more than graze; it penetrates.

"You're acting totally weird, Dalton." I want to say more, but can't.

"Look, Hunter, I've been thinking about this . . . you know, about us, whatever. And I guess I've kinda been trying to say this to you for a long time, but . . ."

"But what?"

He starts to stammer. "Look, man . . . look . . . you know you're my special buddy, and, like, one of the best friends I ever had . . . and . . . what we do is cool, you know, it's OK, but I don't think it's me, man . . . not really . . . I don't know . . ."

"What the hell are you talking about?"

He turns and looks at me for the first time. Those blue eyes that I woke up to yesterday morning . . . they're not the same eyes now. Steely and distant, they look through me and around me; they don't look *at* me.

"Just don't think I can do it anymore, buddy. I'm just not that way. Not like you. I mean, I don't know if you really are or not . . . but . . . well, things are going great with Susan now. And you know I'll always be your friend."

I'm your friend.

Slap.

I'm your special buddy.

Slap.

I'm your friend and *your special buddy.*

Surprise! *Cut.*

"You're so full of shit," I say. "This is bullshit. What's going on with you?"

"I'm sorry, Hunter," he says, sharply. "I knew you wouldn't deal with this too well, but you can at least try to understand."

"What about New York? In September? The apartment?"

"Yeah, I've been thinking about that too, and I've decided I might do better out in L.A. There's more movie work there."

He turns away again; he has nothing if not an actor's timing. I start to reach for his hand, his arm, anything; then I don't. I shove my own hands in my pockets and look down at the ground.

"I gotta go, Hunter," he says, quietly, after a minute or so of silence. "Listen, I'll see you at graduation next weekend, OK?" He doesn't offer me a kiss, of course; he doesn't even offer a handshake. He just turns away from me and sprints back into the Pi Kapp house. As he passes the basketball goal in the driveway, he jumps up and grabs the rim, holds himself there for a second, then drops and thwumps the net on the way down, as if he's just . . . scored. Then he disappears into the frat house.

I stand there for a moment, then turn in the direction of town and start walking. I saunter down Franklin Street, trying to carry myself like a normal person who hasn't just been run over by a truck, because if I think about it, if I give in to it for a second, I'll just—

No. I'll be damned if I'll let him get to me. Fuck him, I'll just go see the movie anyway, I think, but as I head toward the Varsity, I can't concentrate on anything. Everything around me is a blur, like an out-of-focus movie, and the traffic sounds mix with the shouting voices of students and the usually reassuring hourly chiming from the university bell tower—now it sounds more like a death knell. From some distant, open window in the music building, a soprano practices a difficult aria, repeating one phrase over and over, stopping and starting again, trying to get it right. Everything looks and sounds out of sync, unreal, fuzzy. Warped. *Super-cali-fragi-waa-waa . . .*

There's not much of a line to get into *Cruising*. I know I should look around to see who's here to see me going in, but I really don't care anymore . . .

Sitting in the dark theater, I watch the homosexual characters dressed in black leather cavort across the screen; some vicious murderer lurks among them. They disco dance and sweat and do drugs and "cruise" each other—I do know what that means—and some of them die, murdered before, during, or after sex. These are not people that I know anything about, and I don't think I'd ever want to—I certainly don't want to *be* any of them; not a person in black leather, not a drug-taking disco dancer, not a rootless, anything-for-a-high homosexual living in New York City, a place where, the movie seems to be saying, it's very easy to get yourself killed if you hang out with the "wrong" people.

I don't know if any of the other audience members can see me sitting alone in the back row. If they were to turn around and look, I'm sure they would think it strange that, as I watch this weird movie, tears are streaming down my face, as though it were really *Gone With the Wind* and I'd just heard Clark Gable bid good-bye to Vivien Leigh at the door, frankly, as he says, not giving a damn.

IV.

The moderately famous movie critic leaves the screening and heads out into Times Square. It is a gray, chilly October day; it has been raining off and on, and large pools of water have collected at curbs and intersections. It is nearly evening, and the electricity of midtown has begun its spectacular rainbow dance amidst the dirty gray-brown buildings; he loves that he can actually read the signs and theater marquees as they reflect in the rain puddles— muted, pastel neons shimmering in shallow water. As he walks, he dodges them neatly, having spent quite a few years now maneuvering through rain-soaked city streets.

He takes his familiar route up Broadway, heading back to his magazine's midtown office. It is always better, he feels, to write the review as soon after a screening as possible, and he has no particular reason to rush home anyway. He likes working in his office rather than from his apartment; he actually enjoys working late, after most of Manhattan's nine-to-fivers have long since gone home. He is a writer, after all, a critic; it's a "late beat" kind of job.

The movie was long; it had been daylight when he got to the screening room, and even while walking the last few blocks, it has begun to grow steadily darker outside, the early end of the day that is particular to autumn, especially to the city in autumn. Still, this is one of his favorite times of the day in New York, always has been; just before "curtain going up" at the theaters, the last few moments of evening before everything becomes night.

He pauses at a corner to watch theatergoers rushing hurriedly into theater lobbies, many of them arriving at the last minute, clearly full of the anticipation of an expensive evening of live entertainment. It saddens him that people aren't as glamorously turned out as they used to be, in the evenings, though that satiny, tuxedo-and-mink-stole era was even before his time. He knows it only from old photographs and long-forgotten record album covers. He misses it, if it is possible to miss something you never really knew, never actually experienced. He's seen the photos; he believes in what used to be.

The wind is bitter, and insistent, but he is nearly at the office now. The narrow sidewalks are still crowded with city dwellers hurrying and scrambling, inconsiderately sideswiping one another in their agitation to get where they're going. How annoying it is, even useless, to try and dodge them all, especially with their umbrellas opening and folding at a mad pace, as if in some Busby Berkeley production number, as they dash from subway stairs to curbs and corners, to taxis and doorways and beyond. He, of course, is in no particular hurry, seldom is. Turning up the collar on his pea coat, he thinks instantly of the famous photograph of James Dean walking through Times Square on a cold, blustery afternoon. He catches a glimpse of himself in the reflection of a storefront's glass door, and laughs at his own pretension: he's probably much more Roddy McDowall than James Dean.

He passes the theater where one of his childhood idols is appearing in a show. She has not been back to the stage in years, and her return has been treated as a momentous event. He stops to study the large, blown-up photos of her lining the side of the theater. She's still uncannily beautiful, and still exudes that same bewitching presence that allured him so completely, so inexplicably, when he was a child. He wishes his mother had beaten the cancer long enough to have come up and seen this show. How he had dreamed of taking her to see it! Just as she had taken him to see the star's first movie over thirty years ago. He recalls that his mother is the same age as the star—well, she would have been.

He has a friend in the show, one of the boys in the chorus, and his friend has spoken highly of the star, told him how lovely and gracious she truly is. Just before his mother died, on one of the last afternoons that he spent sitting beside her bed and holding her thin hand, he related his friend's stories to her, telling her what the star had been like in rehearsals, how friendly she was, how courteous and kind to everyone. His mother had smiled and whispered that she wasn't surprised; that's how she had always seemed in the movies, too. It was one of the last coherent conversations they had.

He continues on a few blocks to his office building; the rain is lighter now. He passes through the revolving door into the pink marbled lobby, waves hello to the guard behind the desk, and steps into an open elevator, which closes, hums, and ascends: one fluid, noninterrupted pattern of movement that has become for him an almost nightly ritual. He travels silently and alone up to his office on the forty-fifth floor, a height that makes him think of the Rainbow Room and Cole Porter songs and the old movie where the lovers have a reunion on the top of the Empire State Building. It's quite a glamorous height to ascend to on a daily basis, he thinks, even though, once at the top, he goes only to a small, nondescript office. It does have great views, though, overlooking the city from one of its loftiest *You Are Here*s, otherworldly, in its way, *noir*ish. He laughs when he compares it to his own apartment: a third-floor one-bedroom in a Chelsea brownstone, with a view of an air shaft.

His closed office door bears a label with his name printed on it; he stares at it for a moment, as though he had never come face to face with it before. Sometimes he thinks Hunter is a ridiculous name for a man nearing forty; it was fine when he was a child, but even then some people called him "Hunt Boy." He hasn't been "Hunt Boy" to anyone for years. *Hunter.* He mulls it over, stares at the sheer lettering of it. It now sounds to him like a character in children's literature—a minor friend of Davy Crockett's, some kid character in a Disney summer camp drama from the '60s.

Hunter. It's too youthful for the age he is; too youthful, he thinks now, for him.

There are messages on his voicemail, but he is anxious to write his review, get it over with, so he ignores the blinking red light for the moment. He is thinking only of what to write of Dalton Foster in his first starring role in a major studio film. He sits at his desk, and smiles, and rubs his eyes. He thinks how after years of fair to decent supporting roles in both low- and big-budget films, Dalton has finally gotten himself a starring role, a vehicle. A big-time romance, no less! His character, a family man, loses his wife in a car accident, and soon finds himself, in his grief, falling in love with her best friend. Ah, the guilt the poor man feels. It was there on the screen in those big blue eyes, a little weathered around the edges now, gazing down on the actress playing the friend. Explaining to her, sotto voce (having finally lost that southern accent that haunted his performances in earlier movies), how he couldn't love her like this, not when he loved someone else so dearly. Well, at least, the memory of someone else. It had been lousy dialogue; he couldn't help wondering if Dalty had thought so, too. Dalty had always been so fond of good dialogue.

The critic thinks a while, and consults his notes, circling a few key phrases that he had scribbled on his pad in the dark, crossing out other ones. He decides to give his review the tone of a curt dismissal, rather than that of an all-out, juicy pan. Turning to his whirring computer, he begins to type rather quickly, but slows suddenly when he gets to the actors' performances. He types, stops, reads, deletes . . .

He is unsatisfied.

He looks at the clock; he doesn't want to belabor this. He'll probably go out for a drink, or two, after leaving the office; there's a bar in his neighborhood he frequents. He's sure to see someone there that he knows, if only casually; someone to shoot the breeze with, anyway.

He turns to his telephone and again notices the blinking light. He listens to his messages. The first is from a man he has had a few dates with who seems, well, *nice. When can we get together again,* blah blah blah. *Beep.* His father, whom he has called Ed since he was in college, wanting to say hello and report on his latest visit to the doctor; also something about confusion over an insurance claim. Give a call. *Beep.* His brother Henry, thanking him for the silver piggy bank he sent the new baby, saying how much he was sure little Eddie would love it when he was old enough to know it came from his Uncle Hunter in New York. From Tiffany's! *Beep. No more new messages.* After a moment or two of staring out the window, he turns back to his computer and types:

"Dalton Foster, as Stone Michaels, commands the screen with his enormous physical presence and intense, still-vital good looks. After years of supporting the stars, he has finally been given the chance to become one himself. Unfortunately, he is simply not up to the task, and remains unconvincing in the key love scenes with his two leading ladies, who seem to be acting overtime in an attempt to get him to register some emotion, *any* emotion in response to them. (Romantic interest would seem to be what is called for here.) For an actor of his considerable charm and leading-man appearance, this seems an especially damaging thing not to possess in his performer's bag of tricks."

His phone rings. He hesitates for a moment, then decides to pick up.

"Hunter? It's Billy. I thought I'd find you there."

"Billy. Hey. Where are—aren't you performing tonight?"

"Yeah, but I've got a couple minutes. I'm in the chorus, you know. Right now, it's Star Time out there."

"Oh. It's always Star Time."

"Tell me about it. So, did you see the film?"

"Yeah. We'll talk about it later, OK?"

"Sure, fine. I gotta go on soon anyway. Listen, I just wanted to let you know I got Julie to sign the record album for you."

"Wow. Thanks, Billy, I really . . . thank you . . ."

"You'll love this: she said she's *always* glad to do whatever she can to make a critic happy."

"Ah. Imagine that. I should be so lucky."

"She also said you must have played the record a helluva lot to have warped it like that."

"That's a long story."

"I'm sure. Actually, she said heckuva."

"Of course. What did she write?"

"Hang on, I've got it. 'For Hunter . . . So glad to know your mum took you to *Mary Poppins* all those years ago. I'm honored . . . Love, Julie Andrews.'"

For a quick second, Hunter can't really respond to that; he freezes. He feels the sudden catch in his throat—*God, what a cliché I am*, he thinks—but he steadies himself with a hand on the desk. He has learned how to suppress these moments, so he does. Quickly.

"Hunter? You there?"

"Yeah. That's great, Billy. Thanks. Hold on to it and I'll get it from you when I see you."

"Sure. Hey, listen, I'm on in a second here. I gotta go."

"OK. Thanks, Billy. I'll see you."

He hangs up and turns back to his computer screen. He is composed, once again. He finishes the review and files it. With a click, he sends it via e-mail to the entertainment editor. Done.

He turns off the desk lamp, and gathers up his coat and briefcase. He pauses at the window, illuminated by the silvery lights of the city shining into his darkened office. For a few moments, he stares out over them, as he has done so many times before, as he once stared out at the tops of dogwood trees in his front yard from the window of his boyhood room, as he once looked out onto the campus bell tower from a window in the industrial-green hallway of his dorm, so long ago. He's always looking over things, he thinks. Or . . . overlooking things? He laughs out loud to himself: it's a word problem!

The rainy city streams and twinkles and honks below him. He has always loved this view of New York, even before he saw it for himself, even from when he gazed at photographs of Times Square on album covers and in old magazines, imagining it for hours at a time, imagining it in three dimensions—the sounds, the smells—*what does it really look like?* Now he knows.

He watches as lights in other offices—desk lamps, over-heads—are turned off and on in windows across the way. He wonders if other people in other tall buildings are also standing alone in their windows, at this very same moment, looking out over the city . . . he wonders if *they're* wondering if other people like themselves are standing in windows looking out over the city! So many people in such high altitudes, just under the clouds, staring out across the city, their city, the one they know so well, yet filled with people they'll never meet, never even see. So then: a city they live in, but don't know at all.

He stands in his window and counts other windows, as many as he can make out, as many as he can count. He could stand here forever, he thinks, just looking, just looking and counting; looking and counting, but not moving. And that's good enough, he thinks; the city needs people who are merely content just to look at it, to watch it, to regard it from a distance . . . to gaze upon it without ever touching it, to study it, in admiration, as if it were—all of it—nothing more than a rare and famous painting, stretched across an endless canvas, protected by glass.

Perhaps he has always stood here.

DELEGATES

The traffic is thick and stop-start along the Henry Hudson Parkway heading out of the city; it is, after all, Friday afternoon in the middle of the summer. Fortunately, Perry's new Ford Explorer is blissfully air-conditioned, and from my vantage point in the backseat, I feel like I'm at a drive-in theater, since Perry and his new boyfriend, Duffy, are putting on a show up front. This is the scene where they're arguing about what music should be played in the car.

"*I* get to pick the CD this time," says Duffy.

"No," says Perry. "You always pick your own music without consulting me."

He leans on the horn with a violent blast, though I hadn't noticed that the car ahead of us had done anything to warrant the honk.

"Don't be so premenopausal, Perry," Duffy says. "It's just a CD." And with that he chooses one from what I note is indeed his own personal CD collection, contained in something like a photo album, with DUFFY printed in gold letters on the leather cover.

"Rufus Wainwright!" he announces suddenly, flipping the flat silver disc between his palms like a pancake, and here he turns his pretty, youthful little head back to me.

"Do you know who Rufus Wainwright is?" he asks, his eyes fixed on me. It sounds more like an accusation than a question.

I stare back at him for a moment, then turn my own head

around to look over my shoulder. Then I turn back around again. "Are you speaking to me?" I ask.

"Duh!" he says.

"Duffy," Perry says, suddenly grabbing a chance to navigate the car into the faster-moving lane, "adults address other adults by their first names. I realize you probably haven't gotten to that lesson yet in kindergarten this year, but since you're in the accelerated section, I think you can handle it."

Duffy glares. If he were a dragon, steam would be coming out of his nostrils. I'm thrilled; it's like being plunked into a virtual reality production of *Who's Afraid of Virginia Woolf?* with an all-male cast.

"Now try it again," Perry says.

Duffy snaps his head back to me. "JACK-SON," he says, speaking phonetically. "DO YOU KNOW WHO RUFUS WAIN-WRIGHT IS?"

"Oh, you *were* talking to me. Yes, I do."

"You do?" Perry asks, glancing at me in the rearview mirror.

"I read *Entertainment Weekly*," I say. I must choose my words carefully, since it's in my best interests to offend neither Senior nor Junior. It's only Friday, after all, and I am invited up to Connecticut for the entire weekend. Perry has a new country house in Claxton (courtesy of his recently acquired executive status at Salomon Smith Barney) and this is my first visit. And even though their little front-seat drama is fun for the moment, I'd just as soon not have to listen to George and Martha bray at each other for three whole days. Of course, it does occur to me, young Duffy has probably never heard of *Who's Afraid of Virginia Woolf?*, so I must resist future references.

"Rufus Wainwright it is, then," says Duffy, and he inserts the disc into the dashboard's CD player, which sucks it quietly, but immediately, into its insides. Because of my own current state of Intimacy Deficit Syndrome, I can't help but muse upon this as a visual metaphor for a popular sex act.

"Besides," Duffy says, "Rufus is gay. And out. Gay boys should support gay musicians!"

"Liberace was gay," I say, "but we're not playing him."

"Touché!" says Perry. Traffic is moving along better now; his shoulders aren't arching up to his ears with tension the way they were a minute ago.

Duffy turns around sharply in his seat, glaring at me with a deliberately overdone "scorned diva" face.

"Whose side are you on, *Bernadette Arnold?*" he hisses.

"Just call me Switzerland."

"Duff, please be nice," says Perry. "Don't alienate the guest before we even get to the house."

Duffy puckers up his lips and kisses the air in my direction.

"Oh, Jackson loves me," he says. "Don't you, Jackson?"

"Isn't that Perry's job?" I offer.

Perry snorts, and Duffy just stares at me, uncomprehending.

"What-*ever!*" he says, running his elegant fingers through his perfectly tousled, drenched-in-highlights blond hair. His tanning-bed tan and his Chelsea-boy hothouse muscles, all courtesy of the same magic emporium on Eighth Avenue, gleam in the late after-noon summer sun; exactly, I'm sure, in the way he knows they do. I look down at my own biceps, the equivalent of deflated tires, not straining in the least the armband fabric of my polo shirt. Just the sight of Duffy, even from the backseat, causes me instinctively to suck in my stomach; though it's not *un*flat, it is far from meeting the standards of the nightly Abs Parade down Chelsea's Homo Highway. In my own defense, I never aspired to those standards, though that doesn't necessarily prevent one from being intimi-dated by them. I also try running my fingers through my own hair, but I touch more forehead than boyish locks.

Perry continues to drive in broody silence while Duffy sings along to the Rufus Wainwright. He stops singing for a moment only to ask this question to the car at large: "Hey, who the fuck is Liberace?"

. . .

Closer to cocktail time—Perry says the sun goes over the yardarm a lot earlier in Connecticut than it does in New York—he and I are standing side by side at the faux-marble island in his spacious kitchen, arranging cheese and crackers onto serving trays and slicing up limes for drinks, while Duffy is upstairs "beautifying" and "maintaining."

"He's driving me crazy, Jackson," says Perry, unwrapping a gourmet Gouda. "And yet I don't know what I'd do without him."

"But you've only been dating him for five months."

"Four and a *half* months. It just seems longer."

"Oh. Well, in hetero terms, that's the equivalent of three years. Besides, after four and a half months, shouldn't you be more like, 'It's as if we only met an hour ago,' followed by copious blushing?"

"No, it's like I've known him all of my life! Jesus, listen to me. I sound like a Harlequin romance."

"Or a penny dreadful. Oh God, there we go again, speaking in antiquities."

Duffy calls from somewhere upstairs. "I feel that I'm being talked about!" he sings out.

Perry and I freeze a glance at each other.

"Gee," I whisper. "Little pitchers have big ears."

Perry rolls his eyes. "That's not the only big thing little pitchers have."

"Too much information," I say. "And yet not enough. Continue."

"You're a writer. Use your imagination. And make yourself a drink."

We move out onto his terrace, cheese trays and drinks in hand. We're waiting for my old friend Thomas to arrive; he has his own weekend house in Briar Hill, one town over from Claxton. This summer, he's working in a local stock theater, playing one of the leads in a production of *1776*, for which Perry, Duffy, and I have tickets tonight. Thomas called to say he'd swing by Perry's house on his way to the theater.

"Have more, darling," Perry says, tipping the Absolut bottle into my glass. "You must be exhausted from your long journey from town."

"Yes. How divine to *finally* be in the country with the landed gentry."

Perry looks around at his terrace and garden, which overflows with brightly colored summer flowers: petunias, geraniums, salvia, marigolds, impatiens . . . the colors blow together in the afternoon breeze; if you squint, it's like looking in a kaleidoscope. Beyond the grounds, at the far end of the yard, is a calm, silvery lake; an old brown canoe, tied with a rope to a tree stump, bobs gently at the water's edge.

"It really is lovely here, Perry," I tell him, suddenly realizing, in my rush to get a drink, that I hadn't paid the proper weekend guest homage to his new digs. "Your place, I mean. Very Merchant Ivory."

"Do you like it? I hope so. It's only taken me forty-nine years to get a house of my own."

"Worth the wait. It's beautiful."

At this moment, Duffy, another specimen of beauty, appears in the doorway. He strikes an open-armed, welcome-to-my-home hostess pose; very Loretta Young, but that's another reference I resist making. Which is just as well; I wouldn't be able to stand hearing him say: "Hey, who the fuck is Loretta Young?" I probably shouldn't even know myself.

Suddenly he turns surly. "Where's *my* cocktail?" he brays; he's gone from Loretta to Bette Davis in the bat of one elegant eyelash.

"Just sit down, sweetness, and I'll mix it for you," Perry says.

"Thank you. Now Jackson," he says, turning to me, "who is this friend who's coming to visit?"

"Thomas."

"And who is Thomas?"

"He's my oldest friend, actually."

"As old as Perry?"

"Jesus," Perry moans. He hands Duffy a Cosmopolitan. "Drink this. It's a potion to turn you back into a human being."

"What I meant," I say, "is he's been my friend for the longest period of time. We're the same age. Twenty-eight."

Perry does a double take worthy of Jack Benny.

"Oh. And he works with you at the magazine?"

"Duffy," Perry says. "I've told you all this. Thomas is an actor. He's in the show we're seeing tonight. Don't you retain any information that's not about you?"

"In a word, no," Duffy says, but then he winks at me, which makes his remark only a tad less obnoxious. "Continue."

"I've known Thomas for . . . I forget. We met doing summer stock when we were eighteen."

"Twenty-one years ago, for the record," Perry says, under his breath and over the rim of the wide-brimmed glass.

"Ah . . ." Duffy says. "So Thomas is still an actor, and you're not."

"Something like that."

"You gave up the business too, like Perry did," Duffy says. He reaches out to stroke Perry's cheek and flick his fingers through Perry's thinning, brush-cut gray hair.

"Don't remind me of my actor days," says Perry. "I've blocked them."

"I wish I had known you when you were an actor, Perry," he says. "I wish you were still in the business. Then we could go on auditions together."

"As what?" Perry says. "A father-son act?"

"Ooh. Don't let Jackson know all our secrets."

"I don't miss auditioning," Perry says.

"Nor do I," I say.

"Oh, I love it!" Duffy exclaims, setting his drink down. He

stands and thrusts his arms up into what I recognize as the patented, internationally known *Evita* pose. "I absolutely *love* auditioning. You should see the faces behind the table when I go into 'Don't Cry for Me, Argentina.'"

And before anyone can suggest otherwise, he begins to sing it, full-voiced, just as I glimpse Thomas coming around the corner from the driveway. Instantly, Thomas freezes in place as soon as he catches sight of Duffy in mid-performance; he stands at the edge of the house and waits. Thomas is far too polite to interrupt another actor's audition.

I give him a tiny, surreptitious wave just as Duffy goes into the second verse, and he gives a little one back to me too, while he leans against the house, watching. I watch Perry watching Duffy; he is transfixed. Duffy, oblivious to everyone but himself and his voice, continues his number. I notice from the corner of my eye that a lone deer has wandered into the far end of the yard. It too stares at Duffy with an incredulous expression.

As Duffy wails a line—something about Evita being immortal—I discreetly pour more vodka into my glass, and sip, and wait. Many musical minutes pass. Finally as Duffy descends into the third verse, I can't help it, I put my drink down and call out, "Thank you. *NEXT!*"

Duffy stops suddenly. Still holding his dictatress pose, he snaps his head around at me, glaring; Perry's eyes go wide, then he reflexively checks in with the bottom of his empty martini glass. Thomas, still waiting politely at the corner of the house, seizes the moment with his infallible actor's timing.

"Well, hello everybody," he says cheerfully, and saunters up to the patio.

"Ode to Beauty," by Jackson Williford Cooper:

Everywhere I look in Connecticut, I see beauty. Beauty, beauty everywhere! Perry's new house (his new *old* house), a white, 1885 Victorian two-story with a wraparound porch and a red front door, is beautiful. The sloping driveway that winds between two large framing oak trees beside a yard bursting with red, yellow, and white summer flowers and bright green grass is beautiful. Perry, a few weeks away from turning fifty, trim and energetic, a newly bleached white-toothed smile, and a high forehead under a short shock of blondish-gray hair, watery blue eyes behind white-gold wire-rim glasses, is beautiful. Duffy, Paragon of Chelsea Youth, with his bleached-blond hair and sharp, kelly green eyes, a gold earring in not one but both ears, a lean, taut body created by God but improved upon at 23rd Street Fitness, is . . . yes, the sweet little jerk is beautiful. And Thomas . . . well, Thomas has physical attributes, too: he's tall and trim, with dark, Apollo-like curly hair, which once hung shoulder-length during his *Les Miserables* days on Broadway. It's shorter now, and the newly-appearing flecks of gray only add to his allure. But for me Thomas's beauty lies in the fact that he's been my friend for almost twenty years. And that's beautiful. Of course the vodka tonic in the frosted tumbler that I'm currently clutching in my right hand as I sit parked in an Adirondack chair on Perry's terrace— well that, too, is beautiful. Beauty all around me! Beauty, beauty everywhere, and *lots* of drops to drink!

"Isn't there just so much beauty in the world?" I say, after a while, to the three of them—Perry, Duffy, and Thomas—who are also slouched in big Adirondacks but who suddenly seem to be facing me in a circle of . . . what? Is that Judgment? They're looking more like . . . *jurors* than equally inebriated drinking companions. "Isn't everything beautiful?" I say again, getting nervous. "Aren't *we?* Isn't the world beautiful? Isn't *love* beautiful? And friendship? Isn't friendship beautiful?"

And then my Ode to Beauty is silenced.

"You're drunk," Thomas says, in a dry, measured tone, a tone of pronouncement, of finality, as if he were issuing a sentence. He's drinking club soda, since he performs tonight.

"No, I'm not, I'm just . . . beautiful!" I say, but already his tone of voice, the judgey edge of it, the sharply aimed sliver of criticism—*You're drunk*—these are enough to make me start losing my considerable buzz. After all these years, my neurons and synapses know instinctively how to respond when they hear that familiar Thomas tone. Thomas is deeply in touch with his inner schoolmarm.

"Yes, Precious, you are," he says. "But more beautiful when sober."

"Thank you. And fuck you."

"Thomas seems to think you're an alcoholic, Jackson," says Duffy, breezily. "Is that right, Tom-Tom? Is he?"

"Duffy," Perry says. "That's rude."

"Yes, don't put words in my mouth," Thomas says. "I never said—"

"Oh, please," I say. "Sticks and stones. Besides, you know I'm much too fond of drinking to ever let myself become an alcoholic."

"Well, I'm drunk *and* high," says Duffy. "And I *high*ly recommend it." He has changed his clothes once again, this time into spandex shorts, a muscle shirt, and Tevas. On his biceps, he has a caduceus tattoo, the international medical sign of two snakes wrapped around a winged staff, and on his ankle, a tiny red rose over which is painted a small "D." He is puffing on a joint now, having traded in the evil potato for the evil weed.

Perry sips his usual martini—extra dry, two olives. It's his third since five-thirty, but who's counting? Thomas maybe, but not I. Besides, Perry never shows his drunkenness; he just chain smokes Marlboro Lights and grows progressively meaner. Me, I'm a cheerful inebriate. Perry throws a withering glance at Thomas's drink.

"Is that club soda?" he says. "Jeez, Thomas, aren't you the Good Baptist."

"Yeah, what's up with that, Tom-Tom?" Duffy asks, narrow-

ing his eyes while sucking the joint. He is sitting on the railing of
the patio fence, swinging his tan muscular legs back and forth.
"Are you, like, twelve-step or something?"

Thomas looks at him in the most condescending way possible;
warmth and disgust flow in equal measure from his large brown
eyes.

"I'm performing tonight," he says, as evenly as he can muster.
He exchanges a quick glance with me, which I return. Suddenly,
we're like canasta partners; our exchanged glances make me feel
we're in sync again. "I'm working at the Briar Hill Playhouse for
the summer."

"Duffy," Perry says, clearly embarrassed. "We're going to see
Thomas's show tonight. You know that. We *told* you that. Christ."
He lights up another cigarette, and drains the rest of his drink.

"Hey, I just met the guy, I can't remember everything I'm
told, right? Right, Jacko?"

Duffy seems to be under the impression that I'm on his side.

"Right, Duffo."

"Cool," he says. "And what show is it?" he asks in Thomas's
general direction.

"*1776*," Thomas answers politely, but I can see his patience
is on the wane: with Duffy's thoughtlessness, with Perry's smoking, with my intoxication. I try to mentally slap my cheeks to
get unlooped, just to make him happier. As soon as Thomas
announced to the beautiful Connecticut air that I was drunk, I
surreptitiously dumped my vodka on the ground, feeling like a
fourteen-year-old whose dad has caught him in the liquor cabinet.

Duffy continues: "And what is that show about, dude?"

Thomas starts to tell him, starts to talk about the Revolution
and the Continental Congress and the Declaration of Independence, but Duffy isn't really listening, and his attention is
diverted by the neighbor's Jack Russell terrier that has just wandered into our circle, sniffing around. "Oh, looky this! Here,
poochy," he says. "Wanna try a martini?"

It's hard to ignore Duffy's combined ignorance and rudeness; I mean, *1776* is a good musical! And he's an actor; why wouldn't he be more interested? At his age, I gobbled up theatrical shoptalk like candy.

"I should get going," Thomas says, giving up on Duffy's dramatic edification.

"I'll walk you to your car," I say, pulling myself out of the low chair.

Perry is up, too. "So we'll see you tonight after the show, then," he says.

"Yes. Come backstage, then we can head over to my house after that, for a nightcap."

"Oh, nightcap. I love that word." Perry moves to hug Thomas good-bye. "Break a leg," he says, as they embrace. "Do theater people still say that? God, it's been so long since I was in a show, I don't even know the lingo anymore."

"They still say it. Thank you." They kiss good-bye, perfunctorily, and Thomas and I walk toward the driveway, rounding the corner of the house.

When we're out of earshot of Perry and Duffy, he says, "*Welllll* . . . Half-Pint's a piece of work."

"Oh yes, he's a regular Dorothy Parker. The wit and intellect just flow out of him. Like juice from a blood orange."

"So what's the attraction then?"

"Do you mean for Perry or for Duffy?"

"Either. Both."

"Ah . . . well, that's easy. Duffy wants a father figure, or is it 'needs'? I never know the difference. Anyway. A father figure, and preferably one with a little bit of money. *Ka-ching.* Perry needs— or is it 'wants'?—a hunky young stud, preferably one who'll appreciate all the attention, and gifts, he lavishes on him, but appreciation, as we know, would always count as a bonus. So . . . Duffy gets to remain beautiful and well taken care of, but is obliged to put out; Perry has to do the taking care of, but gets to remain culturally and intellectually superior, not to mention one hundred percent sexually gratified. Duffy gets new clothes and CDs and Perry gets a beautiful little trophy boy to carry around all over Manhattan. And, on weekends, all over the wilds of Connecticut."

"Obviously you've given this some thought," he says dryly.

"It was a long ride from the city. I was able to observe quite a bit from the backseat."

"Well, I'm not immune to the charms of youth, I just don't get this particular youth."

"Oh, I don't know, Thomas. I think he's sweet, in a *Tiger Beat* kind of way."

"Speaking of youth," he says, "wait till you see some of the boys in our show tonight. I mean, I feel like their father sometimes, but oh Lord, are they beautiful."

"Beauty is all around," I say.

"Yes, you said that before. Odes to beauty." He kisses me and hugs me good-bye before he gets into his car. He holds the hug for a few extra moments. "It's good to see you," he whispers in my ear. "I've missed you."

"Have you really? Well, thanks."

"No, I mean it. Do you think I don't mean that, Jackson? I have missed you. It's hard to be gone all summer and never get into the city to see people."

"Poor you, Thomas. All alone in your little house in the big woods, surrounded by flora and fauna, working in the theater, attended to by muscular, naked chorus boys running around the dressing room . . . I don't exactly feel sorry for you, Precious."

He rolls his eyes, then reaches for his sunglasses from where they've been nestling in the forest of his curly hair and slides them on. Hopping into the front seat and starting the ignition, he says, "Well, I've missed you anyway, whether you choose to believe it or not. And just for the record, the chorus boys are not attending to me."

Delegates

"Then how will I know," I say, leaning against his window, because I still need to steady myself, "which of tonight's young thespians are your personal favorites?"

"Oh, you've known me long enough; see if you can figure it out. God, Jack, they're so young. Twenty-one, twenty-two. What would I do with one even if I caught it?"

"I don't know, ask Perry."

"Well, I don't want to catch one like that. I'd have to cruelly violate him and then throw him back. And that's so unfair."

"Agreed. Perry can have him. I don't want him, either."

He glances at his watch. "All right, Precious, I'm going. I'll see you tonight."

"Break a leg."

"Thanks. Do try to stay sober, at least for my big number. And try not to be too critical. It's just summer stock, you know."

And I watch him back out of the beautiful sloping driveway—which he does . . . beautifully.

July 1981, Big Rock Mountain Theater, Appalachians of North Carolina

Thomas and I are alone in our room in Mildew Manor, the boys' cast house. We're spending the summer of our eighteenth year doing summer stock, for twenty dollars a week plus meals. It's two o'clock in the morning; Thomas is trying to sleep, but I can't even think about it, since there's a humongous flying cockroach on the loose in our room.

"It must be destroyed!!" I say, using my stage voice. I've got my sneakers in my hands, ready to throw one or both of them at the invader as soon as he shows again.

"It's just a cockroach, Jackson," Thomas groans from his bunk. "You've seen too many horror movies."

"That's right!" I wail. "And horror movies have taught me

185

how to use weapons of mass destruction to save the world!" I brandish my Chuck Taylor All-Stars and scan the room, whirling in all directions, making myself dizzy. I've had one too many Purple Jesuses tonight at our cast party for the closing of *Little Mary Sunshine*—my first-ever taste of a Purple Jesus, and my first taste of alcohol of any kind except for beer. "Oh my God, there it is!" I scream, spying the hideous creature and hurtling my sneaker at it. I miss, but it knows I'm after it, and—*shit!*—it flies up at me, sending me running and screaming into my bed and under the covers.

"Lord, let me kill this thing before you kill yourself," Thomas says. He gets out of his bunk and, with what sounds like a couple of masterly swipes of a rolled-up magazine, ends the life of a summer stock flying cockroach.

"That's why they call it Mildew Manor," he says.

"That thing *had* no manners," I say, from under the blanket. "Did you get it?"

"Yes, Little Miss Muffett. You can come out of hiding now."

He stands next to my bed, holding the dead cockroach in a wadded-up Kleenex. "Hey, Jackson, maybe you ought not to drink so much. I mean, at the next cast party."

"Really? Why not? Didn't you drink too?" I say, in a deliberately challenging tone of voice. The window is open, and the night mountain air is blowing the threadbare red silk curtains across the peeling, crumbling window frame. The wind ushers in faint scents of honeysuckle and mountain laurel.

"Sure, I did. But only two. That's usually enough. And not that Purple Jesus stuff, either. Wine is much safer, just so you know for the future. Besides, we have rehearsal tomorrow, so . . ." He disposes of the cockroach out the open window: "Back to nature," he whispers, almost like a blessing. Then he snaps off the overhead light, a globe with a huge black mass visible at its base—bug corpses from a hundred seasons of summer stock—and climbs back into his bed on the other side of the room.

I prop myself up, watching him. The moonlight shines in clear and silvery-white, illuminating everything. We're both in nothing but our white Hanes briefs; our legs are long and sinewy, deeply tanned from rehearsing musical numbers outside on the rehearsal deck in the noonday sun. I've only recently sprouted some chest hair—a late bloomer—but Thomas's torso is admirably furry with thick black ringlets. I've seen some of the girls in our company looking at him lustfully when he's walking around with his shirt off. Some of the boys, too.

"You're so wise . . . and grown-up," I say.

He laughs. "Mama always says I have an old soul."

"Really? My mother is always saying stuff like that, too. But not about me. I don't think I have an old soul."

"No, you're definitely a little boy."

"Really? Why do you think that? I mean, what about me makes you say that?"

"Oh, Jackson, you don't want to talk, do you? I have to sing in the morning."

"OK . . ."

But it really is much too early to stop talking. "Thomas? One more thing. I was wondering . . . when I couldn't find you at the party tonight . . . where were you? Where'd you go?"

A moment or two passes before he answers. "Oh," he says, finally. "I was just talking to Lee."

"Up in his room?"

"Yeah. Why?"

"Nothing, I was just wondering." We listen to the night sounds—crickets and rustling leaves—outside our window. There's also the faint murmur of a radio, trickling in from someone's room in another part of the house.

"We were just talking . . . it was no big deal," he says, but his voice sounds distant.

"I know."

"Why, did somebody say something?" He sits up in bed and looks over at me, pulling his knees up and hugging them.

"No . . . why would they?"

"Never mind," he says.

"You mean did they say you guys were maybe being weird with each other or something?"

"Did somebody say that?"

There's a knock on our door, and Lee opens it and sticks his head in. He's the director and choreographer of the musicals this summer. Lee is in his late thirties; he's a college teacher from Tennessee. He's cast me in all the musicals, just as he's cast Thomas. He told us privately that we're the only two actors in the company who can get rid of our North Carolina accents when we're onstage, and he thinks we'll both have careers in the theater. Lee is nice and everything, but I have to admit I've kind of steered clear of him offstage ever since he handed me a magazine called *After Dark* and told me he thought I'd enjoy reading it, since it features lots of articles about New York City and Broadway and actors and stuff. What I enjoyed most were the pictures of muscular guys, models, in bathing suits—I think it's kind of a magazine for homosexual people—but I just thanked him and never said anything about what I liked in it one way or another.

"Are y'all OK?" he asks. "I heard a lot of jumping around."

"Yeah, we're fine," Thomas says.

"OK, then," Lee says. "Jackson . . . kiddo, you probably shouldn't drink so much at the next cast party. Do you feel all right?"

"Yes, I'm fine." I don't want him to come over and feel my forehead or anything; that would give me the willies. It's bad enough he's talking to me like my dad, calling me down for bad behavior.

"I'm expecting you in shape at rehearsal in the morning then, young man."

I smirk, but I doubt he sees it.

"Tom . . . you OK?" He whispers this, almost like he didn't

Delegates

want me to hear him. Thomas has told me he doesn't like to be called Tom, only Thomas.

"Yeah . . . I'm OK," Thomas whispers back. It's odd that they're whispering, even if it is two-fifteen in the morning.

"Good," Lee whispers again, closing the door on his way out. "I'll see you tomorrow then. Good night."

We're silent for a long time after that, even though I'm dying to ask Thomas questions. But I don't; I'm too afraid he'll turn around and ask the same ones of me. But there's nothing to tell, really; after all, I have a girlfriend in the company, Shelley, even though we haven't done anything but make out. A little.

"Good night, Jackson," Thomas says, finally.

"G'night."

I can't sleep though, and in a moment or two, I whisper: "Thomas?" I'm resting my head back on the pillow, when suddenly I feel a wave of something hot and clammy rush through my body.

"What?"

"I think—Thomas, I think—"

"Oh God, Jackson." He jumps up.

And he's at my side, helping me out of bed. "Stick your head out the window!"

And he guides my torso halfway out the window, so that my chest and head are all the way outside and my brief-clad butt is sticking up inside. Just in time. Woe unto the poor, thin patches of clover and dirt underneath our window, and any insects that may be lurking there unawares.

Thomas rubs my back while I'm leaning over, which feels good and maybe a little scary; I've never had another guy's hand on my bare back like that. Even as I'm heaving, I'm grateful to Thomas for helping me out, though I can hardly express my thanks with my head out the window. Yet I wonder how different this would feel if, instead of Thomas, one of the other guys in the

company were doing this for me, rubbing my back like this—
Chris maybe, or Greg, or D.J., those athletic blond dancer boys,
the ones I'm always trying to steal glances at in the dressing rooms
when we're all getting out of costume. Thomas is like my brother—
he even treats me better than my own big brother does—so I don't
steal glances at Thomas taking off his clothes. I wonder if Chris or
Greg or D.J. might rub lower than my back, something I think I'd
want and not want at the same time.

"Just relax," says Thomas. "You're gonna be OK."

Oh boy. Maybe. I ask myself if I'd do this for Thomas, if it were
him who was drunk and sick instead of me. I would, yes. But I
know, deep down, it would never be like that; it's always the old
souls who take care of the little boys, not the other way around.

The Briar Hill Playhouse is filling up with the Friday-night audience as Perry, Duffy, and I take our seats. Duffy is carrying on
about how *Rent* is his favorite musical, the only musical he can
"personally relate to." He still doesn't seem to understand what
1776 is about.

"I bet I know other musicals you'd like, Duffy," I say, trying to
be helpful. "The girly ones, like *Mame*, and *Hello, Dolly!* I'll bet
you could relate to those."

Perry kicks me under the seat. "Be nice," he hisses in my ear.
"He's still my boyfriend."

"And why do you think I'd relate to those shows, dude?" Duffy
asks me, looking at me with his studied *I'm focusing on you now*
intensity. His attention always seems to be riveted when a conversation centers on what *he* might do, what *he* might think.

"Well, you know . . . all those feather boas and sequins. You're
a fan of that type of thing, aren't you?"

"Well, I do like *Evita*, so maybe," Duffy says, cocking his head
to the side and thinking. "But I think basically any show before
1980 is, like, totally unimportant. But, hey, you know . . . what-

ever. As long as I'm not bored." He flips his hands, palms upturned, and shrugs, a gesture that says, "Hey, that's just who I am!"

The lights go down, and the overture—played by a lone piano and a snare drum—begins. In a few moments, the "Continental Congress" takes the stage; most of them sport cheesy-looking powdered wigs tied in the back with black ribbons, and they are costumed in waistcoats over blousy shirts, buckle shoes, and white tights. It's clear that the cast features quite a few young, college-age actors—nineteen- and twenty-year olds—playing older characters. A few of them exaggerate "old age" characteristics—speaking in bizarre scratchy voices and walking with pronounced stoops, like old witches in fairy tales.

"Wait a minute," I whisper to Perry. "Aren't they supposed to be playing, like, forty-year-olds?"

"Oh, yes," he whispers back. "That's what they're playing. That's what they think we look like."

I decide this would not be a good time to remind Perry that he's ten years older than Thomas and I. Duffy, for his part, is already fanning himself with his program.

"This is like history class," he whispers. "Bo-ring!" He says this too loudly, and an elderly couple in front of us turns to look at him, and he rudely glares back.

"Duffy," I say, under my breath, "I think you're disturbing them."

"Oh, please!" he whispers. "They *look* like they've been here since 1776," whereupon I cover my face with my hands.

"Duffy, shut up!" Perry hisses.

Duffy rolls his eyes and snorts. "There aren't any divas in this show," he whimpers. "I want divas. Big black women." He snaps his fingers in a circular sweep.

"I know," I whisper, "but try to concentrate on how cute some of the boys are."

"OK, I can always do that," he says, instantly altered, the way a child stops crying when you hand him a toy. "Good call, Jackson. Let's see . . . I want to meet . . . that one and that one and that one . . ." He jabs his fingers in the air toward the stage, nearly rising out of his seat with enthusiasm for this new activity. I gently coax him back down.

"We can meet them *after* the show," I whisper. Fortunately we're in the midst of a rousing musical number, in which the Congress is singing and yelling at John Adams to "Sit down, John!" Which John Adams, of course, refuses to do.

Clearly, that bit of advice doesn't work any better on Founding Fathers than it does on Chelsea Youth.

At intermission, Duffy goes off to the men's room and Perry and I mill about on the theater grounds. I'm drinking coffee, remembering Thomas's edict to be sober for his second-act number. I have been de-inebriated for hours now, of course; the coffee is just insurance.

"He's driving me nuts!" Perry says, as he lights up a Marlboro. "How did I ever get myself into this? It's like baby-sitting. I mean, he's not even socially adaptable, for God's sake. He can't sit still in a theater without talking. And he wants to be an actor? Jesus Christ."

The outside lights start to blink on and off, prompting the audience to return to the theater for Act 2.

Perry looks around. "Where is he? Do you think we can get him back in his seat before they make America an independent country?"

"Not if he's having sex in a toilet stall."

And Perry suddenly looks at me with an awful expression of horror, as shocked as John Adams looked onstage when he was told he couldn't put his slavery clause into the Declaration.

"Perry, I'm sorry, I didn't mean that," I say, putting my hand on his shoulder.

He glances in the direction of the men's room, wrinkling his brow and biting his lip.

The lights blink again, and suddenly Duffy comes rushing up from the other direction. "Are we late?" he says, sounding actually concerned, almost like a normal person.

"You're lucky we're not," Perry snaps, but then he's so obviously relieved to see him that he kisses him on the cheek.

Duffy links his fingers through Perry's fingers and they walk on ahead of me, holding hands all the way into the theater. I'm one of the last audience members still standing outside, so I chuck my red, white, and blue coffee cup into the nearest trash can, and start to head into the theater behind them, but then . . .

Why? Why should I? Really . . . why? I don't want to sit through the godforsaken second act of this miserable production. I don't want to have to make a silly twenty-two-year-old Chelsea boy behave while his lover sits there saying nothing, paralyzed with fear that one wrong word out of his mouth will send the kid skipping into someone else's open arms the next time he's trawling down Eighth Avenue. And Thomas . . . how many times was Thomas conveniently out of town when *I* was in some poor dumb show? And I've not forgotten that both Thomas and Perry had slippery excuses for not coming to my birthday party last year. And my Christmas party the year before that . . .

No. What I want is to head out to the highway and hitchhike myself back to New York, where I could do what I should be doing, which is wearing all black and sitting alone at the end of an expensive hotel bar nursing a martini and looking every inch the femme fatale, or whatever the male equivalent of femme fatale is, projecting a patented air of mystery and glamour and driving the other male patrons wild with my particular allure. Oh, what *is* the male equivalent of femme fatale? Gigolo? *Bon vivant?* Man-child-about-town?

From inside the theater I hear the tinny sound of the orchestra striking up the entr'acte, and I can see the usher is about to close the main door. I realize now is my chance to go, my last chance, actually, so . . . theater or highway? Highway or theater?

I make a run for it . . .

. . . and before she shuts the door completely, I land inside the theater just as the house lights go all the way down.

Oh well, why not? After all, how ironic it would be for me to miss, of all things, the signing of the Declaration of Fucking Independence.

Thomas is playing Edward Rutledge, the delegate from South Carolina. He's the bad guy who doesn't want Thomas Jefferson's abolition clause in the document; he will only vote for ratification if the no-slavery clause stays out. This, of course, is a huge blow to the good guys—Jefferson, Adams, and Franklin—but they realize they have to accept the terms if they are to win the debate on declaring independence.

Thomas is in the midst of his big, dramatic number in which Rutledge makes his racist case to the Congress. He sings and acts it superbly, as he always does, but it's obvious that Thomas is slumming somewhat here at the Briar Hill Playhouse since most of the other actors are college-aged performers, and Thomas is an accomplished, thirty-nine-year-old with Broadway credits. I want to stand up and say to the audience, "Hey, do you all realize how lucky you are to have this guy on this stage tonight?" and then I want to turn to Thomas and say, "Hey, Thomas, do you realize how deeply you're slumming here, Precious?"

But I only join in with everybody else on the solid applause when he finishes his number and then decide to follow the advice I gave to Duffy, to concentrate on the various actors onstage for reasons other than their acting skills. As if playing a parlor game for one, I try to determine which of these youthful thespians Thomas is excited about. It's hard to tell behind some of the unfortunate old-age makeup just who is a young buck and who isn't. Watching the show, I decide that Thomas is probably hottest for the guy playing Roger Sherman, gentleman delegate from Connecticut—Connecticut is short but compact and well-built, and by looking at his eyebrows I can tell his real hair is probably as dark as the wig he's wearing; he actually reminds me of a couple of Thomas's old boyfriends. A definite candidate. However Thomas could also be interested in the tall, sweet-faced redhead (eyebrows matching wig again) in the role of Joseph Hewes, representative from North Carolina. In the show, Mr. Hewes is kind of a wimp, and keeps deferring to Rutledge: "North Carolina yields to South Carolina." I wonder if North Carolina is equally passive offstage; a control freak like Thomas could really go for an attitude like that. Obedient, docile . . . Oh, but Connecticut really is cute; maybe Thomas can have dark-haired Connecticut and leave redheaded North Carolina to me. In the show, Connecticut is always anxious to vote for independence: "Connecticut says 'yea.'" Connecticut has a can-do attitude. Connecticut also has spectacularly broad shoulders.

The one I like best is the hunky delegate from New York, Lewis Morris. I'm ashamed to be so attracted to musculature, but his calves bulging under his white tights are like grapefruits; I can only imagine what is hidden under his waistcoat. New York isn't wearing a wig; he sports shoulder-length blond hair that is obviously his own. In the show, New York is undecided about the voting. When asked for his vote, he always says: "New York abstains—courteously," which gets a big laugh from the audience, most of whom are from the Tri-State area. I can't wait to find out which of these swains Thomas wants for himself, and which ones I might get the chance to meet—and charm. I believe it's still possible. After all, I've been known to ratify a few constitutions myself in my day. My day—has it come and gone, and I missed it? In three months, I'll turn forty; I should figure out if I've already had my day, or if I've still got one coming.

The action is leading up to the big roll-call scene, where the clerk takes the final votes of the Congress. Duffy has behaved pretty well during this act, but all of a sudden he leans over to me and whispers: "Jackson, how does this turn out, do you think?"

I glance at him sideways. "What do you mean, how does it turn out?"

"I mean . . . like, they pass the thing, right?"

I just smile at him, and pat his knee, which I notice Perry noticing from the other side.

"I'd tell you, Duff," I say, "but I don't want to ruin it for you. It's so much better if you're kept in suspense."

"No, tell me now! I like to know ahead of time."

"OK," I sigh. And then I take a long, dramatic pause. "England wins," I whisper.

After the curtain call, Perry and Duffy and I wait outside on the patio, behind the theater, standing among piles of discarded flats, assorted bric-a-brac scenery, sawhorses, and an ancient upright piano. Duffy is still in a good mood—I think he was genuinely relieved to find out that the Declaration of Independence got signed after all—and Perry seems happy that Duffy is happy. Naturally, I'm happy that everybody is so happy. Ode to Happiness.

One by one, the Congressional delegates begin to emerge from the stage door, a Parade of States, as it were. They've traded their three-cornered hats and powdered wigs for shorts, sandals, and tank tops; their young faces are scrubbed free of old-age makeup, and their muscular shoulders are toting what we used to call "dance bags." I wonder if they still call them that. Needless to say, the real Continental Congress of 1776 would hardly recognize themselves coming out of the stage door, these young men who are whooping and hollering and kissing each other good night, some of them even belting out things like "See you tomorrow, girlfriend."

Duffy, of course, immediately recognizes himself reflected back in their living mirror. He is one of them, this is his milieu, and they are speaking his language. He is at Maximum Perk, and I notice he keeps positioning himself in what he must think are sexy "stances." And this little vaudeville is not lost on most of the Continental Congress. They nearly all notice him; first, they glance at the three of us, as a group, and then their gazes settle— not surprisingly—on Duffy. They say it's like that in the animal kingdom too; ultimately, you mate with your own kind.

I wonder if any of them might be more interested in me if they knew that I write the "MAN-hattan" column in *Downtown* magazine. They must read it; I'm sure they do, it's a very popular column in a widely-circulated publication. And my photo runs next to it, complete with state-of-the-art airbrushing. Surely they recognize me . . .

Duffy finally pounces. "You were great!" he says to an athletic-looking blond who has been leaning absently against a pole. Clearly, they have made the proverbial eye contact.

"Now who did you play?" Duffy says, batting his eyes.

The guy laughs, impervious to the fact that he's just been insulted. He's probably all of nineteen years old. I was nineteen once.

"I played Stephen Hopkins," he says, straightening up and smiling, clearly happy to have been recognized, as it were, and exhibiting a sweet sense of pride, however misguided. When he speaks, he reveals an unmistakable Boston accent. "You know, the old one? From Rhode Island? You probably didn't recognize me without the makeup. My real name's Kevin."

"Ah, Kevin," Perry says, jumping in, clearly smelling trouble where Duffy and Rhode Island are concerned. "Makeup. That means you're a *character* actor." Kevin nods his head, then appears momentarily confused. He looks back at Duffy, and smiles again. Duffy smiles back.

Finally, Thomas emerges from the stage door, flanked on

either side by dark-haired Connecticut and redheaded North Carolina. I was right—the wigs matched their own real hair color. If this were *Let's Make a Deal*, I would now be the proud recipient of a new Amana Radarange.

I'm waiting for Thomas outside the stage door. We've just gotten through our opening night of the last show of the summer— *Damn Yankees*. Thomas is playing the Devil, and I, Mr. All American Boy, am playing Joe Hardy, the star baseball player who sells his soul to . . . well, to Thomas! The performance went great; the audience whooped and hollered and gave us a standing ovation. So I should be in a chipper mood, but late this afternoon, right after final dress rehearsal, Shelley broke up with me, without any warning. Of course, I don't even really know how it could be considered a breakup, since we weren't actually committed and we never did much more than mess around. A little. But I liked her. I liked her, and I definitely considered her my girlfriend, until she said, "Jackson, sweetie . . . I just don't think you dig girls." And then I called her a liar, and turned on my heel and walked away from her in a huff. I went out to the woods behind the theater to sit and think.

Thomas knew I was upset before the show, but I didn't tell him why, and he told me to wait for him and we'd talk afterward. So I'm standing outside, waiting for him—his old-age makeup takes longer to get off than my regular makeup does. I'm sitting on the stone fence with my head in my hands when a couple of older guys—probably about forty—pass by me on their way to the parking lot.

I look up and see them whispering to each other. About me?

I pretend not to notice them and look elsewhere, but soon they come over my way. Oh God.

"Excuse me," says the first one. "We just wanted to say that you were simply great in the show tonight. We really enjoyed it."

"Oh, yes," says the other one, equally excited. "You were fabulous. You're very talented." They both have pronounced southern accents, and similar-sounding voices, almost as if they grew up in the same family, though they look nothing alike. One wears thick black-framed glasses and is dressed in a blazer with tan pants and white shoes. The other one, a little younger but not young, has on Wrangler jeans and a flannel checked shirt, with a red bandanna tied around his neck. He sports a thin, sad little mustache that looks like a caterpillar crawled onto his upper lip and went to sleep.

"Thank you," I say.

"We just love coming to the playhouse every summer," the one with the glasses says. "I'm Roger, by the way."

"And I'm Terry," the other one says. "We always stay down in the square at the Crest View Inn. Do you know it? It's just fabulous."

"Yes, and you're Joe Hardy," says Roger, smiling a big smile and moving in a little closer.

"Well, I *was*," I say, and look away. It's clear Roger and Terry aren't hint-takers.

"Listen, Joe," Roger continues, "if you're not doing anything, why don't you come down to the inn and have a drink with us?"

"We'll buy," says Terry. "We know how pitiful summer stock salaries are."

"Oh yes, it's on us." Then they both begin to titter, though I have no idea why. Neither of them has said anything remotely funny, as far as I can tell.

"Well, thanks a lot," I say. "But I can't. We're pretty busy rehearsing and performing and all."

"Oh," says Roger. "Well, come on down later, if you change your mind."

And they don't say much more after that, except good night. I don't watch them walk off, since I'm afraid they'll keep looking back to see if I'm looking. *Where the hell is Thomas?*

I wait for a few minutes longer, and finally Thomas appears at

JOHN ROWELL

the stage door. He's with Lee, which really burns me up; Lee is the last person I want to have hanging around tonight.

"Hey, Jackson," says Lee. "Good work tonight, kiddo. You were terrific."

"Thanks."

Thomas and Lee exchange a little look. I can't believe they don't know that I see it. "Listen, Jackson . . . ," says Thomas. "Are you gonna be up for a little while? Lee and I need to go over some of the choreography in 'Good Old Days.' I guess I didn't get it quite right tonight."

Ah. A sudden reversal of plans, I see. However, the rehearsal sounds bogus; he did the number perfectly tonight, as he always does everything.

"Sure, no problem," I tell him.

"So I'll see you later in the room, then," he says. I look up into his eyes, but he looks away. I look at Lee, and he looks away, too. Of course they look away. I gather up my dance bag and start to walk off.

Lee calls out after me: "Get some rest, Jackson! Good show, kiddo, good show."

There's a trail that leads up along the edge of the woods from the back of the theater to the back of the cast houses—I've gotten to know it pretty well this summer. It's easy to walk along it and stay in sight of the outlines of the houses; through the branches of the pine trees, you can see the lights coming through the windows and hear the sounds of people partying and rehearsing in their rooms. I always stay just inside the edge of the woods as I walk; it's like being onstage in front of forest scenery. And even though the woods are a little scary in the dark, even in this shallow, open part, tonight I don't care. Tonight I don't give a shit. And that's exactly what I yell out to the woods, spinning around with my dance bag still on my shoulder: "I DON'T GIVE A SHIT! I DON'T GIVE A

SHIT ABOUT ANYTHING!" Bears be damned. Come and eat me, for all I care. I wish I had a Purple Jesus.

I come up on the back of Mildew Manor, which I can easily see framed through the spindly pines. Most of the windows in the house are dark—a few of the guys have hooked up with a few of the girls, and they spend most nights with them in their house, which is a nicer place—so the Manor has gotten progressively emptier and quieter as the summer has gone along. There's only one true light blazing in the whole house, on the third floor. I can't help but be drawn to it, especially when I see the silhouette of two men embracing in the open window. They are held together in the window frame, as if in an oil painting, two men, or, more correctly, a man and a boy, surrounded by the light of a yellow overhead bulb.

I watch as Lee holds Thomas close—they look like they might be slow dancing, and Lee runs his hands through Thomas's dark, curly hair. He then pulls him close, and they kiss, and break, and then kiss again, this time holding it longer. Finally, their bodies disappear from the frame of the window, and one of them turns out the light.

I sit down on a tree stump and stare at the windows of Mildew Manor through the wispy branches, which are swaying and rustling in the night breeze. I can't concentrate on anything, and I don't want to think about stuff anyway, so I start singing to myself. I figure it will calm me down. Since the songs from *Damn Yankees* are still in my head, I start with my favorite one, a love duet in the first act—I know both parts—and I sing it quietly until I've gone through every verse. Then I stand up and give myself a round of applause, shouting out "Bravo! Encore!" I bow to the trees. So then, encouraged, I start in on one of the Devil's— Thomas's—songs, until I've performed every verse of that, too . . .

I don't applaud myself this time, however.

I notice that every window in the Manor has gone dark now; everything around me is pitch black, and deeply silent. If the woods *were* a stage set, this would be the moment where a lone stagehand carries out the solitary worklight from the wings and places it center stage, leaving it to burn in the empty theater throughout the night. He would be ready to lock up and go home.

That feels like a cue. I lift my dance bag over my shoulder and exit the woods, trudging slowly up to the dark, quiet house, not singing, and stepping cautiously inside, so as not to disturb anyone.

ᦀ

"You were great, as usual," I say to Thomas, as he works his way across the patio from the back of the theater to our little group of Stage Door Johnnies: me, Perry, Duffy, and . . . Stephen Hopkins, delegate from Rhode Island.

"Thank you, Precious," he says. He leans over to kiss me, and as he does, he whispers in my ear: "Does the show suck?"

"We'll talk," I whisper back.

"I see you guys have already met Kevin," he says, referring to Rhode Island.

"Yeah, totally," says Duffy, beaming; this elicits a nervous glance from Perry and an *aw, shucks* grin from Kevin.

Thomas introduces us to Jake, the compact, dark-haired "gentleman" from Connecticut, and Wynn, the tall, redheaded "gentleman" from North Carolina, who, in their youthful, postshow excitement, appear eager to be complimented—they don't seem like gentlemen at all now, actually, they seem like frolicsome puppies. I tell them I enjoyed their work, but all Perry can manage is the even more slippery, "You know, I'd forgotten what a good musical *1776* really is." Duffy, for his part, chimes in with, "You guys kicked ass. You rock!" causing three of the thirteen original colonies to suddenly light up in his presence. They immediately high-five him: he has spoken their language.

"Drinks at my house," Thomas says, perhaps sensing the need

to change scenery. "I can take four in my car. Perry, if you and Duffy can bring Kevin, that'd be great."

"Sure we can," says Duffy.

As we walk toward the parking lot, Wynn and Jake end up ahead of Thomas and me; the two of them are talking loudly to each other, and with great enthusiasm. Every now and then one of them belts out a line of a show tune, and then they have more discussion. Thomas just looks at me and rolls his eyes.

"Hey, we were like that once, if you remember," I say.

"Yes, but we improved."

As we round the corner of the theater, I see my own personal favorite Continental Congressman, Mr. Morris, gentleman from New York, walking alone, dance bag slung over his shoulder.

"Oh, there's New York," I whisper to Thomas. "Can we invite him over too? I think he's hot."

"Oh . . . Garrett," he says, and I can tell by his tone that Garrett does not come recommended.

"Yes, yes. Mr. New York. The one who abstains. Courteously."

"Yeah . . . you don't want him, Jackson. He's odd. And a loner. He's always going off in the woods by himself. Nobody can figure him out."

"Odd? Odd . . . What is that code for? Does that mean straight? He's straight? Oh please."

"Hmmm . . . well, none of us knows. But we have our suspicions."

"Wait, don't tell me," I say. "New York is undecided."

Thomas sighs. "Yes . . . undecided. Or, perhaps he just hasn't cast his vote yet."

We're almost at the car; Jake and Wynn are already there. Jake is demonstrating what looks like a *pas de bourée*, which is nicely executed, even in flip-flops. Thomas digs in his dance bag for his keys.

"Really?" I say. "Imagine that. Undecided."

He locates his keys, and then looks up at me, staring me straight in the eye with a sly smile.

"Yes," he says, "but he's courteous about it."

At Thomas's rustic little cabin in the woods (Perry calls it "The House That *Les Miz* Built"), we seven boys of varying ages and varying talents and varying claims to chunks of that elusive dream called "A Life in the Theater" can at least agree on one thing, though no one has brought *this* to an actual vote: we like men. We also like: vodka, gin, vermouth, wine, beer, and—God help us—the Patti LuPone CD currently playing on Thomas's stereo.

"Oh, *Patti LuPone Live!*" says the chipper redhead Wynn, who is seated next to Jake on Thomas's battered old blue couch, and who has, I'm starting to notice, an annoying/endearing habit of phrasing everything he says like a question. "Is this great or what? This is the concert Patti did when she still thought she was going to star in *Sunset Boulevard* on Broadway? And she goes into character as Norma at the end? And—"

"And she jinxes it," interrupts Jake, besotted with both red wine and the lure of telling tales of musical theater misdeeds, "because then they snatched it right out from under her nose and gave it to Glenn Close." They are like a comedy team, this little duo of Connecticut and North Carolina, completing each other's sentences with breathless excitement, and then giggling. I've also noticed, and I'm sure Thomas has too, that as of five minutes ago, they've begun to hold hands. Earlier, as Thomas and I were icing glasses and slicing limes at his kitchen sink, he whispered: "I think Jake and I might be . . . well, you know. I *think* he's interested, and I definitely am." Which was fine with me, since I was all set to go about trying to seduce the gentleman from North Carolina. "Maybe I can win Wynn," I said, as I poured an obscene amount of vodka into the drink I was making for him.

Now, with Jake and Wynn holding hands and chirping like little musical comedy magpies, it's looking like Thomas and I are going home empty-handed, as it were. Both of us turn away from drink-mixing at the same moment to catch sight of Jake casually lifting his hand to smooth Wynn's beautiful red hair, causing Wynn to rest his head on Jake's shoulder and close his eyes.

"You mean," says Kevin, from the corner where he's sitting next to Duffy and Perry, though closer to Duffy, of course, "that Patti thought she was gonna do *Sunset Boulevard* on Broadway and they took it away from her?"

The rest of us freeze instantly. No one takes a sip of a drink, rattles an ice cube, or bites into a pretzel. The sudden suspension of conversation, perhaps even of breathing, is truly deafening. Sitting in a roomful of musical theater aficionados and not knowing the tale of Patti LuPone's humiliating loss of the Norma Desmond role in *Sunset Boulevard* on Broadway is tantamount to being a scientist at a quantum physics convention who's never heard that Einstein was responsible for $E=mc^2$.

Finally, I take it upon myself to break the silence and voice what everyone else is thinking, which is: "Should he be allowed to stay?"

Kevin looks confused, wearing the slightly goofy, slightly querulous look of someone who is slowly realizing, with mounting horror, that he has committed a gross faux pas. "Be quiet, Jackson," says Thomas. "Of course he can stay. You can stay, Kevin."

"You can stay, Kevin," says Jake. "Connecticut says 'yea.' " This sends Wynn into a fit of giggles.

"And North Carolina yields to South Carolina," Wynn says, smiling at Thomas, even as he continues to rest his head on Jake's shoulder.

"Not tonight," says Perry under his breath, prompting Thomas to throw him a daggery glance.

"Well," I say, "I'm the official representative now from New York. And, of course, New York abstains, courteously."

"That's no fun, to abstain," says Wynn, with a saucy lilt, suddenly lifting his head and focusing his pretty blue eyes on me. And I'm thinking: What? *Now* you're teasing me? Excuse me, where have you been all evening, North Carolina? And is it your mission to flirt with *everyone* in the room?

"The thing is, Rhode Island," says Perry, blotto from the one-two punch of three martinis and Duffy's full frontal flirting with Kevin, "is . . . that there's a lesson to be learned from the saga of Miss LuPone and *Sunset Boulevard* and how she jinxed herself."

"What's that?" I ask, playing George Burns to his Gracie Allen, Dean Martin to his Jerry Lewis.

Perry looks lasciviously around the room at the young folk.

"Don't count your chickens," he says slowly.

"I think we'll go for a walk," says Duffy suddenly. "Come on, Kev, let's go outside and look at the stars."

"I thought that's what we were doing in here," says Perry, indicating Thomas. I think that like Thomas Jefferson and John Adams, he's been forced to admit a rather large defeat.

"Sure, man, let's go," says Kevin, looking suddenly quite relieved. And they are out the front door.

"Do you wanna . . . go out too?" Jake asks sotto voce to Wynn, though not sotto voce enough that the whole lot of us can't hear it.

Wynn high-beams him back with those big blue eyes.

"We're going for a walk, too," announces Jake, redundantly. And, clutching their drinks, and each other's hands, they, too, head out Thomas's cabin door.

"Watch out for bears!" shouts Thomas, pleasantly.

"And then there were three," I say, looking around from my deeply slumped position.

"Well . . ." says Perry. "This has been . . . enlightening."

"Hasn't it just?" says Thomas. He begins to pick up empty pretzel bowls and dead drink glasses.

"What are you going to do, Perry?" I ask.

He stands up, wobbly and flushed, but as determined as any Boy Scout, even an overaged one. Finally, like the foreman of a jury, he delivers his one-word proclamation:

"Compete," he says. And he, too, finds his way out of Thomas's front door.

"And then there were two," I whisper.

"I had no fucking idea, obviously," says Thomas, "that Jake and Wynn were interested in each other. Give me your glass." He begins to drop in ice and pour Absolut. "Say when."

"That's a switch," I say. "Earlier, it was like, *sober up, sober up!*"

"That was then, this is now." He finishes making my drink, then replenishes his own.

The room is lit only by a few low-burning candles and the glow from a red lampshade on the end table. From the stereo, Patti LuPone receives thunderous applause for her final number, but then that, too, fades to silence.

"The lighting is very romantic in here," I say. "You've done a great job with it. It makes us look years younger."

"That's a cold comfort," Thomas says. "But thank you. Those of us who are about to turn forty salute you."

"We're still thirty-nine," I say, lifting my glass and throwing my head back with pride, a drunk's pride. "Here's to still being thirty-nine."

"Queer, queer!" he says. We clink. Then, slowly, he says, "My God, Jack. Thir-ty-nine . . . for-tee . . ."

"Well, don't say them phonetically!" I shout. "It makes them sound older. Say them quickly. Say 'thirtynineforty.' See? 'Thirtynineforty.' See how much more youthful it sounds when you say it fast like that? It takes *years* off the words."

"You're insane," he says. "And you were insane when I met you a hundred and fifty years ago. God . . . I just realized we've known each other more than half our lives."

I cover my eyes with the back of my hand to shield them from the truth. "Yes . . . almost as long as these . . . *children* . . . have been alive."

"Exactly. What are we doing here? What are *they* doing here?"

"Don't you know? We're team teachers at the Days of Wine and Roses Nursery School."

"Don't berate the charms of youth," he says. "It's unseemly." He gets up and peers out the window. "What do you think they're all doing out there?" he whispers.

"Oh, you know, forging a new union." I manage to hoist myself up and join him at the window. "Declaring themselves independent and free of the old ways. Which seems to be a theme of the evening."

"Hmm . . . I think it's probably more like a gay *Midsummer Night's Dream.* Young lovers running around the woods like nymphs and sprites, undressing and cavorting."

"Exactly. Yes. A bunch of fairies and one old jackass."

Thomas sits back on the arm of his chair. "Poor Perry," he says. "Poor, dear, cuckolded Perry. What's to become of him?" He collapses back onto the cushion.

"Thomas," I say. "Do you remember that night in Mildew Manor, so *very* long ago, when I got sick out the window?"

He groans. "Lord, child. I've never seen anybody throw up more violently in my whole life. I had to go out and hose off the ground the next morning."

"A belated thank you, then, for taking care of me."

He smiles and lifts his glass in my direction.

"What *I* remember," I say, "is that you were rubbing my back. And I was thinking, God, Thomas is so great, and . . . and . . . so sweet, handsome, such a good friend . . . all of that . . . of course *now* it seems like the perfect porn film setup, both of us there, alone, just in our briefs. The next shot would have been your hand sliding down my back . . ."

He laughs. "Yes. *Summer Stock Boys.*"

"Except—not to sound ungrateful at this late date—but I remember thinking, what if one of the dancers were rubbing my back? Chris, or . . . whatever their names were. I would have been so turned on."

"Oh God, yes. And it's true. If you had been Chris, I would have gone for the gold, baby."

"Ah. Then it would be Chris sitting here right now instead of me."

"Wrong. He would have been on to somebody else in a month. We were eighteen! Please. I'm *glad* it's you sitting here."

"But . . . can you imagine if we *had* ended up lovers instead of . . . this . . . we could have saved ourselves a lot of time. And money."

"Time, money, bad dates . . . and all those lovely two- and three-month relationships through the years . . ."

"Especially those."

He gets up for more ice.

"Thomas," I say, "speaking of good old Mildew Manor . . . do you have any idea whatever happened to good old Lee?"

He turns around holding the ice bowl, and looks at me for a moment with a blank expression. "Lee. God, that's amazing. For a second I almost couldn't remember who you were talking about."

He brings the bowl over to the coffee table and sits back in his chair. A candle burns itself down into its little self-made valley of red wax, and dies.

"Old Lee," he says. "Old Lee was exactly the same age you and I are now, you know. How frightening is that. God, I wonder what did happen to him."

"No doubt he's probably still choreographing *Damn Yankees* somewhere and trying to seduce the chorus boys."

"Oh, Jackson. You're drunk again, Precious. You're drunk, and you're mean. But it's OK. You're safe here with me."

We sit quietly, drinking, staring into the corners of the room; every now and then we glance back at each other, just to check in.

"What made you think about Lee?" he asks, after a few minutes.

I look into those big, searching brown eyes for a long, held, exquisite moment. "Oh. I don't know," I tell him finally. "Just crossed my mind, that's all. But, look, he's already gone. Poof!"

He smiles, and looks down.

I hold up my glass. "More vodka, please, Precious," I whisper, lifting my foot to his knee and giving him a gentle kick. He pours, without a word.

Laughter comes from somewhere outside. I keep looking at Thomas, but he's staring off now, lost in the thought of . . . something. More and more laughter floats in through the window, laughter that might have once been described in a Jane Austen novel as "gay."

"Ah, listen to the fairies," I say, holding the icy tumbler against my cheek.

"Yes," he says, dreamily. "Well, here's my Ode to Youth: *fuck* youth."

"I wish we could," I say.

"Alas. Maybe someday."

"Perhaps . . . but then again . . . perhaps not." And we clink glasses.

Then we sit quietly for a while, saying nothing, just drinking, and more sounds of laughter and crickets and rustling leaves filter in from outside . . . and then the scent of honeysuckle and mountain laurel, ushered in on a breeze which blows the threadbare red silk curtains against the frame of a dilapidated old window where a boy in his underwear leans out, while another boy, also in his underwear, stands behind him rubbing his back, just rubbing, *gently, gently,* and that same hand moves from my back to the hand that I now have dangling across the arm of the chair, and Thomas takes my hand in his, and squeezes it, and then holds it, for what feels like a long, long time.

WILDLIFE OF
COASTAL CAROLINA

Friday, 10:30 A.M.

The all points bulletin that I have to share with the citizenry of my town of Duck Island this morning is this:

"I, Talbert John Moss, have decided to end my self-imposed exile of nearly two weeks in which I have stayed in the bed mostly day and night. I am up and walking around now, and I am ready to be myself again. I know you all will be gladdened and filled with joy over this fact. Some of you anyway. Thank you to everyone who prayed for me during my exile, and thank you to everyone who brought food to my doorstep, especially the barbeque and the ham biscuits, the iced tea, and the two-liter bottles of Diet Coke. Much appreciated. I will see you soon. Love to all— or at least to many, T.J."

I think I might even call up our radio station WAVE (this is the beach, after all) and ask them to read my statement over the air just like that. It's hard to know how they'd take it, though; they don't exactly have Rhodes scholars and Mensa candidates working over there. As is always the case, I fear my words could be misinterpreted by persons lacking a sense of humor, not to mention a sense of irony. Lacking both a sense of humor and a sense of irony is something that, in my humble opinion, applies to about 95 percent of the citizenry of Duck Island. It's as if at some point—some point before I got here, of course—a horrible epidemic like bubonic plague came along and wiped everybody's senses of humor and irony clean away. The Humor and Irony Plague, I believe it was called, the one that hit poor old Duck Island, in the mid-1970s, or thereabouts. That's my theory, anyway; they ought to consult with me before they next update the North Carolina history textbooks; I have a thing or two I feel should be included.

But I guess *some*body around here has a sense of humor, because this morning my alarm clock radio (set to WAVE) woke me up with this: "Now here's a song being sent to Talbert Moss from a secret admirer who wants to say, 'Talbert, I love you, and I hope you'll be feeling better soon.' And so do we, Talbert, buddy, so do we. Now here's Miss Dionne Warwick singing the 'Theme from *Valley of the Dolls.*'"

And I'm thinking: *Valley of the Dolls?* It *is* my favorite movie, after all. And, come to think of it, I *have* been kind of acting like Patty Duke's character in the movie, Neely O'Hara, because in order to stay in the bed for almost two weeks, I have had to drink the occasional Amstel Light and take my share of Extra-Strength Sominex, and the cumulative effect of that did start to make me feel like some boozy, blowsy ol' Hollywood starlet who lays up in the bed all day and night, weepy and hagged-out, insulting people all around her in foul-mouthed and unrepentant ways, eventually refusing to take any calls or visitors . . .

So I listened to the song, with Dionne singing all about getting off this ride, getting off this merry-go-round, all that carnival imagery that I think is intended to imply dizziness and a feeling of being disoriented, and I certainly started to see how that applies to me. I got to thinking that was a pretty nice thing for somebody to do, actually, to call up WAVE and dedicate that song to me because they cared enough about me to try to help me get up and get out of bed. The more I thought about it, the more I decided it really was a *sign* that I needed to get up and get moving again. A sign—yes. If not from God, at least from Dionne Warwick, and everybody knows how connected to the psychic and spiritual worlds she is.

So I was really taking in Dionne Warwick's message, really feeling it in my bones, really thinking how it just might be the thing to jump-start me. But then I heard the newsman come on with this: "There are still no leads in the disappearance of Donny Tyndall, the six-year-old Duck Island boy who was reported missing two weeks ago—" and then I had to snap the radio off immediately.

That was just so not what I wanted to hear, though I wasn't surprised to hear it.

Donny. Little Donny . . . when I first found out he had gone missing, well, that's about exactly when I decided to go into exile. It was just more than I could take, the thought of something bad happening to Donny. He was—and still is—my friend. And I knew things weren't too good for him, really, so I guess I shouldn't have been so shocked, but still . . . that news made me sick to my stomach with nothing but pure fear. I've always felt that if you're afraid of something that much, then it almost *has* to come true, so you'd better try real hard to beat that fear back and increase your odds for some kind of happy outcome, which is why I got out of bed this morning. After all, my laying in the bed wasn't doing Donny or anybody else a bit of good, and I know I should be doing my part to help find him. I repeat—Donny was, and still is, my friend. No matter what.

So I got up, and made my bed for the first time in nearly two weeks, which felt like a step, if not in the right direction, because how do you ever really know what the right direction is, at least a step in *some* direction.

Now I'm standing in my kitchen staring into my open refrigerator *desperate* for a Diet Coke only to discover that there aren't any. I must've drunk all my gift Diet Cokes, and there haven't been any doorstep deliveries in the last couple of days. There is only one pitiful pink and yellow can of Tab, whose sad expiration date I believe is extremely close to the time of the Berlin Wall coming down. But this might be a sign, too, since the 1980s were good for me, socially speaking; it was a decade in which I had not one, but two, long-term boyfriends.

The Tab doesn't taste all that bad, really; as my mother is always saying, "At least it's wet."

That reminds me that I probably ought to call up Mama and Daddy and tell them that I'm out of the bed, but I'll do it later. Maybe after an Amstel Light.

I take the Tab out onto my back porch. Already it's a hot day; the humid, salty air blows all around me. Standing here in nothing but my boxer shorts, it actually feels good, even though I generally hate the heat and opt to preserve myself almost exclusively in air-conditioned environments from March to October; like certain animals and plants, I need a cool climate in which to function. Staring out over the low dunes now, I notice the tide is out and the ocean looks smooth and calm; it usually does this time of year, late October, when hurricane season is nearly over.

I watch the seagulls skittering around on the khaki-colored sand; they're so goofy, how they run to miss a wave when it comes lapping up on the shore. The waves rush away from the gulls too, as if they just came up to steal a quick kiss from whoever happened to be on the beach, only to run away from them like a shy child. Since I haven't been outside in a while, watching all this natural activity makes me think about how many beautiful things there are at the beach, or anywhere, really, when you look for them, and that is sometimes a very hard thing to remember when radio stations and local newscasts can only tell you how screwed up and awful everything in the damn world is, and I'm not just talking here about missing children but about everything else, too.

WAVE, in particular, just seems to love harping on armed robbery, car bombs, murder, petty theft, homelessness in our county, the sad state of agriculture in southeastern North Carolina, all that. But here's what just kills me about WAVE and its employ-

ees: After reporting all this negative, horribly tragic stuff, stuff
that anyone with the least bit of human sensitivity is going to
have their day just completely ruined by hearing about, they have
the nerve to turn around and play songs like Captain and Tennille's "Muskrat Love," or that "Piña Colada Song" (now there's a
number that would actually *encourage* a body to drink and drive)
or—and this strikes me as the worst—"Maneater" by Hall and
Oates. I swear somebody down there at WAVE just loves "Maneater." Now it doesn't take an Einstein to figure out that if you
were the manager of a radio station in a town where a little boy
has lately disappeared, in a place, mind you, where hungry
wildlife and perhaps awful child snatchers are probably lurking
around every corner of the shopping mall and various Quick
Marts, you probably, if you're any sort of a compassionate person,
should think twice about giving the thumbs-up to keeping "Maneater" on the daily playlist.

This is the kind of thing I have to deal with down here, so
that's why staying in the bed, my bed with nothing but me in it,
has been the most appropriate, and safest, place to be as of late.

Suddenly, I think of my reminder to myself to call Mama and
Daddy.

On my way inside to the telephone, I catch my reflection in
the one window on my back porch and I can see that I look like an
absolute mess—not that I care all that much, really; looking a
mess is expected when you're coming out of self-imposed exile.
Most days, in nonexile periods, I'm not so bad, actually; I'm five
eleven and weigh a hundred and sixty pounds; in the men's exercise magazines I belong to the "fit and trim" category in their little charts. I'd date me. But the sad reality is that I don't have the
Paramount Pictures hair and makeup people fussing over me and
making me look like a million bucks on a daily basis. So I look like
what I look like, which this morning is disastrous, most definitely
not like the Paramount and MGM goddesses of yesteryear—Jean
Harlow, or Norma Shearer—or whatever male version of those

women would be, since I don't mean to present myself as some kind of drag artist.

Inside, I sit down in my captain's chair, and, using my Sam's Club long-distance card (I'm glad to see it hasn't expired yet), I dial Mama and Daddy, but get a busy signal—they haven't yet taken up with call waiting. Maybe they're trying to call me at the same time, and the wires are crossing. Daddy would call that a coinkie-dink.

On second thought, maybe I don't want to talk to anybody yet, unless it's somebody who can tell me that they found Donny and he's doing OK. And it's not like I haven't had *any* human contact over the last two weeks. Yes, the phone has certainly rung, and various people have certainly been by, though I mostly would only peek out at them from under the covers to see if they had brought food, or maybe a CD or a video. The doctor came, Reverend Julian Stubbs, in the midst of praying for Donny Tyndall, came to pray for *me*, Mama and Daddy drove down from where they live in the middle part of the state, and I simply told them all the same thing, which is: "I just don't feel like getting up." And they all said: "Talbert, are you sick? Are you depressed? Do you need to go to the hospital? What do you want us to do?" To which I said, as sweetly as I was able, "Will you please, *please* ask the disc jockeys at the WAVE station to reconsider their daily playlist and stop playing insensitive, inappropriate material?" And they all looked at me like I was talking out of my head, but now I believe that somebody finally understood my wish, and called up WAVE; hence Dionne Warwick and *Valley of the Dolls* at 9:15 on a weekday morning. It could be any one of a number of people around here who might have done that—and all of them would be more than happy to let me know they had done it so as to curry my favor and pass themselves off as a good friend slash samaritan. If I go out and start talking to people again today, as I think I might do, I'll see if anybody owns up to placing that musical order for me and my well-being.

While sitting in my captain's chair, trying to decide if I should try Mama and Daddy again or just let them call me, I take a good look around at my tiny little house, my "shack by the sea," for the first time in two weeks. I'm glad to see it hasn't changed much during my self-imposed exile; I'm sure Mama straightened up the place when she was here, or maybe my friends Trey and Kelly came by and cleaned it. God bless 'em, they all know I utterly despise domestic work. I'm just happy to see my seashells are all still here, plus the stuffed sailfish my grandfather caught in 1958, which I am happy to see is still hanging intact above my couch. Hell, I'm even happy about this circa–Berlin Wall Tab in the refrigerator. I'm feeling a whole lot better.

That is, until I turn on the TV.

Because wouldn't you know the first thing I see, after missing every local newscast for two weeks, is that god-awful *Carolina in the A.M.* show, with that woman host I cannot abide, Claudia Davenport Shields, who was Miss North Carolina about a hundred years ago (well, probably in the early '70s, and before that, she was the statewide Miss Flue-Cured Tobacco for three years running—I know that because she will mention it on the air at the drop of a crown), and who still to this day sports pageant hair, big and poofy and as blond as Tweety Bird, and it hurts my eyes to look at her, not to mention having to look at the obvious little nips and tucks she's had done to her face—oh yes, I can always tell when surgery has occurred; I have a sixth sense for detecting plastic surgery. But the thing I hate most about Claudia Davenport Shields is how she tries so hard to speak and sound like a real network journalist, like her idol, Jane Pauley (she's always talking about her too), when we all know Claudia was born and raised in the pitiful hamlet of Cliston, whose populace grandly thinks of itself as living in an actual town, which I personally feel is a *generous* way of describing a landscape that includes one solitary stoplight, a self-service post office, and a run-down old Tastee-Freez sitting on the side of a long-shut Pure station at the edge of a tobacco field.

And that is just exactly what Claudia Davenport Shields is: *Tobacco Trash*, and as true Tobacco Trash she cannot get rid of that accent to save her natural life. And the worst thing: Claudia is always having to do little sponsor spots on her show, most of which are for PET Milk, whose simple slogan is this: "Get PET." But Claudia, ex–Miss Flue-Cured, the veritable pride of Cliston, and Coastal Carolina's pathetic answer to Jane Pauley, always says it so it sounds like this: "*Git . . .* PET."

I watch Claudia make a fool of herself conducting an interview with the mayor of Duck Island, my mayor, I should say, whose name is Hiram Clark.

Claudia: "Mr. Mayor, we're so honored to have you with us today. I know you took time out from your busy schedule just to come to the studio."

His Honor: "Well, Claudia, you know I always like to visit with you all here at *Carolina in the A.M.*"

Claudia: "Thank you, Mr. Mayor. Now, what I want to ask you about this morning is, of course, what's on the mind of everyone here on Duck Island and Marsh County, which is the investigation into that poor missing child, Donny Tyndall. Now Mr. Mayor—"

And I listen as Claudia and the mayor just repeat the same old information with no new developments, and with Claudia, of course, acting real concerned and condolencey, which is simply wrong since I know Donny is still out there somewhere. Claudia is a master at putting on "serious" faces and nodding her head to indicate comprehension.

But now Claudia has moved right along—heartlessly, to my way of thinking—to a segment about how easy it is to macramé pot holders from scraps of yarn you might have lying around in some drawer somewhere, and what an excellent Christmas gift that would make, et cetera et cetera, and I just have to snap bottle-blond Tobacco Trash right off my TV set, as who wouldn't when faced with that kind of sadly insincere faux journalism.

I get up and start pacing around the room. I'm so mad, so mad that I want to throw things, and maybe even cry, because now I'm convinced I'm going to turn out to be as bitter and hateful as my grandmother Florence Moss was when she got to the age of forty, a legacy of spite and hatefulness which lasted to the end of her life (eighty-eight, which meant forty-eight years of crotchety meanness and the ill winds of bad moods blown at everyone who came within thirty feet of her), and here I am thirty-four years old, which is not all that far from forty, and I'm thinking why did I bother even getting out of bed, and to hell with Dionne Warwick's *Valley of the Dolls* philosophy. Maybe I like being on that damn merry-go-round all the time, what the hell.

I decide this is as good a time as any to try Mama and Daddy again—either they'll just make me madder or they'll calm me down, and I'm game for either one.

"Hello?"

"Hey, Mama."

"Talbert? Oh my Lord, Talbert, are you all right? I can't believe you've called me. What in the world? Don't tell me you're out of the bed?"

She doesn't give me a chance to answer, just starts screaming out for Daddy, who must be in another part of the house, probably fixing something that might not even have been broken in the first place just so he didn't have to stay in the same room with her all day long.

"Dixon! Dixon, it's Talbert!"

And she adds, real loud, so that I, and perhaps a few neighbors, can hear: "Our *son*, Dixon! He sounds like he might be outa the bed, which would be a full-blown miracle! *Dixon!* Good Lord, what are you doing? Pick up the extension phone in Mama's room. It's a miracle, I'm telling you. Dixon! *Dixon!* Pick up the damn telephone!"

And obviously Dixon manages to get himself to the Miracle Hotline, and I'm thinking how Dionne Warwickish and Psychic Friends–like this is.

Daddy: "T.J.?"

"Yes, it is I, Daddy."

"Well, I'm glad to hear it. You feeling better, son?"

"I guess so."

Mama: "Talbert, tell me something. Are you finally on some sort of a medication?"

"Oh, nothing special," I say, in a calm voice, looking down at my nails for a "nonchalant" effect, though of course there's no one to witness it. "Only a few over-the-counter dolls. Mostly, I just felt like getting out of bed. I guess it's just the Lord's will." I like to say things that I know Mama likes to hear.

"Well, perhaps it *is* the will of the Lord," she says, because she knows that I can get just as sarcastic as she can, and that we can give it back and forth to each other. "Anything good that happens is the Lord's will, Talbert."

"What about the bad stuff that happens, Mama?" I say. "Is that the Lord's will too?"

"Talbert, don't get me riled up in a theological discussion, I'm in the middle of cleaning the house and I don't have time to think. Perhaps if you had warmed any kind of a church pew in the last six months, you wouldn't need to be asking big theological questions of a lay person like myself. You need to go talk to Reverend Stubbs—"

"Loralee, please . . ." Daddy says, much to my relief. "T.J., you sure you're all right?"

"Well, Dixon," Mama says, "he said he was. If he picked up the phone, he must be! It's not up to us to question the Lord's mysterious work."

"I want to hear it from Talbert, if you please."

"Yes, Daddy, I feel fine."

"Well, I am relieved and mighty glad to hear it, son, I'll tell you that."

Mama says, "No one will ever again look me in the face and say one doubtful thing about the power of prayer, I'm telling you that. Because I have prayed for this moment, and I mean I have prayed and prayed . . ."

"Well, Mama," I say. "I am so glad I have answered your prayers."

And I manage to escalate things in the direction of a mutual good-bye, telling them I'll call them later before Mama can remind me that only the Lord answers prayers, not mortal man.

Still in my boxers, I go to my front porch and pick up today's newspaper. On the front page is yet another photo of Donny, one I haven't seen before, one of him and his awful mother, taken at Christmastime with them posed next to one of those artificial all-silver Christmas trees. He's clutching a doll, a G.I. Joe or something, and grinning at the camera.

I throw the paper into the garbage can without even opening it and go back in the house and drain the last of my Tab.

I must have been crazy earlier, thinking this Tab was good, because it tastes like pure-tee poison now. I sit in the captain's chair and cover my eyes with my hands, and stay there like that for a minute or so, because I can't get that photo of Donny holding G.I. Joe out of my head.

I go back out onto the porch and pull the paper out of the garbage can and take it back inside. I lay it on top of the stack of all the other unopened papers—I realize somebody has been bringing them in for me and stacking them up for the last two weeks.

Every last one of them has Donny's picture on the front, with the words "Still Missing" splayed out underneath.

God Almighty . . .

Where is Dionne Warwick when you need her most?

Noonish

If you've ever gone for a long period of time without taking a shower and putting on clothes, you know that when you finally clean up, it feels like you've been sprung from prison or something. As I bathed, shaved, exfoliated, all that, I was glad to be reminded of what I really look like, to see that I'm not hideous, after all. And even though I don't consider myself movie-star good-looking, though I wish I were, I'll do in a pinch. My hair is about the color of a cured tobacco leaf (though I certainly am not Tobacco Trash), a brown color about one shade lighter than what people so often call mousy. I have an average face, I guess, not a face someone would visualize when they're having idle sex fantasies, per se, but not one that, if they were next to it in bed, would make them scream "Oh, get out, get out of my bed, Cyclops!" My body isn't bad, either; in fact, I'd say it's pretty good; I had been lifting weights every day at Duck Island Health and Racquet before my exile.

Once outside the shack by the sea, I walk the sandy path down to the ocean and stare out over the water, and then close my eyes and let the late-fall salty wind whip me all over. I think how I could just take off my clothes right now and swim out into the ocean and drown, like James Mason did at the end of *A Star Is Born*, because he just couldn't fathom how disappointing his life had become, even though Judy Garland was slavishly in love with him. However, I believe there would really be no point in my doing that, when you think about the fact that James Mason's character at least at one time had a great career, while I, on the other hand, am still waiting for mine to *gel*. (I'm also waiting for someone to be slavishly in love with me, though I don't want to seem greedy.) But I suspect, when all is said and done, that I'm much more the Judy Garland type than the James Mason type, more likely to be the one dressed in evening clothes who tearfully cries into a microphone, "This is Mrs. Norman Maine," than to be the one who washes up dead on the beach with seaweed in his ears and dressed in an unflattering bathing suit.

Now I'm behind the wheel of my 1989 Datsun, which I call the Dirt Devil, since it's compact-sized and cherry red, and I'm greatly relieved to discover the motor still runs—Daddy probably started it a time or two when they were down here. And that's just the kind of thing he'd be thinking about too, anything with an engine or dependent on a part that you can only get at an automotive store. I don't frequent automotive stores myself; I'm a mall person.

I feel like a new man, and my mind is racing about various things. I careen the Dirt Devil down Beach Drive and turn onto Yaupon Boulevard for the first time in two weeks. I don't know why, but I feel so encouraged to see that someone, probably some lonely, horny teenager, has spray painted the big city limits sign so that it now reads: "Welcome To *F*uck Island."

"Oh mah God," says Tammy Buttry, from her usual outer office/reception area perch when I walk in the door of Bledsoe Real Estate, and her eyes go all deer-in-the-headlights at the sight of me, though she quickly starts trying to act nonchalant and friendly, saying *"Welll* . . . hey you, let me give you a *biiig huuug."* And she does, wrapping her fleshy arms around my neck and nearly choking me to death with the smell of some cheap Sam's Club perfume. But I know she's secretly disappointed to find out that I've actually recovered from my exile, that I didn't have to be carted off in a straitjacket to the Dorothea Dix Hospital in Raleigh after all. And I'm sure she's absolutely *aching* to pick up that phone and call everyone who knows us on the Island to report that I'm up and around and to say *Well, I just can't believe it, I thought T.J. had a complete nervous breakdown, didn't you?* until she gets somebody to agree with her.

"Well hey to you too, Tam But," I say, which is what I call her, and which I know gets under her splotchy, milky-white skin something fierce, even though I say it with undiluted sweetness.

She smirks a little smirk right back at me, and I can tell she's about to say something that will be mean deep down and sugar-coated on the surface.

"T.J., we were all so worried about you and your . . . your little time-out," she says, oozing concern. "Are you feeling better?"

"Yes I am, Tam But, and thank you so much for your card," I say, oozing sincerity right back at her. Poor Tammy; she has never forgiven me for beating her out in auditions for *Nunsense* at the Duck Island Playhouse, in which I broke the gender barrier with my highly acclaimed performance as Sister Mary Amnesia. (Well, I was highly acclaimed by the Wilmington *Star-News*, though maybe it doesn't count so much since the reviewer, Stephen Brickles, has a thing for me and is always trying to get me to go out with him.) One day soon after that, when I was on the phone trying to get a condo deal to go through, I heard Tam But in Rollie Bledsoe's office, all pitiful and crying on his shoulder, saying: "It's not fair that T.J. is a guy and he gets to play Sister Mary Amnesia! It's just not faiiiiiiiiiiirrrrrrrrrrr, Rollie!!!! WAAAAAAAA!"

"Is that you, Talbert?" Rollie calls out from the inner office. "Come on in, come on in."

"I'll just go talk to Rollie now, Tam But," I say, heading for Rollie's knotty-pine door.

Tammy glares at me sweetly and says: "I'm glad you're feeling better," but I can see her hand is already beginning to creep up to her Rolodex; she just can't wait to start making calls. God, that girl is so small-town. It's pitiful.

"Come in, Talbert," Rollie says, shutting the door behind us. "I have a paycheck for you."

Rollie's desk is littered with ham biscuit wrappers and rental and lease agreement papers and 7-Eleven Big Gulp plastic cups. There is a large framed photograph of Rollie with his wife, daughter, and son enjoying a camping trip in the woods; a setting which, unfortunately—and I hate to be mean—makes them look like the innocent family in a horror movie who goes on vacation and is never seen nor heard from again.

"Thanks for understanding my predicament, Rollie," I begin.

"You know, sometimes all you need is some rest and then you're back in action."

"Yeah," he says, and he pauses for a long time. "Well, it hasn't been real busy since you've been gone, Talbert. You know, now that the summer craziness has died down and we're into the off-season. I believe Tammy and I can probably handle most everything around here for a while."

I smile, and then look down at the floor. I know what's happening; I don't need a house—or a condo—to fall on me. "Oh . . ." I say, still looking down, knowing I should put up a little more of a struggle about this, but, hell, I didn't like this job, anyway. He's probably doing me a big favor.

"I'm sorry, Talbert, it's just that we don't really need three people here in the off-season. Business just doesn't warrant it." At least it sounds like telling me this actually pains him, so I can't hate him too much.

"No, no problem, Rollie, I understand . . ." I say, looking up from the floor.

"Talbert, you're . . . you're a fine fellow, you are, we just . . . you know . . . it's . . ."

He's lurching now, stuttering out the same information, just in different sentences, trying to couch the blow I guess, and I don't really want to stick around and listen to it. For my own sake, I'm going to remain noble and dignified, make him think that losing my job doesn't really matter to me, that I'll take it on the chin and rise above it. I gaze out the window, and then into the middle distance, heavy-lidded but magisterial, instantly calling up my own personal reserves of smiling-through-tears, with visions of Mildred Pierce and Stella Dallas filling my mind—wounded and broken, but head held high.

He's still rambling, saying something about "Maybe next spring, when tourist season kicks back in, we can see how things stand, if you're available . . ."

"Sure, Rollie, of course, thank you," I say, if only to shut him up. And even though inside I feel like Joan Crawford, or Barbara Stanwyck at her most beaten-down, I extend my hand to him in a good, strong masculine way, firmly shaking his short, pudgy one, and looking him squarely in the eye. He isn't completely a weasel, and I wish I could hate him more than I do. Truth is, Rollie has always been pretty nice to me.

"You know, Talbert," he says, walking me to the door. "My wife and I always enjoy reading your articles in the *Quacker.* We always check to see what you have to say about a movie before we go see it, we really do. Even though we didn't agree with you about that last Steven Seagal movie; I mean . . . it was just fun to us. Man, that guy . . . whew, he can kick some butt, can't he?"

"I'm not a fan of Mr. Seagal," I say.

"Yeah, well, I gathered that from your review there, pardner. Hey, maybe you can get Ralph to give you a few more assignments over at the paper."

"Well, thanks," I say, maintaining composure worthy of a spring debutante, "but I'm working very hard on finishing my novel, and I'm going to be directing and starring in a show over at the Playhouse, so I've got a lot going on." Rollie has no idea that I've just gilded every lily in the pond.

"Oh, well, sounds like you do, then. Now you come by and see us, Talbert, don't you be a stranger, you hear? And you take care of yourself."

"Will do," I say, anxious to get out of Bledsoe Real Estate.

He shuts the door behind me, giving me a chance for a moment with Tammy, who, I now figure, has known all along that I wasn't getting my job back.

But of course, in true Tam But form, she is *radiating* saccharine sweetness as I walk past her, and as she opens her mouth to say something—something I guarantee would be unnecessary, inane, and probably ungrammatical if I allowed her to say it—I throw up my hand to silence her, and I whisper: "When you speak of this, years from now, and you will . . . *be kind.*"

Her mouth just freezes in mid-O. I have silenced the Tam But.

And though I know she doesn't get any of my references, at least she can tell it's an exit line, that I've made it *my* moment, not hers. And I walk out of the office proud, dignified, *head held high,* as behind me the thin screen door thwacks anemically against its frame.

And on the porch, to no one in particular, I hold the paycheck in the air, and say to the nonexistent crowd clamored before me:

"*This . . . is . . . Mrs. . . . Norman . . . Maine!*"

1:15 P.M.

I deposit my check at Coastal Savings and Loan, though I make sure to do it in the ATM anteroom so as to avoid seeing people I know inside the bank, especially my friend Kelly, who works there as a teller; she would want to take me to lunch. I'll see them all soon enough; I need a careful reentry, one of my own design and execution.

I slide back into the Dirt Devil and decide, spur of the moment, to head out to Charlotte Watkins's house. Something I heard myself saying in Rollie's office has given me an idea I want to pursue—funny how sometimes when you tell a lie it makes you want to go out and make it true—and I am so grateful to be back to my old self, to be back in touch with my own special inner creative spark and to be receiving signals from it that make me want to go out and *do, do, do.* In my bed during my self-imposed exile, I didn't hear my spark call to me at all, not even once, and that only added to my fear about Donny. But now, cruising around my sleepy little one-fish town in the Dirt Devil has given me a new focus, despite losing my job, and I am Making Plans.

I tempt my fates and turn on WAVE to see if they have any new musical words of wisdom for me; what suddenly fills my car is Diana Ross singing "Ain't No Mountain High Enough," which is OK, I can get some inspiration from that, but then when the song ends, the local news on the half hour begins with: "The search continues for Donny Tyndall, the six-year-old boy who has been missing for two weeks. Law enforcement officers say a three-county-wide manhunt has turned up nothing new—"

Immediately I flick the dial to the only other station you can get in our town, the Christian station WGOD, and they're playing the Happy Goodman Family's rendition of "I'll Fly Away," and to make myself feel better, I start singing along with Sister Vestal, imagining her beehive do and powder blue muumuu and white patent leather pumps tapping the studio floor. *"I'll fly away . . . I'll fly away . . ."* but then an ad comes on for Marsh County Christian Day School, an institution of lower learning that I can't abide, because it is funded by archconservatives and because I have always believed the rumor that little Mindy Kazyre went around town telling, which was that teachers at MCCDS would occasionally introduce snakes into the classroom. I stop singing and turn off the radio.

While I'm sitting at the stoplight (there is more than one around here, but barely), waiting for it to change, who walks in front of the Dirt Devil but Claudia Davenport Shields, fresh from the TV studio, I guess, dressed to what she obviously thinks is the nines and the height of lady journalist couture, but in the glaring light of day that hair looks brassier than it does on camera, and her makeup is heavy and stagy-looking. Oh, I am just dying to roll down my window and yell out: "Hey, Claudia! It's *get* PET! *Get* PET! *Git* it?" But I realize it's probably not a good idea for me to trash the biggest local celebrity to her face, since I am endeavoring to become a local celebrity myself, and I may need her promotional help at some point if I'm to accomplish that.

Up ahead, on my way to the outskirts of town where Charlotte

Watkins lives, I decide to turn onto Myrtle Street to say hello to
Hazel Toomey and Jessie at the Biscuit Break. I haven't had one of
Hazel's biscuits in two weeks, and she was good enough to send
me a card with a free-biscuit coupon while I was convalescing.

I decide to go up to the drive-thru window because I think it
will be more of a surprise for Hazel if she sees the Dirt Devil
slowly creeping into view.

Hazel pulls open the glass window as I approach.

"Well looky here! I thought that was you, Talbert Moss! Oh
Lord, child, how in the world are you? We was so worried about
you, you sweet thing. Give me a kiss."

And Hazel leans awkwardly out the drive-thru window, forc-
ing me to lean awkwardly out of my window, so she can plant one
on me. Hazel is in her mid-seventies, and has been making biscuits on Duck Island for fifty years. This morning, Hazel's big,
frowzy gray wig sits cocked at an unnatural angle, sort of on an
incline toward the right side of her head, and I want to reach up
and adjust it for her, so people won't make fun of her for the rest of
the day. Hazel's been through chemo and lost all her hair, but she
doesn't seem to think anybody knows that. No matter what, she
still gets up every morning to come in and start rolling that dough
at four-thirty. Suddenly, thinking about that makes me feel kind
of ashamed to have been laying up in the bed for two weeks like a
sick person when I wasn't truly sick. I vow to make up for lost
time.

"What in the world was wrong with you, did they say?" Hazel
asks, looking at me over the tops of her ancient silver-plated cat-
eye glasses, which are attached to a chain hanging around her
neck.

"Oh, just a bug, I guess. I'm fine now, though." I'm not sure
who she means by *they*, but I have no way of knowing how local
gossip has spiraled out of control. I'm sure it's been said I've had
everything from pneumonia to Lyme disease to sleeping sickness
to Lord knows what. Fortunately, I still have traces of my end-of-

summer tan, and my days of rest have left my eyes clear and white and blue, plus I still have summer blond highlights in my hair. I also have good calves, which is fortunate, because I near-about live in khaki shorts and deck shoes, no socks, all through the spring, summer, and fall. I've always felt that I was presentable to both men and their mothers.

"Thank you for the coupon, Hazel," I tell her. "I'll have a ham and cheese biscuit."

"You got it, sugar pie. Coming up, you just wait right there."

Just inside the drive-thru window, next to the cash register, I see that Hazel has posted a new sign that reads: "*Employees must wash*"—and here she has pasted a cut-out illustration of the Praying Hands—"*before returning to work.*" This is odd, because it's only Hazel and Jessie who work here. Hazel must have suddenly gotten the notion that Jessie is unclean, or perhaps she put it up to remind herself. Also, in the window, facing out, is a small poster of Donny Tyndall, with his little smiling face and blond head of curls, clearly an Olan Mills kindergarten portrait. Above, it says: MISSING. Then: *Donny Tyndall, age 6, last seen in the vicinity of Dodd County. Reward. Please contact Marsh County Sheriff's Office.*

I stare into his little eyes for several seconds, and then I feel my own eyes start to sting and—

"Well, look what the cat done drug up to the pick-up window," says Jessie, appearing suddenly, opening up the glass and looking askance at me like I was something out of the prison reformatory program. She is wiping her flour-covered brown hands on a rag.

"Hazel said that was you, but I had to see it with my own eyes. Boy, I heard they were about to pack you off to Dix Hill."

"Well, Jessie," I say, suddenly feeling slightly defensive. "Reports of my death have been greatly exaggerated."

"Uh-huh. I never heard anybody say anything about being dead, just that you wouldn't get out of the bed for two weeks.

What in the Sam Hill was wrong with you, laying up there in the bed like that, Talbert?"

"I was . . . I don't know . . . I just didn't feel well . . ." I don't like being questioned so point-blank like this. Where is Hazel with my biscuit? She at least seemed glad to see me.

"Sounded like a movie-star disease t' me," Jessie continues, eyeing me up and down. "Laying up in the bed like that, well and healthy. Shoot. Your mama came by here, I never felt so sorry for anybody in all my life, worried sick, didn't know what to do. You ought to be ashamed, making folks worry about you like that, when there wasn't nothin' wrong with you, and you a fully grown man . . ."

I bite my lower lip. I thought people around here would be happy to have me back dancing among them, favoring them with my cheerful, revived self.

"Well, I'm sorry, Jessie," I say, looking at her. "Don't you ever get depressed or anything?"

She looks back at me all hard and sarcastic, and then says: "Are you kidding me, Talbert, or what? Shoot. Hell yeah, honey, I get depressed, but I come in to work." Then she lowers her voice to say: "What's Hazel gonna do, sick as she is, if I don't come in here and help her run this place?"

Hazel appears back in the window, squeezing in next to Jessie. Yes, that wig is definitely listing. Oh, it's so damn sad. I think I'm just gonna break down right here, this has become the worst part of the entire day.

"Here you are, Talbert," Hazel says, handing me a small white paper bag. "Now, honey, give me your hands." There are two other cars behind me in the drive-thru line, but I don't think she's noticed. I pass my hands through the window. Hazel's gnarled, bony hands grasp and rub mine, and she closes her eyes.

"Let's us just say a little prayer thanking the Lord that you're doing all right, and let's pray for that Tyndall boy, too. Come on Jessie, let's all hold hands . . ."

And the two of them pray, with lots of *Oh Lord's* and *Yes, Lord's* and *Praise Be's* all coming out at me through the little window, and the people behind me in line are starting to honk their horns, which seems to me a sadly inappropriate musical accompaniment for Hazel and Jessie's lamentations; I know I ought to turn WGOD back on just to provide the right musical backdrop for our prayer session, but mostly I just want to get out of there and eat my biscuit. Finally I wrest the moment away from them with a big "Amen!" and the Dirt Devil and I peel out from the drive-thru with a big rubbery screech that I hadn't intended, but don't have time to go back and apologize for.

2:00 P.M.

The biscuit makes me feel better, and I'm reminding myself that by day's end, I will have convinced the all-powerful, all-important Duck Island Playhouse artistic director Charlotte Watkins to back the fabulous theatrical plan that I'm about to lay at her feet. I don't really like Charlotte all that much, truth to tell, but she does pull the strings at DIP and I know she thinks I'm talented. Still, I wonder if she has forgiven me for getting all the good reviews as Sister Mary Amnesia in *Nunsense* back in the spring. Charlotte directed our production, naturally, and also conveniently gave herself the starring role of the Mother Superior. But here is what Stephen Brickles wrote in the *Star-News:* "As Sister Mary Amnesia, the brilliant, talented, and handsome Talbert John Moss gives a performance that is, well, unforgettable (ha, ha), but as the Mother Superior, Charlotte Watkins is, decidedly, inferior." I saw Stephen in a bar after that, and as I warded off his brazen overtures, I said, "No more Rex Reed for you, mister." I'm sure he thought that was ungrateful and I know the next time I'm in a show, he'll crucify me.

The Dirt Devil and I race out onto Highway 17, which mostly

cuts through scrubby pine woods filled with yaupon trees and droopy Spanish moss and oleander and that ugly pampas grass, which I say is the Devil's weed because it'll just about cut the pure-tee hell out of you if you as much as touch it. Between the hollowed-out places through the trees, where little roads have been built, you can see, in the distances, the ocean on one side, the Intracoastal Waterway on the other. Two years ago, Highway 17 was named in the *Guinness Book of World Records* as the site of more roadkill per mile than any other highway in the Southeastern United States. And the Duck Island Chamber of Commerce, bless their hearts, actually quoted that in brochures, as if that might be some kind of attractive feature to entice vacationers to come to Duck Island! Imagine that as a selling point for potential tourists: *Come on, Joyce, let's take the kids over to Duck Island this summer so we can sun, surf, and eat some good roadkill.* I'm convinced that all the local Rhodes scholars who don't work at WAVE work at the Chamber of Commerce.

Seventeen leads out to Surfside Beach, which is where Charlotte lives in her veritable, though now slightly decaying mansion, which was part of her take in her last divorce. Charlotte funds much of what goes on at the Playhouse with her own money, which is why she directs and stars in everything, and probably why the local critics resent her so much. She has finally started doing character parts, though, which is a good thing since she is way too long in the tooth to keep playing things like Reno Sweeney in *Anything Goes*, or—get this—Eliza in *My Fair Lady*. Stephen Brickles said they should have retitled it *My Fairly Over the Hill Lady*.

Soon enough, of course, the Dirt Devil and I encounter roadkill: a long, thick copperhead snake smashed and strung out across the highway. My grandmother Florence Moss died at the age of eighty-eight from being bit by a copperhead that was hiding behind a refrigerator on her back porch, and people rudely said that there was something ironic about that, seeing as how she was already so full of poison anyway. I worry sometimes that I carry what my mama calls the Moss family's "mean gene," but I think I have more of what Daddy says is the craziness from Mama's side of the family, the Rideouts. During my self-imposed exile, I thought a lot about killing myself, maybe not like I actually was gonna do it, but more like the ways you *can* do it. When I was a child, about eight, my mother actually did, as they say, "make an attempt." And of course, with my nose for drama, I was the one who found her. One hot summer Sunday, Mama trotted out of the house completely naked, but sober as a judge, and lay down on an entire, thriving village of fire ants in our backyard—just lay there waiting for them to eat her alive, or whatever fire ants do. Stark naked, except for her bedroom scuffs and big Jackie Onassis sunglasses. I followed her out there. She looked like a female version of Gulliver in Lilliput, tied down and trounced upon, not by Lilliputians but by the ugly, red, fire ants. I asked her what she was doing, and she said, "I'm just taking a nap, Talbert John, you just run along. Mommy loves you. These fire ants don't bother me." And I began to cry and then I tried to brush the ants off her body—I had never seen her naked before that I could remember—and I kept brushing and trying to get her to get up and the ants kept coming back up but she wasn't helping me get them off, and then I started to scream for Daddy to come help me— "Daddy! Daddy, come here!"—and out of the corners of her eyes behind the sunglasses, I could see big tears starting to roll down, mingling with the rivulets of sweat on her cheeks and neck because it was so hot, and that's when Daddy found both of us, and made everything all right again. To this day, people still whisper: "That's Loralee Moss. Tried to kill herself once by lying down on a village of fire ants." I keep trying to forget about certain bad events in my life, but the more I try to forget them, the more they just keep playing back over and over in my head. As Mama herself would say, "That's the way the Devil works."

I get to Surfside Beach and to Charlotte's driveway, which is about a half-mile long leading up to the mansion, the site of many good cast parties in which I was cheered and toasted as the Dustin Hoffman of Duck Island Playhouse. (Charlotte would always say, "Oh, I guess that makes me the Meryl Streep!" to which I always wanted to say "You mean Meryl's grandmother," but I never did, I just took the high road.)

I pull in behind Charlotte's black Lincoln Continental (which she also received as part of her last divorce settlement) and I'm thrilled to see that Charlotte's personal assistant slash maid, and my friend, Printemps Decoupage, is here. Printemps's car, an old Volkswagen bug, is parked next to the Lincoln, and I happen to know Charlotte doesn't really think that is appropriate with regard to the employer-employee relationship—she thinks Printemps should really park around to the side—but that is all a part of Printemps's newfound "Woman of Power" assertiveness. Five years ago, Printemps was known by her birth name, which was Delores Jackson, and Delores was perfectly happy to identify herself as the maid of the richest white woman in town. That, of course, was just fine with Charlotte Watkins too. But then four years ago this fall, Delores went down to New Orleans to take care of her aunt who was sick, and while she was down there, she met this drag queen in the French Quarter who called himself/herself "Printemps Decoupage." Delores began spending all her time with the original Printemps, who was still working in the drag shows, but who was dying of AIDS.

Now what I think is that Delores actually fell in love with Printemps, although she's never told me that, exactly. But Printemps was good for Delores, and gave her lots of assertiveness talks about living up to her true potential and stuff, and he/she told her to stop referring to herself as a maid and to think of herself as equal to her employer, and when Printemps died that winter, Delores took his/her name as a kind of tribute, and came back to Duck Island a new woman, all empowered and full of righteousness and everything, and had her name legally changed to

Printemps Decoupage. And boy, if you don't think some of the white people around here had a problem with a formerly shy little black girl transformed overnight into an assertive, beautiful, empowered African-American woman with an exotic name . . . I, of course, thought it was magnificent. Printemps is a walking Oprah/Sally Jessy/Ricki Lake show rolled into one, and I think she's totally fab.

Charlotte's front doorbell is musical, which means it plays the first few notes of some randomly selected show tune when you push it. And I always play "Name That Tune" with myself when I come here. Before pushing the doorbell, I say, "Well, Jack, I can name that tune in . . . five notes."

("Well, name that tune!")

I push the doorbell and I hear a slow, legato *Da-da da-da*, then a quicker *da da da da, da da da da da* . . .

" 'If I Loved You . . .' " I say, hearing the clock tick.

(Studio audience applauds, and I win the Sarah Coventry jewelry.)

Naturally, it's Printemps who answers the door.

"Hey, Printemps," I say cheerily.

"Well, if it isn't Eve Harrington," she says. (Printemps learned the gay reference vocabulary from the drag queens in New Orleans.)

"Shhh . . . don't let Charlotte hear you say that. She might think it's true."

"Talbert John, honey, do you think Miss Lady has forgotten that you stole all, I mean *all*, her thunder in *Nunsense?*"

"Well," I say, with a trace of Eve's effrontery, "I can't help it that I'm so fabulous, now can I?"

Printemps harumphs disgustedly, but I know she gets a kick out of me and my me-ness, because I'm the closest thing she has around here to some of those boys she got to know in the French Quarter.

"Is she home?" I ask.

"Yes, honey, she's home . . . come on in."

Printemps ushers me into Charlotte's grand foyer, with its clean, shiny floors of enormous black and white terrazzo pattern and Louis Quatorze gold chandeliers hanging from cathedral ceilings.

"Girl, you've done a good job of these floors," I say, as innocent as Huck Finn walking into the Wilkes's house.

She immediately cuts me a slice-and-dice look, then arches her back, feline-style, and glares at me, but mockingly.

"No, no, child, you will not come in and insult Printemps with your little plantation-style jokes," she says, wagging a long, exquisitely manicured finger at me. "Printemps will personally see to it that you are offered only chorus roles at the Playhouse from here on out."

"I was never in the chorus," I say.

"Yes, honey, but there is a first time for everything." And we burst out laughing.

And I love her for this next thing, which she whispers: "I'm sorry you were depressed, honey. I understand. We all get the mean reds, baby." (The drag queens must've turned her on to Truman Capote too.)

"Thanks, Printemps. I missed you."

"Yes, child. All the children miss Printemps when Printemps goes absentia from their world. I'll summon Miss Charlotte."

I poke around in some of Charlotte's rooms, because I know she likes to keep people waiting and it will be a while. Prominently featured on many of Charlotte's walls are huge, blown-up photographs of her stage performances, most of which have been in community theaters of North Carolina, but you would think, if you didn't know any better, seeing these dramatic photos, that Charlotte has had a theatrical career on the world stage to equal Helen Hayes's. There's Charlotte in *A Moon for the Misbegotten*, Charlotte in *Streetcar*, a younger Charlotte as Daisy Mae in *Li'l Abner*, and—oh, God—the infamous Charlotte as Eliza Doolittle in *My Fairly Over the Hill Lady*.

"Is that my darling little Sister Mary Amnesia?" I hear Charlotte intoning from the foyer, her rich voice embracing me.

"That would be she," I call out, as if giving an onstage cue to an actress about to make her entrance from the wings. Exactly.

"Hello, darling!" she says, sweeping into the room, big and grand, arms outstretched, with an affected flourish that suggests she has been studying Diana Rigg a little too closely while watching imported BBC programs.

"Hello, Charlotte," I say, kissing her first on one offered cheek, then on the other.

She is wearing a black cashmere sweater and black cigarette pants plus low-heeled black pumps. Somewhere along the way someone told Charlotte: "Actresses wear black."

Her hair is dyed red, and she is in full makeup, even though it's early afternoon. Printemps has told me it takes Charlotte two hours to dress and make up for the day, even when she isn't going anywhere. Charlotte is always quoting people who say she resembles Arlene Dahl or Cyd Charisse, which is why she keeps her flat brown hair red, and why she goes Full Glamour even on weekdays. When she's performing, she gets to the theater four hours before curtain to begin getting into costume and makeup.

"Come in, come in," she says, hooking her arm in mine and leading me into her living room, walking slowly and deliberately, but full of *inspiration*, like Auntie Mame escorting her nephew Patrick up the stairs in her New York apartment.

"Talbert, Talbert, I've been on the phone all morning with the members of the board, it's just exhausting! You of all people know how I try to bring the very best kind of culture to this town that I possibly can, and . . . well, it's so sad, really. All they want is Neil Simon this, Rodgers and Hammerstein that. Now, mind you, Messieurs Simon and Rodgers and Hammerstein have been very good to me in my time, but, Lord, I just think we should do some Mamet, some O'Neill, some . . . I don't know. *Rent.* We should do

Rent!" She looks at me intensely, right in my eyes, but in the way of someone who's been directed to look at someone like that. Funny how all of Charlotte's gestures read suspiciously like over-rehearsed stage business.

"What do you think, Talbert?"

We are in her main living room now, decorated to the hilt with antiques and gaudy, overstuffed, floral-print sofas.

"Well, Charlotte, I think it might be a while before Duck Island is ready for *Rent.* But that's just my opinion."

"Oh, no, you're right, you're right, you're so right," she says, looking away suddenly, then releasing a heavy sigh. "I just dream big, Talbert, that's just the way I am, the way I've always been. Dream, dream, dream! The bigger the better! Let nothing stand in my way! Well . . . a house full of photos and memories. You can't take that with you when you go, can you?" And she gives me a "forlorn" smile and "sadder but wiser" eyes.

If I didn't know better, I'd think Charlotte was preparing to play Madame Ranevskaya in *The Cherry Orchard,* getting ready to leave her precious mansion for the last time.

"Now, sit down, sit down," Charlotte says, suddenly breaking the mood and plopping down briskly and businesslike, putting her glasses on and looking at me. "Printemps said you had something you wanted to discuss with me."

"Yes, I have an——"

"Oh wait. Oh, Talbert, I'm so sorry, I just remembered. You've been sick, darling."

I look down at the floor. I didn't want to have to talk about my self-imposed exile with her; I figured she was probably way too lost in her own world to care, or even know, about my period of absentia.

"Well, yes, but I'm better now," I say.

"Was it that nasty Hong Kong flu or something? I hear it's just terrible."

I know Printemps wouldn't have told Charlotte about my taking to my bed for fear and depression, so I just go along with whatever Charlotte thinks it might have been.

"Yeah, the flu. It was awful. But I'm better now. Now listen, Charlotte . . . I've had an idea."

"Yes . . ."

"I have something in mind to adapt, and then stage, for the Playhouse. I think it could be a big hit."

A long, meaningful pause. "Oh, I see. And what would that be?"

"I want to write and direct a new adaptation, my own, obviously, of *The Little Prince*. You know it, don't you? The book by Antoine de Saint-Exupéry about the little prince who—"

"Oh, yes, of course," she says. "Of course I know *The Little Prince*, darling. Hmmm . . . well, that's cute . . ."

"It's a wonderful story," I continue. "I mean, *I* think it is, and I think it's great for adults as well as children. And it would give a talented local child a chance to make his stage debut, and that would be great publicity for the Playhouse. I know a child who can do it, too. He'll be wonderful. And we could have a few songs also, like, turn it into a mini-musical. Billy Squiers, the organist at First Methodist? He's always wanted to write the score for a musical."

She takes her glasses off and leans back, staring up at the ceiling, biting on one of the earpieces of her frames, "listening" and "contemplating."

"Well, it's an idea, certainly . . . it certainly is an idea," she says, finally. "When would you want to do it?"

"It would take me just a couple of months to write it, maybe not even that. I have a lot of time on my hands." I say this because I suddenly remember that I no longer have a job at Bledsoe Real Estate.

"Yes . . . yes . . . well, I love that you're thinking about things like this, Talbert. Really, such initiative. Such ambition. Of course, I'd have to see the finished product before I could show it to the board, and probably it's a little late for the upcoming season. But why don't you write it, darling, and we'll have a look."

She kind of slaps her hands on her thighs, as if to signify that this meeting is over. I can tell my idea about *The Little Prince* doesn't really excite her. I should have known better. I should have approached it from the angle of "There will be a wonderful part for you . . ." I feel a cold sweat break out on my forehead, and even though I haven't sold my idea in the best way, I still think I can convince her. I keep going.

"I really have a vision about this, Charlotte. I really think it could be quite a good show . . ."

"Oh, yes, I'm sure it could be, darling," she says, standing up and motioning for me to do the same. "Now you just work on it, and in six months, whenever you feel it's ready to be looked at, you just let me know. All right? And thank you, thank you, Talbert, for all your work for the Playhouse. We'll have to get you onstage again soon, won't we? You were such a big hit with the press as Sister Mary Amnesia."

Printemps appears in the doorway, as if on cue.

"Charlotte, Dick Buttry is on the phone for you."

"Oh, I have to take that. Talbert," she says, leaning over and kissing me on both cheeks, "thanks so much for dropping by. Good for you, darling, good for you. You keep me posted on your little project."

And she breezes out of the room with a cursory, "Thank you, Printemps," making a big deal of pronouncing it very French: *Prawwnnn-tauuuun.* I'm sure that she still refers to her as Delores when Printemps isn't around to hear her.

"How did it go?" Printemps asks, walking me to the door.

"Like shit, basically," I say.

"Now, little one, don't you get discouraged by Miss Lady and her shenanigans. You know better than that. Listen to Printemps. Where would Printemps be if Printemps allowed Charlotte's foolishness to undermine the exquisite glory that is Printemps Decoupage?"

"Printemps would still be Delores Jackson."

"Yes, honey, and we know Delores is dead. Delores is long

gone. There is no Delores, only Printemps. And there is only Talbert, too, you remember that. You get out of Talbert's way so Talbert can take care of Talbert, do you hear me, child? Believe, honey, believe in the power, the possibility that is Talbert."

And she kisses me good-bye and goes back in, I presume, to continue cleaning Charlotte's house.

3:20 P.M.

I should go home and get back into bed, that's what I should do. I don't feel like seeing anybody else. I realize now I *liked* being in that damn bed, and sleeping and not waking up much. I missed the Dirt Devil, but that's all—I certainly didn't miss any people, that's for sure. To hell with them all, I say.

Still, there is somebody, one last person I want to see today before I go home and re-exile myself.

The Dirt Devil and I cross the bridge that takes us from Surfside Beach back to Duck Island. I head away from the ocean to the Intracoastal Waterway side, down to Squaw Pond Road, to the very end, where Trey and Kelly live in a tiny little cabin in the piney woods. This is the time of day Trey usually comes in from his construction job, about two hours before Kelly gets home from the Savings and Loan.

When I pull up in the yard, I see that Trey's truck is parked out front, but Kelly's Toyota is gone. This is what I expected, and what I hoped for, nothing against Kelly.

At the unlatched screen door, even before I knock, I look into the tiny little living room and see Trey asleep on the couch. The TV is tuned to *General Hospital* and there is a half-empty bottle of Michelob on the coffee table. Trey's big, lanky frame is stretched out the length of the couch; he is dressed in blue-jean cutoffs and a white workshirt with the sleeves cut off and the front unbuttoned. He is barefoot, his workboots and socks tossed onto the floor next to the couch, and his big feet are hanging over the edge of the sofa, facing the screen door. He looks like big, dark-haired Apollo taking a rest from running errands half-naked all over Athens; just watching his broad, hairy chest lift up and down in his sleep is reason enough to stand here for several minutes, quietly, which is what I do. And then, remembering time constraints, I open the door and gently let myself inside.

"Hey," I say softly, standing over him, not wanting to frighten him with touch. "Trey. Wake up."

He opens his eyes, kind of in a flutter, and then into a slow, sleepy stare. He takes me in for a second, and then sits up.

"Tal," he says, looking at me, waking up. "You're walking."

"Yeah, hard to believe, I know."

"Damn." He rubs his eyes, and runs his hands through the back of his longish hair. "Thought we'd lost you for a while there, bud."

"Well, I don't know . . . maybe you did, for a while."

He leans back on the couch, his hands behind his head. "So . . ." he says.

"So what?"

"So what's the deal? Are you OK?"

"I think so," I say. "I just . . . needed a break . . ."

"Oh, is that what it was?"

"Something like that."

He takes a long pause. "OK. If you say so, whatever."

"Yeah."

"You want a beer?"

"Uh-huh." He gets up to go into the kitchen, and, as he passes me, quickly runs his hand over the top of my head, through my hair. His big hand on me like that makes me take a sudden sharp deep breath—it's been a while since I've been touched. I mean by someone other than myself.

"Have you seen Kelly?" he asks from the refrigerator, twisting the screw-top on a Michelob. "She's been worried about you, fucker."

"No, I haven't . . . I mean, I know she has. I think she came over and cleaned up. I think I remember that."

"Yep," he says, returning, handing me the cold, sweating bottle. "She said you were pretty much in a drugged-out haze."

"Right . . ." I take a long swig of the beer; it burns cold down the back of my throat.

Trey sits down again, next to me on the couch, but one cushion length away.

"Is the Dirt Devil OK?" he asks.

"Yeah, seems to be. Why?"

"Well, I came over and started it a couple of times so it wouldn't sit idle for so long. I mean, when it looked like you were planning to stay in bed for a while."

"Oh, wow, I thought Daddy did that . . ."

"Nope. Me."

"Well . . . thanks. Thanks for . . . thanks for doing that."

"Yep." He swigs from the bottle, and then I do too, again, which makes me feel suddenly stupid, like some monkey-see monkey-do little brother. We sit there for a few minutes not talking; on the TV, an angry blond girl is screaming at her hunky boyfriend, something about money, something about a diaphragm, something about "before it's too late!" I'm too nervous to really follow it.

"Mind if I turn this off?" I say, picking up the remote and aiming it.

"Nope," he says, looking me right in the eyes.

I turn off the TV, and suddenly the room goes quiet, except for our swigging and breathing. I think maybe I shouldn't have come now, and start to think about how to leave.

But then I think about how good it felt when he ran his hand through my hair a minute ago. I do that to myself sometimes, run my hands through my own hair and pretend that it's another guy doing it—maybe sometimes, even Trey. But it's so much better when somebody else actually does it. I'd like to see if I can get some more of that.

I set the bottle down on the table, on one of Kelly's crocheted drink coasters, and scoot myself over closer to him, causing our knees, both bare in our shorts, to deliberately touch. One time he pushed me hard off the couch for doing that, and told me to get the hell out. Today, he allows it.

"I missed you," I say, then remember to add "buddy" at the end of it. "I missed you . . . buddy."

He snorts, and swigs. "I bet. I'll just bet you did, fucker."

I hate that word, but I'm not going to tell him that. Some things you just reserve expressing opinions about. Out in the yard, Trey and Kelly's dog Buster barks at a truck of loud kids, whooping and hollering down the road, probably just let loose from the school day. I reach over and start to rub his thigh, slowly, because you have to go slow with him so he won't suddenly freak out (he's even shoved Kelly a time or two, the way he shoved me. She told me that. All I could do was to sit there and listen and nod my head) and he leans back again, shutting his eyes and he . . . well, he allows this, too. So far so good—for me.

"I missed you so damn much, Trey," I say, and I'm afraid I'm going to start to cry.

"Hey, come on, Tal," he says, suddenly sounding nice again, which I'm grateful for, and he puts his arm around me and pulls me closer to him, and it feels OK just to lean against him, big-brothery, instead of getting horny for him; it's probably better this way, truthfully. But then he whispers in my ear, all hoarse and sweaty: "Give me a fucking kiss, buddy . . . you know you want to."

And he's right. I do. I want to so bad. I move my mouth up to his, remembering to go *slow, slow, don't get too excited, don't make him mad, don't make him hate himself for doing this.* And I just kind of turn off everything in my mind, all my thoughts and feelings, and let my body do all the work on its own.

"Are you OK, buddy?" I ask him, whispering back. "Are you OK, Trey?"

"Yeah, fucker. Don't talk."

And so I just take the plunge; maybe I'll be pushed and kicked, maybe I won't, I'll risk it. My hands move over his big, muscled body all at once, and it's as if some crazy puppet master was pulling strings above my head, making my hands go places that they probably shouldn't. My legs slide all over his, and I'm not even thinking about it now, just feeling it; we're just two big boys doing it, just *doing it*, and all we are is legs and arms and muscles and tongues and feet and hair and chests—bumping, rubbing, kicking, thrusting, sliding, and *Damn, this feels good*, it feels great, it feels like sports, like about the only sport I was ever any good at. It's hot, and it's wet, and it hurts, and it feels good too, like beer that burns cold in your throat, and the only sound in the room is our grunt, grunt, and moan like two exhausted football players, or like wild animals, and underneath us, underneath our frenzied movements, the couch creaks loudly, like cicadas freaking out on a hot August night.

And then . . . it's over. Is it over? It's over when *he* decides it's over.

Yes. It's over.

He just stops, just like that, and chucks me on the chin with a little "gotcha" laugh.

"Whoa, dude," he says. "You're too much. You're just too fuckin' much, man."

And he gets up to go to the bathroom, pulling his shorts up, whipping his cut-off, cut-out shirt over his right shoulder like some tennis champ walking off the court, proud and cocky, his back turned arrogantly to the roar of adoring fans.

When he comes back in the room, I am pulled together again too, and though I could use more, what I really want now is just to leave. Usually, afterwards, Trey starts talking about stuff, like football, Kelly, cars, Duck Island, construction work—whatever—

in his friendly, good ol'-country-boy tone that doesn't have much to do with what has just happened between us. Let's just say afterglow is not in Trey's repertoire. But now, he just looks at me and shakes his head, not smiling but not frowning either, and saying "Tal . . . dude!" and going into the kitchen for another beer.

"What?" I ask.

"I don't know, man . . . why do you always wanna do that?" He takes a long, measured swig from the bottle, searching me for an answer.

"What? Do what? I don't know . . ." He's never been analytical before, and I can't decide if this is some kind of enlightened progress on his part or just that old hidden wall of anger and shame about to come crashing down again.

"You know, fucker."

"I don't. Why would you ask me a dumb question like that? Because it feels good, I guess. I mean, it does for me."

He sits across the room from me now in a broken white wicker armchair, propping his feet up and drinking. "Does it? Does it feel good?" he asks.

"Of course. Of course it does. Damn right it does. Doesn't it?"

He snorts—sort of. "Hell yeah, it feels good. To me. I'm just wondering there, pal . . . if it feels good to you. Because I ain't too sure that it does, if you know what I mean."

I don't say anything to that, but my heart starts jackhammering.

"Look at me, Tal. Hey, buddy . . . I'm just a big ignorant country boy. But I'm a big horndog, too. I don't have to tell you that. I've just always been that way. So . . . it doesn't mean anything to me one way or the other if we do this or if we don't do this. I mean, you're here, you want it, whatever, that's fine with me. You're my buddy. The difference between us, bud, is that you really care about it and I don't."

I look up at the ceiling, look all around, anywhere but at him. "Gee, are you always this romantic?" I ask, finally. "Do you talk all this sweet-talk to the sheep too, after you finish with them?"

I look at him—he's glaring at me now; I know I shouldn't have said that. I pray he won't hit me, won't break the beer bottle and come after me. I don't think he will, but I pray anyway.

He keeps glaring, holding the beer and not drinking. There's a glint of rage in his eyes, and his jaw is set. Shit, he's furious. I should have kept my big mouth shut. I glance sideways at the door; I'm pretty sure I could dodge the beer bottle if it came flying, and I think I could make it out of the house if he lunged at me.

He sets the beer bottle down, still glaring . . . I brace myself, ready to bolt.

"I draw the line at sheep," he says, finally. "Goats are another story."

I exhale. He just busts out laughing.

"God, you're an asshole," I say, wiping sweat off my forehead.

"Yep. And that's why you like me so much, little fucker," he says.

"The hell!" I say, which I know sounds completely dumb. It's not even a completed thought, and I pride myself on completed thoughts. He's got me too nervous to be articulate.

He hoists himself out of the chair and comes over to me.

"Come 'ere," he says, picking me up and pulling me in close to him. He rubs my back, and strokes my hair, and I lean down a little and bury my face into his chest, which is sweaty and hairy, and I hold on to him as though my life depends on it. Maybe it does.

"I'm not nearly as dumb as I look, bud," he says, whispering in my ear.

"You don't look dumb to me."

He claps me on the back, then gently eases himself away from me. He lifts my chin with his thumb and index finger, almost like a dad would. "Don't get attached, T.J., OK? Don't make me have to kick you out, man. 'Cause Kelly and I love you, little fucker. You know that."

"You have a funny way of showing it."

He laughs. "Big Tal . . . Big Talbert . . . you go home and think about it. And you don't need to get into bed to think about it.

Ain't nobody around here wants to go through waiting on you hand and foot like that all over again, especially me. OK?"

I don't say anything. I guess this is like being broken up with, but the rules and the players are completely whacked.

And I start for the door and Trey says "Big Tal" again, and slaps me on the butt, like a coach. "Hey," he says, suddenly. "Did you hear about that kid?"

"What kid?" I say, out the screen door now and standing on the front step, which is nothing but two cinder blocks piled on top of one another.

"That little Tyndall boy. They found him in the woods this afternoon, way the hell up in Dodd County."

My stomach lurches, and the inside of my head starts to swim . . .

"What? What happened?"

"I don't know, something about his daddy came down here looking for him out of the blue and his mama sent him away to her boyfriend's friend's house up in Dodd County or something to make it look like kidnapping so the daddy couldn't have him."

"And then what?"

"Uh . . . I don't . . . something like he must've run away from the friend's house, something like that, and then he got lost up there in the woods, I don't know. They didn't have too many details. Damn, isn't that fuckin' pathetic? I'm tellin' you, T.J., trash will always act like trash."

"Well . . . is he . . . is he hurt, or is he . . . OK?"

"Nah, man, he's dead. He'd been mauled by some damn wild animal, a bobcat or something. Sucks, doesn't it? Just a little kid. Fuckin' bobcats."

5:30 P.M.

It's late afternoon now, and getting dark earlier, this being October. I've come home to sit on the beach in front of my house, just to stare out at the big, old, mean, beautiful Atlantic, trying to decide what to do next. All those hopes and plans I had when I started out this morning . . . I was so excited about everything. None of it matters much to me now.

I knew Donny Tyndall, but just barely. He was my friend, though. Because if you ever met Donny Tyndall, even for just a little while, you'd have felt like you'd known him for a long time. He was just that way.

Two weeks ago, I had just finished showing a condo on Yaupon Boulevard to this rich but nice young couple from Winston-Salem looking for an off-season beach getaway. They liked the condo, and agreed to take it right on the spot, so we went back over to Rollie's to draw up the papers. On my way home, I stopped at the 7-Eleven because I had a craving for a Cherry Slurpee. But first I went over to the magazine rack and just started looking idly at the magazines, mostly *Entertainment Weekly* and *Us*. The only other people in the store were the cashier, a big guy named Larry, and this cheap-looking but kinda pretty blond woman who was clearly flirting with him. Anyway, while I was reading something about Julia Roberts's latest romance, the woman's little boy comes over and stands next to me. He was a beautiful child, about six or so, with big blue eyes and a huge mop of bright blond curls. He had on light blue overalls over a white T-shirt, and child-sized construction boots.

"Hey," he said.

"Hey there," I said back. "How are you doing?"

"The 7-Eleven man gave me a Slim Jim," he said, and held it up to show me.

"Really? Well, that was nice of him."

"Yeah," he said, and then looked long and hard at his yellow-and-red-wrapped Slim Jim. "You want some of it?"

"No thanks. It's yours, you should have it."

"OK. Okey-dokey."

And then from over at the counter, his mama called out for him. "Donny?" she said, and he ran back over to her.

She looked down at him, hard. "Didn't I tell you not to bother people? Stay here!" Then she called out to me in a thick, swampy accent: "Was he botherin' you, sir?"

"No, not at all. We were just talking. It's OK."

She turned back to Larry, who was leaning against the counter, his enormous butt sticking out from under his red and green 7-Eleven apron. "Won't never do what I tell him," she told him, though I could hear it too. "Just all the time going up and talking to people he don't know. He's just like his daddy—ain't got no sense."

Then, in a few minutes, Donny came back around the counter, slyly creeping back toward me, grinning, knowing he was disobeying his mother, but she was so engrossed in redneck-to-redneck conversation with Larry, she didn't seem to notice. I guess she had figured that, *one,* I didn't mind talking to her little boy, and *two,* that I didn't look like some crazed kidnapper type, and *three,* that it got him out of her hair so she could devote all her time and energy to flirting with other like-minded rednecks.

"Hey," I whispered, like a secret agent.

"Hey," he whispered back, and laughed. "My mama's funny, ain't she?"

"I guess so. Your name's Donny?"

"Uh-huh. Donny Tyndall. That's my daddy's name too, but he don't live around here. Does your daddy live around here?"

"No, he lives somewhere else too. My name's Talbert John Moss. Some people call me Talbert, some people call me Tal, and some people call me T.J."

He looked at me for a second. "I like T.J."

"OK. Then that's what you can call me."

And we started talking about where he went to school (he was in kindergarten), and he said he lived in a trailer park at the end of the beach; he said he loved living there. And while he was talking, he ate his Slim Jim, continuing to offer me some of it, and then he asked me if I liked animals.

"I like some animals," I told him. "Most animals, I guess."

"I love *all* animals," he said. "I want a dog, or a kitty cat, but my mama says we can't have one where we live at."

Then he said, "I like flowers too. Do you like flowers, T.J.?"

"I sure do."

"My mama and I have a big rosebush in a big tractor tire right up out next to our trailer. And we water it about every day and it used to have some big red roses on it, but they're all gone now. But you could still come over and see it sometime. You wanna come over and see it?"

"Uh-huh . . . yeah, sure, I sure would, Donny," I told him. "I'll come down to where you live sometime, if it's all right with your mama, and then you can show me your rosebush, OK?"

Then he motioned for me to come down closer to him so he could whisper in my ear.

"I might run away," he whispered.

"Run away?" I whispered back. "Why?"

"I think—so I can see more places."

"Oh. Well, that's a good reason then, I guess. It's good to see more places."

"Did you ever run away, T.J.?"

I thought about that for a minute. I knew I should say no, that he wouldn't really understand if I said yes, since I'm a grown-up, but he was looking at me so seriously that I just felt at that moment I couldn't tell him any sort of a lie about anything.

"Yeah . . . I ran away once. I mean, actually, I've run away a lot of times, I guess."

"To see more places?"

"Yeah . . . that's right. To see more places." And he just studied me with his little blue eyes, and I could see he was taking it all in.

"Donny Tyndall!" his mother hollered out again. "Didn't I say not to bother the man?"

And we shook hands, and I waved good-bye to his mama and to Larry on my way out—I had decided to forget about the

Slurpee—and Donny said, "Bye, T.J." He watched me from the glass doors of the 7-Eleven, and kept on waving good-bye as I got into the Dirt Devil, and I could see his little golden curly head bobbing up and down excitedly as I pulled out of the parking lot.

To be honest, I hated to leave him there. The whole way home all I could think about was turning the car around and going back to get him and take him away from his mama and her redneck world—I guess you could call that kidnapping, but in this case, I would call it kid*saving*. And I thought about how I would read to him all the time, and take him to G-rated movies, and teach him songs and help him make stuff and then teach him to read for himself. All the way home, I thought about those things, about how I could be a good surrogate daddy to Donny and keep him out of the clutches of ignoramuses like Mr. 7-Eleven over there. And I vowed to myself that I would go to see him and be his friend and just help him along as much as I could, as much as his mother would allow me to, and just thinking about all of this made me feel so much better about everything else. Really, it did.

Two days later, I turned on the TV to see Claudia Davenport Shields talking about a missing child, and then Donny's mother was on, being held and comforted by a glum-looking Larry. They were standing in front of her trailer, and she was screaming and crying hysterically about "My Donny! My angel Donny!" and I turned off the TV and got up and walked around my little house, and I started to feel dizzy and weak-legged, like I'd been on the Tilt-A-Whirl too long, but I couldn't do anything, and I couldn't eat and I wanted to call somebody but I couldn't do that either and basically all I wanted to do was to go back to bed, and maybe say some prayers, and that's what I did. But then the next day came and I felt the same way all over again, and then the phone started to ring, but I stayed in bed and refused to answer it. People began to come over, and I sort of saw them, but by then I was taking sleeping pills, so mostly I just stayed in bed, and I stopped even remembering to pray anymore, barely even remembering to get up and eat something, which some days I didn't. I usually had a beer or two, though.

Still, I would always set my alarm for the next morning, just in case I felt like coming out of exile when I woke up, but then when I would hear WAVE come on, with their stupid, inane songs and idiot chatter, I would just shut it off and go back to sleep, if I could, but even if I couldn't, I stayed in the bed anyway . . . and stayed and stayed and stayed . . .

Until this morning.

And now, I'm sitting here on this tiny little patch of beach, and it's dark out, and I'm shivering slightly and my face is wet, and I want to scream and yell, but I can't seem to do it; all the words I want to say stick in my throat. I want to say to the sky and the ocean that I'm sorry, that I should never have told Donny it was OK to run away, I should never have told him that I'd run away myself. Oh, God, why did I have to tell him that? Why did I have to meet him in the first place? Why did I just happen to go to the 7-Eleven that day? I didn't mean to tell him it was all right to run away, I mean, it isn't . . . it never is. Grown-ups don't tell children it's OK to run away, only other children say that, to each other. I didn't know he was listening to me. Not like that. Oh, God . . . why?

Why . . . why . . . why . . . why . . . why . . .

I lie back in the sand and wipe my face with my sweatshirt sleeve, which is wet and sandy. Next to me is a flashlight, and I've also brought my old copy of *The Little Prince*, too. I pick it up and look at the cover, with the drawing of the blond little prince standing on the crater-filled planet. How I hoped I could make it into a play for Duck Island Playhouse: *The Little Prince* starring Donny Tyndall. I swear, even this morning I believed I could make that happen, I believed Donny would be found and be OK, and that we were going to officially become good friends, and I believed I could make this book into a play starring him.

I flip the pages open to my favorite part, and with my flash-light in one hand I read again what the Little Prince says to the aviator: *"You—you alone will have the stars as no one else has them . . . In one of the stars I shall be living. In one of them I shall be laughing. And so it will be as if all the stars were laughing, when you look at the sky at night. . . . You—only you—will have stars that can laugh!"*

I close the book, and turn off the flashlight, then lay both of them on the sand.

Whywhywhywhywhy . . .

Suddenly I am filled with a horrible desire to tear off all my clothes, and so I do, every stitch, and I run down to the water's edge naked as a dog and then I wade in a little ways and hurl myself into it and fall face first—the shocking, splashy cold of it washes all over my body—and I think how it *is* just like James Mason at the end of *A Star Is Born*, except he kept swimming—that's it—he kept swimming. And here I am—just drifting.

I pull myself up and stand, trying to find footing on the shift-ing sand. I look up at the sky, and the stars, and down at the black, white-tipped waves crashing all around me, and now my throat opens and I start to scream and yell and finally, *finally*, I start to cry, and deep down I know how awful I must look: thirty-four years old and naked, standing in knee-deep ocean water, clutch-ing my chest and shaking with huge, loud pitiful sobs, but I can't help it. I just hope no one can see me, or hear me. Or . . . maybe I do hope they can see me and hear me, I just don't want them to come rushing down to me and ask why I'm naked and screaming. *Please don't ask me that! No! Please don't!* I want them to know why without having to ask.

But they never will, will they? So what I should do is to just start swimming and allow myself to be carried away out to sea, and all the while I'll just be saying good-bye to everyone and everything, or *not* good-bye: I'll be saying *fuck it* to everyone and

everything—*Fuck Island!*—as I sink down deep into the Atlantic
Ocean, *go slow, slow, don't get too excited.*

But this is not my Norman Maine moment. It's only knee-deep
ocean here.

I lower myself back down slowly in the water, until I'm
crouched on my knees, and I bob my body up and out of waves,
and I remember again what I've always known about myself,
which is that I really am much more like Judy Garland than
James Mason; it just isn't in me to swim out into the big black
sea and die there. I'd rather be the well-dressed martyr at a press
conference . . . I'm pretty good at that, after all, pretty good at
standing up and facing down cruel cameras and distorting micro-
phones, *head held high.*

So I stand up in the water and scream out *"This . . . is . . .
Mrs. . . . Norman . . . Maine"* over the roaring surf, and it's like a
tree falling over in the woods, nobody hears it, because I'm all
alone out here, but just doing that makes me laugh and now that I
know I'm not going to swim out into the Atlantic, I allow myself
to simply float back toward the shore, just calmly taking in the
sensations of the seashells and seaweed and the undertow as they
knock and pull against me, and wash over my whole shivering,
moon-white body. And even though I know the water is dirty, it
feels clean and pure, and I say, in a voice that isn't screaming,
"Please God, please make everything turn out all right. Please
don't forget about us down here on this little island. And please
don't forget about me."

Lying here, I suddenly realize that nobody I saw today took
credit for dedicating the "Theme from *Valley of the Dolls*" to me
this morning. I guess I'll never know for sure, then. Some things
it's probably good not to know about . . . I have my suspicions,
though . . . I'll keep thinking about it, trying to figure it out. Mysterious work.

And so I'm planning to lie here in the shallow water for a long
time, staring up at this big old night sky, looking and looking, and

praying some, too; I believe that soon I'll be able to know which is the one star that was promised to me, the only one that makes any difference to me at all, the one star that can laugh.

I'm sure I'll see it, eventually . . .

I'll be here until I do.

ACKNOWLEDGMENTS

I am deeply grateful to the extraordinary teachers I've been fortunate to work with over the years: Max Steele, James Wilcox, Jonathan Dee, Benjamin Taylor, Wesley Gibson, Josh Henkin, Alice Mattison, and Amy Hempel. I am especially thankful to Susan Cheever and Jill McCorkle for their encouragement and support. Thank you always.

My thanks also to Hilary Bachelder, Amy Boutell, Melanie Cecka, Brendan Costello, Reid Jensen, Amanda McCormick, Susan Rosalsky, and Lan Tran for insightful readings and advice, as well as friendship.

Much love and appreciation to all my friends and classmates at the Bennington College Writing Seminars.

Profound thanks to my agent Leigh Feldman and my editor Chuck Adams, not only for their wise and generous counsel but for their friendship as well. Many thanks also to Kristin Lang at Darhansoff, Verrill, Feldman, and Cheryl Weinstein at Simon & Schuster.

And a lifetime of thankfulness, of course, to: Betty Herring, Ginny Ross, Elizabeth and Rob Fitzgerald, Natalie Muldaur, Earl Black, Gary Rzasa, Keith Bulla, Mark Hardy, Paul and Lois Shepherd, Bob Plasse, Jon Imparato, Eric Thal, Nixon Richman, Al Hornstra, David Bottrell, Wendell Laurent, Richard Storm, Arnold Levine, Christine Butler, Kerby Thompson, Frank Cerbo, Jack and Martha Fleer, Peter Kaiser, and John Avino. Very special thanks also to my aunts, uncles, and cousins.

And for David and Katherine, Griffin and Anderson, and my mother and father: love and gratitude, always.

ABOUT THE AUTHOR

John Rowell is a native of North Carolina. He holds a B.A. from the University of North Carolina–Chapel Hill and an M.F.A. from the Writing Seminars at Bennington College. He lives in New York City. This is his first book.